ASCENDENCE

Cover art and design by Samantha Harrison

Raven's Lantern LLC, Orange, CT 06477

© 2017 Dana Perry

All Rights Reserved. Published 2017.

Printed in the United States of America

ISBN 978-0-9972619-1-2

For my mom,
because crazy is genetic.

ASCENDENCE

By Dana Perry

 Raven's Lantern LLC

Chapter One

Wind howled through the tree tops, causing the branch underneath me to shudder and groan and my hair to claw furiously at my eyes. I spat out the wayward brown strands, which were remarkably similar in color to the dead leaves below, and was forced to release my grip on the branch above me and rest the entirety of my weight on my knees, which were getting scraped raw in the thin yoga pants I was wearing.

I knew there was going to be a gathering of bloody scratches there later, but right then I was more concerned about the excess blood flowing to my head. I'd probably look more like a flatfish than a human if I face-planted from that high up. Even though I may have made a few comments about wishing for a smaller nose, that was not my preferred method of obtaining said goal.

Pines are not known for being strong wood, but that fact had not stopped me from recklessly scaling the trunk. At that moment, I was dangling face-first from the sturdiest looking branch I could find, which was about as thick in diameter as my calf.

Another violent gust of wind slammed into the tree, bending it with an audible screech and setting me off balance. In a swift and desperately instinctual attempt to maintain equilibrium my hands shot out to catch my

1

ankles, contorting my body into a rather uncomfortable D-shape. I grinned at the challenge.

I was having fun. Oodles of fun. Trust me, dangling from a tree right before a storm hits is what any sane person should be doing. People just don't realize it because they settle for the mundane route for most things. They don't look for more. While my friends were probably off studying, I was red-faced and shivering two stories up in a tree and loving every minute of heart-pounding excitement.

"Show-off!" a familiar voice shouted from below me.

Ah, yes. One of my friends definitely was not studying right that minute. On the lowest possible branch of the tree sat Jessica, her head lolled back so she could see me. Her raven black hair fluttered lazily in the wind, looking model-perfect. Judging by the way the wind was making it thrash around me, mine probably looked like the offspring of an octopus and a porcupine.

She continued to speak despite my lack of answer. "You know, when I said we should hang out, I meant shopping. Under no circumstances did I mean we should come out here in the middle of a flippin' thunderstorm and sit in a tree like a bunch of hippies."

I rolled my eyes at her dramatic pouting. She was enjoying herself, somewhere deep down.

"I'm *climbing* a tree, unlike you," I teased. "And I'm way too angry to be a hippy. So, you were saying? The evidence you've finally lost your mind?"

Jessica rolled her eyes at me. "If anyone's lost their mind, it's you. Can you even hear me upside down?"

I smiled sweetly, my face probably beet red. "Oh, of course! Only your words are reversed."

Jessica laughed and continued telling me about the

dream she'd had last night. "There were so many birds! The sky was like...black with them. And then, one by one they started to fall. And then Mitch was there, but he was running away from me and the birds cut off my vision, so I couldn't see him anymore, and I was *so* freaked out. Then, you know, I woke up. But now I'm still freaking out."

I gave an appreciative nod before flipping over. The bark of the tree dug into my spine a little bit uncomfortably, insistently prodding. Jessica continued speaking.

"Do you think it was a prediction? I mean, you are like, the town psychic."

I laughed at the last part, a smile splitting my face. A bird, startled by my outburst, took wing. "Me, psychic? That's a bit of a stretch. I really only ever dream about demons. And look," I pointed at the sparrow that I'd spooked, "your dream has already come true!"

A piece of bark flew from below to bounce off my thigh, but Jessica had joined in on the laughter. I continued to tease her. "Don't be angry! It'll attract the flock!"

Our laughter faded and she took false interest in her phone with its shiny pink and silver case. If she didn't put it away soon, it'd drown in the impending rainstorm. Her brightly colored nails tapped the screen. "The only thing I'm angry about is the lack of service here. How do you even—Ick!"

She flailed desperately, launching herself off the branch. If she'd been any higher, she would have been feeling it in the morning. As it was, she fell gracelessly on her butt and scuttled away, crab-style. I gripped the tree trunk and hoisted myself into a sitting position, clinging on for dear life as the dizziness hit.

Once it had passed, I dismounted the pine as quickly

as possible. Pieces of bark scraped at any uncovered skin, which didn't hurt, but I knew from experience it would leave angry pink gashes later. I climbed down the tree at lightning speed, joining her on the ground.

"What's wrong?" I asked, my eyes darting between her and the vacated branch.

Jessica breathed heavily. "There was a spider!"

I put my palm to my forehead. "Spiders are everywhere. Don't worry, they don't eat much."

That was the wrong thing to say. Jessica's dark mane tried desperately to catch up to the swinging of her head as she searched for more of the creepy crawlies. I grabbed her arm and pulled her up off the ground. "Come on, I'll show you a 'selection' even better than at the mall," I said in an attempt to distract her.

Her calm and collected façade was mending itself before my eyes, the way a vampire straight off a fresh feed would heal its wounds. The cell phone was in her hand again, but the screen was blank. "I don't suppose you are talking about a new pair of shoes, are you?"

I smiled. "Nope."

Clouds whizzed above us, but they had become such a huge, menacing mass it was hard to see them moving. Jessica had warily relocated her phone to her back pocket when a flash of lightning was cast out of Thor's hammer. I continued to wind my way through the pines.

I took a spider web to the face, but I didn't show it for fear of Jessica's...well...fear. Discreetly brushing the sticky strands from my cheek, I walked on until I found what I was looking for. Curled prickers concealed juicy wild blackberries low to the ground in front of me. My hand snuck through the thorny exterior and extracted the ripest.

I held them out to Jessica. "Tada."

Her face scrunched up. "You found those in the middle of the woods. What if they're poisonous?"

I picked one up and plopped it in my mouth. "They're blackberries, Jess. Totally safe. See? Not dead."

She grabbed one cautiously and eyed it, holding it up to a nonexistent light like one would with a hundred dollar bill. Then she put it in her mouth and chewed. After a second or two, she was eyeing the rest of the berries in my hand. She reached out for another.

I raised my eyebrows and smirked. "You think you can hog—"

I was cut off by an earth-shaking pulse of thunder. I knew that heaven's rumbling meant the dark clouds above were ready to spill their wet cargo all over us. From the terrified look Jessica cast my way, she knew it, too.

"Run!" she shouted, bolting away from the house and deeper into the woods.

Her track-and-field record was nothing against my years of experience in the woods. I caught up to her in seconds and grabbed her wrist.

"Wrong way."

She said something which was most likely an expletive, but the thunder stole it. We ran like the lightning streaking the sky. I grinned wildly while she lost her signature pout. The adrenaline was pleasing to her, as well.

That is, until the first droplets of rain began to trickle down, smacking into the leaves in a fashion that made it sound as if the woods were applauding us. I wanted badly to just sit down and enjoy the spectacle of the rain slicing through the air, but it was clear that was the opposite of what Jessica was thinking.

She let loose a yell of frustration. "I'm supposed to be going out with Mitch tonight and now my hair is ruined!"

I looked over my shoulder at her. Her hair might have been wet, but it was still perfect. "Oh man, you're right. He just might mistake you for a kapre."

Her eyes were glued to the ground so she wouldn't trip, but she gave it a glare for me. "No one besides you knows what a kapre is!"

"Humanoid hairy man tree. Sometimes invisible," I yelled as we ran.

Jessica tore her gaze off the ground to give me a squinty-eyed look. Makeup was starting to run down the creases by her eyes. I stuck my tongue out at her and then bit it as my foot hit a rock at the wrong angle and my ankle lolled to the side before I could right myself.

I sighed. I had definitely added some blue bruise-flowers to the smattering of red scrape-vines on my arms and legs from tree climbing. Tomorrow was going to be another long-sleeved day to cover up. That is, unless the rain magically healed me, which was unlikely but not in the slightest impossible. Water has many healing properties.

Dashing on the quickly saturating ground, footsteps chased by thunder, I held one hand above my head and tried to will the rain away from me. I imagined it separating in the purplish sky above me, coming to land near but not on me. Apparently, my hydrokinesis skills were not up-to-date, because a fair amount trickled down my face and in my hair.

Not that I was hydrokinetic anyway, but a girl could wish. By the time we reached the sliding doors on my abode, I was noticeably dampened. Jessica bolted to her car and hopped inside, smiling at me. She wiggled her fingers in lieu of a goodbye.

"Next time, the mall!" she yelled as she started the car and drove off.

The clicking of my dog's toenails on the wood downstairs rang in my ears like the ticking of a clock's second hand, making my homework all the less bearable. The sound stopped for a moment, silenced by the carpeted stairs. When Nyami's wet nose nudged the door open, I was rereading a paragraph for the fifth time.

I smiled at the silly golden retriever, who sniffed at my soaked, lank seaweed-esque hair. The rain had done wonders for it, along with the leaves that were entangled in the back. I gingerly plucked them out.

The fact that I was out in the storm wouldn't have been taken kindly by my parents, but luckily they'd both been involved with work. The mechanical *whirr* below me signaled that the garage door was opening and one of their arrivals was imminent. Nyami's ears twitched with excitement, and she left me to go greet whoever it was.

"Some big bad river god you are," I muttered. I'd named her after a water deity of the Zimbabwean Tonga tribe, but she just wasn't as scary as the fabled half-fish, half-crocodile Nyaminyami. I loved her all the same.

With her gone, I started back on my task. I made it a solid two questions into my social studies packet before I was interrupted by a raven's throaty caw. My ringtone.

More subtle than a wolf howl, I mused. It had helped me out a few times when I had accidentally forgotten to put my phone on vibrate in class. I checked the tiny display screen

7

to see if it was anyone worth flunking a homework grade for. Bold black letters stated 'Jeremy'.

He was definitely worth my time. Jeremy was my best friend, despite many accusations by our fellow peers that it was more than that. Although said accusations had begun to annoy me to no end, I could grudgingly admit that they had good rationale.

Jeremy would have fit the mold for bad boy perfectly with his dark, unruly hair, long and lean body, and warm brown eyes, if it hadn't been for his unusually giddy temperament and mega-intelligence. I flipped open my phone to read the message.

Hey. It was one word, simple, yet infinitely more interesting than the textbook I was getting ready to chuck out the window.

To what do I owe this honor, Mr. Bellevue?

Did you hear that Marcus got hit on the head with a can of soda? He had sent.

Who the heck is Marcus? Was my eloquent response.

I don't know, but I guess he was lucky it was a 'soft drink'! Ha? Ha? Get it? I groaned louder than socially acceptable for one locked away in her room, but what're you going to do?

Hardy har har, Genius. What dark corner of the internet did you siphon that from? I was snickering a little, but no way was I going to let him know that.

Fine, fine. Killjoy. Now, less quick, what do you know about obtaining immortality? This was not too unusual of a request, seeing as I was practically a walking dictionary of all things supernatural.

Through ritual? Through sacrifice? Which religion? You've got to be a little more specific. I replied.

Sacrifice. That one. I mused he must be trying to validate some show's or book's representation of the subject. Normally, the questions would be more along the lines of 'what is a chupacabra?' Still, I did not hesitate to respond.

More specific. What is providing the immortality? A deity? Is it just immortality, or could it be along with other effects? Had to narrow down the field. People had been searching for immortality for ages.

Hmm, I'll have to think that one over. Give me a minute. Curious, but not alarming. Jeremy was harmless, the sun to my moon. At the very least, his ever-present tan from his Native American heritage made him look like he'd gotten plenty of sun, while the moon could have taken paleness lessons from my own ghostly complexion.

People tended to alter their paths to greet him in the clogged hallways of our high school, whereas with me they parted as if I was poisonous to the touch. It actually worked pretty well for me, because my mind frequently focused on the internal world rather than the external. If only lockers and table corners would do the same as my classmates, my legs wouldn't look so much like they'd suffered a squid attack.

Can't make up my mind, but guess what? Jeremy asked me. I began to ask, but there was already another message popping up.

Jessica told me that someone moved into

9

that little shack at the top of your road.
She thinks that there's someone living there
that's about our age. And since you two are on
the same road...I expect you to get all the
details.

Sometimes Jeremy was more of a teenage girl than I
was. *Most* of the time Jeremy was more of a teenage girl
than I was. It didn't surprise me that Jessica had neglected
to tell me this herself, as she practically ran the school
gossip ring. Lots of stuff to keep track of. I guess when your
mother is the mayor of the town, you can stick your fingers
in many different pies.

Mhmm, right. What do you think I'm going to
do? Peer in their windows? That might come off as
a *tad bit* stalkerish. We discussed a mock battle plan for a
while, but eventually I had to get back to homework.

However, thoughts of that little cabin in ruins persisted.
My curiosity was piqued. This section of town was not
exactly a place where people considered moving to. In
fact, this town was not a place one would consider moving
to. As rural as rural could get while still having a human
population, situated right on the edge of a huge state forest
so dark with pines and so far reaching that every few years
someone walked in and never returned. With steady black
bear and coyote populations and miles of hilly terrain, it's
not surprising some of the bodies were never found.

I decided to stay my thoughts until Monday. When, if
the new occupant down the road actually was a student,
I would observe carefully. Until then, I would surrender
myself to dreams, the highlight of my days. Window open,
moonlight unobstructed, and lights off, the tentacles of
sleep wrapped around me and pulled me deep, deep under.

10

The deep crevasses of the bark beneath my feet were comforting as my toes curled in anticipation. That action should have caused bloody furrows to crawl over the hardened soles of my upper foot as the bark met yielding flesh, but in this place it would take much more than wood to call forth my blood. No, not many beings had the capability to harm me. The ones that did were armed with fang and claw and fire, and burned with the rage of a thousand suns.

I should know, I was staring at one.

The huge, ursine form lumbered beneath me. With a pelt as black as tar and heat waves emanating from it, even a human could have distinguished it from the smaller and much less deadly black bear it was imitating. Its huge nostrils expanded as it greedily gulped the air, sensing my presence. Hidden in the tree, it would only be a matter of seconds before I was located. If I was as soulless as the beast beneath me, I might have taken the opportunity to attack from above. As it was, I decided to wait with eyes to the sky in search of any omen not to proceed. None came.

In fact, I'd say the ground-shaking slam of the bear's paws hitting the tree trunk and the heaven-quaking roar it unleashed subsequently were pretty clear go-aheads. I thrust my open palm to the side, and called my blade. I did not have to look at it to know the exact moment it shimmered through a golden veil into existence. My hand wrapped around the hilt, feeling the heat of the short sword's unearthly fire crawl up my wrist and permeate my veins.

Wherever the beast's claws skimmed the tree it withered and blackened as if scorched by fire. As they dug in, murky lines spread upward like venom through veins. The shadow

11

bear heaved its weight up, climbing more slowly than necessary. It almost looked like it was in pain. All of its limbs shuddered and seemed to grow heavier the further it traveled from the ground, as if it was bound by invisible shackles pulling it back toward the earth's core.

Despite these setbacks, it continued the arduous journey toward me. Any branches it passed grew shriveled and leafless, eventually crumbling to ash and floating downward. The tree did not have long before it collapsed into a giant heap of soot. Still, I waited. As the being drew closer its invisible flame flew off of it in waves, only noticeable when my own soft, undulating golden light touched the edge and intensified to keep the darkness at bay.

In reality, it was my sword's golden light evoking the light inside of me at the nearing threat. If any humans were to watch me now, they'd see a faint shimmer surrounding me like an aura. They'd see my eyes immersed in a sea of pale gold, no iris or pupil to be found. If they were particularly observant, they might even see how the radiance was most tangible around my sword and in two long strokes off my shoulder blades.

Then they would run.

As the bear would be doing if it did not possess its single-minded drive to exterminate anything light or pure. It was only a branch below me, close enough where I could smell its fetid breath. Its eyes were almost hollow-looking, the same color as its pelt, and they darted to my calf. Its cavernous maw opened and shut repeatedly as if it were already feasting on my remains. Or perhaps it was merely re-chewing the bloody gunk stuck between its teeth. It saddened me to ponder the origin of the gore.

The creature extended a clawed paw toward me,

preparing to snag my leg and tear it to ribbons. A slight tremor of nerves caused me to shiver. A small doubt entered my mind. The possibility of miscalculation made my eyes widen almost imperceptibly. But then I heard a loud, resonating bang and a sound not unlike pine needles trickling onto the earth.

The whole tree shuddered before spinning to the side and descending to the ground. I had a split second to take action. Anything left in the tree when it collided was sure to be fatally wounded. It might seem that the bear and I would share the same grisly fate. There was only one difference.

I could fly.

The bear could not.

A flash of pale light later, I was relishing the pull of air on my extended wings. Billowing and white, yet shrouded in gold, I could feel the strain of every feather as they caught wind. Moving them felt like moving an arm through water, slightly difficult but rewarding. My feet lightly crunched leaves as my wings retracted and I landed, one palm clutching the earth for balance.

Several sharp, splintering snaps resulted from the first branches of the tree of ash hitting the ground. The light substance flew, diminishing vision and coating me in grime. There was a wetter, thicker crunch as the demonic entity met the forest floor shoulder first. Its own bones had shattered and stuck inward like glass, making it ooze its dark essence on the humus beneath it. Anything in contact with that dark essence burned.

I approached, vision still impaired by the gray haze. The creature was almost pitiful now, as it shuddered with each dying breath. If I hadn't known only its physical form would perish, that it would be haughtily satisfied to have the

13

situation reversed, or that left unchecked this beast would annihilate anything and anyone with purity by means of its jaws, I might have taken pity on it. But as it was, I drew nearer to deliver a quick death blow. It was the highest mercy I could grant.

I came close enough that the soles of my feet were scorched by its hellfire. Gripping it by its golden hilt, I raised my sword and—

Screamed as the creature's knife-like fangs pierced deep into my calf, severing muscle. My sword whipped downward in a clean sweep and lodged itself in the lungs of the bear. Once it pierced the earth through the opposite side, rumbling drowned out my involuntary whimpers. A chasm opened, swallowing the demon in a great burst of fire. It took merely a blink of an eye before the ground knit together its punctured flesh and appeared unchanged, sans the ursine beast.

My relief was short-lived as the darkness began to pulse from the wound in my leg, decay creeping swiftly toward my heart.

Chapter Two

What an awesome dream! I was delighted; dreams of the not-quite-angel—the Protector—were the best kind. Who wouldn't want to fight demons in their sleep? I attempted to jump right back into it, but something was scratching at the back of my mind. Actually, something was scratching at my back. I sat up and opened my eyes.

I was met by unfamiliar surroundings. I felt pulsing, frantic and irregular, beneath my right hand. I gasped as something moved in the darkness. A small, hard object bounced off my forehead. It left an unsettlingly wet imprint.

I attempted to scramble backward, but I didn't realize one of my hands was centered over my heart in a slightly open fist. I flopped backward instead, my unsupported shoulder smacking another unidentified thing behind me.

My hand flew back and hit the offending item in an unintentional slap as I tried to regain balance. The lightness of the resulting thud told me it was wood. I exhaled all of my adrenaline in a long sigh when I realized that the wood behind me and the carpet below me added up to one thing: I was in my bedroom. Albeit on the floor, but safe. I had been sleepwalking.

A long, wet tongue covered my nose. I sputtered out a laugh. "Nyami! You almost gave me a heart attack!"

Her tail thumped the floor contentedly. She looked

between me and the small red ball she'd dropped on me, waiting for my sleep-addled brain to get the message.

I groaned. "Let's play 'fetch the zzz's' instead."

I smiled to myself as I got up and plopped back down on my bed, smug. Nyami leapt up and squashed my legs under her weight, but my mind was elsewhere, mainly back on the floor. I'd done it again.

Somnambulism lends more weight to the dream. It puts more emphasis on the content, maybe even indicating a sign or omen was lurking. Admittedly, I had been doing it with irregular frequency since I was a child, but it was still a surprise when it occurred.

It was also a surprise when my alarm clock began its shrill mechanical screeching the second my head hit the pillow. I contemplated smashing it, or perhaps dumping a bucket of water over it. I could very easily picture myself laughing maniacally as it fizzled and sparked through its last moments.

I made a deal with myself: if I could get it to explode using telekinesis, I'd just screw the whole school day.

Forty minutes later, I was starting the walk down to the bus stop with a pounding headache from scrunching my face up and rubbing my temples at a clock. It was only then that I remembered I was supposed to be in super-secret surveillance mode for a new student who might have moved in down the road. The whole sleepwalking episode had me on high-alert, and the possible new arrival was the only atypical thing that'd happened in days. That meant I couldn't just shirk my duties. I had a personal responsibility to check it out.

Luckily for me, if there was a potential high school student up the road, we'd be sharing the same bus stop. That made my work so much easier. I just had to wait there and board the bus like any other day. I perched on a rock and attempted to look natural, listening behind me rather than looking. There was something moving around softly in the woods to my left, but no tell-tale slap of sneakers on pavement.

Slightly disappointed, I hopped on the bus when it came and plopped down in the only completely open bench seat left. It appeared Jessica had missed our ugly yellow transportation to prison, because I usually sat with her. The bus began to pull away, so I pulled out my clunky cell phone to text Jeremy the bad news—he had been misinformed.

Just as I was making plans to investigate the dilapidated house down the road after school, the bus braked abruptly. I had to thrust my palm out to keep from head-butting the seat in front of me.

Thinking a deer or some other critter had jumped into the road, I peered out the window. My pulse spiked to see a tall, blond boy had emerged from the woods only a few feet from where I had been perched on the rock. His backpack looked too small strung on his back. His arms were lined with visible muscle, all the more apparent when he thrust one out, the palm of his hand calloused.

His movements betrayed no franticness, but it was clear he intended for the bus to stop. I guess his telekinetic skills were a little better than mine, because the brakes screeched something hellish as we rolled to a standstill.

When the doors opened, he stalked right up to the steps with a sure, steady gait. Headache forgotten, I watched as he tilted his head side to side to search for a place to sit. His gaze zeroed in on the open seat next to me, close to the only one left. He walked up the aisle and inquired, "Can I sit here?" The deep, rumbly quality his voice had was pleasing to the ear.

"Sure," I said, proud when it came out strong rather than squeaky. I scooted over to the window, close enough that the cold of the fall morning bit through my shirt. I watched him from the corner of my eye. Even through the blurred edge, I could tell he was good looking. Something about how he held himself, though, reminded me of a wolf. Perhaps it was just the leftover leaf litter strewn on the top of his head from dashing through the woods.

Now that I noticed that...Gosh darn it, I couldn't leave it there. Who wants to start their first day with a leaf on their head? I awkwardly half-reached out half-pointed.

"Umm...You brought a little tree with you," I stated. My hand was still awkwardly hanging, unsure if I should remove it myself or wait for him to brush it off. He chuckled, a low rumble.

He reached up to brush the litter off. "What I get for being late."

I retracted my hand. I figured I was on a roll now, though, so I might as well up the awkward.

"So, I'm Leah. Are you new?" I asked, well aware of the answer.

I could tell from his short sentences that idle talk wasn't exactly his thing. "Just moved here."

I think he realized the same, because he continued. "My name is Lucas. Most people just call me Luke."

Now the internal debate began. Do I ask questions? Is that too much prying? Gah. People were not my thing. But then again...He might not be people. A new person brought a whole slew of possibilities. Perhaps he was an empath? A vampire? Oh, no, I had it. With that entrance, he was totally a werewolf. This I just had to investigate!

I subtly eyed him, looking for signs. Factoids from different myths and lore exploded in my head like fireworks. "Are you from around here?"

His shoulders were relaxed, but his gaze was full of intensity. His eyes found mine and did not leave. Though they were a delightful shade of blue-gray, the urge to look away was almost overwhelming. However, to look away was to submit, and I was not a submissive person in any way, shape, or form.

"Few hours north of here. Maine," he finally said. I was still so captivated by his gaze that I almost missed it. Unfortunately, that left me floundering for a reply.

"Oh, that's cool," was all I could think of. I figured that any more questions would be an intrusion, so I left it at that. I allowed my eyes to slide off his, but to the side, not down. Down is submission, side or up is stalemate.

I returned to my peripheral vision studies. He definitely looked like someone raised by hard work. His left hand was open, and I could see the calluses coating it. His flannel shirt bore a worn plaid pattern. He did not look unclean, but there was something under his short-cut fingernails. Some dark color. Perhaps dirt? No, not quite, it had a reddish tint.

Blood.

Things had just gotten a whole lot more interesting.

"He's totally a werewolf!" I half-joked, half-informed

Jeremy as we were walking toward our meeting place. Every day, after the bus let us off, we stealthily circled behind the school and into the woods. There was a beautiful stream-fed pond about a minute's walk in, obscured from sight by densely packed pines.

Today, it was a sight to behold. The rising sun caught all the ripples on its surface and turned the whole thing into a cauldron of gold. Combined with the verdant evergreens and the deciduous trees' freshly recolored leaves, this place was like an artist's paradise. Jeremy had been eager to sketch it for months now, never seeming to have the time.

Jeremy laughed, but not in a harsh way. He chuckled like what I had said was merely an inside joke between the two of us. In some ways, it was. He was my sounding-board for all things not fit for public discussion. It was not a rare occurrence when I leaned over, gestured to a person, and whispered, "Telepath?"

He was also nearly the only one I'd told about my dreams, at least in depth.

"What makes you say that?" he asked in a mock-curious way. He began to walk along the edge of the pond, being careful to avoid getting his feet stuck in mud. Leaves crunched as I widened my stride to catch up.

"He came running out of the woods this morning. But the thing is, I've been thinking—" I ignored Jeremy's mock gasp. "I was pretty vigilant this morning, listening. If he was so late he had to dash through there, wouldn't he have made lots of noise? I definitely would have heard him," I stated. I knew it wasn't conclusive evidence, but it was enough to excite me. Jeremy, on the other hand, looked like he found my speech adorable. I decided to bring out the big gun.

"He had blood under his fingernails." I watched for his reaction. A strange look passed over his face, one I couldn't decipher. It was quick, though, because his smile burst out again after a moment.

Jeremy's teeth flashed. "Maybe he's a vampire."

I laughed. "No way! He took tons of sunlight to the face on the bus ride here and didn't flinch, he isn't exactly pale, didn't seem effected by my heartbeat, and didn't react to my bag of tricks."

I gestured to my backpack, which had a little draw-string bag inside full of miniaturized totems from many different religions and cultures. In the supernatural world, it was as good as an arsenal. I even had a miniature printout of an exorcism spell. This girl came prepared.

For some reason, he got that funny look on his face again. "Maybe you should stay away from him? You know, he doesn't really sound safe."

I was taken aback by the seriousness of his tone. Did he really think a new student was a danger to me?

"I can handle myself just fine, Jeremy," I snapped with a little more aggression than I planned. I knew he was just worried about me, but I'd never been able to handle being ordered around much. It made my teeth clench. He seemed to realize his error instantly and grinned again, trying to alleviate any negative feelings.

"Oh, it's not you I'm worried about, it's the new kid. Luke, his name was? I'm afraid you are going to kidnap him and lock him up in your basement for the next twenty years as a supernatural specimen," he retorted. I choked down my laughter and gave him a playful shove. But I might have shoved just a little too hard, because he staggered a step to the left.

Unfortunately, there was no land to the left, only water. He did a sideways belly flop-type maneuver and water rose up in a magnificent fight against gravity. It cascaded down in a circle around where he had gone under. I waited for him to rise, gasping a shocked laugh. The water wasn't that deep toward the shore, only about ten feet. Any person with swimming abilities should have been able to surface instantly.

But not one with a backpack bursting at the brim with heavy textbooks. After a few silent seconds, this realization struck me.

Panicking, I shucked my own bag and kneeled down to see beyond the glare of the sun. Still seeing nothing, I stuck my face in, eyes quickly locating the human shaped blur of color streaking toward me. Before I could react, Jeremy surfaced inches from my face, heaving huge, ragged breaths.

"Oh my god, are you okay?" I screeched. He did not reply as he started to cough violently. My heart was a hummingbird caged, crashing over and over again into my ribcage. Jeremy extended his hand to me, signaling for me to pull him up and over the bank.

I quickly complied, grabbing his hand and reaching behind me to grab a root as leverage. Before I could, however, I felt a sharp yank from Jeremy's side, the force of which rolled me straight into the freezing Vermont water. The shock of the cold was almost enough to make me inhale the instant I hit it. It took a second before my brain turned on and screamed 'surface'.

My sneakered feet hit something solid underneath me, and I used it as a spring board. A few strokes later, I could breathe again. And, despite the copious amount of water in my ear, I could hear. Jeremy's laughter was loud enough that I wouldn't be surprised if the whole county could hear as well. Wiping water and what little makeup I'd been wearing out of my eyes, I couldn't help but to start laughing as well.

"What did you do that for? It was an accident, I swear!" I croaked out, still laughing too hard to say more than a few words at a time. Both of us treaded water, though when his hand accidentally brushed mine, I couldn't feel it. My skin was numb with the cold.

"I'm going to need some help getting my backpack out of the mud at the bottom, and since you put it there, you have to help," he said, but his naughty grin showed that having me fetch the bag had been an afterthought.

"You're such a...Meanie!" I exclaimed in a particularly expressive display of vocabulary and maturity. Blame the freezing water.

"Meanie bobeanie, and don't you forget it." He winked. "Now, grab a strap and help me pull my bag up from the abyss."

He ducked under the water and I followed suit, keeping my eyes open to locate the backpack and pick where to pull.

Only one problem though, it's nearly impossible to get leverage without a solid surface underneath you. Well, that and the fact that the solid thing I had utilized to break the surface might very well have been the bag, seeing as the mud's greedy mouth had swallowed the entire bottom of it.

Yanking proved fruitless, only getting our feet stuck in the muck as well. We returned to the surface to revise our plan not only wet but mud-soaked.

"How are we supposed to do this?" Jeremy whined. His normally springy curls were acting like they felt gravity for the first time, flopping over one of his eyes.

"You know, if you hadn't dragged me in I'd have been able to grab a branch and use it to pry up your bag," I teased as I waggled my finger at him. Nearest to us, the bank was smattered with wet rocks and roots, climbing it would have us embracing the ground in no time, face-first. We'd have to swim over to where the shallow stream fed in to be able to get out.

Jeremy had an intelligent gleam in his eyes. "You know what? That's a great idea!"

I looked at him, unsure exactly how that was a good idea as we were both currently swimming and neither of us had a stick.

He continued, the plan forming. "Why don't we search here for some tree limbs? There have to be some fresh ones on the bottom from that storm yesterday."

Ignoring the cold water brain freeze, I nodded my assent and dove under, scanning for anything dark. I spied something that looked nice and thick almost immediately. I surfaced and took three deep breaths before diving into the darkness a few feet below.

I wrapped my palm around the smallest part and began to wiggle it. Mud flew up, making me close my eyes to fight against the rough grit. Now sightless, I was relieved when the branch came loose. Twigs clawed harshly against the inside of my wrist, but I ignored the pain as I lugged my catch up to the surface. It was surprisingly heavy. I had to put my second hand on the smooth underside.

The second I surfaced, I knew I done screwed up.

"I said a branch, not a fu—" Jeremy began to yell before my little 'branch' extended its giant neck and went for his head. He flinched and went cross-eyed as the snapping turtle's beak snapped shut less than an inch away from his nose. I jerked my arms backward and nearly lost my shoulder as it came back to make me its new crunchy munchy.

"Are you crazy? Put that dinosaur down!" Jeremy's voice was at the highest pitch I had heard it to date. I put as much distance between me and the snapper as I could while still holding it and slid my hand out from underneath.

Jeremy halted me with a shout. "Wait! Don't let go!"

"Let it go, don't let it go. Make up your mind! Why on earth would I not let it go?" I said, with a twinge of hysteria in my voice. A little twinge. Shut up, I'm tough.

"I am not letting you put that thing where it has access to my crotch!" he yelled, already swimming toward the shallow side of the pond. Dang, he could boogie faster than a seventies disco band.

"Ah, hello!" I yelled, "Forgetting anything?"

The turtle's back claws were really starting to dig into my skin as it kicked in an attempt to free itself.

He shouted from the shore. "Oh, my bag? Satan can have it. Now put his spawn back in the water!"

Water rolled off his body in thick streams which hit the ground hard enough I could hear it clearly from twenty yards away, pounding like a throbbing drum.

"I meant me!" I hollered.

"I don't know, sing it a song! You always said you liked animals!" he said with his hands cupped to project his voice.

"I never said they like me," I whispered, staring at the snapper. "Hello, Mr. Turtle, please don't bite me." The snapping turtle eyed me warily. At least its neck was retracted.

"I have an idea, stay there!" Jeremy said excitedly before

running into the trees. A minute passed, or perhaps it was only a few seconds, before I thought, *screw it*. I was going to torment Jeremy relentlessly about him fleeing as quickly as a cheetah with its tail on fire, but later. I had muddier problems to deal with.

Dragging in a deep breath, I closed my eyes and dug deep. Where was my flame now? The fearlessness, the power, the sense of purpose...Yet I couldn't even convince myself to let go of a puny, mortal turtle. What was the worst it could do, bite the tip of my finger off? I'd live.

With that thought, I pried away my fingers one at a time, not because I was afraid to go any faster, but because I was testing myself. How many fingers could I peel off before emotions crept in again? Turns out, it was six. As soon as one hand was off, my heart went from beating like a hummingbird to diving like a peregrine falcon, straight down to my stomach.

With a strangled *kyah* sound, my arm flung the turtle forward and let go. Instead of turning around to snap at me, it swam away swifter than I thought would be possible for an animal so bulky. A blink later, it was indecipherable from the benthic murk. I watched it with a sort of wary admiration.

After a small eternity, I turned around and swam toward the shallowest point in the water. I really could have walked, but I was not putting my feet within the range of another angry turtle. At the bank, I strained to heave myself up. The combined weight of the water, the mud, and the adrenaline crash desperately attempted to tug me back into the pond.

I managed to roll up onto the solid, dry ground by grasping at handfuls of moss underneath the layers of leaf

litter and dead pine needles. In this state of mind, I wanted nothing more than to melt into the detritus and sleep.
I would even consider taking root like a dryad. Becoming a towering oak tree, arms flung upward in a desperate struggle for the sky's embrace...Oh yes, that would suffice. I might even—

"Leah!" Hands gripped my shoulders with crushing force. "Are you okay?"

I opened my eyes with a jolt, revealing Jeremy's eyes wide and panicked. He had some sort of wooden contraption next to him.

"I'm fine, no thanks to you!" I grumbled and hauled myself into a sitting position. "What the heck is that?" I inquired, nodding at the bundle of sticks.

"Oh, I built it to scoop up the turtle. See? It has a little basket end over here in which I'd grab it, and then I'd pull back this long branch so the bottom would come out—" He halted at my look. "Guess it wasn't necessary, huh?"

"Well, seeing as I don't have my hand down a snapping turtle's throat, yes, everything is okay." And with that, I wasn't mad at him. It was hard to stay angry at someone like him for long at all.

I shrugged it off. "Let's go to class."

His brows drew together. "Soaking wet and covered in mud?"

"Yup, I have a math test to take," I replied without hesitation. Jeremy smiled and extended a hand for me to hoist myself up.

"Wait a minute!" I exclaimed. "We still need to get your bag."

"That thing? It's probably turtle chow by now. I don't think anything in it'll still function. Lucky I forgot my phone this morning," he retorted.

"Use the little...snapper trapper thing you built to grab it!"
And we did.

Five minutes later, we whooped and hollered as the
bundle of sticks dragged up Jeremy's sludge-ball of a bag
from the depths. We shared a celebratory hug that sent
mud and water flying before collecting all of our materials just in time for us to miss the bell commencing second
period.

We fled the scene in a giddy haze, encountering no
problems upon entering the building, at least not of the
administrative kind. We went our separate ways, to our individual classes. The few students in the hall gave me a wide
berth, some even clinging to the lockers as I passed. Funny,
when I looked over my shoulder at Jeremy's retreating
form, the majority of females—and even a few males—grav-
itated toward him, despite the fact that he was as absolutely
filthy as me. I shook my head and smiled to myself.

I was late. When I arrived in my second period English
class, I found that the usual empty seat next to me had lost
its vacant status. Luke was there, and when his gaze met
mine, his eyebrows took their chance to make a launch for
the moon. I slid into my seat, unfazed. He leaned toward
me.

One corner of his mouth twitched up, a miniature
smile. "Is it normal for people around here to come into
class soaking wet and mud-streaked?"

"If there's one thing you are going to know about me,
it's this..." I paused for dramatic effect.

"I'm not normal."

28

The world spun around me, pulsing waves of darkness confusing my senses. The demonic fire wove its way through me, the pain even more blinding than that of the physical wound left behind. The bite alone rendered my calf torn and useless. Puncture wounds gaped like a cave, to the point where one could stick a finger through it and clean out the other side. Each hole was burnt to the point where not a drop of blood heeded the call of gravity. Blackness and blistering pain began its journey upward, meaning to turn me into ash the same as the tree, a sickness and corruption of the soul.

My lips pulled back in a silent snarl of pain. The darkness traveling through my system in thorny tendrils was impure, decay. Everything I was meant to silence in this world. There was only one thing I could do to combat the desecration of my very essence: cleanse myself in the same way I had cleansed the demon.

The golden sword shone in anticipation, shifting from a mortal form to something less tangible. It was a weapon that no longer pierced flesh, but soul. I lifted the blade straight to the sky like a salute to the heavens before turning its tip down and plunging it straight into my chest.

Pain. So much. Warmth, fire, light. Lightness—was I on the ground? Eyes closed. Noise. The wind? A scream? Myself? No matter. Spinning was more important. The whole world spins. Then stops. Images flash. Past. Present. A house. More of a shack. Rotted. Human figures. Men. Secrets, dark ones. Raven says it, and so it shall be: The bridge draws near. The two worlds shall merge.

My eyes rolled in my head, unseeing as my very being was stripped and purified. My breath came in quick gasps that combined with the chorus of phantom and real sounds surrounding me. I felt as though I was being stroked by thou-

29

sands of razor-edged wings, sliced and reduced until only light was left, blinding.

All at once, the pain released. I let out a stuttered gasp as my senses flowed back into me, no longer concealed by pain and brightness. The crunch of leaves below me sounded foreign and startling as I moved my limbs experimentally. My palms were empty, the sword that had saved me nowhere to be found. I stood up, favoring my unhealed leg.

The wound in my calf gave a painful jerk as I bunched up my muscles and kicked off the ground. The angelic sword had left me once the unholy fire was burned out of my system. Demonic flames worked like venom, a speedy poisoning of the soul. Luckily, the angelic fire from my blade had combatted it, leaving only the torn flesh behind.

That ancient sword was gone, off to wherever ancient swords go when they aren't being called upon to deliver demons back to Hell. It was not my sword, not technically, but the number of times it had saved my life and the life of others made me partial to it. I even referred to it by name: Haldis. Though whether the name was by my design or the realm above's subtle thought suggestions, I'd never know.

My wings snapped out, catching air. The wind ruffled the feathers in such a manner that it felt like small, delicate bubbles popping on the surface of my skin. There was no longer a reason for me to be in this forest, and already I felt the stirrings of the pull forward. Soon, there would be someone I must protect somewhere to the west. They were not in danger, or at least, not yet, so the abilities bestowed upon me by Haldis were fading.

The light around me was growing dimmer, beginning to diminish since it was no longer needed. I estimated I only had a few minutes before I could pass as human, albeit a slightly off-looking one. I had to use my time wisely.

I climbed higher into the sky, swerving around the branches extending their leafy fingers toward me as if to shake hands. In what seemed like seconds in the thrill of flight, they spread out, leaving more space. There was a small clearing with a lake situated in the center, glistening from the sun. I was grateful for its presence once the last wisp of my borrowed light evanesced into the sky and I began to plummet.

I fell. Years of experience had me instinctually curling into a ball, the form I had to use to minimize the damage of impact. Do it right and you only get some broken bones. These flesh wounds healed quickly and the pain was tolerable. Do it wrong...Well, that was not pleasant.

However, if I played it right, I could go without breaking anything this time around. I uncurled and straightened, using my familiarity with aerodynamics to arc forward into the position that would deposit me into the water the smoothest. I had less than a second to react to the entire situation.

My hands sliced the water in front of me, which soon enveloped the whole of my person. The lake was deep, even more so than I had imagined. I sank straight to the bottom, where it was cold enough to give a human hypothermia. When I called out to the water spirits, the patches of gooseflesh subsided.

Even better, they smoothed over with scales.

The loose clothing I wore was forcibly ejected as the silvery scales rose to the surface of my legs and melded them together. My feet stretched and thinned, and I gasped at the momentary pain as the skin of my neck was sliced as if by an invisible knife.

Once those slits began to function as gills, I was able to draw a deep breath. I opened my eyes and marveled at the clarity as a third, clear eyelid slid up to cover the more vulnerable surface of my eyeball. I should do this more often, I mused. Not that it was my doing, exactly.

No, it was some force...Other. Elemental. Shifting forms like this was not entirely uncommon for me. It was almost as if the natural spirits recognized my mission and sought to aid me.

If one were to delve through my memory, they'd find many moments where I was broken of body after a particularly gruesome fight or fall, laboring to reach some unknown destination where I must protect an innocent. While the forces of light healed my soul, the spirits of earth and other Elementals would work on my body, morphing it into a vessel more capable of getting where I needed to go.

I'd have liked to believe it was a sign of gratitude, but one never knew with matters so complex. Just like the raven I had seen earlier, it could have been an omen from either Heaven, nature, Hell, or perhaps even myself. I had been in the midst of a cleansing by fire, burning away the taint. Pain that intense may cause hallucinations.

Either way, I was grateful when the stretching of bones and skin ceased and I was left with a new form. This one was quite interesting, a blend of fish and human that frequents human mythology, a mermaid. The pull on my tail fin was delicious, a pleasant tug of muscles as I propelled myself forward. Water swirled off the smooth scales as I made for the swirling sky.

Once at the surface, the skin of my throat knit back together. I did not have time to breathe before I felt an incessant tug at the center of my chest, making my heart beat irregularly. The source of this distress was close, even more so

32

than it had been when the sky dropped me.

Using the long, sleek tail that was already beginning to revert, I moved closer to the shore. The pull was strong, so much so that I could almost sense the threat moving in the brush just barely obscured by shadow. Something lurked there, of that much I was sure. I expected the beginning stir of my inner flames and was surprised when I found none.

Why was I left with only my own, small aura? Where was Haldis? This event was unprecedented. I had never been left completely defenseless in a time of danger. Haldis never failed to aid me in vanquishing demons. That must mean the threat was not of a demonic origin.

I was soon to find out. My freshly human toes lightly tapped the ground as I effortlessly hoisted myself onto the grassy bank. I debated attempting to be stealthy, perhaps to climb a tree or crouch behind a bush, but it was too late for that. I was met with a low, earth-rumbling growl.

I walked calmly toward the noise, verdant grasses springing beneath my toes. I shifted to a jog and quickly met the forest's edge. The second the shadow of the canopy hit me, I could see the dark gray outline of an animal watching from a nearby thicket.

Golden eyes gazed out, darting swiftly from me to the nearest escape to something unseen behind it. Low noise poured off it in waves, getting louder in spurts accompanied by snarls. From what was visible, it seemed to be a large timber wolf, but not unnatural in any capacity.

Yet I felt in my bones that something was not right. I approached, not fearing the minor damages the creature could inflict on me. It was not demonic, therefore if it did anything short of devour me, I could heal.

Before I got within ten yards, however, the beast sprang

from its hiding place and ran, faster than it should have been able. It disappeared in a blur, but not quick enough for me to miss the streaks of a rusty color lining its muzzle and chest, coating the white, brown, and black.

I only had to glance at the spot it once occupied, now vacant, to see why the wolf looked as if it were painted by the sunset. Copious amounts of blood matted the forest floor. Little rivulets that pulsed slowly and sluggishly poured from the open wounds of an unconscious man, expanding the puddle inch by inch until the tips of my toes were stained scarlet.

Next to him lay a woman, faceless where she'd been consumed. Her only recognizable feature was her long, blonde hair and the hiking boots she wore, too tough to be chewed off. Her stomach was an empty cavity.

I didn't have time to take it in. It was too late for me to help her. I knelt down in the pool of gore and extended my hand above the man, whose blue eyes were unfocused and turned heavenward. It took three breaths of my own to realize he no longer drew his.

Chapter Three

Our printer was broken again, much to my dismay during the last minute scrambling before school. I swear, either my father had spilled coffee on the printer's innards again or an impundulu had been targeting our house with its lightning strikes. Neither likely culprit was around to interrogate, however, and I still needed a printer. So, I set off for Jeremy's house.

My car was the only source of noise in the pre-dawn day, chugging along. The beautiful, rose-colored atmosphere created by the sun just under the horizon was almost worth having to get up so early, but not quite. The gas gauge in my car was about as low as my energy, and as empty as my wallet. Hence riding the bus most days.

I'd texted Jeremy, so he greeted me with a smile on the front porch. The instant I went inside, I was tackled by a mini-torpedo.

"Miss Leah! You're here! Did you come to play with me?" Benjamin shouted, much too excited for this hour of the morning. His black curls brushed just above my hip.

He was in a good mood today, to my relief. Benjamin was a little too prone to seeing monsters for his own mental health. When Jeremy had first told me about it, I'd been certain that Benjamin had the clairvoyance found in most youth and lost by the teen years. That was still a working hypothesis, though, as to date I'd never found anything off about their house. However, Benjamin seemed to appreciate my efforts and he had taken to calling me 'Miss Leah' in some form of respect. My relief that he was getting some peace sent a wide smile across my face, but it was diminished when I remembered I was on a schedule.

I was saved from having to tell him so by a familiar voice in the kitchen. "Well, if it isn't my fourth child! How have you been, Leah? Want some pancakes?"

Rosalind Bellevue peeked around the corner, only narrowly avoiding a collision with Benjamin, who'd gone running at the promise of pancakes. Her curls, blonde unlike the rest of her family, waved faintly in the breeze he created. Her smile grew as she spotted Jeremy and me in the entryway.

"If I'd known you were coming, I would have baked something," Rosalind apologized.

My mouth dropped. "At six in the morning? This is not a time for baking!"

She just shrugged and nodded toward Benjamin. "It is when you have little ones."

The other little one, Melinda, was nowhere to be seen. I wasn't surprised. She was a couple of years older than Benjamin, but about five times as sneaky. I kept an eye out for her as I headed toward the stairs.

Rosalind called out to me over the clink of Benjamin's fork hitting the plate as he gulped down his delicious-smelling breakfast. "How are your parents doing, Leah? Has your mom got that promotion yet? I've been too afraid to call and disturb her when she's working so hard."

I shook my head and started climbing the stairs to the office with Jeremy, who had a satisfied little smirk on his face for some reason or another. "Not yet, but she's work-ing her butt off, leaving home early and coming back late, so she'll get there. Don't be afraid to call her and ask her yourself. She'd love to hear from you!"

Rosalind said something in reply, but I missed it. My almost subconscious search for Melinda had resumed. My light brown hair swished over my face as my head swept side to side. I investigated all the dark corners and hidden crannies, but wasn't rewarded with even a suspicious streak of color.

Jeremy, as usual, had interpreted my unusual behavior. "You know she's not going to leap out of the shadows and shank you, right? She's eight."

I raised my eyebrows, not entirely convinced. "Can you prove that?"

Jeremy smiled, a mischievous smirk. "Of course. I could go dig up her birth certificate easily enough."

I sighed as we filed through the doorway into the office. A stuffed fish hung on the wall, one of many, and the sun-light that flickered off its scales not only seemed to animate it, but cast the whole room in a shimmery light reminiscent of being underwater. It also made the glass eyes of the huge bull moose glitter manically, an effect that elicited a double-take from me, even as I continued the conversation.

"I was more talking about her super-secret stabbing ability," I informed him, even though he knew darn well.

An office chair squeaked as it swung to face us. "Whose super-secret stabbing ability are we discussing?"

My grin widened. "Cole! What are you still doing around?"

I blinked when I realized how that sounded, especially to a man like Cole Bellevue, Jeremy's father. "I mean, not that I'm not glad you're here, I totally am, just I'm not used to seeing you around in the day anymore."

The yellow and green Vermont Fish and Game Warden patch on his uniform was a testament to that. I eyed it with envy, trying to imagine myself in a similar uniform, but though it brought me temporary happiness, it faded away almost as quickly as when I tried to imagine myself working in the auto shop with my own father. I tossed my future out of my mind. It wasn't that important, anyway. What was, however, was the essay I had to print. I got to work on that while Cole continued the conversation.

"Yeah, this morning was really busy, but I'm off for a little while now. Don't have to do patrols until nine," he explained. My curiosity was piqued.

"What happened this morning?" I asked. Though slower than molasses, the printer was printing, so I let it do its thing while I further investigated the moose. Its palmate antlers were so wide I felt I could lie in them, curled up, if I wanted to. It didn't look to be the most comfortable, though, so I passed on that opportunity.

Cole Bellevue chuckled softly under his breath, drawing my gaze to him briefly. His skin, darker than the rest of his family, was unmarred despite his active profession, a quality my easily-bruised skin lacked.

"An older lady called about a rabid wolf. When I got there, it was nothing but a skinny coyote that hit the road almost immediately. She had her TV turned all the way up, and I could hear some news story about two people getting mauled by a bear. Must have just been frightened," Cole explained. This triggered an internal debate about whether it'd be worth it to have wolves here, cause, let's face it, wolves are cool, but if they came along with rabid ones and mass hysteria…. The printer, oblivious to the countdown before school, continued to work at a snail's pace.

"Oh, I almost forgot! I picked something up for you the other day in the woods, Leah. I know you said you wanted to try some. Let me go get it," Cole said as he stood and left the room.

I returned to watching the moose. There was something in its eye that was making me uneasy. I moved my face closer, watching it distort and take up most of the surface.

Jeremy's words interrupted my thoughts. "The eyes are sort of creepy, aren't they?"

I shrugged without giving up my vantage point, not quite so affected. "Maybe the duck's eyes are creepy, but I think that ducks are just creepy in general. What makes you say otherwise?"

He leaned closer, as if he was looking into the moose's other eye. "I don't know…It's almost like they despeyes us."

It took a second for the pun to click because of my intense concentration. "I despise *you*."

It was in that moment I registered why the marble eye of the moose was flashing purple.

I spun around. "Oh! Hi, Melinda! I didn't see you…" I trailed off as she disappeared; wholly unconvinced she wasn't just a phantom. Jeremy confirmed my sanity.

"Wow, I think that was the longest conversation you two have ever had," he said sincerely. I was of the same belief.

"One day, I'll get her to like me. Okay, well, maybe getting her to *tolerate* me is a little more reasonable."

Jeremy did not look convinced, but our conversation was cut short by yet another in the busy household.

"Cole, you *are not*, under any circumstances, giving that

girl a wild mushroom! What if it's poisonous?"

"I double checked it, I swear, this one's completely safe. And edible."

I didn't need to be in sight to imagine Rosalind's right eyebrow shooting sky high. "Do you not remember what happened last time? Hmm?"

The printer beeped once, finally done. Jeremy shoved the essay in my folder as I grabbed my car keys, and we took that as our cue to leave.

I grabbed some bagged, maybe-edible mushroom on the way out.

There was a faint flapping behind me, a steady pulse of something smooth beating through the air at regular intervals. My mind conjured the image of a vampire bat honing in on its target, small tongue darting in early anticipation of the blood it would lap. When the source of the noise landed square on my desk, I realized this creature was out for more than just blood. No, this was much, much worse.

This was an essay assignment. They just kept coming. Now, I had wrangled a few of them before, but it was a harrowing process. Adds years, I tell you. And as I returned my mind to the English classroom, I could barely keep from moaning in disappointment. Even worse, it was a partner project.

Normally, that'd be nice. An excuse to get together with friends even. But someone like me does not have an overabundance of possible choices in the friend department. A quick scan of the room revealed that the person I knew the best in there was Luke, which was quite pitiful considering I had gone to the same grammar school as most of the others.

I looked down at the paper and eavesdropped on the people around me, especially Mr. Wolfie in the seat next to me. He did not call anyone right away, but I could hear a group of girls in the back daring each other to partner with him. The bravest one separated from the herd and approached.

"Hey Luke, I'm Sarah. Do you have a partner?" the tall brunette asked, angling just so to best highlight her skinny physique. The smile she threw his way was honest and open. Her friends giggled in the corner, making small bets about silly things, like if he'd say yes or if she'd score a date. He didn't seem overly impressed, however. His eyes were slightly glazed as if he was elsewhere in his mind, a look that had featured on my face many times.

He glanced my way, but I wasn't too sure he was even seeing me. "Actually, I was hoping to work with Leah."

My thoughts froze, little blocks of ice stopping the flow. It seemed the same happened to the pretty brunette, because her mouth opened and closed a few times like a fish on land. Luke seemed to realize that he had accidentally insulted her and rushed to fix it.

"We live close together, same bus. Be easier..." He looked at me pleadingly, with a slightly frazzled look in his eyes. Something was off about him, but I couldn't tell what. I mentally filed it away, making a note to myself to look at the moon phases. When he gazed back up at Sarah, one corner of his mouth twitched down slightly, but it seemed to be more at his own behavior than hers. He must have been pretty out of it.

I searched for something to say, because now not only was Luke watching me, but the brunette and her flock of

41

friends were giving me the stink eye. She looked slightly hurt, like I had purposefully inserted myself in the way of her flirting. I started to say something, though I don't know what because I had the mental capacity of a rabbit at the moment.

I got lucky, because before I could stammer out some sort of apology, she spun on her heel and stalked off to her friends. I really hoped I hadn't just made an enemy, but right then I had more pressing concerns. It seemed I had caught a break from the usual last-people-left pair up.

"Sorry. Working with you is okay? Seemed easiest. Have to stay around the house for a while...." Luke trailed off.

For what, exactly? Werewolf party? Why don't I have a ticket to that shindig? I wondered, my mind leaping to all the insane possibilities.

When I took into consideration that this guy could be a wolf for all I knew, I realized working together was a grand opportunity. I was quick to secure it.

"No, no, it's fine! Saves me from having to do this alone," I stated, giving him a quick smile. *Great, you just established yourself as a social outcast, in case he hadn't noticed,* I sniped internally. "So what is the assignment about?" I looked down at my desk to read the paper and Luke did the same. It was creative, my favorite type of project, but it looked difficult.

It called for two people to do an activity together, something of their choosing but new to both parties. Then the partners would write a two-part essay, with half from his/her own view and half what they expected the other to feel. From the few dislocated snickers floating around, it seemed many people interpreted the instructions as something a little less innocent than the examples of 'stargazing' and 'playing an instrument'.

I lifted my head up to watch Luke rather than the paper, which I'd already read three times. "Huh. Does anything come to mind?"

He had succumbed again to the faraway look in his eyes, but this time accompanied it with a wry smile, lifting at one corner. After a second, his expression became an undisturbed lake. Nothing in particular was going on at the surface, but I knew something was lurking underneath.

"Can't think of anything off the top of my head, but is it okay if we do it tomorrow? There are...certain things...I have to do Sunday. It'll give us more time to work on the writing section," Luke said, although the second part seemed almost like an afterthought.

Suspiciousness increase to 88% capacity. I was definitely going to have to check the moon phases.

My first instinct was to wait for him to come up with an idea, but one was already wisping around in my skull, not yet tangible. "Sure, as long as we figure out something to do."

In a flash, that little smoke-like wisp had burst into a full-grown blaze, quickly outshining any other fledgling ideas. Oh, this was going to be fun.

"Don't you think that's a tad bit dangerous?" Jeremy inquired, mumbling through the wrap he shoved in his mouth. Lettuce screamed in agony as its watery appendages were split and swallowed, resulting in a loud *crunch-crunch* sound. He did not seem as enthused about my project plans as I was.

"I think my track record with this type of stuff is pretty good," I retorted, shoving my own mouth full with a ham and cheese sandwich while raising an eyebrow.

"Leah, that's like comparing a spring breeze and a roaring hurricane! I'm pretty sure maybe once seeing a spirit is different than actually hunting them down in an old, abandoned building." He smiled as he said this, knowing full well he was in for one heck of an argument. Any other day, I would have been on him like a chupacabra on a goat, but my brain was already churning out another idea. It seemed like I was just chock full of good ones.

"Then why don't you come with us? I'm sure I'll need someone as big and strong as you to catch me when I faint like the southern belle I am," I drawled, batting my eyes in a way that most likely appeared closer to epileptic than flirty. Perhaps if we weren't living in Vermont, it would have been slightly more realistic. It did the trick though, because he laughed and pushed up his sleeve to flex his muscles while making some ridiculous squinty-eyed, lip-puckering face he must have assumed was macho.

Then a serious look fell over him and he rolled his sleeve back down. "So what you are saying is that you want me to come with you to some old, creepy building that probably is infested with god-knows-what and wave flashlights around trying to attract the attention of a spirit which may or may not throw me into a wall or possess me?"

I leaned closer, putting my elbows on the table and moving my lips right next to his ear. "Yes."

He chuckled, released from his serious spell. "Good."

And that, my friends, is how you convince someone to willingly take the role of spirit bait.

I walked out the main doors of the school with Jessica and her boyfriend, Mitch. Mitch was eyeing me, but not in a sinister way. His dark brown eyes flickered between me and Jessica, trying to make the image of us walking together meld. I didn't blame him. He wasn't the first, wouldn't be the last...and wasn't the only one, at that current moment.

Jessica was oblivious, as usual. The metal of the pin in her dark hair clinked together with every step she took, notifying all those around us that she was present. The thought of deliberately tossing away my anonymity in such a way left me uneasy, but I supposed just walking near Jessica, who truly did not need that clinking pin to draw envious stares, was doing just the same.

The things I do for my friends. I sighed and tossed the debate out of my head. A little discomfort was far worth it.

I wasn't sure that I knew any of the people Jessica was currently gossiping about, but I nodded along and gasped at appropriate moments, because it was clear she was enjoying herself. A sudden, shocking thud above our heads stopped all three of us in our tracks, which allowed the source of the noise to tumble down over Jessica's head and face. Feathers flew before any of us comprehended that a bird had just hit the sprawling window above the entryway of the school.

Jessica yipped and danced out of the way of the flapping bird, whose motions were slow and jerky. I moved the opposite way, toward the creature in distress. The stream of students that had been exiting the building coagulated in a rough circle around the bird and, by extension, me. I only had eyes for one thing as I moved forward, however. The bird went still as I approached and scooped it up, carefully.

45

Immediately it enlivened, thrashing about and pecking at my hand. I gently inspected its wings, ignoring its assault. A low, amused voice rumbled from in front of me, and I found my circle of isolation had been breached.

Luke smiled at me, a small, soft twist of the lips. "Live a little longer, if it's biting like that."

He was right, and my inspection turned up no broken bones. I wordlessly opened my palms to let the little ball of warmth between them free, and the finch barely blinked at me before taking off, free from the paralyzing shock that had kept it on the ground.

My senses returned to me with the sound of shuffling feet. The crowd around me dispersed, but their words floated around me like ghosts.

A nervous giggle from somewhere in the crowd. "Well, that was weird."

To which her friend retorted. "That *girl* was weird."

"Witch," someone said, or perhaps it was many some-ones. "She brought it back to life."

But they were just the few. I took shelter in the benign chatter, the homework, and deadlines and parties. Luke was still there, and I could only imagine what expression he was seeing on my face. A hand on my wrist yanked me away, weaving deftly through the crowd.

"One, that guy is cute. I had to pull you away before you blew it," Jessica started. Some bird feathers had caught in that pin of hers, so I reached forward and plucked them out.

"Thanks for the vote of confidence."

She continued with both the tugging and the speak-ing. "And two, you know exactly what this means. The bird dream! Get the cards."

I groaned. "Jess, it's just a game. These people think I'm weird enough already."

Jessica turned quickly, calling out. "Mitch, would you mind getting the…"

She trailed off when she realized that he was no longer behind us, having been intercepted by some of his buddies. She shrugged, because that worked just as well to get him out of the way. Her eyes lit upon mine, and I swear, there was a fire brewing in her irises.

"Leah, don't think I don't notice the way you sneak around and slip through people's gazes. I know how you act, like you're some invisible observer. But, hello, you're human. If people couldn't see you, something would be very, very wrong. People think, so it makes sense that occasionally, they'd think of you. Can't be all positive, can't be all negative. It is what it is. Now, cards please?"

I sighed and did as she asked, pulling out my tarot deck. Shuffling them was natural, their glossed surfaces gliding over one another until the deck seemed new, unpredictable. I handed them to Jessica who, knowing the drill, cut the deck three times before handing it back to me. I laid the first card on my knee, for lack of a better surface.

"Six of wands, reversed," I said, tugging at the grass below me semi-unhappily. I didn't think this card would exactly assuage her fears.

She prompted me onward. "And?"

"A large betrayal. Treachery and fear resulting from letting someone in that you shouldn't have." I smiled in a half-hearted attempt to lighten the mood. "I guess those dang birds don't have your back."

The world was in stasis. The trees did not forfeit their leaves to the wind, nor did the brushstroke frost crunch under the footfalls of the forest-dwellers. Sky-reaching grasses took up this swatch of land, painting a bare bulls-eye in the middle of the otherwise endless woods.

At the center of the target was I. I was not enveloped in the protective golden glow I had come to expect, but was instead in a simple, seemingly human, corporeal form. No danger nearby, then. The fighting stance I did not know I was holding relaxed. I was alone, no eyes to witness me.

The brittle heads of grasses tickled my legs as I started walking toward the edge of the clearing. Even after a minute, the trees did not seem to get any closer. In fact, it seemed as if they shied away from me, as if I were contaminated with something they did not want to touch.

I mused over the strangeness of this phenomenon, for I had always been welcomed by the forest prior. As I watched, a wind was winding delicately through the canopy like an anaconda through water, more precise and guided than any gust should be. It left its sunlit throne to descend to the edge of the field.

The grass whistled as the wind threaded through it, getting louder as the stray gust grew closer. When it reached me, it stalled for a minute and grasped at my hair like an overeager child. I was smiling faintly and debated whether or not to fly along with it when it became harsher.

Clumps of grass tore free from the earth and flew by me, pelting me with dirt from their roots. I turned to see what had made the gust so violent and saw that it had acquired hurricane force in the middle of the field. Grass spun around—and through—a dark shadow in the eye.

The forest's avoidance made sense now. This apparition was the cause of it, not I. Even without being able to distinguish features, I could tell this was a vengeful spirit. A dark aura pulsed around it, one that was not demonic but was definitely not a force of light. This spirit was out to do harm, and judging by the steady intensification of angelfire around me, out to do harm to a human.

The wind settled, exhausted from its attempt to purge the shadow. The disembodied soul stood still in the center of the grasses and then it was no longer there. Simply gone in the blink of an eye.

Then the screaming started, and golden fire pumped through my veins. I was off the ground before it had me completely, but I did not dip to the earth again. Instead, I was a bolt of lightning soaring across the field and into the woods.

My wings passed unscathed through the trunks of trees, for only something of angelic or demonic substance could touch them in this early stage of manifestation. I was so close that when the scream stopped I could hear the person's ragged gasp before everything fell silent.

I found the location of the human in distress by heading toward the darkest part of the forest. In this area, light did not filter through the canopy as it should. I swooped in, landing square in the center. My undulating aura fought off an impressive amount of dark fog and illuminated the source of it all.

A human girl was quivering; mouth opened to the sky as the dark entity from before entered and pushed itself through her every pore. It was trying to rip her soul straight from her body so it would be the vessel's sole occupant. From the glazed look in her roaming eyes, the spirit was succeeding. Black crept over the whites of her sclera.

49

I landed in front of the girl without a sound, though it wouldn't have mattered if I had made all the noise in the world. The girl looked like an insect attempting to fight off a spider bite, writhing as paralysis slowly took hold. I knew I did not have long.

"Spirit, I command you to leave this vessel. Failure to obey will result in immediate soul-cleaving," I warned verbally, unable to use telepathy with something so unlike myself. I did not receive a response and I was not going to waste any more time when an innocent was being killed in front of me.

I opened my palm to the sky and Haldis came readily, willing to serve against the threat of corruption. The golden flames I had cast before were mere sparks when compared to the inferno that came with Haldis. Since spirits are not demonic, but once human, I could not simply force it out with flames. It had no physical body to burn, manifestation or otherwise, unlike the demons I so often encountered. There was only one option, a terrible, tricky last resort.

I plunged Haldis into the girl's chest. No skin fissured and no blood pumped out, because I had plunged the angelic sword right into her soul in much the same way as my wings had gone straight through the trees earlier.

Her screams before were nothing next to her screams then. Black smoke evanesced from her mouth in little bursts as tarnished parts of her soul were excised, along with the attacking spirit. Her screaming took on an eerie quality and doubled as the spirit agonized through her, trying desperately to cling to its recently acquired host.

The spirit had no chance. It poured out of her, so weak its aura was completely snuffed out. It seemed to dissolve into air, likely not gone but dormant. The girl, however, without the spirit to keep her upright, collapsed.

I caught her and lowered her to the ground before kneeling and pulling Haldis out. It returned to its mysterious dwelling place almost immediately, leaving me alone with the young brunette. Her eyes were bloodshot, calling out their green hues. The girl was gasping, desperately heaving air into her convulsing body.

There was not much I could do but wait. If her soul was closer to being pure than corrupted, she would live a normal, if not improved life. If its composition had large quantities of darkness, the soul would be too fragile to maintain a body. I prayed she would live.

Her gasps stopped suddenly. Her body quit shaking. However, I smiled. From my vantage point, I could see her chest rising and falling in an unpronounced but rhythmic way. Her eyes had closed in sleep rather than remained open in death. She would be just fine.

With the recession of danger, the angelfire pulled away. Even though she was technically no longer threatened, I picked the sleeping girl up and carried her out of the woods. She did not so much as mutter her dissent as we swayed forward, still in a slumber so deep it might take her a night or two to wake.

I knew instinctively where to bring her, following a faint trail of her aura. I did not have far to walk before she was returned safely, looking as if she had taken a rest on a reclining, blue-and-white striped lawn chair. The residual aura evanescing around it told me that was something she had done in the past. I left the small neighborhood at the edge of the woods feeling sure about her safety and well-being.

I disappeared into the forest and walked for a long while, eventually getting back to the point where it all began. Wind whistled through the grass, playful once more. The trees stood around the circumference, still and guarding. There was one difference, however.

Eyes to the sky, a dark mass blotted the horizon. Bright flashes crawled through it and pumped like blood through a heart. The cloud wasn't crying yet, but it looked ready to burst at the seams.

A storm was coming.

Chapter Four

Audio recorder? Check.

Video camera? Check.

Trail camera with infrared? Check. (Thank Odin for Cole Bellevue allowing me to "borrow" these)

Digital camera? Check.

Flashlights? Check.

Dowsing pendulum? Check.

Bag of tricks? Check.

Lovably annoying best friend? Check.

Mysterious neighbor? Erm...In progress.

Truth was I had forgotten to collect his phone number, email, or anything at all that I could use to contact him. What I hadn't forgotten to check, however, was the moon phase. I added another penny to the werewolf fund when I found out the full moon was on Sunday.

Either way, it didn't help me get into contact with him. There was only one choice left, it seemed. I would show up on his doorstep toting about eight different cameras and a knapsack full of various equally unexplainable spirit communication/protection charms.

It was quicker to get to his house as the crow flies than by walking the main road, so I set out as soon as I gathered all the equipment. With a tripod slung over one shoulder, trail cameras bouncing off my hips, and a drawstring bag on my back, my gait was uneven and a smidgeon painful.

Perhaps I should have driven, but it was a shame to waste such a beautiful evening. The sun shone strong through the canopy of pines, highlighting each bead of moisture like a glistening silver bullet. If I had more time, I would have stopped to investigate each one of them. Unfortunately, I had a schedule to follow. It was best to set up the cameras before dark to make sure everything worked.

After a short time, the dilapidated cabin was in sight. I slowed down a bit, observing it. The structure itself was uninteresting, just very old. It didn't hold my attention for long. No, what I was looking for was any sign of the inhabitant. If I was truthful, I was looking for any sign the inhabitant had succumbed to lycanthropy.

Unfortunately, having my eyes on the house meant that they were not on the ground. Even at my slow rate of speed, I managed to trip over a pesky root and slam down on my butt. Twisting around in order to get up, my tripod smacked into the bark of a nearby tree. The resulting resonance cracked like a gunshot, making me flinch even further into the leaf litter.

I felt like such a moron for it. A scarlet flush crept up my neck like a tide was coming in. I scurried up, clinging to a sapling with deer-nipped buds. Once standing, a second clash almost brought me back down on my knees. My heart pounded as my head swiveled to find the source.

There was no way that noise was an echo of mine, it was too loud and too late. It seemed almost deliberate, the distinctively hollow sound of wood against wood. Instantly a theory popped into my mind, but it was impossible. I mean, it couldn't possibly be—

Thunk.

THUNK.

Two progressively louder knocks wiped away the doubt and allowed me to think clearly. I whipped out my cell phone and debated using the outdated camera on it, but ultimately concluded it wasn't worth it. Any image that dinosaur produced could easily be recreated by a toddler with a stick of chalk.

Instead, I punched in one of the few numbers I knew by heart and hit dial.

"Ready to g—" Jeremy's steady voice began, but I cut him off.

"Jeremy. I think there's a sasquatch in these woods," I whispered quickly, not wanting to scare it away. I had never been fully on board the bigfoot/alien conspiracy train, but no way in hell was I going to miss out on evidence like a newbie. If only I had something to record with....

"Leah, weren't you the one who told me not to eat the random orange mushrooms that—" Jeremy began.

"I just told you there is a bigfoot here! I got wood knocks in reply to me banging my tripod—" and then it hit me harder than a golem's fist. "My tripod! I'm such an idiot! I have like six different cameras on me!" I smacked my forehead with the heel of my hand before I knelt down and began to free all my electronics from their cloth prisons.

I shoved the phone between my shoulder and ear for a second before it slipped down to the forest floor. I knew it wasn't broken, though, because I could hear every couple of words and occasionally a few phrases that Jeremy said. My frantic camera set-up had mismatched and muffled words as background music.

Click, main video camera in place.

"High as a..." Jeremy muttered.

55

Whir, digital camera on and ready to go.

"Are you even..." His voice was muffled, like a wind-storm with nothing to blow against.

Snap, the audio recorder was on. It was unlikely a squatch would howl outside of night time, but I had just gotten a wood knock in the middle of the afternoon, hadn't I?

"Should I call the..." I wasn't even truly paying attention anymore.

Scrape, the tripod with main video camera mounted on it was in place.

"Only you..." Why had I called him again? *Definitely going to have to break this dependency, it isn't healthy,* I thought.

Zip, all non-essential things went back in the bag. I didn't have enough time to set up the trail cams.

"Kidnapped by yetis..."

I grabbed the phone and stuck my face behind the lens of the tripod camera.

"How many times have I told you yetis are mountain-dwelling creatures in Nepal, Idjit?" I hissed, trying to keep my voice low. My eyes scanned the surrounding woods.

"Oh, you're still alive. That's good, I guess. Now, what the heck is going on?" He didn't seem overly concerned, so I had no problem simply hitting the off button. I'd text him later.

Right then, I had to focus on opening all my senses. I tilt-ed my head so that I could get an approximate height along with distance and position if it were to knock again. I didn't have to wait long before I heard another loud bang of wood against wood. It was behind me, so I pivoted around the cam-era, turning it with me. I was then facing Luke's house.

Something brown poked out from behind a tree at the edge of his yard and then quickly darted behind it as something black peeped out about a yard above. The black disappeared just as the brown had and another wood-on-wood thump had me gritting my teeth to keep from squeaking in excitement.

I had to change positions. There was no way I was going to let a tree block my line of sight to quite possibly the world's most elusive creature. But how to do it discreetly? I didn't want to make a noise that might scare it away.

My hand was moist as I unfurled it from the digital camera and let it dangle on its wrist strap. With two hands, I lifted the tripod straight up and then crept with it from rock to rock, careful not to crunch any leaves or sticks. Not a peep escaped my feet or my tripod.

Well, that wasn't exactly true. I may or may not have stepped on a wiggly rock and went down hard, lightly scraping my forehead as I laid my cheek on the ground. I didn't even bother getting up for a few seconds; rather I just let out a sigh I felt should have been hurricane-force strong. How on earth had I fallen twice in such quick succession? Normally I was light-footed when winding through the woods.

The deep-throated caw of a raven had me spinning my head so forcefully I was surprised my neck didn't snap. My eyes lit upon two pairs of eyes, one black and unfathomable up above, and one a shocking grayish-teal. The shadow-filled eyes belonged to the raven which had drawn my attention. However, as far as I knew, sasquatches did not have blue eyes.

I might not have known any squatches with blue eyes, but I sure as heck knew the person watching me. Luke, his arms and face striped with dirt and fingers wrapped around the handle of an ax, had a confused wrinkle between his brows and examined me for half a second before striding toward me. The ax was deeply embedded in a log thicker than me and with a gnarled knot on the side.

I felt the urge to grind the heel of my hand into my forehead yet again for my stupidity. Do you know what you do when you get stuck in a knot while splitting firewood? You set up another piece of wood underneath it to smash the log down on top of, pushing the ax head through it. I was no stranger to this type of work, nor the wood-on-wood sound it produced. My father had been a real fan of stockpiling firewood when I was younger, but in recent years, there just had not been the time. This lumberjack, however, was not my father.

"Are you okay?" Luke called. There was something off; it was almost as if he spoke louder than necessary. It wasn't out of concern, though I could see traces of that in the lines of his face, but like he was warning someone of my presence. He reached me and extended his hand, coated in a fine layer of dirt and wood fragments. I took his pleasantly rough palm and was lifted effortlessly to my feet.

"I'm fine, thank you. I was just coming to get you. Ready to do our project?" I brushed myself off and attempted to discreetly press the stop recording button on the video camera, but found I didn't have to because the preview screen said 'standby'. In my haste to film the supposed sasquatch, it seemed I had never even started to record. A bigfoot could have done the Hokey Pokey in front of me and I would not have had any evidence whatsoever.

"Oh, great. What're we doing?" He cast a semi-suspicious glance at all of the stuff I had brought, but it seemed more on the curious side rather than wary. His posture was a little more relaxed than it had been on the bus and in school. I pondered whether to take his relaxedness as proof of my werewolf theory, but it could easily be chalked up to new kid nerves, even though I was having a hard time imagining Luke as nervous about anything.

"Well, umm, I thought it might be fun to run down to the library and try to get evidence of the paranormal?" I could feel myself blushing with embarrassment so strongly I knew whatever cuts or blood I had on me would soon be just a drop in the sea of scarlet. Why had I thought it was a good idea to bring a guy I barely know to an abandoned library in the hope that some wayward spirit had meandered over from the neighboring graveyard?

Luke scrunched his eyebrows and looked at me. Really looked at me, eyes going all the way down and then back up to rest on mine. I could see the mental recalculation in that gaze, like when someone looks at the same thing every day for years, but could only draw a general outline with his or her imagination filling in most of the glossed-over details. He looked at me like he had held his picture up for comparison and found that his drawing and I were as different as a river and an ocean.

But then he smiled all the way up to his eyes, causing little crinkles to appear at the corners. He stepped closer and grabbed my tripod, easily dismantling it and slinging it over his shoulder.

He gestured out in front of him. "Lead the way."

I stood there for a second with my head cocked, but quickly blinked myself out of it and turned to the left, angling back toward the road. As I walked forward, he kept pace easily.

When we reached the road, I marched across the unpaved gravel without hesitation and straight into the woods on the other side. It was the same situation as it was with Luke's house; time favored the woods rather than the road. Luke hesitated for a beat, but then he was at my side again faster than an exposed vampire running for cover at dawn. If I'd expected him to ask questions, I was disappointed.

I had two options of route from here. Well, technically three, but following the roads would make us late to meet Jeremy at the library. So that was out. The other two were different game trails in the woods. One cut straight to the library, going up a steep incline we were likely to have to climb. The other wound leisurely around the little hill, making it an easier trek but much longer.

I opted for the first because if I could do it, a werewolf could. As I'd hoped, Luke was able to do everything I did with ease and we made it up without any major injuries. We walked in silence. At first I felt the need to fill it, but after a while the crunching of our soles against the leaves was enough.

The rocks littering the path fled under my feet, and I heard one or two bounce off Luke's calves on their descent. He never made a sound, not a single grunt. As I looked up the incline, however, I couldn't help but wonder how many of them were castaways from the graveyard above.

The library was as menacing as ever when we reached it. The old building had been around for ages and had not been well cared for even when it was operational twenty-five years ago.

Thick vines crawled up the side of the building and pulsed like living veins when a gust of wind blew over them. Other vegetation crowded the foundation, taking every opportunity to breach the library through worn away chinks or broken windows. The surrounding woods shrouded the cemetery next to it, enough where we'd need a machete to fully investigate it. I decided to save that for later.

The effect of the vegetation on the skeletal building was eerie, almost as if the library itself was possessed. I took the creepiness as a good sign. Soon, the slam of a car door broke me out of my reverie.

"Is this private property?" Luke bent down to whisper in my ear as Jeremy leapt out of his truck. I must have forgotten to tell him Jeremy was coming. Whoops. Before I got to inform him, Jeremy approached us.

"You ready for some smudging? Ritualistic chanting? How about some head spinning?" Jeremy teased, scooping one equipment bag off my shoulder. His smile dimmed down to a polite one, and he introduced himself to Luke.

"Hi, I'm Jeremy," he stated, not anywhere near as warm as before. Luke nodded and extended his hand.

"Luke," was his simple introduction. They shook a little harder and longer than necessary. I had to stifle a groan because I had not expected the dominance competition. Both of them stared each other in the eye, not looking away even when I meaningfully shook my equipment.

"Sorry to break up this piss-party, but we've got stuff to do," I jabbed as I walked by them, not entirely sure they would follow. Luckily, it didn't take long at all before I heard them both laugh and fall into step behind me. It was likely that Jeremy had made some sort of face or gesture mimicking my bossiness to lighten the mood. A small, proud smile made the corners of my lips turn upward almost indiscernibly.

The doorway screamed like a banshee when I pulled it open. Dust motes swirled out of the new opening in a mad rush for freedom and I had to blink my eyes furiously to keep them out. Stepping in, I was surprised to see shelves full of books were still in their orderly rows.

I suppose it made sense, because the library had been closed due to structural instability. Moving the heavy book cases would have required heavier equipment and, of course, money. Luckily for us, the book cases still holding strong meant the floor would be able to support our lesser weights. Having the titles still there, though, just added to the air of abandonment in the place.

I had been on the premises before, but I had always assumed the door was locked so I never ventured inside. Don't tell the boys, but I had been planning to climb up one of the vines and through a window. With the door wide open, it made this little excursion seem less like a B&E operation. I mean, technically it still was, but whatever. It was in the name of science!

The room I stepped into was painted grey and gold in the late afternoon light. The sun slanted at an odd angle through the vines coating the majority of the windows, making dust dance and shadows twirl along the faded brick walls. I knew then I was going to have to be precise in my set up, for I didn't want any fake orbs or suspicious shadows that were actually dust motes or ivy leaves shimmying outside entering my shots.

From what I could see, this main entry space had two small rooms connected to it by narrow hallways. Off to the side, a gray-white door with little flakes peeling off it partially obscured a descending stairway. A creepy basement? Fabulous. We were sure to get some action there.

The boys filed in behind me, saying nothing as I surveyed the surroundings. Perhaps they were waiting for me to tell them what was what, as I was obviously the most experienced in this area. However, I doubted it. I couldn't picture Luke as anything but a leader, a right-and-proper alpha. Most likely, they could feel the strange heaviness to the air here, a silence so oppressive I couldn't shake the feeling that I would be struck for breaking it.

However, the sinking sun forced me to shove words out of my mouth. I tried not to flinch at the loudness, even though my voice was barely more than a whisper. "Okay guys, I think here is a nice place for base camp. We don't have any active monitors, but it would be nice to set all of our stuff down in a place that is central so it can be easily reached."

I thought for a second before continuing. "It would be ideal to set up one camera in both of the smaller rooms on this floor. You two can put one in the far corner of each room, the one that faces the majority of the room and the hallway. Don't forget to hit record," *like some doofus had done earlier.* "Get started on that while I do this area."

"At your bidding, Your Highness," Jeremy sniped with a smile as he grabbed another camera from me. Luke didn't say anything, just loped off to do his job. If he was uncomfortable or confused, he didn't show it. Then again, I didn't think I'd know even if he was showing it.

I grabbed a trail camera and found a bookcase to perch it in. I made sure to flick the switch so it would not only take a picture, but record a one-minute video when something interrupted its infrared beam. I wasn't entirely sure if a ghost would trip it, but it was worth a shot.

None of this was an exact science. In fact, most would argue it wasn't science at all. Looking around, I kept on expecting to see a shadow or hear a whisper. I had to remind myself that it took a lot of energy for spirits to manifest themselves in ways that are visible to ordinary-yet-open people like me. It was at times like this when I wished I could be a psychic medium, clairvoyant, or even the almost-angelic being from my dreams. I'm sure they would be able to spot ghosts easily enough.

Despite my petty desires, I was still woefully reliant on technology to tell me when something was amiss. The boys returned almost simultaneously, both casting suspicious glances at all the dark corners of the library. I told them to wait while I set up our remaining camera in the basement.

"Help yourselves," I said as I gestured to my bag in the middle of the floor. Kneeling by it, I extracted one flashlight and clicked it on. It wasn't necessary to use them on the main floor yet, but that basement looked darker than tar. I realized then I probably should have brought a few more cameras, because all I had left now was one trail camera and the digital. Oh well, I would make good with what I had.

I stopped and turned around before entering the dark. I tried to tell myself it wasn't fear, but because Luke had made a sort of soft chuffing noise under his breath. I addressed it with a smile.

"Got a problem?" I teased. I placed my hands on my hips a little awkwardly. It's hard to look brave when your fingers were clutching a flashlight just a tad too tightly to be normal.

"Sure it is safe? One of us could...." He trailed off when he saw Jeremy's attempt at a stealthy head shake warning and my rising eyebrows and cocked smile.

Both Jeremy and I laughed. He knew very well that I would twist Luke's words into a challenge, and any hope of one of them accompanying me to set up the camera was lost. Jeremy began to instruct Luke in the art of dealing with me the second I turned my back and began to walk down the stairs.

The chilly air hit me like a blast to the face and made me remember I had forgotten to bring thermometers. Although I reasoned most of this cold was merely because I was now underground, spirits are known to manipulate the temperature of areas as they draw energy to manifest. I resisted the urge to put my palm against the wall or railing for balance because I knew I'd come into contact with tons of creepy crawlies.

The steps felt surprisingly sturdy underneath my feet, a fact which I was immensely grateful for. I kept my flashlight trained straight ahead, unwilling to move it from the staircase because I knew I would trip and cartwheel down the stairs the second I moved the beam away.

I let loose a little smile of victory when I reached the bottom. I slid my flashlight side to side, creating a mental map of the room. I'd need it later. It was kind of strange. All of the larger furniture was left, but anything small was gone. From the looks of it, anything that would have required dismantlement and/or multiple movers to bring it up the narrow stairs was left behind.

There was a single bookshelf against the wall. It was shorter and a little wider than the ones in the main section of the library. It was even a little darker than the ones upstairs. I figured it must have been some sort of personalized shelf, not for the general public. The volumes there were thicker than my calf.

The large wooden desk in the center of the room solidified the idea that this might be an office rather than a storage unit for the library like I had originally thought. It was strange to have such a huge desk in the center of everything rather than on the wall, but I didn't pay too much heed to that fact.

There were no other objects in this gloomy area, so I could not resist approaching the desk. Multiple drawers lined each side of it. None of them were locked, so I gave into the desire to take a peek. I held my breath as the first one squeaked open.

Nothing but dust. Disappointing. The second one revealed the same results, as did all of the drawers on the left side and the first two of the right. The last one, however, did have something.

It wasn't what I was looking for, but after yanking furiously to open the drawer a big wood spider scurried toward me. I gave it the evil eye, but it was lost on the creature. It crawled up the side and on my hand before dropping to the floor and scuttling off. I watched it go and began to shut the drawer. But I stopped when I thought, *wait, something is off.*

It took me a second to realize what struck me as odd. How would a spider of that size get into a drawer stuck tight? I pulled the drawer out entirely and noted a little black hole in the bottom. I put my flashlight under the drawer and the light did not travel through.

"Huh," I muttered under my breath. "I wonder if...."

I turned the drawer upside down and was rewarded with a solid scraping sound from inside. I sucked in an excited breath. Was there something hidden inside it? A long, thin crack extended on a diagonal from corner to corner on the bottom. It reminded me of the way mud looks when it dries, all plated and broken. I chalked it off to natural decomposition of the wood, not the secret way in.

I righted the drawer and looked again at the small hole. I needed a pencil or something small to stick inside and pry it up. Without any luck, I searched the desk again for a writing implement. I looked down at my hands, which were ashy gray with dust and dirt coating them.

Finally, I elected to wedge my pinkie in the hole and use my nail to wiggle it loose. My littlest finger was just small enough to fit in, and the uneven edges of the hole bit into my flesh. It felt like tiny devils jabbing at me with pitchforks, but I angled my finger so the pressure was pushing up. I was rewarded with a thunderous crack as the wood unstuck from the sides.

Because it was such a low-tech system I wasn't expecting classified government documents, but I could not stop the excited smile from spreading over my face and my hands from clapping together in excitement. A chill crept up my arms, spreading gooseflesh in its wake as I remembered where I was.

With a muttered apology to any spirits I might be offending, I extracted a worn manila envelope from the newly opened cavern. It seemed that it had been bleached over time to the same gray that coated my hands. In the middle in barely legible cursive was just one name:

Helen.

A love letter? Business briefs? Probably library dues. My mind whirred to figure it out. There were too many possibilities to discount and not enough evidence. I could feel the bulk of a decent amount of papers inside, and two small and cylindrical things near the bottom. Still I hesitated to open it; it seemed a violation of a dead man's privacy.

I hugged it to my chest, careful not to put too much pressure on any one area, for it would surely rip. Then I quickly accomplished my mission of setting up the video camera at an optimal angle. Taking the stairs two at a time, my flashlight bounced erratically in front of me until I came to a halt in front of the doorway. I could hear the boys' hushed voices, but I couldn't see either of them.

"Don't think that's a good idea," Luke half-whispered with a questioning edge.

What isn't a good idea?

"Trust me, she'll like it. It'll be funny," Jeremy retorted, but he seemed a little disappointed, like he had expected Luke to commend his brilliance. I took this as my cue to open the squeaky door.

"Hey guys, you ready to go?" I called to both, but then my eyes honed in on a brown smudge at the crease of Jeremy's lip and his hand darting behind his back. My eyes narrowed.

"Of course! Just let us—" he started. I cut him off with a raise of the pointer finger.

I wiggled my finger in a reprimanding manner. "You raided my secret chocolate stash."

"Well, it isn't secret anymore. That's for sure," Jeremy replied with a cheeky smile. I fought the urge to lift a different finger and rolled my eyes. Somehow, though, I didn't think the chocolate was what they had been referring to.

"Let's get this show on the road. Because you two are about as useful as sawdust without training, we're going to do the first room together," I commanded. *I'm going to have to do this more often,* I thought. *I like being alpha.*

I walked forward into the left hallway and paused, whispering instructions. It had gotten dark out and our flashlights cut through the gloom perfectly. I made it clear that since we had cameras in every room, our true purpose was not to see a ghost but to use our other senses to perceive them. It would also be beneficial if our presence served as a lure to wayward spirits.

I began instruction with a call and response session. I flicked off my flashlight and the boys followed suit after some whining from Jeremy.

"How am I supposed to defend myself if I can't even see them?" he complained. I was quick to point out that he'd have trouble seeing a non-manifested spirit in broad daylight, so having the lights out wouldn't be much different.

"Besides," I explained, "taking your eyes out of the equation heightens your other senses."

"I'm supposed to smell a ghost?" Luke interjected. Jeremy jumped at the chance to answer, wearing a proud smirk on his face. The fact that he knew the answer at all brought a proud smile to my own face, because it was I who had taught him.

"It is harder to manifest physically, even more so to make oneself entirely visible. It's relatively simple to manifest a scent that the ghost was associated with in life, such as a perfume or smell of smoke, because all that requires is making a few measly pieces of air, rather than bending light," Jeremy said in his instructor voice, which was my cue to get started. If I didn't, he'd probably start telling us the specifics of how scent is perceived and the olfactory bulb's place in it and yada yada yada. Heard that lecture before.

"All right, we start by introducing ourselves. Hi, my name is Leah," I stated as seriously as I could. Luke followed suit.

"Hello, my name is Luke," he continued. His voice reminded me of an oak, strong with a hint of roughness. It was a voice that could leave you scrambling to obey or just sound deliciously like distant thunder, depending on the mood of the speaker.

It might be the wolf, I reasoned.

"Lord Jeremy the Third, at your service," was Jeremy's brilliant input. I heard a faint shuffle in the dark and knew without having to see that he had taken a bow. I glared in his general direction even though he couldn't see me.

"If there are any spirits present, we would like to communicate with you. Could you give us a sign?" I asked.

In the absence of light, it looked like the dark coalesced in certain spots, writhing to and fro in some sort of agitated dance. I had to close my eyes to keep from flinching when these images came too close. Despite my desire to see spirits, I knew these were merely tricks of the mind, a prisoner's cinema.

I flicked the audio recorder on. I should have done it in the beginning, but I was distracted. We weren't hearing anything now, but that did not negate the possibility that someone was trying to talk to us. Sometimes it was easier to catch EVPs, Electronic Voice Phenomena, than to actually hear it with our dull human ears.

Human... I wonder? No, it was almost too good to be true. Humans may have terrible hearing when it comes to spirits, but dogs and cats are noted to be extraordinarily perceptive. I'd think the same would go for a human with wolf hearing, a werewolf. Just as I turned my head in Luke's general direction, he began speaking.

"Are you male or female?" Luke asked, following suit.

I was surprised he knew this was the next step, because I hadn't yet told them to try to ask personal questions to incite a response. I didn't quite know how to process the information. I decided to store it in the back of my mind, unsure what its significance was.

We all waited with racing hearts and skipping breaths. I

thought I might have felt a chill, but I didn't dare break the silence. We proceeded in this pattern, asking a question and waiting before asking again, until I ran out of standard procedure questions. Discouraged by the lack of responses, I had to remind the boys I'd go over the audio and video with a fine-toothed comb later tonight.

I told the group to split up now that they were educated in the ways of the spirit. Jeremy stayed in the first room, Luke took the opposite hall, and I took the main entry. I waited until I could no longer hear the shuffling of Jeremy and Luke moving around to head toward the stacks.

The beam of my flashlight, which had seemed so broad and strong at home, looked far too narrow and dull. My every step kicked up dust, which whorled in a dizzying display in front of my face. I could not help but think that they looked like orbs, the small circular manifestations of spiritual energy. With the dusts' frantic swirling and the closeness of the dark wooden shelves, my mind conjured the image of a predator's jaws snapping shut over its prey. Prey which happened to be me at the moment.

The floor boards moaned softly under each of my footfalls like the building was being roused from slumber. I shuffled forward as silently as possible, ears perked. Light flashed once through the bookshelf and I almost believed it was something otherworldly until it happened again and I realized it was just Luke taking pictures in his corridor.

I rounded another shelf, halfway expecting something to jump out at me. My heart galloped faster of its own accord, and I cursed the blood pounding in my ears. I stopped to help lower the adrenaline in my veins, but the noise of footsteps did not stop. No, I realized, there was a separate groaning noise coming periodically from the ground in the aisle to my right.

Three solid steps on the other side of the shelf, then a pause. It was only a foot away, separated by an impenetrable veil of books. *Or maybe not so impenetrable*, I thought as a book from the top shelf began to slither forward.

The book peeked out over the lip of the ledge, and I began to shake. First my hands, then my legs, then my insides filled with electric bees as I watched the book crawl closer and closer toward me. My brain shut off completely. After what seemed like a millennium, the book tipped and I instinctively attempted to snatch it out of the air.

It fumbled off my hand which I had forgotten contained a flashlight and tumbled painfully onto my toe. I yelped and began hopping on the opposite foot to alleviate the pain. Not at all because I was scared to pick up the book and was stalling. Not even slightly. Nope.

I'm ashamed to admit my hand trembled like a leaf in the wind. I half expected the book to leap up and bite me, or maybe flop open to a certain page which held the secrets of the universe. What I was not expecting was an old, worn Stephen King novel which did not even twitch as I collected it.

I quickly scanned the covers and spine, hoping for a clue. I picked up nothing but the smooth surface. I flipped through the first few pages and found them equally ordinary. The text was not altered; there were no notes in the margin, nothing. Zilch.

Should I put it back? I questioned. I felt like I was missing something, so I tucked it under the crook of my arm and stood up. But as I did a gust of stale air reanimated itself and crawled across my skin like a zombie crawling from a grave. I tried to turn, I really did, but a foreign pressure held me facing forward.

I could *feel* the presence behind me, its hands on my arms, its gaze on my back, even its breath whispered over my skin, coming closer and closer to my ear until I could no longer struggle. I was paralyzed.

"*Sound good,*" the entity behind me said in tones more like the wind than any voice I had heard before.

My mind snapped.

I flailed desperately, using reserves of strength only accessible to humans in fight or flight mode. My elbow shot back to hit something surprisingly solid and I was released. My scream tore out like an alarm, and I launched myself straight backward, leaping blindly to get as far away as possible. My back crunched against a bookcase and I fell, hitting the floor knees first.

But I was not the only thing that fell. No, the tribal drums beating in my ears gave way to a thunderclap of wood hitting wood. The pressure at my back disappeared. A splintery cracking was strong enough to shake me to the core, dropping me to the floor before the floor itself dropped.

My stomach was in my throat and my hands shot out like frightened birds as my knees folded under me and my elbows, knees, head, and the floor all let out a synchronized bang and then…blackness.

But it didn't last. No, nothing lasts. Although my eyes opened to darkness, my other senses did not. The first thing I noticed was the warmth underneath me, a strange thin one quickly penetrated by the coolness further under that. Then I realized my forearms and thighs felt like they had rolled down a hill of cacti. When I gasped and air filled my mouth, I could taste rust.

Something was wrong with my ears, because I could

hear all sorts of noises. Either that or a flock of seagulls started their cawing cacophony right behind that pile of rubbish. I think the rubble was blocking the door and the seagulls were too stupid to realize that they could simply fly through the hole above me.

I wished I had wings. *Oh wait, don't I?* My mind fuzzed and I blinked a few times, confused. But I could remember it very clearly—a golden sword to match golden wings and golden eyes and an aura that looked like golden flame but moved like the ocean. And it was me. Undoubtedly so.

So why am I lying here? I managed to roll over onto my back, but my legs did not desire bending. Any sort of exertion just made the muscles twitch and more heat soaked my pants. The room flashed a few times, and then the shadows coalesced in the corner. The silhouette seemed to get closer, taking long, stiff strides.

I could feel my eyes start to burn away, gold spreading from the pupil to the iris and continuing through the white. The stronger the flames got, the clearer the shadow became. Blurred features appeared on his visage, but nothing more than a strong nose and jawline.

He drew close, so close that I was certain he would have begun to burn had he been demonic. Even so, I was not certain this spirit was free from darkness. Shadows seemed to leap from the surface of this apparition, curling toward me like hot steam off a cold lake.

I did nothing as it bent down, folding into itself, and approached my face. I was not paralyzed by fear. No, my disinclination to movement came from just the opposite. I had not a single drop of terror in my veins.

"*Don't trust. Murderer,*" *whispered the spirit almost unintelligibly. Rage saturated his voice and made it low and warbling. I cocked my head closer.*

"Who?" I asked. It was entirely possible the spirit had encountered a demon, which would mean it was time for me to spring into action. However, Haldis would have traveled here if there were any true danger. Perhaps the spirit's logic fled with his body. Or, an interesting theory, perhaps this spirit met his end by the blade of a fellow man, now long deceased.

The disembodied soul's eagerly awaited reply was cut off by a cascade of rubble from the stairway. The shouts of familiar males made me blink rapidly in confusion.

"Leah!" shouted one of them. But Leah who? Could Leah be the murderer of whom the spirit was talking?

The dark haired boy barreled down the cluttered stairs, tripping on almost every step in his haste. The fair one was not far behind at all, choosing to bypass the stairs and leap directly to the floor. When the first came into my personal spotlight, I gasped.

"Jeremy," I breathed, and suddenly I could feel no golden light at all. What I did feel was a heck of a lot of pain. It hit me all at once, like a tidal wave, and my eyes unfocused.

Jeremy's strong hands were on my upper arms, squeezing like a constrictor. He was saying a great many things at a loud volume, but it was like I was underwater. Out of the rush I could only pick out one phrase said over and over again.

"Stay with me," he begged. There was a deeper, softer noise and Jeremy looked behind me. He nodded.

Hands came from the darkness, much rougher and from a different direction than Jeremy's. Despite their roughness, their touch was tender. I was lifted slowly off the ground. My head curled against a shoulder, and I saw the lighter shirt being tainted by the warmth trickling from me.

Those stains will be a nightmare to get out, I thought disconnectedly.

I started to fade out with that thought in mind and with Jeremy's voice echoing through the room. He wasn't talking to me anymore, rather into something glimmering in his hands. I didn't have enough concentration left to care about what it was. I closed my eyes and let the darkness pull me under like a warm blanket, safe.

I had journeyed into the small town at the edge of the woods to check up on the girl, yet everything had melted away until I found myself in a cold, enclosed space. Steel chains slithered across the floor, metal links clinking with every serpentine movement. Two rose up like cobras before wrapping themselves around my wrists and forearms, while another descended from the ceiling and looped my neck, pulling up so I was forced to crane my head up.

A solid jerk froze all the restraints where they were, locking me into position. The walls of this place were shrouded in darkness even though they were near me, for the light above was dim. I did not struggle; it was not the time for that.

Somewhere outside, a raven cawed.

The ceiling was sadder than I was, leaking a steady drip of water onto the side of my face as if it was offended at my lack of tears and was trying to put them there. I welcomed the water's caress like that of a concerned aunt, helping me find the strength to see this through.

Haldis was like a phantom limb, my hand gripping where the handle would be if this situation was more dire. Human steel would not fatally harm me and was not in a position to harm an innocent, so the angelic sword was absent. It was a necessary drawback. Though Haldis would be very useful in this situation, having it now might prove more harmful than beneficial if it was needed elsewhere more urgently.

I would need to be resourceful to get out of this situation. The cement didn't allow for much of a connection to the living earth underneath. The air in there was stale and silent, unwilling to devote the energy to thrust into a gale. It wouldn't be of much use, anyway.

My angelic fire was weak without Haldis to draw it out, and so it couldn't shear steel. It worked more like water than a flame, dousing and extinguishing hellfire on contact. It would not melt or burn other materials, unless it was something at the soul level.

The only things I did have were the droplets from the ceiling. The water dripped at a rate slow enough to leave only the barest of puddles, more of a damp spot than something that had true depth. Still, I could use it.

"Water spirits," I called, the chain around my neck clinking tight as I tilted my head to catch more water on my face. "I ask for assistance."

At first, nothing happened. The collection of droplets tumbled off my jaw and onto my neck as they would normally. Then more came to keep me company, dropping at a slightly accelerated rate. I didn't question the usefulness of these extra drops, I knew better than to do so with a force that had always helped me prior.

That would insult them, and these Elementals tended to hold grudges. I did not know how sentient they were nor if they were separate or just one uniform element, but it was not my place to find out. I readily and thankfully accepted their help. I had learned a long time ago not to investigate the matter too closely.

The tempo of the water increased until it was a stream, thin but steady. It splashed into my eyelashes, turning my vision simultaneously blurry and crystalline. I felt my hair pulling free of the noose around my neck as the pieces outside the chain grew heavier and wetter. Now I had enough room to take a deep lungful of air.

Water stuttered over my nose as I did this. Dripping down and running over my shoulders in a manner that should not have been possible. It worked under the coiled chains and allowed me to spin both my arms and wrists. However, freedom was not imminent. My hands were too large to pull through the chains.

The possibility of severing them occurred to me, but I discarded it as the chain around my neck was still tight. I would not be very useful headless. The Elemental that controlled the line of water was thinking along the same lines, because the intensity of the stream of water increased until there was as much of it under the chains at my wrists as possible.

Then it crackled as it started freezing. Everywhere the steel touched succumbed to frost, the expansion of the ice slowly, but surely lifting the chains off my skin. The difference was only a fraction of an inch, but it was all I needed. I yanked.

Ice shards drew blood as they shattered, but I didn't care about the pain. The patches of my skin under where the water froze were red and chunky, well on their way to being damaged. Luckily, it was neither irreparable nor detrimental. With help, they'd fade.

My fingers worked their way underneath the chain collar

at my neck, futilely pulling. I had no doubt the chain would crumble in my hands if Haldis were here, yet I was still alone. I heard a sizzling above me and saw the stream from the ceiling had frozen into a massive icicle.

It hissed as its base boiled and then froze once more. The cycle repeated like the seasons were lasting mere seconds, winter to spring and summer to fall. They were weakening the ceiling by contracting and expanding it in a short period of time. Already fissures were spreading like the reaching appendages of spiders.

I wrapped both of my hands around the links behind my head and jerked it down with as much force as possible. A chunk of concrete pulled free, along with the base of the chain. I moved before I could take the brunt of it, but the mass clipped my ear and collar bone, drawing even more blood.

I unwound the chain from my neck with muted satisfaction, but it was quick to be extinguished. The minor feeling of victory faded away when the door to my prison opened. My captor stalked in, cloaked in shadow.

Chapter Five

Porcupine attack, sewing mishap, and dirty dancing with a pricker bush. Oh, and tagged by a vampire coven. Can't forget that one, too. I built an army of entirely plausible explanations to give to people when they took one look at my arms and legs that were riddled with tiny holes and ugly bruises.

It would be a long sleeve day for at least a couple of weeks, but now that the mid-fall air was starting to have a bite to it, I didn't think anyone would notice. The scrapes I had received that day in the storm were microscopic compared to the ones I harbored at the moment. One on my forearm even required a couple of stitches. Most of my injuries were made by being impaled on splinters from the floor and bookcase. A few had to be surgically removed, but they were thankfully tiny. I was told that I passed out from blood loss, and any confusion I experienced was caused by my blow to the skull.

I was lucky I hadn't woken up until I was in the hospital, because I would have died of embarrassment if I was around when they loaded me into the ambulance. Even still, I had wanted to sink into the underworld when I woke up to see my mom's pink eyes and her worried tugs on a strand of her blonde hair with a garbage can full of tissues next to her. Makeup colored the corners of most of them. When I glanced at the clock, I thanked the spirit guides that it was still Saturday, albeit late.

My father's eyes had been clear, but the lines on his face had deepened to the point where it had looked like he was in pain himself. Smudges of oil coated his dirtied work clothes and face, and I couldn't help but imagine him literally dropping everything to come make sure I was okay. My eyes prickled just thinking of him speeding out of the auto shop like a bat out of Hell, worried about me. I shoved aside the thought of my mom doing the same. How long had they been here for?

And it didn't end there, no sir. For each day I was stuck in the hospital, Jeremy brought me a flower. Which, luckily for my guilty conscience, only amounted to two. True to form, these were not regular flowers, either. Each one had some sort of myth or old wives' tale based on its healing powers. I laughed as I tried to place them, often having read about them but never having seen them in real life.

Occasionally, his eyes would slide down to my arms and legs, and he would wince at their pellet-smattered appearance. I was thankful the doctor pronounced me concussion-free, because that would be just another thing for people to pity me over. It left me with quite a few questions stuck in my head, snagged like a bag that floated downstream until it wrapped around a stick.

Even though I took the brunt of the fall on my forearms and knees, my head did tap the ground. Hard enough to cause a hallucination? No clue. There was no way in hell I was informing the doctor of my experiences in the basement of the library. The psych ward was just a floor above, after all.

It was only logical that I started a new super-sneaky

mission to figure out what actually happened. With two now, of both the werewolf and dream variety, I was sure to be a busy girl. And speaking of werewolves...Luke.

If I had been surprised by his dedication when I was laid up in the hospital, I was even more so by his daily home visits once I was out. He didn't bring flowers or anything like Jeremy, but his presence and his steel-like aura calmed me. I think seeing me heal calmed him in turn. It kind of worried me that my biography of his life would be three sentences, maximum, but I was beginning to trust him. It also kind of made me happy, even if his enigmatic self perplexed me.

Though Luke had been kind while I was in that stale white bed, stopping by both days just to assure himself I was okay, he would take off when Jeremy entered. I caught the two of them staring icily at each other as they passed in the doorway and it made me wonder what the heck had happened between them.

Boys. So filled with testosterone. I'd deal with it another day when I was back up to full butt-kicking power. If Jessica were there, she probably would have enjoyed the show, but hospitals weren't exactly her thing. I wasn't mad. Her frantic text messages and calls were more than enough to assure me she was worried about me. To be honest, it was kind of nice not to feel like I was greatly inconveniencing someone.

For now, I wandered aimlessly around my silent house with Nyami close on my heels. I had a couple of days to relax before I went off to school and I was planning on doing just that. This freedom was hard-earned. And, of course, the product of a sheer landslide of luck, though mostly bad.

The phone rang, its sudden, shrill tone making me jump. The motion pulled painfully on a few of my larger injuries, but I moved to collect it anyway. Sure enough, the caller ID let me know it was my father. I answered it immediately, not even considering letting it slide. I owed that much and far, far more to my parents for their worry.

The line opened to mechanical whirring and grinding, distorted by the phone. "Hi, Dad. What's up?"

He coughed a bit, likely trying to fill his lungs with air not as heavily infused with the smell of gasoline. "I'm just calling to check up on you. How are you doing? Do you need me to pick up anything?"

I made sure not to twist or move around too much so that my voice came out clear and strong. "I'm doing much better, Dad. No need to worry about me."

His breaths came more lightly, barely registering on the phone. "I don't know if I like you hanging out with that boy. Did he make you do this?"

I blinked, knowing that he wasn't referring to Jeremy. "Luke? How could he? I had to drag him there. I thought it would be a fun idea for an English assignment."

My dad sighed. "I just feel like maybe I should meet his parents first, before you go traipsing around with someone you don't know. He could be dangerous."

I could hear someone shouting for my dad in the background, beckoning him back to work. "I think he's okay, Dad. I don't think he'd visit me in the hospital if he wasn't concerned for my well-being. And besides, I brought Jeremy with us to the library anyway."

I could tell he wanted to argue a bit more, but the time was up. "All right, all right. Just...take care of yourself, sweet pea. I don't want you getting hurt."

I nodded even though he couldn't see it. "I'll try to stay inside for a little while, Dad."

I hoped he could hear my sincerity. "Good, your mother and I appreciate that. I have to go now, though. I love you."

"Love you, too," I replied and hung up the phone.

Not even ten minutes later, my mom called and a similar conversation ensued. I was saved from having this conversation in person by my parents' ridiculous work schedules, a fact I couldn't truly be happy for when it meant they were gone so often. In the phone call, my mom made sure to remind me that if I left the house, I was to text her, but the woods were off-limits until I'd healed.

Unfortunately, the entire house smelled of lemon cleaning solution, so strongly it felt like it was permeating my brain with every breath. My mom cleaned when she was feeling just about anything negative, so the entire floor of the house was spotless and the fumes were intense. I'd like to think I could tell how sucky of a kid I was being by the level of cleaning scent-induced lightheadedness I felt. This one was way, way up there. I couldn't even imagine the level of industrialized clean the house would have been if she wasn't working so hard on being promoted within her corporation.

Roaming the halls at home wasn't going to last, but for now I was trying to atone for my sins. To avoid the stink of cleaning product, I curled up in a patch of dying sunlight next to an open slider door with a young adult paranormal fiction novel and had almost submerged myself in the shapeshifter horror. It was only a minute before I realized there was something else I should have been reading.

I leapt to feet and winced as my poor, scab-speckled calves protested. Nyami, who had curled up next to me and melted into a big puddle of golden fur, also protested with a startled yip.

"Sorry, girl, but I just remembered something," I told her even though I was fully aware she couldn't understand me. I wasn't a telepath, and certainly not one strong enough to break the interspecies barrier and communicate with animals.

I hobbled to my ghost hunting equipment, sitting in the bag I had brought. The whole thing was still coated with dust. It was also quite a bit lighter than it was when I had brought it to the library, because the cameras had been totaled when the ceiling fell on them.

Luke, who had been kind and brave enough to return to the rubble despite my warnings otherwise, returned what equipment he could salvage. Jeremy took one look at a picture of it I had sent him and described the broken cameras as 'the love child of a robot and a grenade gone terribly wrong'.

I rummaged through the contents and grinned ear to ear when my hand hit a smooth, thin envelope with one irregularity at the bottom. *Strange, I thought there were two when I first found it.* Either way, I thanked the gods that Luke had thought to pack it even though it clearly belonged in the library. I extracted the worn thing and plopped back down next to Nyami, who stuck her nose in the air and whined.

I had no hesitation this time around. I opened it and gingerly extracted the first thing I felt, which was well-preserved paper. It was—shocker—addressed to the same Helen as on the outside of the envelope. From the 'my beloved' in front of her name, I assumed the person who had written this had been a little more than a friend to her. I mumbled sections aloud to Nyami as I read.

"My beloved Helen, I have done the research you asked

of me regarding your brother's sickness. I must warn you, my conclusion is neither conventional nor easy to accept. Please bear with me as I attempt to explain myself with the information I have gathered from my collection of tomes, just as you have through...Blah, blah, blah sentimental mush...Oh, here it starts again, Nyami.

"You told me before you left to aid him that your brother was unclear about the nature of his ailment. Through your periodic reporting, I have managed to gather this list of symptoms: fever, flashes of fury, discontent to remain indoors, chills, gaps in memory, and sensory illusions. I searched all the medical encyclopedias this library owns, Helen, and even some it didn't. None contained an all-inclusive explanation.

"Nevertheless, I did not cease searching. I know more now about the medical practice than any fellow who is not a doctor ought to know, yet still I did not have answers. Believe me, Helen, I searched even more fervently once you told me of your sibling's rage and destruction that night just a few weeks ago. How he broke out of your well-meaning restraints and fled until the daylight brought him back to you...."

Was he ever going to get to the point? This man, or at least I assumed he was a man, was dancing around his diagnosis like mentioning it was too terrible to bear.

I skipped quite a few paragraphs, scanning lightly for anything interesting. My eyes glossed over a word so familiar to me that I almost didn't notice it was out of place. It tugged my subconscious, summoning me to read it over and over again until I was so shocked I had to read it out loud in order to make sure it was real.

"Lycanthropy," I whispered to Nyami. "I believe your

brother is afflicted with...lycanthropy."

I stood up, placing the letter on the table. I floated down the hall, not registering any sensation. I forgot to feel the pain of my arms and legs. I blinked and then I was in front of the bathroom mirror, my own gray eyes staring back at me. I gripped the cold edges of the sink in front of me and leaned closer.

"Lycanthropy," I whispered, and my breath danced along the glass.

"Lycanthropy?" I questioned, but there was no one to answer but myself.

"Lycanthropy!" I shouted, my mouth splitting open so wide the girl in the mirror looked like she was baring her teeth. I laughed then, loud enough it almost eclipsed the rumbling, low sound that slipped under the bathroom doorway.

I froze, my elation snuffed out. I opened the bathroom door a crack and recognized the fluctuating, continuous noise quickly even though I had never heard it in real life. A dog's growl is unmistakable. I ran out, scared to death Nyami was in trouble. It was too easy to picture an intruder taking advantage of her amiable nature to hurt her.

When she wasn't in the patch of fading sunlight next to the screen door, I started yelling.

"Nyami!" I screamed, and was rewarded with growling and a flash of motion outside. I put my face up to the glass, hand resting on the open screen just a half foot to the left. My breath crawled over the glass like a ghost trying to manifest, taking a misty form right before fading back into oblivion. I quickly halted my exhale, trapping it inside for fear it would yet again obscure my vision. The pounding of my heart made it impossible to exist in that breathless stasis for long, though.

I inhaled greedily and was rewarded with another flash of color. I stumbled over myself as I shifted a foot to the right, pushing the glass door out of my way to see better. I leaned my weight against the screen like an over-eager hound pulling on its chain.

I couldn't believe it.

Even with my face smushed against the sliding door and tendrils of hair sneaking over to obscure my eyes, there was no mistaking the figure at the edge of the woods, not even twenty yards away. Amber eyes caught my gaze, and my already skyrocketing heart rate shot through the roof. A long, muscular gray-brown body trailed behind the eyes, leaving no doubt in my mind that what I was seeing was not by any stretch of imagination one of the skinny coyotes found around these parts. The old lady that called Cole was on to something.

My fingers twitched, itching for my camera, but I knew the second I so much as blinked the wolf would be gone. It seemed almost circumspect as it shifted its gaze from me to the sun, like it was taking inventory of every pine needle dotting the snow-coated evergreens between it and the sky.

When its lips peeled back and it emitted the loudest, most soul-shivering noise I had ever heard, I jumped, smacking my forehead against the mesh and emitting a slight squeal of surprise. All the hair on my arms rose with gooseflesh as I shivered at the sound of a hundred emotions combined into one.

Before I could regain my composure there was skittering behind me, a sliding of claws on hardwood as something massive smashed into my legs and sent me crashing through the thin screen into the dusk.

I've been thrown to the wolves, literally, was my only thought before my already battered limbs smacked against the ground and I rolled. Eyes foolishly open, I flailed my limbs to make myself stop.

Hello, Ground!

Hello, Sky!

Ground, my old friend, how have you been? No time to talk, gotta roll.

And hello to you, Wolf! Wait a minute...

I managed to stop without too much pain, but my tumbling had eaten up another ten yards of distance between me and the canine. My gaze zeroed in on a patch of fur through the underbrush, and slowly the shadowy silhouette of the animal materialized. Large portions of it were obscured by needles and leaves, but I could see the triangular head clearly.

Strangely, the more I could see of it, the less my pounding heart influenced my brain. I was calmer then than I had been at any other point in the past few days. The wolf seemed to be doing the same thing I was: eyeing each other and slowly, subtly, trying to back away. I knew better than to get too close to a wolf that howled before dusk.

The growling returned, but it came from behind me. I started to scramble up, suddenly remembering the one simple fact that wolves hunt in packs. A huge, furry mass eclipsed the setting sun for an instant before landing in front of me. I opened my hands in preparation of clawing and fighting, but there was no need.

Rather than a second wolf, sunlight shone off a very familiar golden fur. As soon as I saw her, my memories clicked. Nails behind me on the floor? A wolf could not have entered the house. My dog had tried to protect me, but wound up putting me right at the danger's feet.

But now, it was I who threw my body against hers. I quickly wrapped my arms around her chest, pulling her close and preventing her from approaching the wolf. The growling peaked as the wolf flicked its ears back, lowered its head, and joined in; its amber gaze locking on Nyami like it was unsure whether she was an actual threat or misguided prey.

I knew the situation was a time bomb. I slowly rolled up onto my knees. I was so tense the air felt like glass, like if I moved too quickly it would shatter and shards would rain down to score the earth. I grabbed Nyami by the scruff and stood up. She vibrated under my hand, a byproduct of both nerves and growling.

Or maybe it was me shaking. I was genuinely unsure. I continued to back up, keeping my feet low over the ground. Nyami lessened the intensity of her growl and followed suit. The new position gave me a direct line of sight to the wolf's muzzle, which contorted into a snarl.

Those teeth...They were not the pearly whites dipped in scarlet that Hollywood often portrays. They were a mottled shade of yellow, separated by dark hunks of tartar. Even so, I feared what the massive canine teeth could do to Nyami if they caught hold of her.

The wolf's lip slowly slid down as its growl trailed off. After Nyami and I took a few more steps, there was a flash of motion in the underbrush as the wolf spun and dashed off, hardly making a sound. I walked backward up the hill to the house, not stupid enough to turn my back or run away from a predator of such caliber.

When my heel hit the siding, I let loose a small gasp of relief. I reached for the slider and almost fell on my butt when my arm went straight through gap where it had been.

Below my feet, the screen had popped off the tracks, but it was thankfully whole. Easy fix, but it wasn't my concern right then. I herded Nyami in and shut the glass door, effectively sealing us from the outside world.

The post-adrenaline crash made every step of mine feel like swimming in mud, but I hastily climbed the stairs. My second shadow came with me, and both of us sank down onto the floor of my room. My whole body stung, and I knew I'd have to check later to see if any stitches had popped.

Even my eyes burned, but when I grabbed a mirror I found that they were not the angelic gold I had hoped for, but instead were watery with tears threatening to spill. I wiped them away and tried to convince myself it was an uncontrollable after effect of fight-or-flight, not a product of any weaker emotions.

The questions I had were a flock of starlings in my head: many, fluttering, and difficult to grasp. First and foremost, how would a werewolf have teeth in the condition of a natural wolf? It just didn't make sense. None of the research I ever did said anything about wolves growing plaque as they shifted.

Think about it. There's no way a human could get away with teeth that unhealthy, at least not around here. Though I had only seen quick flashes of Luke's teeth, I knew I would have noticed if they were that bad. The only way to call the wolf a werewolf was if it had not shifted to human in years and years, and I had seen my prime suspect bipedal yesterday.

So I expanded my conclusion range. What if it wasn't a werewolf at all? I supposed it could have been a normal wolf, but those weren't usually found in Vermont. Until today, I had never seen one, and I practically lived in the woods. So, why now?

There was no reason, nothing new here to bring it...Unless—My mind stopped whirring for just a minute as two of the pieces of the puzzle clicked satisfactorily—the wolf was drawn by the presence of a werewolf. Now, I'm not saying it was there to bow down to its new wolf overlord, but a werewolf in your territory is enough to make anyone's hackles rise. Perhaps a stray wolf had wandered down and stayed to check out the competition?

It was flimsy, but when I rose, I felt more at ease. I must have been down for a while, because Nyami was snoring softly and the floor had made imprint-graffiti on the visible parts of my legs. Even though it was nowhere near my usual nocturnal sleep schedule, I crawled under the covers of my bed and let the mental and emotional fatigue pull me under.

The figure standing before me wasn't a beast. There were no fangs nor claws nor fire to rend my flesh. It was decidedly human, but darkness caressed his profile like he was accepted as one of its own. His aura flickered around him in thin, almost intangible lines. His soul so permeated with darkness, I knew him to be one of the Corrupted.

It was apparent that this human had not a shred of purity left. Dirt and other, more difficult to place stains coated his clothing and face. Wounds on his cheek, what looked to be scratch marks from a human hand, were beginning to fester. His eyes were simultaneously glassy and hungry, the empty, yearning stare of the once-possessed. His gaze was louder than any scream. I jerked in reaction to it.

He took my jerk for weakness and attacked instantly.

Brandishing a knife, a simple kitchen ornament, he aimed for my newly exposed neck. I yanked the chain with the concrete ball on the end, making it swing around to hit his exposed flank the second his knife kissed my throat.

Blood does not pick sides. The shallow scratch in my throat—barely more than an artist's brushstroke—made for a warm choker before it slid over my collarbone and went further still. The man had been thrown off balance and lie bleeding from shallow gashes on the sight of impact. Both of us held still, unwilling to make the first move.

It was he who broke the stillness. His knife flashed out at my closest ankle, only to shoot sparks when the blade hit chain. I leaped out of the way of a second blink-fast strike, now in a preferable position to flee. I took the opportunity, bolting as fast as my form could take me.

It was a mistake. Almost instantly, a blade caught my shoulder and threw me against the wall. It didn't stick into the rough surface, but it did poke through the shallow flap of muscle it was caught in. I pulled it out with a sharp intake of air and wielded it in the opposite hand.

My attacker had a smile on his face, but it was as if some spirit had tugged and tugged until his face was contorted into that shape. There was no joy in the expression, no emotion at all. The light above us gleamed off his bared teeth but left his eyes as unexposed black holes. It was with that I knew there was little reason for mercy. This man had no chance at redemption.

I had the weapon, but the man was uncaring. The celestial artist continued to paint in sanguineous hues down my neck and shoulder, seeming to tempt the stranger closer. He lunged at me with hands grasping like talons and his mouth open wide.

His teeth clicked together next to my ear as I turned and rammed him with my good shoulder, throwing him against the cement hard enough that little crumbles came to join him. He rose almost instantly despite the force of the blow.

His grin was still plastered on and it struck me that in his barren emotional state, feeling pain might be better than feeling nothing at all. I ran again, making it to the doorway before his hand reached toward me.

This time, I didn't hesitate. I drove the blade straight through his palm and into the soft wood of the door, continuing to run even as his howls faded into the night. I thanked the water Elementals with every exhale as I dashed further away, doubts nagging at me.

I couldn't help but see the visage of the girl I'd saved from a spirit, one I reasoned must be one of the disembodied Corrupted, flash over the memory of my captor. She could have shared his fate if I had not drawn out the tainted soul. The nearness of these two attacks, both by beings I had not encountered in quite some time, planted a seed of worry. Something was shifting, and I did not know how to handle it.

Did the man deserve a certain death by my hand? Should I return to finish him?

I felt a pull from the east, removing the option from me. My footsteps grew lighter as I turned in that direction and my ocean-like flames extended with each step. Within seconds the molten gold had spread to my eyes. My lightened steps became nonexistent as I took to the sky, ready to face a foe I had no qualms about sending to Hell.

Chapter Six

If Luke's and my shoes became a rock band, rotten tomato sales would increase at least 40%. The completely unsynchronized slap of our treads was the background tune as we walked toward the bus stop. The road wasn't wide enough for two and the stray car, so Luke strode on the grassy berm next to me.

We kept up an easy camaraderie as we meandered to the soon-to-be-filled stop. The topic of conversation was unimportant, only able to stay alive by fully exploiting any tangents that came up. I listened eagerly, keen to learn his secrets, but he seemed genuinely interested in me, too. Well, me and my crazy stories. His mystery was untouched as he questioned me, barely leaving much room for my own questions.

It might have been my first day in school after the library fiasco, but it definitely was not one of our first conversations. After all, falling through the floor didn't get me any more than a two-day extension on that essay—which, to me at least, seemed a little stingy—so he'd stopped over for us to work on it while I was under house arrest. I wasn't at peak performance, but I was tired of being cooped up. Wednesday, here I come.

"What is the oddest thing that ever happened to you?" Luke inquired, and I smiled. My eyes danced to the side as I remembered what seemed to be quite an extensive list.

I gave myself more time by retorting. "You realize you are asking the ghost hunting girl, yes?"

"Coming up with a crazy scheme like that, no way it was your first time..." He stalled unable to find the right phrase, or perhaps the least offensive one. I smirked, not used to having a friend around who had such concern.

"Twirling my toe in the crazy pond? Going gaga under the moon? Flying with the fae?" I filled in, using some of Jeremy's select word choices about my love of the supernatural. Luke's surprised laugh rang out, more of a rumble really, and he almost lost his footing on the uneven ground.

"Guess that's one way to put it, yeah," he said.

"Well, just two days ago—" I began, but stopped instantly when something gray streaked through the trees behind him and leapt out in front of me. I didn't think, just reacted.

I pulled Luke off the berm and shoved him behind me, my nails digging into his flesh. A second too late, I realized I had made a huge mistake. The horrible, terrifying monster I was protecting Luke from was none other than a gray squirrel.

"Ahh...There a reason I'm hiding from that squirrel?" Luke questioned from behind me. The squirrel in question ran across the road as the bus approached.

"It was the aliens!" I yelled playfully and just a little too loud, trying to save face. For some strange reason, I don't think that helped. I rushed up the bus steps, expecting escape from the awkward turn of events by sitting with my usual seat-mate, Jessica. Not that I wanted to sit with the gossip queen, and I say that in a loving way, but I'd be obliged to because of our many years of friendship.

My feeble plan crumbled when she wasn't on the bus

yet again. I scooted into the last remaining seat and made room for Luke, who managed to look more majestic just sitting down than I had managed in all of my seventeen years. I wasn't that upset Jessica had slept in, or, more likely, convinced Mitch to give her a ride. It gave me even more of a chance to redeem myself and sit next to Luke. Even if the plaid shirt he was wearing had little wood chips on it.

Those wood chips plinked against the floor as he shifted to look at me. I couldn't help but notice their little suicide was caused by the rippling of his muscles under the shirt, dislodging them. I looked back up to his face and found that his mouth had turned slightly downward, at first making me think he'd caught me looking.

His attention was elsewhere, though. Murmuring surrounded us. It was a rare occasion when two sleep-deprived students had an animated and lively chat this early in the morning, but it was almost unprecedented that the whole bus full of kids would be having such a conversation. With all the voices around me, it was difficult to single out just one to focus on.

I tried, but it was like listening to a swarm of bees. Many names were being thrown around, most I recognized. There seemed to be no facts, however, as almost all of the remarks ended in that elevated pitch people use when they ask questions. I flicked my eyes over to Luke and found he was looking at two people in particular.

The two girls sat three seats ahead of us in the opposite row, so it was difficult to strain their voices from the rest. I didn't know how Luke had done it without being told what to listen for, so, as always, I put another coin in the lycanthropy piggy bank.

"They are everywhere! In just one night Julie, Angelica,

Megan, and Brian saw them. What could it mean?" a freshman girl with a hot pink bow in her braid asked her friend.

"I don't know! We haven't had wolves in this town since, like, forever!" the second girl responded.

While her timing was a little off, she was correct. It had been decades since a wolf wandered down all the way to this more southern part of Vermont. I leaned forward, forgoing any pretense of not eavesdropping.

"And now four people in different places saw them in one night. What are the odds...? Maybe old lady Juliard was right about seeing a rabid one. Can you imagine? I'm not going anywhere near those woods anymore. Oh, one sec. Just got a text." The pink bow became the only visible part of the girl as she ducked her head down to read it.

She popped back up from her text with extra spring. "You'll never believe it. Clarice says she saw one, too!"

"Clarice? I doubt it. She was probably drunk out of her mind," the other grumbled, and then the topic of conversation switched to the less interesting Clarice and her scandalous acts.

Luke and I were definitely listening to the same conversation, because we both leaned back at the same time. Neither of us spoke, which was pretty dang lucky considering anything that came out of my mouth right now would make as much sense as a naga on a bicycle.

I spent the rest of the ride in sort of a daze. The incident with the wolf had become blurry in my memory, hazy like an interrupted dream, but it was all brought back into crystal clear focus. I could have sketched every strand of fur on its muzzle with my eyes closed.

When I stepped off the bus, I was so distracted that I stumbled a little and skidded down the last two steps. I caught myself just in time to avoid a face-plant, but I still would have tipped over if a strong, warm hand hadn't snagged the crook of my arm.

Unfortunately, that was right where one of the nastier cuts from my fall resided. I sucked in a quick breath and made a muffled *mmph* sound from the pain. Luke realized instantly what had happened and retracted his hand. We moved out of the flow of people heading off the bus.

"I'm sorry. I forgot and just wanted to make sure—" he started before I interrupted him.

"No need, it's not like I have a blazing neon sign above each scrape and bruise. Thank you for helping me." I started to turn a little awkwardly, and then added, "I've got to go. I meet Jeremy by the pond every morning. I don't have much time, so I don't want to be late," to appease his questioning look. We did, after all, have first period together, as I had learned the day after Jeremy and I had taken our accidental swim. It'd make sense if he was wondering why I was headed in a direction that was most definitely not our shared Calculus.

I couldn't read the pull of his face. "See you in class."

He expressed too many, or perhaps too few, emotions to pinpoint. I'd like to say that there was a little bit of lighter emotions and a tiny, tiny pinch of icier ones not aimed at me, but I'd never been much good at reading emotions, anyway. I would not make a decent empath.

"Bye!" I exclaimed with a little too much enthusiasm. I hoped I hadn't seemed too rude, but Luke didn't seem overly mopey so I decided not to worry too much about it. I'd met him only a week or so ago, after all. Older friends were more of a priority. I made a mental note to get the three of us together again and get rid of whatever reservation was bugging him.

I jogged the rest of the way to the pond to be on time. I hated the bump of my heavy backpack against my lower back, the repeated motion pushed against lingering bruises there. It wasn't the pain that bothered me so much, but the sense of limited mobility. If I had to bolt, could I? Out maneuver something far faster than I? No, I mused, I could not.

No matter how much I wanted otherwise, I was starting to believe that the episode in the basement of the library could have been the product of blood loss and a blow to the head. If I had felt something, even the tiniest spark when I faced the wolf, I'd still be wholeheartedly on Team Haldis. Now...So little evidence can only take a person so far.

I was still in a shadowy mood from that line of thought when I came to the pond. Today, it was not liquid gold. The overcast sky reflected so it looked like a rip in the ground, a portal to a sky beneath the Earth's surface. I was tempted to throw a pebble in it, but did not want to shatter the illusion with its ripples.

It took me a second to realize something was missing. I turned to find Jeremy not even a foot away, frozen in some sort of bizarre half-scrunched position with a wicked smile on his face. He straightened when he saw me looking, his grin losing its more mischievous tone.

"Dang, I was going to jump you and squatch call right in your ear," he admitted, snapping his fingers once in the classic 'aw shucks' manner.

I could tell from his mischievous grin he would likely try it again. "It wouldn't have ended well. My nerves are still fried. I probably would have elbowed you right in the stomach."

"You'd do that to a poor, defenseless sasquatch?" Jeremy pouted, and I rolled my eyes.

"Nah, I'd do it to you," I teased. Shush, that response totally made sense.

"Some friend I have. Here I go out of my way to bring a recuperating buddy a gift, and she threatens to beat me," he muttered.

My thoughts wrapped around the word 'gift', stuttering. "What do you mean? I didn't ask for anything. I mean... Thank you?"

Jeremy turned around, unzipping the fresh backpack he was wearing. I guess the old one hadn't been too salvageable, then. "I know you didn't ask for anything, Miss Show No Weakness. I just thought it would lighten the mood."

He reached back and drew out a large rectangle covered with a paper bag.

"Open it," he commanded, and I was more than willing to comply, curiosity eating me up. I tore off the brown wrapping and felt a cool, smooth edge. I flung off the rest of the paper and started to laugh.

It was a framed painting with Jeremy's familiar signature scrawled in the bottom corner. The earthy green and brown hues hit me before the actual content of the painting, transporting me instantly to my home away from home. That, combined with the realism of the painting, plopped me right back in the familiar scene.

A brunette girl was down in the leaves, adopting the classic knee-as-a-rest position used by surprised hunters that need stability for a shot without the time to lean against a tree, bipod, etc. Instead of a gun, she wielded a camera. Various items, including a tripod, some shiny electronics, and a tiny cloth bag hung over her shoulder bandolier style.

The wind teased her hair in such a way that you could see only the profile of her face, but she appeared to have no expression other than a fierce determination. Trees sprung up around her, almost completely obscuring what she was filming. The dark head and shoulders of a bigfoot poked out from behind a thick pine.

I raised my finger to touch its fur before I remembered I wouldn't be able to feel the texture. The whole painting was just so stunning, I couldn't even wrap my head around how something could perfectly capture both the look of individual strands of hair and the look of smooth, flat leaves with just a few strokes. I had seen Jeremy's work before, but this almost stole my breath.

It was realistic enough that I was forced to stop myself from revising my memory to fit this image rather than the real deal. Even with the minor errors, like the picture-me's blatant disregard for the tripod and the absence of Luke's house in the background, it was surprisingly accurate for something that Jeremy wasn't even there to see.

"This is amazing," I breathed. "Thank you so much."

"It was nothing, really. I just thought it would be fun, and I needed something—" he started.

"Shut up," I told him playfully as I wrapped my arms around him. He stiffened for a second, probably in shock at the uncharacteristic action, and then hugged me back. I pulled away when my elation wore off enough that I could remember we were on a tight schedule, especially after our involuntary skipping of first period last week.

"The bell is imminent," he intoned when I pulled away. I nodded and we headed to school.

First period doubled as homeroom, allowing for the circumambient whispers on the bus to explode into more full-fledged conversation. It was a lot like what happens when you put bacteria on agar and shove it in an incubator, except an exponential growth of volume instead of colonies. The conversations' moods seemed to be different this time. Less pure excitement. New news?

There were only two voices that weren't adding to the fray. One would be mine, and the other would be Luke's. *I guess it is kinda hard to talk when you aren't physically present,* I thought as I stared at his empty seat, *although not impossible.* Without him to talk to, I listened to the buzz.

You'd think the fact that no one was whispering would make it easier to eavesdrop, but no. The increased volume only made for an increased headache as I tried to single out the voices with no luck. Then, one of the voices singled me out.

"Leah, have you heard from Jessica at all? I think she's mad at me. She won't text me back."

I craned my neck to face Mitch, Jessica's boyfriend. He had stubble on his lip that really wasn't working out for him. I gave the lip caterpillar a quick glance before looking him in the eye. "No, I haven't, but you know how she is. She probably dropped her phone in the sink again."

He shrugged, not looking convinced. I gleaned from his words that Jessica hadn't ridden here with him this morning. And from his lack of communication with her, I doubt he knew she wasn't in yet. *She must be mourning her broken phone.* The thought put a smile on my face.

We both fell back into the buzzing. I was debating taking a nap on the desk, but did not want to wake up in a puddle of drool and the center of attention. From the corner of the room, the words, "I bet the wolves ate her," drifted over, catching my attention. Before the girl could say anything else, the announcements began and it was like someone hit the off switch on every person in the room.

That in itself was odd, because my peers almost never bothered to pay attention to the announcements, but it was even more so when the principal's voice floated through the speaker rather than the typical student announcer. His tone was grave.

"I regret to inform the student body that an AMBER Alert has been issued for one of our own. A junior, Jessica Sanford, has been missing since Sunday—" I blinked slowly, unable to process. Jessica was missing?

I stopped listening without meaning to, engulfed by my inner emotions. This was my *friend* they were talking about. And I, oh god, hadn't given her absence a second thought. The announcement barely scratched my awareness as tears pricked my eyes.

"—shreds of clothing were found on the wooded border of the Sanford family property. Foul play is suspected. If anyone has any information regarding her whereabouts, please contact the police at—"

The police?! My breathing hitched and then doubled for a few seconds. Just how much trouble was she in? *Who took her into the woods? Is she still there? Is she even alive?*

No, I banished that thought instantly. I just couldn't take it. Jessica had been my friend since grammar school. When images of blood in raven hair and brown eyes blued in death poked unbidden in my mind, I lost whatever resilience I had built up over the past few harrowing experiences.

I got up and made for the door. I think someone shouted

after me, but all I could hear was a sharp whining, like my own, personal alarm bells. Moving blindly and desperately, I didn't even stop when I bounced off some person, spinning them around with great force. My heart blurred over their words, beating frantically. Someone called my name, but I continued on, slamming into the push bar of a side door. My nose kissed the glass. I didn't slow down until I had made it all the way across the parking lot and into the woods.

When I could no longer see anything but trees, I slowed to a less frantic-looking jog and leapt onto the lowest branch I could find. I was careless in scaling it and the bark frayed the edges of the bandages on my forearms and poked at bruises. I climbed further and further, stopping only when I got high enough where the branches could barely hold my weight.

I sat there, catching my breath. It seemed like the tree was, too, because it swayed under me and the light breeze. High enough where someone walking through the woods would not notice me, I tried to calm down but it was no use. I was heading close to full panic mode.

Then the situation hit me and fury at myself rose to the surface. I was sitting in a tree when Jessica could be out there, cold and alone. *I was hiding from my stupid feelings* and she could be under threat, locked up, or injured. I took a second, one that I felt I couldn't afford, to flatten out the debilitating emotions.

I reached behind me to find my bag of tricks, to be comforted that there were at least a few, albeit unlikely, situations I could handle, but I only grasped air. I had left my bag in the classroom. I slumped against the trunk, deflated.

All the things I usually found comforting about being up here turned against me. The bark, the chill, even the air itself all seemed to work to dislodge me. I couldn't stay that way. I was too nerved up. I climbed my way down the tree, frustrated by the slowness of my descent. My collection of scratches grew, but I didn't pay heed to it. Any pain I was in didn't matter.

My feet smarted as I leapt off of a branch much higher than I should have. The deeper cuts on my legs pulled at the effort, already irritated by my climb. I didn't pause though, entirely intending to march back into the school and grab my bag before heading back out, no matter how much screaming and yelling was required.

I took my first step and smashed into someone for the second time today. Almost before the thought of who would be out here had finished crossing my mind, I registered just who I was out here with.

"Please...Don't..." I did not have enough coherence to throw three words together, let alone transfer my thoughts through speech. Luke didn't say a word, just lowered one shoulder and pushed a bag strap off. Then he reached back and grabbed the whole thing, holding it out to me like an offering. My backpack.

I took it without a word and extracted my bag of tricks, rolling it between my fingers and relishing the feel of each charm, talisman, totem, and object in there. I slung the bag over my own shoulder, nodded at Luke, the only action I could do without showing weakness, and started walking.

I didn't know where to. I didn't particularly care. I knew if I headed up the incline, I'd reach an endless forest. Down, I'd hit the road and civilization. But which way would Jessica be? My fist clenched tightly against my bag, causing a rough cut of one of the crystals in there to scrape against my heart line.

It was a second before I saw Luke had fallen into step
with me on the left. He moved a step ahead of me and
pushed a little closer, so I maintained the distance between
us by doing the same. It was only after this happened a few
times that I figured out he was leading me without leading
me, altering my path just enough that I would be heading
straight home.

I complied absently, as much as the storm in my chest
wanted me to do something, anything but give in and go
home. I knew that I needed to think, to formulate a plan,
and the mindless walking did just that. That flame never
died, not even an hour later when we arrived at my house.
I trudged down the driveway slowly, still fighting myself.
My gait skipped a step as a plan hatched and I came back
into awareness, but the frenzy of my mind had not died, not
even close. Luke paused at the head of the driveway, unsure.

"Leah, there any way I can help?" he asked, his voice
laced heavily with concern and with what could be tiny
traces of wariness or regret. I loved him for offering, and
understood what he meant and was trying to do. I don't
think he entirely expected, it, though, when I responded.

"I'm not the one who needs help." My words hung in
the air. That wasn't what I had wanted to say. My plan slid
into words slowly, disjointedly.

"Cole Bellevue," I said, as if Luke would understand. He
waited for me to continue, though I think the time it actually took may have been disproportionate to my conception
of only a second or two.

"He's a game warden. He's going to search the woods
for her. I can help. I can go with him," I explained.

Luke didn't hesitate. "I'm coming, too."

If my mind wasn't so frenzied, I think I would have

smiled. As it was, I wasted no time and called Jeremy.

Cole Bellevue knew I was more stubborn than a bull, so when his truck rumbled up our driveway an hour later, it wasn't much of a surprise. He didn't put up a fight, just loaded me and some kid he'd never seen before into the back of his truck like it was an everyday occurrence. Of course, I think it helped ease his mind that my parents, who had even more up-close and personal knowledge of my stubbornness, saw me off personally. My father approached him and started a conversation.

"Thank you for taking her," my father said, sincerely.

Cole still looked slightly unconvinced. "Are you sure? Did your wife agree to this, too?"

My dad just smiled a little bit sadly. "You know how Leah is. She'd be out there by herself, and I can't stand for that. With you, she'll be safe. Marianne agreed with me when I called her, though she wasn't too happy, either. She couldn't leave work when she's being so heavily scrutinized for that promotion, though."

Cole sighed. "I'll take good care of Leah. Tell your wife she'll be back before eight."

My father clapped his shoulder before turning away. "I appreciate it. And Leah, you stick with him, you hear? Not a foot out of place. I heard about those wolves in the woods, and now this. For now, until that clears up, you stay out of there unless you're with someone, preferably Cole."

I would have thought out my reply if my mind wasn't still in the process of sewing itself back together. I didn't want to lie, but my full compliance was unlikely, especially for an extended period of time. "I will, Dad."

The driver's side door closed about the same time the front door did. I snapped to attention, ready to be in action. Luke sat as still as a stone, but his presence next to me was comforting. When Jeremy, in the passenger seat, turned his head to look at me, he looked like I felt. Needless to say, it wasn't pretty. There were no bags under his eyes, and his tan skin was resistant to paling, but his lack of animation almost made him seem foreign to me. Jessica was his friend, too.

The truck rumbled to life without hesitation and we took off. The silence was thick, choking the air. Or maybe it was just my nerves that felt like a hand around my throat. I couldn't particularly tell at that point. I knew the route by heart, until Cole turned off too quickly and we pulled into a patch of woods.

He knew my question before it was asked. "Lots of people are at her house, and they've found nothing. The media is driving Mayor Sanford and her husband crazy, when the worry itself would be enough to push anyone over the edge. People are starting to think it might be a political kidnapping, but no ransom has…Well, the important thing is that we're expanding the search area."

I wanted to argue, but he was right. If her property had been combed over by a thousand eyes, what good would I do there? The idea shook me to my senses, making me realize I'd been fixating on a mental image of Jessica, alive and well, emerging from her house. I didn't want to get rid of that fantasy and the hope it created.

Cole said something into the truck's radio and jumped out, followed by the rest of us. I turned in place, my footsteps muted by the dead pine needles on the ground. The

DANA PERRY

road was still illuminated duskily, despite a lack of street lamps. The woods, on the other hand, seemed impenetrable with darkness, a premature night due to the heavy pines. Cole noted this and rummaged through the pile of odds and ends in the bed of the truck, finally reaching into a box and extracting three flashlights. He took a larger floodlight for himself.

Jeremy put his hand on my shoulder. "We'll find her."

Will we? I wasn't as sure, but I could see my own desire for it to be true reflected in his eyes. I simply nodded, and his hand fell back to his side. Cole beckoned us forward, and Jeremy was the first to walk behind him. I followed and Luke walked behind me to end our little line.

Within a minute, the road was out of sight. Tree branches, my exuberant friends, lacked their normal vigor and instead seemed to be giving me consoling caresses. Even though we were in the dark and I hadn't seen eye-shine, I felt like a hundred gazes weighed my steps. Our flashlights cut in useless arcs, only serving to make the shadows writhe around us.

Normally, I would have been exhilarated by this primal world. Right then, however, I could only think of the chill in the air and how cold it'd be if I didn't have my thick green jacket on. It wasn't quite winter yet, but fall Vermont nights can be frigid. Who knew what Jessica was wearing?

"Cole?" I asked, my voice louder than a gunshot in the darkness. "Where do the police think she is?"

Luke straightened, attentive. Jeremy got caught up on a root, but I grabbed him before he fell.

Cole slowed down and turned to face us. In the eerie, patched lighting, we must have looked like demons. I think, at least, we looked like slightly hopeful demons.

110

Cole sighed. "I'm not a police officer, just a game warden. From what I was told, which wasn't much, there were a lot of signs of a struggle, but the trail ends in the woods. No one else's DNA and no other torn fabric was found."

I think all of us were shocked when it was Luke who spoke. "Human or animal?"

Cole rubbed his close-cropped beard absentmindedly. "Human, almost certainly."

The scream that racked my eardrums was almost certainly not human. All of us spun to face the noise as it died into the night.

I didn't think as I plunged into the darkness, running toward the noise. It'd sounded so primal. So unnatural. No one shouted after me. I realized that all footsteps had fallen in line with mine. The flashlights in our pumping arms threw light wildly and uselessly, but all of us were of the same mind. It was close. Close enough to be Jessica.

I leapt over roots and rocks, wind whipping my hair behind me. My head felt airy, like it would pop off if I jumped too high. The others had fallen behind me, but not by much. A nagging thought pricked at my mind. I'd heard the sound before.

Jeremy's desperate voice ripped at both the night and my heart as he shouted, "Jessica!"

I abandoned that nagging feeling and I took up his cry. "Jessica!"

Cole and Luke followed suit. Our voices merged into a chorus of hope, more blinding than the night. She was close, I could feel it.

Something flashed in front of me, undeniable movement. My heart stuttered and I grabbed a tree to halt my momentum. My lungs sawed in and out as I registered the identity of the small streak of color. My knees grew weak as that niggling thought came to the foreground.

The others stopped behind me, sweeping their flashlights over the blank area I stared at.

"It was a fox," I said.

Just a fox.

Demons were changing destinies.

They were kamikaze marksmen, taking out strategic individuals whose absence would cause a shockwave to tip the scales a bit without caring that I would eliminate them for it. This was a whole new approach, signifying a shift in the demon hierarchy I knew nothing of. It was slowly becoming clear that they were not single agents fighting in generally the same way because they had generally the same cause. There was a higher power at work here, or perhaps it should be called a lower power.

The patterns had changed. I was used to the purest being assassinated so that their darker counterparts outnumbered them, but my last few missions had not been protecting the purest. These latest demons went after the humans who were related to or involved with those who had the potential to do great good.

If slowly picking off those that the uncorrupt held dear did not shatter their purity, which it rarely did not, the demons would slowly move in on the individual. It'd be little things they did, wanting to change but not kill. To torture the light straight from their souls. They were building an army of Corrupted souls, either embodied or disembodied, one human at a time.

They'd start with night terrors, horrid dreams of blood and loss that kept the victim awake and whittled away at their health. Then they'd cause uncharacteristically delicate misfortunes. Anything that could go wrong would, but these instances would build up and up until a person's mind broke like a weary dam.

It was happening right before my eyes.

I watched. It pained me to do so, but I needed to know what the demons were doing. I needed to stop this madness.

Before me, I saw a demon turn tangible just long enough to cause an exhausted middle-aged man to fall and twist his ankle. He sat there, nursing it and gingerly putting weight on it. The deep lines around his eyes crinkled as he surveyed the pain, so similar to the furrows my fingernails dug in the painted windowsill. I clenched my hands to keep myself restrained, but the man had no such issue.

Though the pain should have been manageable, the older man did not rise. He lowered his head like he was debating never rising again, watching the shadows dance in the corners and hallways of his own home, his only company. I wondered if he could see them, or if he could only sense their sinister presence as a heaviness settling on his skin.

A light flared, sudden and dramatic. My head whipped toward the source and I saw that I could wait no longer. A Corrupted soul had pushed something flammable onto a stove, left on in a moment of tormented absentmindedness. I smashed through a lower window with my elbow and leapt inside.

I pulled the man out before the flames washed over him, but without a doubt the demon watching in an oversized rodent form had been planning on letting the man burn just long enough for his mind to slip. It watched me from the shadows, eager to finish its mission, but unwilling to draw closer to me when I blazed with angelfire. The elder was a dead weight in my arms, but I managed to carry him out of harm's way before the rat demon had decided to run.

I quickly dispatched the monster with Haldis, avoiding the caustic gore that shot from its throat when I sliced it. Only minor scratches and burns dotted me, but the sinking feeling in my chest pulled me further from the physical sensations.

The man didn't respond when I knelt next to him. Mentally and on the spiritual level, the damage had been done. Holding my breath, I did the only thing I could think of…I plunged my blade deep into his chest.

It produced a hissing noise that grated against my senses, and my hope was lost. His soul had suffered too much damage. It was like trying to suture a gaping hole, just not enough left to work with.

He burned, after all. In angelfire instead of hellfire. The man was so close to being Corrupted that the majority of his soul burned like the oil it resembled. The tiny portions of it that clung to purity departed in a glittering haze, rising slowly. I felt very little satisfaction as it faded away. I comforted myself with the knowledge that he would not turn out like the lost one who had held me captive, nor would his disembodied soul remain to possess another innocent.

The problem could not be solved on the scale of individuals. There were, of course, still demons chewing on good peoples' innards, but it was almost as if they were supposed to serve as a distraction. I handled those horrors all the same, but I personally felt every conversion of a good person. The demons had gained foresight, choosing to create evil rather than simply destroy good.

It was my job to put a stop to it. The change must stem from something, something which I was determined to eliminate. I knew the risks that came with any demon call; death for me meant the end, no second chances. That wouldn't matter to me, but I was the first line of defense against the beasts of Hell. I'd be replaced, but time and therefore lives would be lost.

I drew a deep breath, but no comfort came from it, only lost time.

Chapter Seven

It was when I had almost set my bathroom on fire trying to attempt a locating spell with a map and some matches that I decided my attempts to find Jessica were doing more harm than good. That had been my last resort, after the normally lively dowsing crystal had been too jittery in my hand to be conclusive and my subconscious did not give up any clues that I might have missed when in trance.

I felt trapped, stuck in the worst way possible. I could do anything I wanted physically, but none of it would help the sensation in the slightest. I was in a prison of my own dang mind, unable to flee no matter how far I actually ran.

I opened the window to hide my mess, letting in a frigid breeze in the process. I told myself the flimsy smoke swirls still rising from the map were the reason my eyes were stinging, but I knew it was a lie. The open window greedily gulped at the discolored air, until nothing was left of my misadventure except for a lingering scent and some charred remains in the trash bin. Without realizing I had moved, I found myself on my bed, perched on the deep blue duvet.

But I could not remain idle. I decided that making progress on something, anything, was better than driving myself into the ground. With this thought in mind, I reached under my bed and pulled out the manila envelope from the library. Or I *tried* to pull it out, but ended up patting the carpet where it should have been.

I rolled off my bed, not bothering to stand up first and regretting my laziness when I hit the ground with a solid *thump*. I put my head flush to the floor despite the itchiness it brought. Nothing obscured my view to the other side except for a lonely cobweb and a bit of a hump in the middle where there had been excess carpet, making it look like a Mongolian death worm had tunneled through.

As if I wasn't panicked enough, the letter was gone. *Spectacular.* I had not the slightest clue as to where I could have placed it if it wasn't under the bed. I recollected that I had put it under there to save it from being folded to fit into the small chest I had in my closet. Maybe I had slipped up and stuck it in there anyways?

I crawled over to the closet, still too lazy to stand. In the far corner, where my neglected dresses went to collect dust, sat the partially obscured wooden chest. I used the designs on the edges to pull it forward and into my lap, where it quickly cut off my circulation and was then put back onto the floor. It wasn't locked in any way, but I had put so many wards in there nothing unwanted could touch it.

I cupped my hand under the lid as I opened it, careful to remove any excess salt that fell over the edge. Salt, I had heard from multiple sources, was one of the best wards against dangerous spirits and other nasty things. Even with the extra salt brushed away, I could see my little artillery was lacking the envelope I was searching for. It also, as I had discovered before, lacked anything capable of helping me find Jessica.

What it did have, however, were the surviving cameras from the night at the library. I dug around for the audio recorders first so I could save the best for last. I was pretty sure I was going to get a spirit on film on the main floor, unless that whole ordeal was a massive hallucination. That was always a possibility.

I pulled out the three audio recorders I had and was surprised to find that two were empty. When I thought about it though, it made more sense, seeing as I had turned into Humpty Dumpty less than fifteen minutes into the actual investigation.

All I had was the call and response we did as a group. I tapped the play button and sat back, listening to all of our voices filling the silence. When the very first question rolled around, I held my breath to make sure I would be able to hear even the faintest whisper.

Turns out, I didn't need to hold my breath. A *whooshing* sound spread across the room, grainy and indistinct. I held the recorder up closer to my ear, unaware it did not originate from the device. Boy, I froze up pretty quick when I looked up and saw my mother in the doorway, the manila envelope from the library pinched between two fingers. I glared at the recorder in my hand as if it had betrayed me.

"May I help you?" I asked with an overdose of innocence as I discreetly hit the pause button on the recorder. No need for her to hear just what I'd been up to that got me into such trouble. I'd been roasted like a boar on a spit about the subject, but had used half-truths to wiggle out. The look in her eyes told me I wouldn't be wiggling anywhere this time around.

Her right brow twitched. "Explain."

I knew I had it coming then, because the open ended question is the most dangerous type. If I said too little, it would seem like I was keeping secrets. Too much, I'd just dig myself deeper and deeper. There was only one easy way out.

I didn't say anything. I'd learned from years of being awkward that if one person doesn't fill the silence in a conversation, the other normally volunteers something. In this situation, it worked like a charm. Or maybe a bit of Devil's Breath, if you're a Bokor.

"Where did you get this? Why was it under your bed?" she asked with equal parts curiosity and concern. *Good*, I thought, *I can play up the curious side.*

"Library," I stated, purposefully keeping it short so I wouldn't limit myself later.

"You stole this? Why? Is this the new craze with you kids? Did those *boys* make you do this? I can't believe—"

"Mom."

"—you! I put up with the crazy things you bring home, but what is a mother supposed to think when they vacuum their daughter's room—"

"Mom."

"—and find a dusty silver bullet and the ravings of a madman under the bed! Are you okay? Are you on drugs? Are those kids forcing you into the occult?"

"Wait, there was a silver bullet?" I questioned, throwing myself into a more engaged sitting position on my bed. One of my legs dangled off the edge of my mattress and began to tap the bed frame quickly enough to punctuate every other word.

"You mean you took this without looking through it first? Why did you take it in the first place then?" she inquired, a little bit less enraged now that she knew her daughter wasn't about to go Rambo on the local werewolf population.

"Well, I mean, I *started* to read it. But then I," *busted the screen door like it was nobody's business and almost got*

119

swallowed by Fenrir's minion, "...lost attention," I explained.

"Then explain *these*, Leah Grace Walker," she mandated as she pulled out a hunk of dried plant from the package. My breath stalled in awe when I saw the distinctive purple flowers, bleached and withered by time.

She held a nice-sized hunk of wolfsbane. I thanked the Loas that it was encased within another bag, because the toxins could spread easily through the skin. *Jeez, this guy was not taking chances. All the bases are covered*, I thought. If only I knew how to get her to give me the envelope back, I could sorely use its contents. Not that I'd have the desire to kill a werewolf that came at me. In reality, I'd probably embrace lycanthropy with open arms. Well, depending on the type....

"Are these drugs? Are you *smoking* this stuff? Is that why it smells like smoke in the bathroom?" my mom queried, dragging me out of my thoughts.

"No, Mom, really. They aren't. That's—"

"Don't lie to me!" she snapped, and then her face softened a little, her hand drooping as she asked, "Is this because of Jessica?"

I stiffened, and my foot stopped beating like a heart that stalled.

"It's wolfsbane, Mom," I droned, so careful not to let too much emotion into my voice that it came out with too few.

"Why would someone...Oh. The crazy man put it in there for the girl's supposed werewolf problem," she realized, her eyes widening and shoulders losing their stiffness.

I confirmed it. "Yes."

"That still doesn't excuse you from stealing this," she reiterated half-heartedly.

"Steal it from who, Mom? No one has been in there in over a decade. No one will miss it," I protested. Her airy sigh told me I had won. I decided to try and extend the luck just a little farther.

"Can I have the stuff back, please? The mystery is helping to distract me, especially since you don't want me in the woods without a buddy," I pleaded. "I need it. Especially now." My eyes watered a little, involuntarily. I could tell by the slight frown she adopted what she was going to do before she did it, and a huge burst of relief almost knocked me flat.

"If the police come knocking, don't come crying to me," she relented as she put the envelope on my dresser. Then she added, "Are you sure you don't want to talk a little bit about Jessica? I know you must be hurting," in a much more somber tone.

"Actually, I think I might go out for a bit," I said as I got up from my resting position and embraced her. "But thank you."

She held on to me, and I was truly grateful for her presence. "Are you sure that's the best idea?"

I nodded. Up this close, I could see the beginnings of a few new wrinkles around her eyes. Guilt made me bite the inside of my lip, but it was just another drop in the ocean.

"Yeah, I'm going to go crazy if I stay in one place. Well, crazier, I guess," I said, and she smiled slightly.

I disengaged and made my way back out of the house, where the screen door sat innocently in place, as if nothing had happened. I wasn't fooled.

The grass on the back lawn had a serious need for a haircut and it tickled the spaces between my toes as I walked. The sun was being particularly motherly today, heating the earth as a hen would her egg. Its light painted only the uppermost part of the trees a vibrant gold.

I should apologize to Luke for being such a jerk yesterday, I mused. It was one task I knew I could handle, so I didn't hesitate to cross the lawn and start walking down the street. It would have been smart to bring shoes, but that thought occurred to me too late.

I hopped along the shaded parts of the road, careful to avoid the heat from the sections that had roasted all day. I bounced back and forth in a sort of impromptu dance set by the light, unaware of just how strange it might look to an outsider until I saw an outsider just down the road. The onlooker continued to walk the opposite way I was, cutting straight through the sunlight and walking in my direction.

Though I couldn't see his face at this distance, I had a good sense of who it was from the loping way he walked and, if I was honest, mostly by the plaid shirt and work boots. It helped that the sunlight made his dirty blond hair a light wheat color.

When the distance between us was smaller than the distance between me and the wolf had been, he crossed over to my side of the road. I smiled and greeted him.

"You know, the sunlight doesn't bite," he informed me with a small smile.

"It does when you aren't wearing shoes. I swear, when the road sits there in the sun like this, it gets hotter than Hades," I explained and then instantly regretted it when his gaze flicked down to my filthy toes. Fabulous. I'd managed to make myself look like a hillbilly in front of a cute guy.

His brows drew together, but only slightly. "Then why don't you wear shoes?"

"Shoes are for the weak," I teased, but then sobered up

quickly and tried to accomplish what I came here to do.

"Look, I walked down here to apologize for yesterday. I'm sorry for being so rude to you. And thank you so much for bringing my bag..." I trailed off to gauge his reaction.

Somewhere above us, a mourning dove cooed. The sound broke my concentration just enough for a nagging doubt to slip in. I barely knew this guy. As friendly as we might have been, my knowledge of him was summed up by knowing his name and the state he came from. Oh, and his address. And one or two assorted stories from his past. But that was it. I didn't have the slightest clue how to read him.

Except...He'd done so much for me, and I was beginning to take his presence for granted. I breathed easier when he was around. Even his usual solid, comfortable silence soothed my nerves. I might not be able to read his emotions as clearly as I'd like, but I was beginning to trust his actions. Even if he was a werewolf.

"Leah, you found out one of your friends went missing. How were you supposed to react?"

Guilt still prodded me. "I know, but—"

He cut me off. "Could have turned around and punched me out to your heart's desire and it still would have been understandable."

"Understandable? Maybe. But it was still rude of me," I countered. The corner of his mouth quirked up. I set a goal right then that I'd get him to smile all out.

"Won't give an inch...How about you make up for this 'rudeness', then?" he suggested.

"I thought I just did?" I said, but it came out as more of a question.

"I refuse to accept an apology for something that didn't happen," he stated stubbornly, and I swear I could *feel* the

123

alpha he was projecting. I'd be lying if I said I didn't flick my gaze down instinctively.

"Then what do you want me to do?" I asked cautiously. I didn't think Luke was going to screw me over, but I had heard one too many stories of favors and the like going wrong in myths and fairy tales. Who knew how conniving a wolf in human's clothing could be?

Luke nodded his head toward my house. "Have anything that needs doing right now?"

I shook my head and he continued, "Hoping to take a break from yardwork. You fish?"

He said it like a challenge, as if he half expected me to reject the proposal on principal. He should have known better. In an area as rural as this, where malls and entertainment were slim pickings, fishing was a common way to spend the time.

"I can do you one better. I've got poles for the both of us at my house, so we don't even need to walk back to yours," I informed him. Truth was, my family had possessed one or two to mess around with on hot summer days, but I had purchased two lightweight Ugly Sticks so that I wouldn't have to keep borrowing Jeremy's gear every time the two of us went out. He always managed to reel in a whopper that made mine look like half a fish stick, but I liked to tell him no fish he'd caught yet had surpassed his ego in size.

I led Luke back to my house and asked him to wait a minute while I collected all the necessary gear. I grabbed two rods, my tackle box, and a bucket just in case we foul hooked something and was almost back out the door before I realized shoes would be helpful for this excursion. With my luck, I'd probably hook myself in the foot.

When I emerged, my hands were full of equipment and

I had the tackle box under one arm.

"Let me take that," Luke suggested or commanded. I couldn't tell which. Either way, he moved to take the box and the bucket.

"Really, I'm fine. I can manage it," I argued feebly. He had already unwound my grasp and removed the bucket.

"I insist."

The tackle box went next, and I shifted so I had a rod in each hand.

"Such a gentleman," I mocked playfully. That one corner of his mouth pulled up, and I took that as my cue to start leading the way. I knew of a little place not far from there where we might be able to catch a few brook trout. We cut through the backyard and entered the woods in a cut near where the wolf had been.

I watched him from the edges of my vision as we passed the site. It was easier because he had moved up to keep pace with me rather than trail behind like a duckling. *If* he were a werewolf, he should be able to smell the wolf, right? And *if* he were to smell it, he might have a reaction. That is, *if* he didn't expect the wolf to be there. The 'if's were breeding like bunnies in my head, so I shoved them aside for the time being.

He didn't have a perceptible reaction. We marched forth, my fishing poles moving like sidewinders to avoid snagging on grabby branches. I must have walked into three different spider webs, but no way was I going to throw away my cool card. I brushed them off discreetly and a little bit spastically.

It was only a matter of minutes before the sound of trickling water led me to a little creek I had frequented as a child. Wet moss glimmered on the bank like emeralds. Already I could see a flicker of movement under the surface.

The rippling water didn't reflect the sun as well as the pond behind the school did, resulting in a patchwork of gold, silver, and green reminiscent of a mermaid's tail.

"You want to make a bet on who catches the biggest?" I chaffed to break the silence as I held out one of the rods to Luke.

Humor glimmered in his eyes, making tiny lines spread from them. He took the rod I offered him. "Bet what?"

I flipped over a rotting log and snagged a worm, impaling it on a hook.

"Hmm," I hummed, tapping my finger in thought. "If I win, I think you'll have to jump in." I knew from experience that water was freezing year round. That hadn't stopped me from swimming in it when I first found the place, but I had come out with head to toe goosebumps. I'd laugh my butt off to see the look of shock on his face when he hit the surface.

"And if I win?" he asked, seemingly unfazed by my suggestion. Either that or he thought victory was assured.

"Have you got any ideas? That's about as creative as I get," I admitted.

"If I win, you have to answer five questions for me, honestly and unrestrained," he concluded. I kicked myself mentally. That would have been a perfect thing to have used on him. It didn't make too much sense that he was deploying that tactic, since I would have answered most questions without such prodding, but whatever. It worked in my favor in the end.

"You're on," I declared as I tossed my line into the stream. The *hiss* of the line spinning off the reel and the slight *plop* as the worm hit the water were a familiar combination of sounds. That combination doubled as Luke cast

126

further upstream.

It was funny how different fishing with Luke was than it was with Jeremy. With Jeremy, there'd be an endless fountain of chatter and taunts, only ever broken by the splashing of a catch when one of us hooked something. Even then, the silence would never last long because we'd go right back to taunting and teasing each other over the new development.

With Luke, the only time that wasn't silent was right after a catch. When he reeled the first one in, a brook trout no bigger than half again my pinkie finger, I was the one who broke the silence.

"What's that, three-fourths of a fish stick?" I jested. I still hadn't caught anything.

"Something like that," he replied as he unhooked it and threw it back in. I thought it was a deliberate attempt at closing down the conversation until I managed to catch a fish even smaller than his and he spoke.

"What's that, quarter of a fish stick?" he teased as I struggled to keep a hold on the slippery fish. I grunted in reply, focused on the task of finding the balance between enough pressure to keep the fish still, but not enough to hurt it. It seemed I had grabbed it just a tad too loosely, because it flailed just as I was managing to slide the hook out.

"Ouch!" I yelled out of more anger than pain as the squirming fish caused the hook to spear the edge of my finger. The fish was free, at least, so I tossed it back in. I could hear Luke cast again next to me.

I showed him the hook in my finger. "I think I won the bet."

It wasn't deep at all, just lifting a layer of skin so that it looked like the hook had a thin white rope over it. Probably wouldn't even bleed, but I was larger than any fish I could have caught.

"Don't know about that," he remarked, "seems I have the upper hand."

If he were Jeremy, I thought, *that would have been an intentional hand pun.*

"How so?" I asked as I unhooked myself. I bent down to rinse the wound in the water. He responded by giving his rod one quick tug, and a couple of leaves rained down to kiss the water's surface. I looked up and saw the line glimmer like a glowworm's silk straight up into the pine above us. I started to laugh like mad.

"I guess you do win," I admitted between laughs. "Now the question is can you release that catch?"

"With a long chainsaw," he conceded, nodding as if he was actually considering it as a plan of action. It made sense. He definitely operated in a more lupine fashion than simian. I couldn't picture him climbing the tall rocks that were lifting the tree high above us. That meant it was up to me to unhook it.

Not that I would under normal circumstances. Nah, I'd probably just cut the string as high up as possible if there was no way to shake it out. Here, however, I felt I had something to prove. A petty way to up the alpha, a little prod after the staring contest on the first day was a draw.

"Watch and learn, ground-dweller," I taunted as I wrapped my hand around a suitable yet sharp handhold. My legs were soon to follow, walking up the face of stone and clinging to the surface. I relished the capability of my muscles to do this task, lifting me with little to no strain.

I moved quickly, my subconscious pushing me to impress. I was used to climbing trees, so the mini cliff served as more of a challenge for me. A few times, my hand slipped because of the detritus in the crevasses I was using and I had to call out to Luke to make sure he moved out of the way of the small chunks of rock that bounded toward him like overeager puppies.

To my relief, I was done with the rocks in no time. All that was left was to free the tree's captive. I'd only need to go a few yards up because the rocks had made up the brunt of the height. I could see the hook only four or five closely knit branches above my head.

Even so, I moved in such a way that my upward progress didn't always seem upward to me. Sometimes I wove flat between two lovey-dovey branches, sometimes my feet were at a higher place than my head was, and sometimes I was just stepping up, using higher branches to steady myself as I moved my feet.

It wasn't as adrenaline filled as when I was out in the storm, but the sensation of Luke's eyes on my back added its own sort of jitteriness. I got high enough to see the hook without issue and shimmied toward it. It wasn't difficult to dislodge, but it took quite a bit of wiggling and a little bit of cheating on my part, removing the bark.

"Do you think the dryads will be mad at me?" I asked, forgetting who I was talking to.

That became all too evident when I got a confused, "What?" in reply.

"Never mind," I said as I freed the hook. "Heads up!"

Luke deftly plucked the string from the air, spinning it over a finger until the hook was in hand. He then reeled in the slack and caught the hook on the pole to keep it in position. He put the pole down and stood near enough to the rocky base of the tree that I couldn't look down at him without getting twenty double chins.

Going down was harder than going up. My impatience grew as my speed decreased. I didn't want to look like a sluggish zombie. No, I wanted to look like all my movements were cool and calculated, yet graceful. Like a dancer at home in the trees. Or perhaps an earth spirit.

It seemed I was not destined to be either, because in my preoccupation I stuck my hand right into a pile of sticky pine sap. The residue left my hand looking like an echidna because of all the pine needles stuck to it. I brushed it against my pants, trying to get rid of my own personal abstract art.

I must have rubbed it just a *teensy bit* too hard, because that leg lost its footing. It wouldn't have been a problem, except it threw off the balance for the half of me that was still on the tree. My left leg twisted up and off the branch as the right half of me succumbed to gravity, and the scales of bark I was gripping with my remaining hold came loose under my palm.

I don't think I realized I was falling until my foot smashed into something before I hit the ground. I had curled into a crouching position and touched the leaf litter in no time, both my feet smarting and all of my scrapes protesting. The leg that twisted hurt a little bit more than the other, but it was akin to stubbing my toe. I was unhurt, but from the pained grunt behind me, it was clear just what, or rather who, I had fallen on.

I spun around to find Luke on the ground. His eyes were squinted almost shut as if he were staring at the sun. One of his hands hovered over the opposite shoulder. It was a silly thing for me to think of at the moment, but I couldn't help but draw a connection between his hand and a fly. Every time his hand touched his shoulder, he'd grunt and it'd lift up again, unable to hold the position. Like a horsefly scared by the twitching of a horse.

When his hand lifted, I could tell something was off. His shoulder lay funny, and there was a small bump that was sticking out where the skin should have been smooth. *Holy chindi on a tumbleweed,* I thought, *I just dislocated his shoulder.* I got up from my crouched position and drew closer warily, like I could scare the rest of his arm off if I got too close.

"Mother of—" Luke inhaled a quick breath, his teeth clenched. "Will you...give me a hand with this?"

"I don't know what to do!" I said with a touch of desperation leaking out. I stared at the offending bump and willed it to submerge back into its socket. Luke used his good arm to sit up and put his back against the rock, wincing when his shoulder bumped around.

"Not a...big deal. Come here," he coaxed, breathing heavily. He waved me over with the hand that had been fluttering over his shoulder. I approached and knelt next to him.

"Your shoulder is dislocated! How is that not a big deal?" I questioned anxiously. It seemed I was more worried than he was.

"Nothing I haven't...done before," he assured me with a strained smile, but it looked much, much more similar to a wolf's snarl. "Grab my arm?" he asked in a rush of breath. I did as I was told.

"Ninety degrees," he managed to get out after a momentary inhale of breath. I knew from the force of it that this would be the point where, if I had incurred the injury, I'd be screaming like a banshee.

I followed his instructions like I thought an extra tenth of a degree would detonate a bomb. He guided me through

131

the process he seemed to have memorized, telling me to pull down gently and to slowly rotate his arm outward.

I could feel it when the joint popped back in, a sudden release in tension that was accompanied by a sharp, prolonged grunt from Luke. I let out a breath of my own as he tested the limits of his arm gingerly, wincing, but not as badly.

My eyes found the sky, an uninterrupted blue that seemed at odds with what had just happened. There was no blood, no more pain, yet I was still concerned. Perhaps I should have pushed him to go to the hospital, but I could tell just from the straightness of his spine he wouldn't consider it.

"You've done that before?"

"I have a brother," was his simple explanation. His head bobbed back in an odd way after he admitted that, moved by some sort of sudden emotion I could not hope to understand. A brother was news to me, though. This little tidbit of information hadn't come up yet. Questions reared from this lump of knowledge like tentacles off the Kraken. It wasn't long before one of those greedy limbs reached out to Luke.

"Really? I haven't seen him around anywhere. Will he be going to school with us?" I interrogated, curiosity corroding my self-control.

Luke's hand seized a rock under him and held it. "I thought I was the one who won five questions," he stated in a tone with too many different taints and flavors to it that I feared I'd never be able to grasp it.

Don't think I don't see what you did there, I chastised in my head, but I didn't push the issue out loud. The mystery around this boy was driving me *insane.*

That'd be a kicker, having insanity at the root of all my

problems. "Do you have anything in particular in mind?"

Luke pulled himself up with his good arm, the right one, and stared at me thoughtfully for a minute. I tried not to falter under his gaze, but it was like my eyes had weights attached to the irises, pulling them forever down. I noted a pill bug attempting to run for cover under the bottom of my shoe, its little legs working furiously.

I looked back up and found myself staring at the slight bulge of his pectoral muscles, looking fully flexed even in a resting position. My eyes were quick to cant somewhere else. *No matter what, you cannot romanticize the werewolf,* I chided myself. I had just worked up the courage to stare him right in the eye and hold it when he spoke, making me curse my inability to take action sooner.

"It wouldn't be worth it if I asked something typical," he postulated.

I raised my eyebrows a hair. "So, what are you planning on asking?"

He didn't seem to know just then. It took a second for him to say anything, and even then he didn't seem the most enthused with the idea. He did, at least, look curious.

I was beginning to realize he never truly adopted a questioning tone, only one that would better fit a statement or a command. "Something you've never told anyone?"

If this was the very first one, I feared for how the others could escalate. My toe lightly swirled up dirt as I pondered what to say.

"How embarrassing does it have to be?" I checked as a whole flurry of images came to mind. This could turn into a 'back away slowly' situation for Luke pretty fast depending on what I picked. Fortunately for me, he just smirked slightly, leaving me to make the rules.

"When I was little," *and continuing to present date,* I added to myself, "whenever I swam, I'd pretend to be a mermaid." *I also used to do various spells in an effort to become one, but no cigar there.* I planted my spinning foot on the ground, bracing myself for something to happen.

Not much did, though. That one corner of his mouth climbed even further up, and he emitted a staggered, soft booming noise that took me a second to place. Laughter, deep in his chest.

"Spirits, dryads, and now mermaids. What's next?" he muttered in a way that was surprisingly disdain-less. Even so, it rubbed me the wrong way, making my next move tremendously under-planned and irrational.

"Werewolves," I stated, fishing for a reaction.

I got one. His eyes widened slightly and the smirk slid off his face. It was almost imperceptible, but it was something. I let a victorious smile simmer to the surface at just about the same time as he regained his. I cut him some slack; it wasn't wise to flash all my cards just then.

"Maybe vampires, too. Oh, how about the Wampus cat? Or a Pontianak!" I claimed excitedly. It seemed so impossible to me that out of all the hundreds and thousands of mythical creatures there were, not a single one was real. I knew that I craved their existence like a plant craves the light. Little bits of evidence were enough to tide me over for now, but it wouldn't last. The world might look grayscale, but if I dug deep enough or flew high enough, I'd hit that patch of color that made everything pale in comparison.

Maybe by that point I'd be stuck in a straightjacket in a stained padded room, but it'd be worth it. All the past struggles, all the past doubts would be utterly flattened under the weight of the new found purpose. What was a bad grade or a screaming fight when everything is life and death?

It's a good thing that my excitement for that didn't differ outwardly too much with the previous statement. Luke didn't seem to notice my thoughts had veered wildly off track. Instead his shoulders moved downward a fraction, possibly in relief or possibly from the ease of pain. It was hard to tell.

"Do I want to know?" he asked as he picked up the bucket and released the water that had filled it.

"Your life depends on it," I replied with a mock serious nod.

I closed my eyes, resting in a stray patch of sunlight. The red seeped through my lids, matching my thoughts. Then the color dissipated suddenly, though I could still feel the sun's warmth on my skin. Black replaced it, along with a feeling of static fur, sharp like needles, brushing my side. The uncomfortable feeling faded and was replaced with all-encompassing flames: Haldis was lending me some power.

It was a summoning. The dark vision and the sensation indicated that the danger was very, very real with this one. I had an inkling of suspicion that this might be the origin of the divergence of demon behavior, no matter how unlikely that was.

My wings stretched, giving me a physical kind of satisfaction. I ran a few strides and then leapt, wings beating and feathers catching a glorious lift. Dust swirled behind me, but I moved too quickly for any to settle in my line of sight.

I carried myself higher. It would be a long trek to get

where I needed to go, passing many lands and an ocean. There was no time to waste. I rose up high enough that the cold and lack of oxygen would kill a mortal. Anyone who saw me from below would see nothing in the day and something resembling a shooting star at night.

I left the wooded area where I had been staying and flew west. I said goodbye to the forest when the trees were forced down as if by the palm of a giant, sinking lower before giving way to shrubs and then to nothing at all. For the longest while, sand dunes rippled beneath me like the undulations of the sea. Then the sea itself came.

Small crests caught my light and threw it back at me, making it seem like a serpent raced under the water below me. With no people in sight, I was able to descend and fly near the water's surface. I wasn't foolish enough to touch it when I was flying at this speed, it'd be like touching an angle grinder.

Its presence was comforting while it lasted, however. There were things to be learned from a force so immense, especially one that had no favorites. The ocean could give both life and death and was uncaring as to who received what.

When I felt the urging intensify, I knew the time was trickling away. If I did not hurry, I'd be dealing death. I'd learned my lesson by waiting.

I arrived at a little home in the middle of a forest of cacti. Its placement was odd, one of a few houses that were completely isolated from the outside world. When I landed on the dirt road, there was no one to notice my unearthly glow. All the houses but one stood dark.

I didn't need the tugging sensation to tell me that was the one to which I needed to go. Many lights flickered within the squat house, their irregularity suggesting many candles were

136

the source. I could hear no noise over the spurting breeze, one that carried—I bent down to snatch one of its passengers—copious quantities of well-groomed flower petals.

From the fact that no wild flowers were in sight and there were patches of freshly overturned dirt at the very end of the street, I knew death had come for this area. It was possible that the human in the lit house was the sole survivor or the only one not to leave after whatever had happened.

I flew to an open window on the back side of the house, squeezing through and entering. I pulled my aura tighter around me as I folded my wings into my back, masking the light I produced. I walked lightly through the dim corridors with the flames of strange looking candles serving as camouflage for my fire.

I opened my palm and the physical form of Haldis came willingly. The gold hilt was strangely cool in my grasp, and my gold eyes took up residence in the reflection on its silvery blade. I crept as silently as I could to a heavy wooden door with loud, belting snores echoing from under it. Candlelight was emanating from the crack left open.

I gave myself a line of sight to the bed. A man slept sprawled, with his feet hanging off either side of the mattress. The thick blanket on top of him should have made him sweat, but he had it curled up around his shoulders. It had an odd color scheme, entirely light except for the foot, which had a dark splat pattern. A dog with many patches of different colored fur rested there.

It would have been an innocent scene if shadows didn't writhe in the corner. That, and if the dog on the bed wasn't bleeding out all over the blanket. What I had assumed was a patch on its neck was a gaping chunk of nothing where a large bite had been taken out. Quick, lethal. The man was *unaware.*

A shadow separated from the wall and moved toward the bed, taking shape. The darkness coalesced until it took the quadruped form of a black mountain lion. Its thick claws made no noise as it stalked closer to the man and his dead dog. The demon approached the man's bare feet, sniffing.

Then it flicked out a broad, rough tongue and crossed the exposed skin. The man started from his snoring and mumbled, but didn't awaken. The beast repeated the action and the man mumbled the name of his dog.

"Lily, stop that," he insisted sleepily, moving his foot. I took that as my cue to intervene.

Quicker than sight, I was in the room and on the demon's hide. I swiped with Haldis, the motion meant to back the demon up. It inched back, but barely. It accepted the blow, which would have sent a weaker demon back to Hell, with only a flick of the eye.

Then it unleashed a scream that sounded like a mixture of a natural mountain lion and crackling embers. The scream of rage, not containing any pain, solidified the fact that I was not dealing with a run-of-the-mill demon. I had to get it away from the victim.

Its claws raked my ankle as I shot out and hit the puma's shoulder with as much force as I could muster. The beast went flying straight into the wall, which crumbled like it was made of tissue paper. I leapt out of the hole left in its wake.

The mountain lion was not stunned by the fall. It was waiting for me surrounded by a mob of newly-dead cacti when I got to the bottom, leaping for my throat. I stabbed wildly with Haldis, which audibly scraped against the demon's shoulder blade. My skin burned as the demonic fire touched my face. I took satisfaction in the burnt fur smell wafting off my adversary as he suffered similar burns.

My other hand reached behind the black cougar's neck and arrested its momentum. Its teeth came down on my bicep, gouging but not removing it. Charred flesh cauterized the wounds, but Haldis' aura quickly set on healing that. I yanked the ruff of fur I had caught down, flipping the demon.

It retained the mountain lion's natural reflexes, so it landed on its feet. The recovery time was quick, but not quick enough to completely avoid my strike. Haldis made quick work of the demon's paw, cutting straight through the foreleg.

No blood spilled from the wound, but shadowy tendrils flew with the severed appendage and caused the vegetation near where it landed to fold in on itself and lose its color. It leeched life from everything around it, and though the sand seemed unaffected, I knew countless numbers of organisms residing inside shifting burrows had just died.

The smoke poured from the amputated front leg, effectively hiding the creature in a spot darker than this night had birthed. The demon should have been exorcized by that point, yet it seemed to have limitless strength. Under my gaze, a shadow appeared within the shadow, a pulsing heart of darkness.

"Protector," the demon accused in a voice of shattering glass. It took effort not to cover my ears and even more to decipher the word. A demon had never spoken to me. I had not even fathomed the possibility. "I am the Rashtka."

I lifted my blade, in no mood for exchanging formalities. "What is your business with this human?"

A strange chuffing sound came from the center of the cloud. I strengthened my stance in anticipation of a surprise attack. The smoke was starting to disperse, flanking me as its range increased. I was wary of an ambush from the sides as I *approached the center.*

My luminescing eyes flicked imperceptibly when the Rashtka spoke in that terrible crunching voice again.

"I will feast on your corpse, Protector. Suck the marrow from your bones. Your heart, so pure, so pretty...I will swallow it whole."

"You can do no such thing from the Pit," I assured as I swung my blade into the darkest patch. Haldis cut through the gloom with a hiss, but hit nothing. There was nothing to hit.

The Rashtka had escaped.

Chapter Eight

Going to school while your friend was missing was like being a low-level patient at a psychiatric ward. I felt simultaneously ignored and observed, a strange combination. There were girls who were closer to Jessica than I was, and they sucked up most of the scrutiny and sympathy.

In a way, I was glad. I didn't want to be under the microscope. I'd had my fill by the time the day ended and was more than ready to get away. I had the perfect distraction planned to get my mind off it and to make me feel useful.

I was going to get to the bottom of Jeremy's and Luke's hard feelings for one another. I had seen a seed of a possible friendship at the library, and I was going to do my darn best to make sure it bloomed.

The plan was simple: bowling.

It was competitive enough to keep both of them there yet nowhere near as dangerous as our first stint together. That way, there would be nothing to remind either of them of whatever had caused the divide. As long as I kicked their butts, there wouldn't be any victorious gloating to offend either of their masculinities.

I set my devious plan into action with a few texts. Luke had given me his number after our fishing excursion, so I would no longer need to knock on his door like a timid puppy when I needed him. I sent the same, simple text to both of them.

Want to go bowling?

I got a reply from Jeremy almost instantly.

Does the Earth revolve around the sun?

A second text flew in from him right after it.

This physics homework sucks. I wouldn't mind if you used a bowling ball to put me out of my misery.

If you aren't nice, I will. Luke will be joining us. I warned.

His reply speed was a little slower this time.

On second thought, this physics work does look pretty tempting.

If that response had come from Luke, I would have been thrown off, possibly taking it as serious. From Jeremy, I knew he was just fooling around. He'd still be there.

Jerk. See you at 7 at the usual place. I typed and then put the phone down.

It was less than a few seconds before it cawed again.

Why did the werewolf get arrested at the butcher's shop?

He took a lycan to the raw meat? I tried as a preemptive strike. No such luck.

Ooh, I like that one. The correct answer is he was chop-lifting.

I let that conversation die with a smile and a shake of my head. I managed to crank out my own packet of mind-numbing physics and was about to launch into the soul-dissolving calculus when my phone rang. The thunderstorm sound emanating from it let me know it wasn't a text. The display lit up with Luke's name.

"Hello?" I greeted uncertainly as I answered.

"Never liked texting. Figured I'd call. Bowling?" he answered my unspoken question for why he didn't just text me back.

"Yeah, tonight at seven? There's a little bowling alley about twenty minutes away. I can give you directions? Or you can look it up. It's called Well's Bowling Alley," I rushed, not letting him answer in my haste. It was when I paused for breath that he responded.

"Seven's good. I'll look it up," he affirmed. I smirked inwardly at the fact that I had him hooked. He couldn't escape easily once I mentioned who else was coming without giving me an explanation.

"Jeremy will be there, too. I think we'll be able to avoid any major injuries this time around, though," I said in a feeble attempt at humor. I wasn't surprised when no laughter came from the other end of the line.

"He knows I'll be there?" he asked after a small pause. He sounded almost a little incredulous, like he expected the answer to be 'no' because 'yes' was inconceivable.

"Yup. I'll see you at seven," I reinforced, making sure there was no way out of my little trap.

Luke's voice was slightly confused at the abrupt end to the conversation. I got a small amount of glee from the fact that I had been able to throw him off his groove. "Bye?"

"Bye," I ended the call.

My ingenious plan seemed to be working perfectly. I made sure to arrive fifteen minutes early so that I wouldn't have to break up a fight on arrival. I didn't think it'd come to that, but it was like caging a wolf and a panther together. Nothing good would come of it.

I stepped out of my wheezy gray car and slammed the door with a little more force than I needed to. Scattered summer jobs only go so far to pay for something as expensive as transportation, and this particular junkyard graduate couldn't get any more beat up if an elephant did the Cha Cha on top of it.

Nothing to lose, then. I locked it and tread out on ground that seemed to consist equally of pebbles and cigarette butts. Most of those were likely the result of the tobacco shop with the flickering sign to my left, but I'd bet a few came from patrons of the bar at the other end of the plaza and a few more from the miniature convenience mart sandwiched between.

I wouldn't want to be caught without Haldis in the small alleys that crisscrossed behind these shops, but the lit area was pretty safe. Even so, I hightailed it inside, taking up residence at the cleanest table I could find. It wasn't long before the chair next to me squealed.

"Let's set the rules right here, right now. No voodoo, no hoodoo, no witchcraft. If I wake up tomorrow without clothes on and no memory of tonight, I *will* hunt you down," Jeremy teased as he pulled on some particularly clownish rental shoes.

"And *why* would you be naked?" I questioned. My own rental monstrosities were falling apart at one toe.

He wiggled his eyebrows. "My irresistible good looks."

I was saved from forming a witty retort by Luke's appearance. My eyes caught his over Jeremy's shoulder, so I was only able to see the patrons' reactions to him by periphery. It was enough. Luke was a storm cloud and people treated him like he had a solid presence. A chubby toddler with pigtails stopped and stared, while two rougher-looking college-aged students quickly shifted to give him a wide berth.

Just goes to show you, humans have more senses than

they realize. Luke's gaze rested solidly on Jeremy's back until he swung around the table to sit on my other side. I wouldn't say it was an aggressive stare, just a loaded one, like a dam ready to give. I was quick to intervene.

"Let's play, shall we?" I hefted a medium-weighted ball and advanced to our lane. The boys followed suit. Silence billowed around the two, but I suspected they were communicating something to each other while my back was turned.

My bowling ball curved wickedly to the right, only hitting three pins in the first frame. *So much for being the victor, eh?* I mocked myself as I sat back down.

Jeremy turned toward me and smiled, actually showing teeth. "I guess the voodoo dolls aren't helping you much, are they?"

I rolled my eyes. "Voodoo dolls aren't even voodoo."

"Then why call them voodoo dolls?" Jeremy argued.

I smirked at his prodding. He loved to volley back and forth, but this was one I'd win. "Why call a koala a koala bear? People thought they looked a little similar the same way people thought all witchcraft was voodoo."

Luke sank back down and Jeremy got the cue to take his turn. "Interesting discussion."

"Can you tell me what the deal is here? With you two?" I abruptly changed the subject. I was itching to get to the bottom of the dissonance between Jeremy and Luke.

"I..." he paused, as if unsure where to go. A little crinkle appeared in the corner of his eye. He shook his head. "Not my place to tell."

I wanted to shake him until he spat it out, but Jeremy tapped my shoulder. I looked up at the leaderboard. I had three, Luke, that jerk, had gotten a strike, and Jeremy had eight pins down. I reluctantly relinquished my torn-up seat and threw the ball.

I tried to rush through at first, thinking if I rolled the ball harder I'd finish quicker and get my answers, but I soon heard my companions' voices mix into the ever-present ambient noise. I rolled the next ball so slowly it barely made a dent when it hit the pins. I was too busy trying to pull their words from the crowd.

There is only so long someone can stall a bowling game without looking suspicious, and I walked that thin line. I was forced to turn around and interrupt what seemed to be nothing other than an average conversation. I knew better than to miss what it truly was: progress.

"Doesn't make sense," Luke told Jeremy's back as Jeremy collected his bowling ball.

Jeremy didn't turn around, but adopted a little swagger to his step. "I'll explain after I'm done with this strike."

That lucky idiot was saved from having to walk back in shame when his word held true. Meanwhile, I continued to prod Luke for answers to no avail, receiving a lame, "You should ask him."

There was no way I would be satisfied getting stuck in the equivalent of the eternal loop of ask your mom/ask your dad. When Jeremy returned, I shoved him into his seat and remained standing. I had to muster every fragment of alpha I had in me to keep from backing down with both pairs of sea blue and stone brown eyes focused on me.

"One of you is telling me what the deal is with you two. *Now*," I demanded, folding my arms. Both of them looked at each other, but with different stares. Jeremy's was almost a little nervous as he considered Luke and what he might say, while Luke gave him a once over and seemed to make

146

up his mind. He eyed Jeremy for a second, possibly conveying his intentions and forcing him to react.

Jeremy sighed and cast his head down a little, both of the gestures at odds with his usual easy-going demeanor. "Have you looked over the library footage yet?"

My arms fell to my sides and I tilted my head a little in confusion. "Not yet, why?"

"You'll see. Do it when you get back," he advised sheepishly. Luke, on the other hand, let a little bit of tension slip out of his posture. He still held himself rigidly, but I had yet to see him relax from that default. I guessed that he had been mad at something that Jeremy did in the library or the fact that he didn't own up to it, but I was not entirely sure. It could have been a simple dislike all the same.

"Will that alleviate whatever the heck is going on between you two?" I asked, unwilling to settle for non-solutions. The two troublemakers looked at each other and shrugged. I took that as a yes and left them to pick up my bowling ball.

What will I find on that film? A quick spat? Why would they not admit to that? Maybe one confessed his eternal love for the other and got rejected. I snorted at that. Who would think a dusty death trap of a library was a good place to ask someone out?

In the end, I had what I had been hoping for. The answer hadn't revealed itself yet, but I had the means to get it. Turns out, it had been under my nose the whole time. From the more relaxed conversations that slowly formed between Jeremy and Luke, it was clear something had been fixed.

My ultimate bowling victory plan failed. Jeremy came out on top while I was last, but no one seemed to be complaining. There definitely wasn't any sort of brawl or resentment that resulted from it. Everyone went their separate ways like civilized people, or werewolves. I don't discriminate.

Personally, I was halfway to my car when I realized my throat was desert-like in its dryness. I glanced back at the bowling alley longingly, thinking about the snack bar's bottled water, but couldn't shake the idea it'd be weird to go back in simply for that. The gas station style mini mart it was, then.

The moon had tossed its dark blanket over the sky. The street lights and the storefront neon sign illuminated the parking lot fairly well, but I couldn't help noticing that the impenetrable darkness obscuring the alleyways made them look like gaping maws. I gave them a wide berth on the irrational fear that they'd swallow me up.

I blinked a few times as my eyes adjusted to the bright shop interior. I made quick work of my task, collecting the water and bringing it up to the half-asleep older fellow at the register. I'd gulped down half of the cool relief before I exited the mart.

When I left, the brightness adjustment worked in reverse. I couldn't see crap in the dimly lit lot for a couple of seconds, but when I could it was like a dark mist had extended the range of each looming shadow. It was seriously creepy, but I was determined not to let it get to me.

I walked brazenly into the shade, trying to convince myself it was not different than if it had been illuminated. This was a point where my paranormal knowledge did not come in handy. I could all too easily imagine a gremlin, demon, or even a yara-ma-yha-who flown in from Australia just waiting to pounce. I shivered at the thought of the yara-ma-yha-who's blood red suckers reaching for me.

A voice made me flinch and then freeze in place. I ran my hand over the raised goose bumps on my arm to calm myself. *Alleyways have echoes. It wasn't close. Besides, what's the worst a voice can do to me?* I reasoned with myself. I wiggled my toes and walked forward again.

I took a single step before a light caught my eyes. Small and round, it flitted up in the air. It was at the level of my head when it suddenly pulled back. A will-o'-the-wisp? Those little clouds of light normally lead people off the paths in swamps. It didn't make sense for it to be here.

Before I could advance or retreat, a hand shot out and caught my wrist, pulling me into the darkness.

"I've got your little girlfriend right here," a voice growled right next to my face and into the light. A cell phone, not a will-o'-the-wisp. My captor turned it around on me, leaving me blind. My eyes squeezed shut in response, and I was struck with the sudden, terrible image of the same thing that was happening to me happening to Jessica. *Is this the failed abductor back for another round?*

"Not bad, although I'd say her nose is a bit too big for my tastes, brother," the male purred. His voice seemed to have a roughness to it, making every one of his words sound savage and a slight bit cocky. It rubbed me the wrong way, even though having a stranger haul you into an alley wouldn't rub anyone the right way.

I reacted by chucking my uncapped water bottle at his face. It bounced off and sprayed harmlessly, but it was enough of a shock to get him to drop my wrist. I darted away, but he caught the back of my shirt and a few hunks of my hair.

Immobilized, I swung my elbow out blindly and connected with something much less fleshy than I was imagining. The man behind me grunted involuntarily, but didn't let go. He shoved me against the brick wall and pinned me there with one arm.

His other hand touched his rapidly discoloring cheekbone. It didn't seem to pain him much, but he looked a little bit thrown off. "You sure are feisty. Like a kitten. You know what? That's what I'll call you, Kitten."

As he spat those words at me, I could see who I was dealing with for the first time. He had the darkest shade of brown hair possible while still being qualified as brown. His eyes were the opposite, so light they looked almost gold. He was built more like a bear than a man, not entirely unattractive, but bulked out with muscle. I could barely make out a lighter pattern on his collarbone and shoulders, like a complex tattoo.

My eyes darted up once more, as I squirmed experimentally. His arm pushed me harder, making my spine grind against some gritty substance on the wall. His eyes were predatory, locked onto mine like a falcon. His nose had an almost imperceptible notch in it like it had been broken and then set the wrong way.

My fist connected with it.

It was thoughtless, instinctual, and borderline stupid on my part. It felt like a twig snapping underfoot, so silly and little, but blood gushed from his newly re-broken nose in a frighteningly quick spray. Because of our nearness, much of it got on me, clinging to my shirt and my fist. Some slid down his dark jacket and quickly disappeared.

He swore, his free hand coming up to staunch the flow. His lip curled back in a way that *promised* he was going to strike me or worse.

"Stop fighting me!" he demanded, his voice altered by the plugged nose. I didn't have much of a choice.

My upper chest was still pinned under one muscular arm, and he had wizened up enough to shift it so both of my shoulders were immobilized. One of his boots stomped down to cover both of my feet. I braced myself, knowing I was in for more pain than I had ever dealt with before. My eyes squeezed shut.

Then I felt lightness. It was so sudden, I thought for a moment I was no longer alive, that he had twisted my neck or pulled a gun so quickly I hadn't gotten to feel any of it. A loud crash had me jerking out of that stupor pretty dang quickly.

"What did you do to her?!" a voice growled before there was another crash. My eyes jerked open to confirm the familiarity of it. My ears hadn't lied.

Luke held the man up against a metal dumpster by his jacket collar. The stranger didn't look scared, or angry, though. No, he looked...smug. I was going to kill him whether or not he had anything to do with Jessica's disappearance.

"What happened to the angel façade, brother? Don't you want to sit down over a cup of tea and sort this out like *civilized* people?" My former captor smirked.

"Eren, I will not ask twice," Luke stated. It was in equal parts a statement and a fact.

The stranger—Eren—sighed. "Don't you see I'm bleeding here? I was the one who got attacked. Shouldn't you be protecting me right now?"

Luke let go of Eren's jacket, but his fist remained clenched. Tension curled up his arm. Eren, on the other hand, looked completely at ease. The blood from his nose was everywhere, but it had seemed to stop flowing. I wondered if he had something up his sleeve, or if he just knew his brother—if I judged the relation correctly—wouldn't hurt him. I could see now why I hadn't been introduced.

"Leah, are you all right?" Luke asked without turning to face me.

The leftover scrapes from falling began to sting with the withdrawal of adrenaline. What hurt even more, however, were my slightly swelling knuckles. No one had informed me of how badly punching someone hurt. My hand throbbed with my erratic pulse. My elbow was even worse, a surefire bruise.

"A little shaken up, but not bad. You mind telling me what the heck is going on here?"

"This is my brother, Eren. Eren, explain this," Luke threatened with thinly veiled rage.

"Step-brother. And I just wanted to meet your gal pal." He shrugged. "How was I supposed to know she was this jumpy?"

Luke protested the two statements, but even when they argued heatedly the brotherly affection was clear. Eren's eyes flicked over to me, but they didn't seem as mocking as his words. No, as he set his nose—the nose I broke—his eyes roamed over me in a way that told me I was under appraisal. Perhaps I was more than he bargained for. I straightened my spine, striving to appear stronger, less like an animal backed into a corner.

"Oh right, well *excuse* me. Next time a stranger hauls me into a dark alley, I'll let him murder me with a smile on my face," I spoke, my tone dripping with sarcasm.

"I wasn't going to murder you," he retorted, his

shoulders angling away from Luke and toward me as I advanced hesitantly.

I scoffed indignantly. "How was I supposed to know that? You're lucky I didn't send my knee where the sun doesn't shine!"

Now *that* made the smile slip off his face. A scowl replaced it. While we had been verbally sparring, Luke had retrieved a discarded object near the wall of the alley. He held the thermos up to his brother, accusing.

Eren folded his arms. "Just a little Jäger. Nothing you should concern yourself with. Legal and everything."

I made a mental note that Eren must be the older brother, which would explain why I never saw him in school and his ability to drink legally.

Luke sighed, clearly at a loss of what to do. His blue eyes kept darting between his brother and me, but he gave different looks to the both of us. He looked warily at Eren, but for me his gaze held more concern. I decided to cut this party short. There was one thing I needed to know first, though.

"What did you do to Jessica?" I demanded of Eren, watching their reactions.

Luke did not have the most expressive gestures, but this accusation brought out one of the strongest ones yet. He lowered his head as if the accusation weighed on him, personally, but the look on his face was plain horrified. There was no doubt in my mind, had there ever been any, that he was innocent.

Eren had no reaction other than a confused twitch of the brows. Although I didn't know him, it seemed pretty clear that this was one crime I could not justly punish him for, no more than any other person in this town. My

153

mind swirled back to shadowed faces of incomprehensible figures, assigning the blame of an action to nobody even though I knew someone had to drive Jessica into the woods. So much for a distracting evening of fun.

"I don't really know who you're talking about," Eren said, confirming my suspicions.

Luke looked me in the eye. "He was with me at the time."

I nodded, accepting his words. Eren seemed to get the gist. Something crept into his facial features, a darkness, or a sadness, or perhaps even disappointment…but then it was gone, like a mask had snapped into place. "I promise you, I'm much more cuddly on the inside. Couldn't hurt a fly."

I doubted that.

My anger at the situation resurging, I stuck my hand in my pocket and assured that my keys were still there. I was half-glad I hadn't thought to use them as a weapon. I would have felt even guiltier if I had left Eren with permanent scars over this huge misunderstanding. The other half of me was debating doing it right now, but I had enough respect for Luke that I banished that thought quickly.

"Well, it's been fun, but I think I'll hit the road. I can't say it was a pleasure to meet you, Eren. Luke, I'll text you when I get home."

Eren smirked, and my hand twitched with the urge to slap him. "See you later, Kitten."

Never mind, I thought, *I'm not feeling guilty one bit.* I turned my back and walked to my car, careful not to move too quickly or too slowly. I pulled out my phone and sent a quick text to Luke, hoping he'd understand the depth of my gratitude for saving me despite the lack of words: Thank you.

The woodlands simultaneously shrunk and bristled, like an animal backed into a corner. Evil had been here recently and strongly enough that a rot had taken to anything living. A curse.

The land whispered to me with thousands of tormented voices. The trees shrieked from their withered positions and the wind howled in mourning, but the most telling noise of all was the silence. No insects hissed, nor did birds chirp, nor did youthful animals mew.

The forest felt infected, sick. It had not been able to fight off whatever event scarred it, so it grew wicked in obvious ways a human could notice. And, from what I could see, there were a few humans noticing at the very moment.

The most perceptive of the group was a young, red-haired woman who was tugging on the hand intertwined with hers. "Let's leave, this place is creeping me out," she complained loudly, her eyes resting on a tree that pulsed with darkness under my vision, but to her was just gnarled and twisted. "I don't feel safe here."

The male squeezed her hand. "It's not that bad, I swear. Everything's just a little off from the storm. Trust me. You'll love this place. It's magical."

The girl sighed, eyeing the tree's uppermost branches. "You don't think that crow's a little spooky?"

The bird in question turned its head. A fine layer of ash trickled off of its dull feathers. It made no attempt to shake away the rest of its covering. It did not make a sound. The girl shivered.

The boy did not look up. "Are you cold?" he asked, concerned.

She shook her head. "No, I'm...Did you hear that?"

"No, what'd you hear?" The boy's voice was starting to sound a little spooked, too.

The girl pointed. "Rustling, that way. I told you I should have brought my gun."

The male stopped and faced it. He forced a chuckle. "The rustling is a good thing. This place was too quiet. And why would you need that thing? What do you think it is? Stalker Squirrel? Creeper Crow? How about Watching Wolf?"

The female did not chuckle at his attempt at humor. "Are there wolves out here?"

The boy shrugged. "Nah, I doubt it. It would be kind of cool to see one, though."

The girl shook her head erratically. "No way! I like my life, thank you very much!"

Something moved in the unnatural shadows behind the girl, low to the ground. I snuck closer, preparing to defend the two. I felt a spurt of angelfire flicker around my eyes, enough to let me know this was not a false alarm.

The male laughed with bravado that rang false. "The scariest thing out here is me."

The girl rolled her eyes and pointed to a tree root the earth had fled from. "That root is scarier than you."

Roots do not slither under faint moonlight. This being froze when pointed at, but continued forth once the girl turned. It had the illusion of elongating, of stretching to proportions larger than life. In truth, the rest of it was emerging from the leaf litter. This beast was at least four humans long. The pull was stronger than usual, even at this distance. The demon had accumulated enough power that, even if I managed to send it back to Hell, it would take only a year or two to return. A weaker demon would take centuries, while the strongest could recollect their essence in under a week.

The anaconda-shaped demon, its strength feeding its boldness, followed behind its prey at a daringly close distance. Upon the sight of its inky black scales shining fluidly, the familiar pressure pulled at me. I inhaled once, drawn out, and in that period a golden aura surrounded me and worked its way through my veins. Haldis appeared in my open palm as my eyes lost their human façade.

The demon hissed from the undergrowth, sensing my presence. The girl cursed and pushed the guy behind her, taking the front.

"I told you something was there!"

The demon reared back to strike her down, mouth open. Its thick body contracted before lashing out at her leg. Its head was nearly as big as mine, and rows of needle sharp fangs were visible. My wings snapped out and pushed me forward in a split second. My hand wrapped around the base of the creature's head.

It thrashed as my angelfire penetrated its thick scales. My hand burned from both exertion and demonic flames. The giant snake began to coil its way around my arm, squeezing hard enough I feared my bones would snap. The hand with a hold on the snake tingled and grew useless as blood flow slowed.

I wasted no time in using Haldis to slice the coils clean off me. Hellish blood ate at my flesh like the most corrosive of acids, but I simply grit my teeth. Screaming would be a victory for no one. Behind me, I could hear scuffling as the two lovers rearranged themselves.

The snake writhed and brought me to the ground with it, despite being sliced up to the point that any living thing would no longer be able to hold its name. Backward-facing *fangs snagged my flesh, feeling like a thousand hypodermic needles being driven into my flesh with a baseball bat. This time a noise did escape me, but it wasn't human.*

I took Haldis and staked the beast right between the eyes. The blade sank deep into the earth and flickered with a pure whitish-gold glow that devoured the creature's darkness. A dark line marred the soil beneath the anaconda, a huge, menacing crevasse. Just standing near it scalded me, but I could not pull away with the damage the bite had done to my muscles.

Gold sank deep into the demon, so deep its scales began to burn off and dance on the wind like ashes. With the angelic flames forcing it down, the demon was pulled straight back into its fiery dimension. Once it had disappeared, only the featherlike scales remained, floating in the air.

I pulled Haldis from the earth, surprised when the blade lingered in my hand. While healing waves brushed my bruised and bleeding skin, I glanced up to see both the male and the female had remained. The male had inserted himself in front of the girl, who had tears streaming down her face. He curled over her, but her eyes were still visible beneath them, watching. A strikingly familiar green.

When my own eyes met hers, she screamed. The boy flinched and straightened, pulling her with him as he bolted forward, away from me. I blinked once, feeling the gold linger in my eyes. I put two and two together quite simply: Haldis and the angelic fire it brings would not linger unless there was still a threat.

My throat was not torn. I used it rather than a more threatening method. "The danger has not passed. I can provide both of you with protection."

The girl grabbed the guy by the forearm and pulled him

faster. Her scarlet hair flashed behind her. Perhaps a threatening method would have been more effective. It didn't matter anymore; I had to save them either way. A little misplaced fear was far better than damnation of the soul.

I extended my wings, taking no time to enjoy the pleasurable stretching of my muscles. I pushed them down at the same time I jumped and leveled myself, taking off without a running start. Their glow matched Haldis' in intensity.

Wings ate the distance so much quicker than feet did. It was barely a second before I swung in front of them. "I am here to protect. Something lingers here, something that will surely corrupt you should you stray from my presence."

Close by, a large cat roared. Both of the humans flinched, curling into each other. A shadow dropped from a rotting tree right in front of the two. The feline raised its two smoky orb-eyes, but not at me, as expected. No, it watched the girl. Her hair flickered from red to brown before my eyes, lengthening from its current pixie-cut, but it was only my memory making the change.

I knew this girl, but there was no time.

The Rashtka's tail twitched back and forth. My mind furiously tried to comprehend how it could have risen again so soon after Haldis had carved it. I stood in place, wary to make any sudden movements.

The young woman did not have the same wariness. She dug her fingers into the male's arm so hard that it bled and used that hold to steer him behind me, although with a wide berth. The Rashtka's smoldering eyes followed its potential prey, but it stood up lazily, almost carelessly, and bounded away with canyon-stepping paces.

I was a Protector. My duty lay with the humans, not the demon. Despite my desperate desire to rid the earthly plane *of evil, my main goal was to protect the pure. In this case, it meant I could not hunt the Rashtka down. I had to ensure the human's safety.*

I didn't have to turn to hear the pounding footsteps moving back down the trail, in the opposite direction from which the cougar had gone, just as I didn't have to hear their thoughts to know they had labelled me a monster the same as the demons.

Chapter Nine

My eyes opened to the diffuse light of morning far earlier than they ever would have naturally. A raven cawed in my ear, disorienting me for a minute. It was only when I regained my waking memories that I heard the caw for what it truly was: my cell.

I had crashed the second I got home last night, the loss of adrenaline taking its toll. I even wore the same clothes, minus the shirt which was smeared in something unidentifiable yet disgusting and a little nose-blood to top it off. That had made its way into the trash.

I groggily reached for my phone, too bleary eyed to even see the words on the small screen. I blinked a few times and tried again.

Hey, I know it's really early and I'm sorry, but Benjamin is refusing to settle down unless you fix whatever the heck he's rambling about. Can you come and work your magic? Promise it won't take long.

Jeremy had sent it. I knew it must have been bad if he was willing to risk my wrath this early in the morning. I sighed, knowing I had no choice unless I was cool with a guilty conscience from potential friend endangerment.

I geared up, moving as quietly as possible. When I looked at the clock in the hall, I saw it was only four forty-three, which meant I had to be as sneaky as possible to not wake the hibernating bears a few rooms over. Something told me that my activities would be looked on with suspicion, especially when I felt the weight of my filled drawstring bag. No, it wouldn't do me any favors to be caught like this.

I rolled my car down the driveway in neutral as another precaution. It only took me fifteen minutes to get to my destination across town, but I was afraid it would be too late. When I pulled into Jeremy's driveway and parked, the front door was already open for me.

I didn't even get up the front steps before getting tackled by a squirmy mass.

"Miss Leah, Miss Leah! You have to help me! They were in the closet!" the little child whined, clearly panicked.

"It's all right, Benjamin. I brought the stuff for you. Tell me what it was and we'll take care of it," I reassured, bending down to hug the tear soaked child.

"They were scary, Miss Leah. It was all black and had red eyes and it wanted to eat me!" Benjamin gasped out between sobs. The poor kid was quaking.

"How many, Benjamin?" I asked, trying to keep him focused rather than crying. His tears had stopped flowing, but the sniffles remained. I could spot Jeremy in the far corner of the room, pantomiming bowing down and worshipping me. It must have been pretty bad this time.

Benjamin mumbled unintelligibly and walked up the stairs, so I followed him to his bedroom. On the way, I passed little Melinda leaning on the doorframe to her room, eyeing me and her younger brother warily. Her oversized pink nightshirt swished at her ankles when she retreated.

Benjamin tugged my hand to pull me into his room and onto his bed quickly. He relaxed a little once he passed over the paper ring the two of us had put around the bed during a previous visit. He had been terrified of the dark men touching his face and had woken his parents every single night for a straight week.

As with before, I had come over and did a sweep of the house, turning up surprisingly little. Benjamin had looked so hopeful that I'd get rid of the "bad men" that I couldn't just do nothing. I acted as if he had been right and the two of us had glued liberal amounts of salt onto each paper to form an impassible barrier around his bed so they couldn't get to him anymore.

Strangely, it had worked, as I'd seen when my printer broke and he was his normal, pancake-chowing self. I didn't know whether the salt line had actually repelled spirits or if it just helped Benjamin through the placebo effect, but I wasn't going to complain.

Cole and I had gotten into a slightly awkward conversation about any wards he might have learned from his native Abenaki heritage. Turns out, he'd known a grand total of zero, having been raised mainly Christian. Bummer. Rosalind had given me an odd glance at the time, but it dissipated and was replaced with a smile when she saw how excited Benjamin became. There'd also been a bag of lemon squares waiting for me when it came time to leave. Unfortunately, my attempts at stalling the nightmares only worked for so long.

It seemed I'd have to defeat the monsters in the closet this time around, the terrorizers of millions of children worldwide. I looked at the offending area as I unloaded my drawstring bag and rifled through. Chuckling, I fingered a silver upward-facing pentacle, knowing it'd do the trick but also knowing it'd rub Jeremy's über-Christian parents the wrong way. I moved that one aside.

Benjamin reached over, curious. He wound his fingers through a delicate olive dream catcher, pulling on the woven vine rim to inspect the feathers on the bottom. The glass beads clinked against each other as he tried to fit his chubby fingers through the holes.

"I don't know if that's—Wait a minute, that's genius!" I held my hand out and Benjamin obediently put the dream catcher in my hand. I held it up by the loop and we both looked at it.

"Do you know what this is?" I asked him, excitement seeping into my tone. He shook his head.

I grinned and grabbed his hands, a grin spreading across his face as my enthusiasm spread to him. "This is a dream catcher. It's said to stop nightmares. But guess how it does that?"

He was silent for a second, thinking. Then he threw his hands up in the air and yelled in excitement. "It gets rid of the bad guys!"

I high-fived him. "Heck yeah!" This kid was pretty smart for a four-year-old. It used to be thought that the source of nightmares were malevolent demons or spirits called mares. This kid had experienced enough nightmares to last him a long while, so this would be perfect for him. I knew that mainstream dream catchers didn't do much, but I had high hopes for this one because it was authentic native and blessed.

Benjamin picked out a spot above his bed and we used tape to lock the dream catcher in place. The eagle feathers at the bottom swayed in the slight breeze coming from the vent next to it. I hopped off the bed and Benjamin came with, standing next to me with one foot comfortably outside the salt circle he had been so desperate to get within before.

His head was tilted back to eye the new ceiling ornament with satisfaction. He was still smiling, but his eyelids were beginning to droop. It was way too early for him to be up, so now that the crisis had passed he was crashing hard. I knew the feeling.

"Is this okay?" I inquired. I got a hug to the knee as a response.

"Then I think it's bedtime, yeah? I'm exhausted." He nodded and climbed under the covers, mute. The corners of my mouth tugged back as I left the room, feeling as though I had done right.

My detour from sleep wasn't over yet, however. When I had quietly shut Benjamin's door behind me, I turned and almost mowed over the shadow in front of me. I jumped and steadied myself with a hand to the wall.

"Sorry, Melinda. I didn't see you there," I apologized and readjusted to move around her with a wide berth.

She wasn't my biggest fan for reasons unknown. In the past, she had left most of the time when I came around. If she didn't, she was like a lurking spirit, watching from behind corners with a glare contorting her young face. The extra four years under her belt separated her from Benjamin and left her immune to any of my attempts at playing nice. Eight-year-olds. I swear, they'll be the death of you.

No glare contorted her face at that moment, however, only open calculation. She stopped me with a tap to my back, as high as she could reach. "Leah? Could you help me, too?"

I looked back at her face, set fiercely by her determination to look strong. Her dark curls pulled higher on her shoulder as she lifted her head to meet my eyes.

I nodded, but didn't smile. I was afraid I'd appear too patronizing and blow this rare opportunity. "Of course. What do you need?"

She relaxed a hair, something I wouldn't have noticed if I weren't studying her. "I want to be safe, too."

It hadn't occurred to me that Melinda would feel vulnerable. She'd always seemed so stoic and put together for her age. I'd forgotten that she was just as prone to fear as the rest of the younger population.

"What do you need protection from?" I questioned, hoping to get a better read on the situation so I could provide the best solution. I didn't want to muck it up.

She didn't answer. She just shook her head and left me guessing. Funny thing with the Bellevues, if they didn't know exactly what to say, they remained quiet. Jeremy was the only deviant from the pattern, not one for silence. Only once or twice had I caught him doing the same when he wasn't sure how to word something.

I reached back and snagged the drawstring bag, an idea already forming. I had a necklace chain with an empty cage dangling from it in the bag somewhere, just in case I needed to wear some little talisman, gemstone, or mythical creature repellent 24/7. I fished it out and held it in the palm of one hand while using a knee to balance the bag so the other could grab the tiny box of stones and gems at the bottom.

I rifled through, finding the one I was looking for with little effort. The marbled surface of the moss agate resembled its namesake in color. It was a protection stone amongst other varied uses, one heavily aligned with earth. I opened the necklace cage and put the small stone inside it.

I held it out to Melinda like it was an offering, searching her face for any sign of her thoughts. Her face was upturned toward me in the same way mine was downturned toward her, studying. She reached behind her neck and did the chain on her own with more deftness than I could have managed.

166

Her eyes never left mine. "May I ask another favor?" she requested and I tilted my head.

"Sure, shoot," I allowed, wondering what it could possibly be.

Her gaze found a particularly interesting spot on the floor. "Can you teach me how to do a love spell?"

"A love spell? What do you need that for?" *Aww, young love. How cute,* I mused.

She shrugged her shoulders. "To make someone fall in love with someone else."

Well, that wasn't exactly what I was expecting. She made it sound like she wouldn't be a participant.

"For who?" I asked, but got no response. I decided to give it to her straight.

"I wish I could help you with that, Melinda, but spells are dangerous. I'm not a witch, spell caster, nor otherwise qualified to perform a love spell. I would connect you with someone who is qualified, but it's risky. Love is a dangerous thing to mess with because it means messing with a person's core feelings. It could go wrong," I explained.

She must have deemed me to be of no further use to her, because she issued me a curt, "Okay, thank you," before excusing herself into her bedroom. I thought at that closed door for another minute before my next customer contacted me.

"I think I'll need a love potion, too," Jeremy teased as he rounded the corner he had obviously been hiding behind. I didn't blame him for wanting to know what was going on. It was smart of him to conceal himself so that his siblings felt the most comfortable.

"Oh, really? I thought girls couldn't resist your fabled good looks?" I volleyed.

Jeremy shook his head with mock sadness. "One girl

stands while the others swoon."

I rolled my eyes because I knew where this was going. "And she is...?"

He raised his eyes to mine and took a step closer. "You."

I put my hand over my heart and went bow-legged. "Senpai noticed me! Jeremy, I'm so glad you've realized I've been resisting falling prey to your beauty for years. I'm even gladder you want to steal my will away with magic to get me to love you. Best. Morning. Ever. But you know what would make it even better?"

He moved closer, grabbed my waist, and dipped me, grinning all the while. He clearly enjoyed the squeak that came out of me with the unexpected move. I half expected him to drop me, but his lean muscle held me with little effort.

"A kiss?" he taunted.

I yawned in his face. "Some sleep."

He laughed and let me right myself. "Good night, Leah. Or maybe I should say good morning? Thanks for helping. I swear I'll repay you in the future."

"Before I die would be nice, thank you," I huffed as I made my way downstairs and out. I groaned when I saw the pink hue glinting off the brass on the outer doorknob. Dawn was upon us. It'd take forever for me to sleep again, and today was a school day. Next to the opening, however, perched a steaming cup.

When I approached it, Rosalind called out softly from the kitchen. "I figured you'd need a little kick start. Only a store bought blend, though, that's all I've got."

I smiled and took a sip. "This is more than enough. Thank you."

I cursed the fading of grogginess as I made my way home. By the time I snuck back inside, I was tired enough to not want to be awake, but aware enough to know it wasn't going to happen. I lied down on my bed despite this, not intent on sleeping. There was something else I'd always wanted to try.

Astral projection had always interested me, but I had been a little too lazy to wake myself up at three or four in the morning like they recommended for beginners. I wasn't going to get many other opportunities like this, so I took what I could get.

I made sure neither my legs nor my arms were touching. My breathing slowed until it matched the ocean's waves in my head. I cleared my thoughts of everything except Jeremy's painting of me squatching that I had put on my dresser. It would serve as a good anchor.

I made sure to remain perfectly still, not giving into the urge to itch or twitch. If I did that, I'd lessen my chances of inducing sleep paralysis. Yeah, I know. Being completely paralyzed doesn't sound fun at all, but I had heard that it was a very useful state to be in for newbies wanting to have an out-of-body-experience, and harmless, which is a bonus.

In order to project, I knew I had to clear my mind, hold still, and wait for some sort of vibration telling me I could go. I focused on my hand as I relaxed and soon it began tingling. It wasn't exactly the 'mild electric current' I'd read about, but I was excited enough to want to lift it and try it out.

I visualized it first, the slow rise of a phantom palm as it split from my physical one. The tingly feeling spread a little farther up my arm, which I took as a good sign. I repeated the process until my shoulder was eclipsed, then worked on sliding the sensation up my neck and to my head.

I was extremely uncomfortable as the chimerical pouring-rain-on-skin feeling approached the left side of my face, creeping up my jawline. It had been at least a half hour,

169

yet progress was slow. It was like a line of men treading through snow. The first man was sluggish under the extra burden of creating the path, but it was easier for all those behind him.

I desperately wanted to press my hand to the side of my face to see if I was merely conjuring the tingles, but that'd ruin my work. My ear was finally surrounded when I couldn't take it anymore. I twitched my fingers to test their corporeality.

The room exploded in noise. A bird screeched an inch away from my ear and I screeched back in fear at the sudden outburst. Something brushed my cheek. I sat bolt upright, opening my eyes just in time for the flapping of wings to fade. The room was empty.

The best way to describe the moment was the calm before the storm. The spidery black rot that had taken over the forest was slowly receding, but it was too late for most of the vegetation. It was dead.

I lingered in the seemingly endless area because I had not been summoned again. My presence helped to combat the demonic imprints left, but I couldn't revive what was gone. All the life was drained from this cursed place.

Or, perhaps not all the life. My bare toe scuffed away a dead leaf and revealed the tiniest sapling, withered but pulsing with an earthy vitality. I knelt next to it and removed the nearby detritus to reveal the wilting sprout.

It lay along the ground as if it had given up its search for the warmth of the sun. I did not blame it. There was no comfort to be had under the shade of the gnarled mammoths above it. I dug my fingers into the cold soil around it and felt thin, web-like roots.

I didn't have Haldis with me, so I could banish the taint of evil around it to a small degree, but I could not heal it. I did know what could, however.

"Spirits of Earth, I request your assistance to aid one of your fallen," I chimed into the silent woods.

Though the decay of the trees weakened them, I did not have to wait long before I felt a pulse rise from the ground. It echoed through me, into my cupped hands. They were using my energy to remove the vestiges of the demonic corruption. The plant twitched, but did not liven. Another pulse came, but this time when the plant twitched it stood a fraction of an inch taller. Even quicker, two more pulses shot out. Their intensity scattered my thoughts, blinding my senses to every-thing except the feeling of power surging. I felt almost as if I had lost the boundary of my body.

The intervals between the pulses decreased to the point that it felt like I was a conduit for a continuous source of energy. Before my eyes, the sprout heaved itself off the ground and waveringly straightened in front of me. Tiny green needles grew out of its reenergized arms, tickling my hands as they grew through the cracks between my fingers.

Then the pulses began to fade until they resembled the beating of a heart. Three strong, slow ones signaled the end of the connection. Dizzily, I rose to my feet and smiled at the little sapling that brushed my calf. When I lifted my gaze, that smile fell.

The earth spirits and I had revived much more than one sapling. The ground was littered with new growth, verdant and lively. Even one or two of the great trees I had thought were deceased had spread their leaves to the sun once more. However, there was one new thing standing that had not been called back by the earth.

171

The girl from the night before stood to the left of me, partially obscured by the freshly green leaves on a low-growing tree nearby. She stiffened when I turned toward her. Her eyes matched the color of the newly fledged plants around her.

"So, you are real," she whispered, more to herself than me.

I answered anyway, eliciting a flinch from her. "Yes."

She looked around like she was eyeing escape routes, but I could tell her curiosity anchored her. "Luis, my boyfriend, denies anything happened. I had to know the truth. I'm not crazy, am I?"

I held still so as to not intimidate her. "No."

"And that other night? I felt so sick for so long, but you were there, weren't you? You did something to me."

I only nodded. Her eyes stopped flicking between all the possible exits and landed squarely on me. "Are you an angel?"

I kept my eyes purposefully averted to not scare her, despite the fact that they bore some false human hue rather than the gold. "No, I am not. I am a Protector."

The female scrunched her eyebrows until her smooth forehead resembled a mole's burrow. "But that is not your name?"

Names. Human concepts. "I do not have one."

The girl looked deeply distressed by the fact, but didn't say more on the subject. "I'm Katherine."

I said nothing. There was nothing to say. The girl took a cautious step forward before taking a hasty one back. "Are you one of those...Smoke monsters?"

My attempt at humor was bound to fail from the beginning. I did not understand emotion well. "I am not smoking now, am I?"

The girl—Katherine—took a step forward and held her

172

ground this time. Her hair had changed yet again, strawberry-blonde strands swished like tiny, lopsided pendulums above her jawline. "No, you aren't. And the trees, you did that? Wait, are you going to possess me? Like a ghost? 'Cause I'm not really about that...No offense."

I tilted my head. "You ask many questions."

She recoiled like I slapped her. "I-I'm sorry. I didn't mean..."

I raised my hand slowly, non-threateningly. "That is not a bad thing. I do not mind answering your question lest it interferes with walking the path of purity.

"I did not heal the trees on my own. I only banished the taint. Other forces healed the vegetation. And no, not the 'smoke monsters', those are creatures of twisted pain and darkness. They do not give life."

A flash of realization unfocused her eyes. "Demons."

She was quite quick for a human, most wallowed in non-belief for far longer. I showed a small line of teeth, something I'd seen many humans do when they felt a positive emotion. "And no, I will not possess you. Only the direst of circumstances could require such a thing. The only reason—"

I started to explain, but was struck down by an oppressive echo of darkness. Angelfire crackled to life underneath my palm and in my eyes.

"I must go," I informed Katherine, who was watching with open fascination. There was no longer a hint of revulsion.

"Wait!" she cried out. "How will I find you again?"

Delicate, light-outlined wings began to form. Their light played over the surface of Katherine's skin, reflecting mirage-like images off of her green eyes. "Hope that you do not, for when I come, I am following the trail of death."

Chapter Ten

I was going to kill Jeremy.

Okay, maybe I'd just slap him, but I swear I'd do it so hard it'd crack like a thunder clap.

I had watched the library footage beginning to end three times, and I had to say I'd have been much happier if Jeremy and Luke *had* engaged in a secret make out session. I was not a fan of the actuality.

It started off so innocently: While I was in the basement, they were having a conversation. After a little while, Jeremy's voice dropped so the camera couldn't hear it. He snagged my chocolate bar at that point, smirking to himself. Luke was shaking his head, not at the chocolate, but at whatever Jeremy was saying.

Jeremy walked off-screen, heading toward the section of library I'd be investigating. He pulled something small and skinny out of his pocket before he disappeared down one of the rows the camera couldn't see fully. He only spent a few seconds there before returning, spinning that skinny item and sticking it in his pocket. A marker?

My shadow appeared as grainy pixels in the doorway as Luke spoke familiar words. "I don't think that's a good idea."

"Trust me, she'll like it. It'll be funny," Jeremy replied, just as I remembered. How naïve I had been to think the grand plan involved the chocolate he stole. I rolled my eyes at past me's reaction.

The call-and-response session in the side room yielded no clues and the same amount of evidence of the paranormal, much to my disappointment. There wasn't a single orb nor a suspicious glance. It was only when that wrapped up that something odd happened.

Luke cut straight across to the other side room with his flashlight never wavering. I made a small note that he could be using wolfish night vision to observe the darkness anyone else would have been pointing the flashlight at. Besides that small oddity, he went where he was supposed to go. I cut out to the middle section, entering the row to the right of the one Jeremy had been in earlier.

Jeremy lingered in the room he was supposed to investigate only long enough to slip off his shoes. Then he crept out, stocking-footed, and entered the same room as my past self. Even though I was out of the view of the camera, I could see my shadow pause. That was when I had heard the footsteps.

Jeremy's shadow elongated, difficult to discern from the dull light of my flashlight cutting through the shelves. His arm looked like a sprout stretching for the sun when it extended. He reached for something on the top shelf. A loud bang ensued. The book had dropped.

My shadow went still, frozen with its head down as in mourning. Only the hands quivered. Jeremy's figure reappeared and stalked into my row, silent. Hands caught my shoulders, his hands. Not a spirit after all.

Well, you know the rest of the story. Lots of banging as the shelf behind me collapsed under my weight and even more noise as the floor gave out, leaving Jeremy at the edge of the rift, finally visible to the cameras. His mouth was open, eyes wide enough the camera could discern the whites. His lips moved, but no words came out.

Then he bolted for the basement stairs, blocked by debris and began to dig, almost nailing Luke with a floorboard he threw behind him. Obviously, my little fall hadn't been intentional, and both of them had panicked. I felt guilty watching them struggle and turned off the footage then. I had seen all I needed to see.

My fury was a bale of hay. No one thinks anything of a bale of hay, it's just a stack of straw, right? Wrong. They spontaneously combust. Like fireworks on the Fourth of July, but with a lot less *dazzle*. I, my friends, was *on fire*.

I didn't have the mood to even think of what happened in the basement. Maybe that was actually a spirit, but most likely it was just a hallucination. Fantastic. I dialed Jeremy's number and waited angrily during the ring tone.

He picked up on the third ring. "Hey."

I wasted no time masking my anger. "Get here. Now."

He sounded more concerned than wary, which didn't help my mood one bit. He better be scared. "Is everything okay?"

It was so dang hard to stay mad at him. I had to end the call before I forgave him. "No one's hurt, just come here now."

I barely heard his, "okay," before I hung up.

I paced until the doorbell rang. I ran down, opened the door, and shut it behind me as a very confused Jeremy attempted to step in.

"Someone call for a—"

I cut him off by grabbing his wrist and pulling him into the woods. I did not want my yelling to be overheard.

I didn't wait till we stopped moving to start my chewing-out. "When you said to review the footage, I was thinking 'oh, maybe they had a spat.' 'Maybe one embarrassed himself.' 'Maybe, if I'm lucky, one got possessed and said something nasty. That I can fix.' But no. None of that. I saw *you* pushing that book and then scaring the crap out of me! What the heck were you thinking?"

He paused, tugging me to a stop. We had covered enough ground that the house was no longer in sight. His shins were torn and bleeding from shallow cuts. He must have been stumbling under my relentless pace, but he hadn't said anything. My steam was running out pretty quickly now that I could see him, I fought to keep it.

He bowed his head in clear submission. "I didn't mean to scare you. And I definitely didn't mean for the floor to collapse. I'm really, truly sorry, Leah."

A growling built in my head, a low rumble that blocked out my thoughts. My anger was pretty much gone, taken by the wind like dandelion seeds. "I'm not mad about falling, Jeremy. That was almost exclusively my fault. I'm mad that you didn't tell me what happened afterward. And why... What even was the point?"

He started rambling, nervous despite the fact I had calmed a little. "Well, I uh...wrote something in the book. I had a whole plan, including a cheesy one-liner that'd lead to me giving you this and hopefully...other things." He reached into a little bag he'd brought, one I hadn't noticed, and pulled out a cardboard box. He held it out to me. His other hand scratched idly at the back of his head.

I took it, my glare turning into a look of suspicion, then curiosity. My nail wedged between the flaps and it popped right open. My mouth parted as I took in the little treasure inside, a brand-new EMF meter, one of the ones specially tailored for ghost hunting, with an array of lights on the top. I flicked it on and was rewarded with the first light's glow. A low electromagnetic field. No spirits here.

I was smiling now, I couldn't help it. I tried to shove the pesky rumbling from my mind. I knew what had transpired, and that was enough to satisfy me. I just had one question.

"What did you write in the book?" I asked. "I actually searched it for a second, but I didn't find anything. And why the EMF? I mean, thank you, it's really, really awesome and I'm totally going to scare up some ghosties with it, but what's the occasion?"

Jeremy looked so nervous still, like I'd smack him. Couldn't he see I was smiling? But there was a determined set to his eyes. "Would you believe me if I said it was International Obscure Gift Day?"

I raised my eyebrows. "No."

His feet shifted and he pulled himself up straighter. No more submissiveness remained. "In the book, I asked if you'd like to go on a date with me."

The smile slipped off my face. I was stunned, and the rolling noise in my head wasn't making it any better. Catching my thoughts was like trying to pluck a minnow out of a river when you wield only a pair of chopsticks.

Oh my deities, things suddenly made sense. The library, the behavior between Luke and Jeremy...Even Melinda's love spell request. If she had known, it'd even give her reason to dislike me.

I knew I was just staring at him, saying nothing, but so, so many things were running through my skull. What even were my options? I knew I couldn't survive long without his amusing input. Which path would be safest? No, screw that, which path did I want?

He was *mine*, irrevocably. But did that warrant romantically? My world felt so off balance, so crazy and tilted and *new*. Jeremy smiled at me, the same smile that had lifted me from my darkest moments and made my lightest possible. Hope glimmered in his eyes. Should I—

The growling exploded in volume.

"No!" someone very far away yelled.

Jeremy's head whipped around to a bush to my right, smile falling from his face. He lunged at me and yelled my name, but it was too late.

These images and sensations will forever remain a brand on my brain:

Jaws closed high over my bicep, biting deep.

Somewhere, a girl screamed. That was me.

Leaves kissed my face and my blood kissed them back.

Feet stomped by me, sounding almost as enraged as their owner's war cry.

My elbow against the ground, blinding pain, but I could see.

Eyes like dark gold flames, both of them.

But no angels here.

Just a man I knew and a wolf.

Its pelt was tan and white and black and red.

Whoops, the red was my blood.

Jeremy inserted himself between me and the threat.

The wolf or the man: I knew not which looked more feral.

But I knew which one would win.

"No!" rang out again. Me this time.

Jeremy's head spun toward me.

The wolf leapt.

It flung him backward onto the ground, vulnerable.

His arms flew up to block it.

I kicked with all my strength.

Too late.

Too late too late too late too late.

Jaws clamped down on his neck.

My kick dislodged the wolf.

His throat went with it when it rolled away.

Gurgling, thick and wet and spastic.

Blood bubbles forming and popping.

Something I shouldn't have been able to see jerked.

The wolf was gone, but I didn't care.

I only cared that the bubbles had stopped popping.

Jeremy no longer moved.

I didn't scream anymore, I didn't have the air. My voice was just as vacant as his eyes. He wasn't breathing, he couldn't breathe. He didn't even try. I knew what it meant. Tears welled up, blurring my vision, but no filter could hide the blood.

Something grabbed me: hands, human. Jeremy? I whispered his name, but the truth was evident. No. I'd never feel his hands again. I didn't care about the pain in my shoulder. The pain in my heart was so much worse.

Tears streamed down my face, but they came off tinted crimson. Not my blood, his. It'd sprayed. I was grossly sobbing, inhaling so violently in my involuntary double-breathing that my face was starting to tingle.

"Are you okay?" Not my voice. Then, I heard the sharp inhale when the head turned the way mine was facing. "Oh, god." And then, "I need to call an ambulance."

I was released. I couldn't see anymore, my sight was blurred. It didn't stop me, I couldn't stay. I couldn't look at the mouth I'd seen smile so many times set in a permanent grimace. I couldn't see the eyes with sun-kissed gold go blue. I couldn't, I couldn't.

I ran.

I had been here previously, when suffering from a wound. Time was as fluid as the lake before me, yet my memories hadn't faded, especially not one so bloody. I'd seen the wolf in the brush, painted with gore to the point it looked ethereal.

It wasn't here any longer. Only one of the bodies still was. The other, from the drag marks on the ground, had been moved in pieces by scavengers making quick work of it. A foul odor rose from this place. Dread curled around my heart, fearing that a similar atrocity could happen yet again.

I wouldn't know. I wouldn't be able to stop it.

I approached the wolf's remaining kill, hoping to glean details of why the creature had been so unsettling, yet not demonic. I would have been defenseless if it had turned against me. I might win the fight, but it would be hard. I couldn't afford threats like this when the demonic ranks were growing in number. This monster, and any like it, needed to be eliminated.

The face was covered in flies, almost nothing left but bones. Light hair remained, but what was left of the throat was—

I woke up sobbing from my fitful sleep and screamed. "JEREMY!"

Chapter Eleven

I wasn't leaving my room until Jeremy opened the door and carried me out. But that wasn't going to happen. Because it couldn't happen. Because if that magic was possible, then all magic could be possible. And if all magic was possible...Luke had killed my best friend.

The wolf had clean teeth. Red teeth, but clean. That image haunted Every. Single. Blink. I didn't see black behind my closed eyelids, I saw scarlet.

I mean, I visited a hospital for a little while to get stitched up. Nothing deadly. An odd spot for a wolf to pick, unless it was aiming for a nonfatal area. But aiming in that way would show a kind of intent I didn't want to consider. What I *did* consider, though, was that the wolf was just your regular old lupine, but sick.

That'd explain the feverish shivers that wrought me and the itchy, throbbing mess the wound had become. Thankfully those symptoms had started after I left close scrutiny. I could rationalize it easily as my body fighting the trauma.

The truth was I didn't care about the wound. When I was informed of just how badly it'd scar, my first thought was: *good, I deserve the reminder.* Not that I necessarily needed it, but I was supposed to feel the pain. Noticing how messed up the top of my arm was made me think of that day.

Then again, everything did. The worst was when the

police tried to question me. The poor guy looked way out of his depth dealing with a weeping teenage girl who was incapable of anything other than blubbering nonsensically, but I couldn't find sympathy for him.

I thought having Jessica missing was bad. This...It was like comparing a planet to a universe. There was no hope. It was done, and I'd done nothing to help him. I knew people were talking about his death. A snatch of a media report on the 'freak accident' had drifted up to my room. People I didn't even know were making my phone caw, texts ranging anywhere from supportive to openly prying for details. They left a foul taste in my mouth, but then again, so did the thick scent of a new coat of lemon-themed floor cleaner, and the smell of blood.

Even still, those mindless texts were nothing, made me feel nothing, compared to when my phone lit up with Luke's number. He called many times, but I didn't think I was ready for what he had to say. I had a strong suspicion he was the one who had called the ambulance. I desperately hoped not, because that convenient timing had my barely repressed supernatural side screaming werewolf. I'd break if that were true.

Then again, I wasn't exactly whole. So when he began to call more frequently than the hunger pangs of a wendigo— no, that analogy doesn't make sense. Wendigoes don't exist. More frequently than...I needed Jeremy for this. I couldn't think of what normal people were supposed to say—I picked up the phone.

I didn't hit the talk button though. I thought I was strong enough, but I was wrong. I just stared. Like a coward. Well, not like a coward, as a coward. I ran. Cowards run. Transitive property, isn't it?

I took a deep breath and submerged into my suffocating thoughts. It was pretty dark down there. Bleak. Hopeless. I'd do anything…but I'd lost the opportunity. Gone, just like him. When I heard a knock at the door, it took a second for me to surface. The door opened, but I didn't bother looking at it.

"I'm as fine as I can be, Mom. Really," I insisted pre-emptively. She and my father had visited so often…One of them home at all times. I loved them, but I wasn't ready to pop up and walk around like nothing had happened.

It wasn't my mother's voice that responded. "You don't look fine."

I stiffened and actually looked at the doorway. Familiar plaid filled my vision. Luke stood there, his broad shoulders almost touching the narrow doorframe.

I sat up straight, my hand going to the hair I hadn't combed in quite a while, but it fluttered back when I realized I didn't care. My eyes were probably red as garnets, too. "How did you get here?"

His gaze took in my disheveled appearance with what I hoped was a lack of judgment. "Your dad let me in. Nice man."

I stared at him in silence. Luke didn't seem offended at my lack of conversation. "You've figured out it was me who found you in the woods?" *He didn't mention Jeremy,* I thought. *Jeremy, whose funeral is tomorrow.*

I answered again with silence. It wasn't that I didn't have anything to say, it was that I had so much I was afraid it'd all come out at the same moment in a terrifying rush of emotions.

He saw that. He read it so easily in my face, it made me all the more upset. "Leah, how are you?"

How does he think I feel? Wound up tight around an

empty core...

"Doesn't matter what you say, just talk," he coaxed. I'd never heard him say so much at once. "Worth it to call this one of my five questions?"

My happiness at the memory of our little fishing trip rang like a betrayal in my ears. My anger rose. "You want to know how I feel?"

Luke nodded. I threw the sweat soaked covers off of me and at the wall. My breath hissed in and out of me, from the pain in my shoulder along with the pain in my heart.

"I *feel*—" I spat, "like my tears are carrying my soul. Like I'm empty. No fire, no nothing. Just empty and sad and guilty. Then people come in and *see me* empty and sad and guilty, and it makes *them* sad and guilty. I can't forgive myself for his death; I *don't want* to forgive myself for his death! It's my fault..."

Luke shook his head. "No."

I snarled, the sound weak to my ears. "That's it? No?"

He was stone. "You can't blame yourself."

Words bubbled up, thick and jumbled. My bloodshot eyes moistened, but all it brought me was rage. I struck Luke in the chest, but we were standing so close there was almost nothing behind it.

He moved, but only to square his feet. "Good, do it again."

"I'm not going to hit—" but then I was staring at the floor as Luke grabbed me and hauled me over his shoulder. It was so unexpected a startled noise slipped free, as close to a laugh as I had come since...well...for the first time in what felt like forever. A few tears escaped, but they were the last as my mind went instinctual.

My elbow found his shoulder blade and he grunted, releasing me slowly enough I could find my feet. My fist

185

found his abs, and he made a grab for my midsection. I deflected his arm with my own and kneed it, but his other scooped me up with ease.

He threw me over his shoulder again, rumbling a contained laugh. After a second, he coughed distractedly, hard enough for him to flinch. I used the momentum to wiggle out of his grip and fly off his back, catching myself on the ground with my palms and knees. I grunted in pain as my torn muscles protested, but that didn't stop me from swinging again at Luke, who had stopped laughing when he heard the pained noise.

He caught my fist in his hand, and then did the same to the other when that one flew at him. One corner of his mouth tilted up. "Got fire in your eyes."

I was breathing heavily, but the pain and adrenaline were absolution compared to the turbulent darkness that had claimed me before. My mouth twitched into a small smile. "Thank you."

Then he noticed my gauze-wrapped shoulder and his eyes widened. "Were you bitten?"

The mood was shattered, but when I took a breath, I felt calm, not empty. At the very least, I felt like a person rather than a vessel for guilt. I don't know where it came from, but the strongest impulse to lie struck me. Downplay the injury. It was completely against my character, but I obeyed.

"Claws," I stated, unable to get the full lie out. Luke tilted his head a tiny fraction and I wondered if he found me suspicious.

He looked me over, noting the straightness of my spine and the dried tears on my cheeks. He came to a decision somehow. I could tell by the unkind set of his mouth. "Leah, I need to tell you something."

No. What else could it be except what I feared the most? *Please don't do this to me,* I begged silently. *I can't lose all of my friends, nor can I remain friendly with Jeremy's murderer.*

"Listen, I know something about that wolf. You need to know, too. So you know what you are dealing with."

No, please. Don't...I can't... I didn't look him in the eye, wanting him to deny my next statement. To laugh at my foolishness. I wanted that more than I had wanted anything in a long time, besides Jeremy to still be alive. "It was a werewolf."

There was no laughter. Not even a raised lip corner. He just nodded once, taking a second to himself. I, on the other hand, was falling. Everything shook, but I wasn't sure if it was my skull whipping back and forth in an attempt to keep the truth away or if it was all inside my head.

Luke clenched his fist and quickly unclenched it. "You know." It was a statement, not a question. Something he'd suspected, yet hoped wasn't true. The tears threatened again, but I denied them angrily.

Luke crossed the floor so silently I didn't hear him. I started when his hand came to rest on my shoulder. As good as it felt, I shrugged it off. "I can't. You...You...You killed him."

He stood up like an electrical current zapped him. Cool air moved across my face as he flinched violently away from the accusation. "You think I did this?"

The water lenses over my eyes dried suddenly, itching. Deep confusion filled me. "Is there another werewolf?"

I may not have been any good at reading expressions, but it wasn't hard to see that my confusion was matched in Luke. "There is only one."

I felt my eyebrows pulling together. "If not you, then who?"

187

Luke pulled in a deep breath. "Eren."

My mouth fell open. "Eren...He did that to Jeremy?"

Luke stood stiffly. "Yes. I'm sorry. We were experimenting. Trying to find a cure. It didn't end well. He turned and escaped."

Those persistent tears were back. Thick and unrelenting. They weren't exactly sad, but bitter. More powerful than bitter, though, more angry. When would they leave for good? "I really am going to kill him now," I whispered to myself. Luke either didn't hear it or he ignored it.

There was something I needed to know before I collapsed. I looked Luke in the eyes. "Jessica. Is she...? Did he...?"

Luke shook his head. "No, he didn't."

I filled my lungs with air, having to open my mouth to do it. The threat of tears had sealed my nose. I rose and sat back down on my bed.

"She might still be alive," I whispered to myself.

If he heard me, he didn't comment. Then he said the dreaded phrase as he hovered next to my bed. "I know how you feel."

My lip curled, despite my lack of desire to snap at him for his attempt at comfort. "I doubt that."

He stared at me in a charged way that made me know I was dead wrong. Then I recalled the way he just waltzed in and knew exactly how to help me...And then I knew. He'd had his taste of death.

"Who? I mean, if you don't mind. I'm sorry, I didn't mean to..." I trailed off, feeling like an abomination.

"Both of my parents," he admitted. Lines deepened around his face as he grimaced. His chin drew downward like gravity suddenly increased. *I'm a terrible person,* I realized. Even more terrible for wanting to ask the question of whether he lost them naturally or if Eren had offed them.

It must have been written all over my face, because Luke answered my unspoken question. "First shift. Almost got me, too, before he reverted."

I shivered as if I'd found myself in a Canadian snow drift. I really looked at Luke's steely blue eyes for the first time since he showed up. The subtle redness around the iris hinted at a lack of sleep.

When I said nothing, he stood up and shucked his shirt.

It didn't take long at all for me to see why. He angled away from me, so I could only see the left side of his body, but it was brutal. There were a few small red spots from our roughhousing, but it was nothing compared to the scribbled mess covering his skin. All over his chest and side were angry red gashes, scars, healed nowhere near as well as Eren's had. From the look of it, they were claw marks, all to the front. Luke had watched the wolf coming and hadn't turned his back.

Eren had stared into Luke's eyes as he tried to tear his brother to pieces.

I swallowed, almost too timid to ask my next question. "If that's true, why do you live with him? How can you bear it?"

He sat down gingerly on the edge of my bare mattress. "He and the wolf are different. Couldn't lose my brother. He's all I have left."

It made sense to me, but I knew I could never again be in Eren's presence. For what he did to Jeremy...I wanted revenge. Luke had shown me that in order to get out of this, I had to fight. Now, I knew my target. But, an idea struck me, if the man and the wolf were as separate as Luke believed,

189

that meant I could have my revenge—without getting arrested for murder. "I think I may have a few ideas."

I really wanted to sleep forever, but I couldn't do that with the images pestering my mind. There was something I was forgetting. Something I should have been doing. Whenever I tried to remember it, all I got were the images that haunted my every nightmare.

Then it struck me. When I'd run on That Day, I hadn't cared about what went with. I'd left Jeremy's EMF on the forest floor. The mental picture of it sitting there, neglected, made me want to writhe in my skin. It felt so disrespectful, leaving it there. Like I was keeping someone waiting. I tried not to dwell on who that person might have been.

But I couldn't just go back to that dreadful place, could I? I had no idea what'd be there if I returned or if I could handle it so soon. For all I knew, it could be a crime scene. *Wait. Crime. Would the police have confiscated it as 'evidence'? If so, they probably returned it to Jeremy's home. To his family.*

Maybe I could break in. Then I wouldn't have to face them. I didn't think I could take it if Benjamin's eyes looked as hollow as mine did in the reflection when a mirror ambushed me. Yes, an open window would do. I'd climb in, retrieve the EMF, and climb out. Simple, only minor heart break involved.

I left my cocoon of blankets and slunk downstairs. From the sound of water and furious scrubbing, I could tell my mother's nervous cleaning streak had not ended. My mourning must have set her off. The hard wood underneath me was sparkling like it was coated in pixie dust.

My feet slid silently over the floor, but my mom whipped around like I drove a truck through the wall.

She whispered something under her breath along the lines of "God *praise* that boy…miracle worker." I assumed she meant Luke, who had been promoted to deity status in my household after he'd managed to coax me out of the worst of it.

She smiled at me. "Hey, sweet pea, how ya doing?"

"I'm fine. I'm going to get some air," I lied. Man, it was becoming a habit.

She looked torn between wanting me to stay and be safe and not wanting to scare me back off to my room again. Unsure which side would win, I headed out the door before I could be stopped.

I was not fit to drive. I almost took out a telephone pole swerving away from an ownerless husky puppy that darted onto the road. A few times, my thoughts drifted back to that dark memory of blood and death and caused me to drift over the unpainted center line. If I lived anywhere but the middle of nowhere, I'd have been a goner.

But I did live in the middle of nowhere, so I made it safely to Jeremy's. No cars were in the driveway, which I took as a good sign. Maybe his family took a little break and went away. I knew they couldn't have gone far, though. Not with his funeral being held in the nearest city the next day.

I circled the building, tugging on all the doors and windows. Nada. I scrounged around the bushes and decorative plants on the doorstep for a hidden key. Zilch. I almost threw my back out trying to pry open the garage door. Nothing.

There was an open window on the second floor. I could

see it, tempting me. The curtains billowed out from the exposed sill and slapped the mesh screen. I could practically hear its inanimate taunts. My stubbornness chose that as my route of entry.

How to get up? Well, luck sure shone my way when I realized I was standing in front of a large maple tree. One of the boughs extended over the roof next to the sill. I was so grateful to trees it was ridiculous. Maybe one day I'd start a tree religion and collect fellow tree crazies from all over the world.

Such high aspirations would have to wait. I bear hugged the maple and shimmied up to the lowest branch. In much longer than it should have taken, I was on the roof top. My bum shoulder complained about how stupid that plan was in the most painful way possible.

The roof was strangely sloped in a way that made me feel safer crawling. I wondered what the neighbors would think of my shenanigans if they peered out their own windows. Was I suspicious enough to call the cops on? Only time would tell. My hands met the mesh screen.

A little corner stuck out. I gripped it with the edges of my nails and tugged, wary of breaking the fragile thing. One of the plastic pins inside slipped out of its socket and gave me a sudden release in tension. My hand shot out to catch the inside window sill before I could dance my way over the edge of the roof and splat on the lawn. It was the bad arm. I had to restrain myself from yelling so loud I'd scare away every bird on the block.

Heaving a deep breath, I reached my other arm in and unhooked the remaining spike. The curtains slapped my face as they fluttered back and forth. I pushed the screen through and crawled in head first while closing my eyes against the onslaught.

I landed about as smoothly as a comet falling from space. I managed to turn this time, though, and crash onto my good shoulder. I grumbled to myself as I got onto my knees.

"Miss Leah?" a young voice chirped in front of me. *Oh crap.*

Benjamin stood there wearing a blue pajama onesie with dinosaurs on it. He didn't seem particularly perturbed that I'd just crashed through his window and was lying on the floor. I was relieved to see that he looked pretty normal, nowhere near as bad as I knew I did.

I let out a tiny smile. "Hiya, Benjamin."

He held his hands behind his back like he was hiding something. "Did you come here for this?"

My smile turned a little more real. "I think you've gotta show me what you have so I can answer that."

He reluctantly pulled out the shiny, black EMF. My eyes widened. "I like the noise it makes. Like a race car."

It did make a noise when it lit all the way up, but I wasn't too sure it sounded like a race car. I wasn't about to tell him that, though. Kids can dream. Benjamin eyed the contraption in his hands with such appreciation I began to doubt my ability to take it from him.

I pulled myself into an upright position. "Yeah? Do you like it?"

He nodded. "Yeah. But Jeremy gave it to you."

His name was like a slap. I flinched. "How'd you know that?"

He didn't answer. He held out the EMF. "It's yours."

I accepted it warily. "You sure? I mean, if you really like it, I can let you keep it."

He shook his head fiercely. "I'm not allowed."

"Okay, Benjamin. Thank you." I accepted his odd reasoning and took the device.

With his hands free, Benjamin smoothed a lock of his dark hair behind his ear. I saw a flash of Jeremy doing the same thing when we were younger and his mop of hair had been more unruly. Just that one, benign memory was enough to bring ocean water to my eyes. I rubbed furiously to keep any of the tears from falling. I didn't want to cry in front of Benjamin, who was being so brave.

Benjamin was more observant than I gave him credit for. He came closer and wrapped himself around me. "Don't cry, Miss Leah. It's okay."

He did me in. The waterworks were strong. Obese tears rolled off my flushed cheeks and soaked his pajamas, but he didn't seem to care. I desperately struggled to pull myself together, aware of how backward the situation was. I should have been comforting him.

Then he pulled away. "Wait here, Miss Leah. I want to show you something."

I nodded, unwilling to speak for the chance my voice would break. He scurried out of the room and closed the door. I rubbed my eyes furiously to get rid of the warped-glass look the room had taken on.

The door clicked back open almost immediately. *Too quickly,* I mused as I looked up. A shadow lurked there, taller than my crouching form, but not by much. Dark hair partially concealed dark eyes with even darker circles underneath.

"You killed him," Melinda told me. My mouth twisted into a grimace, but I didn't say anything. Somewhere, in the logical part of my brain, I knew it wasn't true. But the rest of me was moaning *agreements.*

If I hadn't been so angry with him...So eager to yell at him...So misunderstanding of the situation...So slow to finally understand...So late to realize the growling wasn't in my head...So weak that I was down with one hit...So utterly useless. In the back of my mind, a little voice chimed in: *You aren't anywhere near as useful in real life as you are in your dreams. You may not have killed him, but you let him die.*

There was a bang in front of me. "Go away, Melinda!"

There was the sound of pattering raindrops as she left without a word. Benjamin shuffled closer and yet again closed the door, bringing with him a dragging sound not unlike a snake's movement. Then my vision was eclipsed by gold.

 Not angelic gold. A gold painting. Benjamin had dragged a canvas bigger than him from Jeremy's room. I couldn't even see his little form supporting it from the back.

I threw my hands out to take some of the pressure off him, but it was almost a secondary response. My eyes were on the painting.

It was our spot. He hadn't been lying when he told me he was going to paint it. When I shifted my hand to get a better look at the tree it was obscuring, I was shocked to feel the texture of the canvas rather than the bark of the trunk. I could see individual blades of grass forming an army of green at the base of that tree.

Up in the sky, the rising sun smoldered. That same fire was reflected in the pond I'd stared at so many times, combusting every single ripple. The left side was incomplete, but I could see a pencil outline of more trees and of a suspiciously turtle-like creature on the pond's edge.

The pencil side had multiple light outlines among the

sturdier, definite ones. Some of the darker ones had been painted very minutely, but the lighter ones were untouched. From the repeated characters I viewed, it seemed like he had sketched out all of the places to put the two of us.

In one, we were both lying in the grass. It was something silly we'd done a lot in freshman year before I had realized I brought all kinds of sticks, leaves, and dirt into school with me afterward. It was almost worth it to relax and watch the clouds, though.

Off to the side, there was a version of me hanging upside down from a tree with faint shading to denote my face was flushed from the adrenaline and the blood-rush to my head. Jeremy's back was to the eye of the picture, his head tilted up, watching. One of his hands left his side like he was subconsciously making an effort to prepare to catch me if I fell.

By the turtle, Jeremy held his huge contraption. His backpack was inside of it, coated with mud and dripping filthy water. His face was turned toward me. I had my hands up in the air and a smile that could take on the world.

I blinked without feeling water squeeze under the lid. I wondered why my cheeks hurt so badly, only to feel the burn of a smile sister to the one in the painting. Teeth bared in a happy nostalgia, I felt ready to face the world.

I existed in a world of rage and pain. Light didn't penetrate.

So many screams. No way to reach them all. No way to plug a dam when the whole thing was gone. I thrust myself into the raging current, but it was far too late for any action other than salvaging. I was no savior.

So far north that the land was washed in eternal light for half the year and eternal darkness for the other, I fought amid chaos. Two demon-possessed and a large handful of the Corrupted had caused a chain reaction that escalated into a war within the town itself.

There were no sides as all Hell broke loose, and as the bodies dropped, the number of demons rose. Each brutal kill weakened the barrier between the earthly plane and the one of torment and demonic fire beneath it.

Demons ran into homes and terrorized anyone they could find. Without a care for the shaky cameras trained on them at the beginning stages, they revealed themselves to the humans and reveled as their minds—and their bodies—broke.

The pile of corpses in the road was testament to that.

Haldis whipped wildly through the air, slicing ample amounts of demon flesh. When there was any thought to spare, I mourned how badly things had devolved. Hell spawn swarmed the living like buzzards that were only too willing to drag their prey to the grave. A few circled me, using their numbers to their advantage. No one wielded cameras any-more, most who had dared to get close hadn't survived.

All I could see were the dark hides of demons. There were just too many. An enemy was at my back despite my con-stant turning. I swiped at those in front of me with Haldis, but could only make shallow cuts before the constant heat on my wings turned to a boil with the attack of the demon behind me.

I knew the tactic. I ducked, watching as jaws snapped shut beside my head. Before the beast could blink, I gripped

Haldis with both hands and drove the blade over my shoulder, right between its eyes. It didn't have time to scream as its body burst into flames and rained fire upon me.

A demon shaped like an oversized, crawling bat leapt at my throat. Haldis, though nearly finished with the burning demon, met just enough resistance that my slice didn't make it in the precious millisecond interval I had. My elbow connected with the bat's muzzle awkwardly, and both of us went down as the beast's momentum carried it through.

Its thin, talon-like fingers came for my head before we hit the ground. Taking what I could get, I slashed at its elbow joint with the angelic blade. Haldis' blaze was almost platinum, a blinding hue as it cut straight through with a clinking sound. The arm fell off, and the thin membrane between the fingers burned and floated away like ashes before the charred remainder of bones and flesh faded from existence.

The bat squealed above me, the sound unnatural and bone-chilling. Angelic flames climbed up the remainder of its limb at a furious pace. Another shadow shifted behind it, and from my position on the ground, I was forced to make my own weapon.

My feet planted in the bat's belly and pushed with all their might. My wings slapped against the ground hard enough to add extra force to the kick. The demon consumed in flames flew for the last time, up and up briefly before its body hit the approaching monster. They went down in the same flame.

My back gave a grunt of protest as I launched myself up, landing on a mailbox and then using it as a springboard to get airborne. My wings snapped out despite how I'd abused them as I took to the sky. No demons left the ground in pursuit of me, but it was not for the reason I had hoped.

Demons did not need to roam the grounds. The humans were doing their work for them. I had never witnessed humans as unhinged as those below me. Fist fights were the least of my concern as Molotov cocktails and bullets flew.

One father was having his son shove the rags in the open bottles, pelting them at anyone who came too close. When a shadow flickered with the slithering form of a demon, he lit it ablaze just a second too late. When a particularly rowdy group violently expelled one of its members onto the father's perfectly manicured lawn, another bomb found its way onto his back, wrapping around him like an embrace.

I plummeted from the sky with purpose, landing next to the agonized man shrouded in flames. He screamed as I ripped his shirt off, removing the combusting alcohol. I did not blame him as his screams turned to moans; his dark skin was black and bubbled across his shoulder blades. I had no time to heal him as I sprinted forward, disarming the overeager father.

I tossed out the rag that was lit in the bottle in his hand and watched as his gaze found mine. Nothing registered, not even a hint of emotion. His eyes were wide and unfocused as they met mine, not reacting to the gold that coursed through my veins.

It was like I had unplugged him. He simply ceased to function. He leaned to one side and sunk lower, as if deflating. His little boy clung to him, shouting for his daddy. It was to no avail.

From behind me, the blast of a pistol reached my ears. Faster than human thought, my wings stretched and curled, shielding the family in front of me. The bullet impacted the solid muscle under the bone in my right wing, right in front of where the child's head had been.

Breath hissed through my teeth, almost serpentine in quality. The bullet, which had not gone through, felt like metal fingers slowly expanding in my flesh. The wing drooped, the muscle supporting it failing. Whitish feathers touched the child's face on their descent.

I willed my wings out of their corporeal form and they fell into shifting golden flames. The bullet dropped in the air from where it had been lodged. My limbs felt tired, sluggish, as I knelt in front of the father. My fingers grasped his chin and pulled, forcing the crumpled man to look at me.

"Take your son," I said, pointing to the boy, "and leave. Do not harm anyone else or let harm come to them."

I allowed the tiniest portion of angelic flames to leap from my fingertips. It let loose a subdued sizzle on his skin and he jerked slightly in my hand before relaxing. It was not meant to harm, just as a warning. It wouldn't burn if he wasn't corrupted.

As I stood, he did as well. The child at his knee got excited and started pulling on the father's thick pants, his face screwed up like he was going to cry. The father scooped him up and ran, disappearing down the road, stalking the edge of the woods. They would be safer that way, staying away from civilization.

The group behind me, including the trigger-happy one, had dispersed. Shadows darted in the darkening yards between houses, whether they were human, animal, or demon I did not know.

At this stage, I did not know which possibility to dread most.

Chapter Twelve

The last time I'd been to a funeral I'd been too young to understand. A distant family relative had passed away, so my sadness that day mostly came from the heavy air around the place and the tears of the people that knew the recently deceased. Today was nothing like that.

I wore all black even though I knew I didn't have to. The dark clothing matched the circles under my eyes and my whirling thoughts. I wore no makeup despite the fact that somewhere between my last breakdown and that moment I had run out of tears. I did not sit in the front row; I let his extended family fill that in.

I wanted to hide. I should have blended into the crowd of downturned faces, but it was like I had a huge bull's-eye painted on me. I was both consoled and considered, but I wasn't sure which bothered me more. Words were empty nothings. Like leaves on the wind, they blew by me too quickly to catch before growing indistinguishable from their compatriots rotting in a mass grave.

There were the people who did not use words, but I did not find their stares comforting. I suppose it hadn't been too hard to piece together why Jeremy was behind my house when he died. They might not know the reason, but they might know the cause: me. I received more than a few openly accusing stares.

One of which came from Jeremy's mom. Rosalind and Benjamin walked down the aisle I'd made sure to sit near as an easy escape route. Benjamin reached out for me, but she tugged his hand so we could not make contact and shot me a stare so full of hatred that my mother, who had witnessed the whole thing, felt the need to wrap her arms around me and pull me to her.

"Mrs. Bellevue? Rosalind?" I called softly, longing for just one smile, one of them that could take me back to the time of sunshine and baked treats at Jeremy's, the two of us laughing as we roughhoused in the yard as children.

My lungs deflated as Rosalind moved quicker, anger fueling her steps away from me, snatching my childhood memories with her.

The funeral was closed casket for obvious reasons. I did not approach that terribly significant wooden case when everyone else did. I had too many things to say. A lifetime of words we should have shared, stolen from us. I couldn't help but think of how nice it would have been to feel his arms around me; to hear him whisper one of his lame puns in my ear. The solution to all my problems had been Jeremy. What was I supposed to do when Jeremy was the problem?

I might not have been crying, but I wasn't numb. Every one of those words spoken about him hurt. It wasn't that I found any of the speeches given particularly meaningful, it was that I didn't. Hollow speeches about how talented he was or how smart he was or how loved he was only served to anger me. I didn't claim to know what the dead want- ed, but I knew what he was like when he was living. The speeches weren't it.

It wasn't that he wasn't smart or talented or whatever,

he was. It was just…The speeches glossed over the imperfections I loved so much. Smoothed them out to look neat and presentable, morphing his memory into an angel he wasn't. I mean…I guess what I'm saying is that that version of him, nice as it was, wasn't real. I wanted to remember Jeremy as a human, as he truly was. My memories were all I had left and I wasn't going to paint them all in pretty, easy-to-swallow colors.

Then again, pretty hues might be better than a bright, sanguineous red.

I said nothing, did nothing. I pretended that the priest's words meant something to me, offered me comfort, but it all seemed like empty promises. My mom held my right hand as my left clenched on the wooden pew. My father, who had boxed me in from the aisle whether knowingly or unknowingly, leaned against my shoulder. I wanted to let my mind wander from this place of pain, but the thought of how disrespectful that'd be combined with the knowledge that my mind would wander straight back to That Day kept me there.

Stuff happened. The place where I was changed. There was grass under my sandaled feet and a breeze shaking the dust off my black dress's hem. It was too cold out for a dress, but I really didn't care. Jeremy deserved no less than my most proper attire.

I could remember the first time I ever wore a dress around him. The first day of freshman year, I'd dressed to impress. I was a little nervous that Jeremy, being pretty much my only friend, would abandon me in favor of some more attractive girls, so I wore a formfitting forest green maxi. If it had been a shirt, it would have been right up my alley, but the dress part threw it right into the realm of never-before-done. Jeremy had taken one appreciative glance before raising his eyebrows at my severely uncomfortable expression.

"Not that you don't look like the most beautiful forest nymph..." he had started.

I'd already been flaming at the cheeks. "Shut up."

A smile had permeated his words. "...But I swear to Zeus I just saw an Acheri."

I had rolled my eyes. "Zeus ain't going to help you with that one. Try a Hindu or Buddhist god. Also—" I had reached down to grab my bag of tricks, which had been much smaller at the time, out of my pocket, only to realize I didn't have it.

Jeremy's grin flashed a generous amount of teeth. "Gotcha!" he had exclaimed. "If those disease spreading hill fairies came for us right now, we'd be achoo-y from the Acheri—"

"That one wasn't even remotely—" I had mumbled, not bothering to finish the sentence as he talked on.

"—and the one person who would have been able to save us all couldn't have because she decided to wear a dress without pockets. Pockets, I say!"

We'd mock fought and bantered back and forth about it for a while, but I never did wear a dress to school again, to my profound relief. That was one story that, if told, this crowd would never understand. They'd think that I was disrespecting him, choosing a memory where he was insulting me. They wouldn't understand that he was freeing me to be myself.

A large hand caught my shoulder. I could feel its roughness through the thin sleeve of the dress I was wearing. "I'll leave if you want me to. Had to make sure you were okay."

I hugged Luke without actually looking at him. "No. Stay."
He did.

It was funny how I eyed the woods with such suspicion
when in all reality the thing I should fear was probably a
biped in an all too familiar shack in the woods. It wasn't
like I was going to swear off the woods entirely, but I wasn't
going near the location of the wolf attack any time soon.

I wore the black dress even though the funeral had
ended hours ago. Nyami was tugging like crazy on the end
of a shiny leash I held wrapped around one wrist. Her carefree attitude and the tiny winds stirring against my calves
helped to keep me grounded, but so did my newest assignment: cure lycanthropy. It was already turning out to be a
doozy.

The wound on my shoulder itched like crazy, but a simple Google search told me that was normal. What wasn't
normal was the fact that I was packing every anti-werewolf
spell, charm, and killer I'd ever laid my hands on. I wasn't
taking any chances.

That said, I wasn't even allowed inside Luke's abode. It
kinda made sense. If something went south I had a running start. Also, I was fairly certain some of the things I had
brought had the potential to be deadly. I knew for a fact
that wolfsbane could kill humans, let alone wolves. I sat
outside with my potentially deadly cargo.

Eren, by my specification, was nowhere to be seen.
Luke told me he was restrained—by his own choice—in the
furthest room of the house. I knew I wasn't supposed to be
mad at him, but merely knowing didn't stop the surpris-

ingly violent rage that consumed me at the thought of him. I don't know if I'd ever felt so ready to explode with aggression and nervous tension.

At the least, I'd hit him next time I saw his unbearably cocky grin. At the worst, well...There'd be wolfsbane in his Jäger. Either scenario could end with me six feet under. So, yeah. Not pushing it by allowing any contact.

Luke had already tried all the common items I'd brought. The exotic ones, however, were introduced in very minute amounts like in the most careful of science experiments. First it'd be brought within scent range. According to Luke, all of the items were already within the range, which was bizarre to think about seeing as I couldn't smell them at all, but what I meant is that they'd be brought in closer.

If he didn't burst into flames, the smallest possible dose was placed on non-sensitive skin. Any discomfort was recorded, along with any sign of skin irritation. If there was none, the next step was sensitive skin like the crook of the arm, neck, or face. Then, if it was supposed to be ingested, he'd put a little bit on his tongue.

It was a lot like testing wild berries before you eat them, except with a much less clear desired result. If it didn't do anything it was safe, but safe wasn't exactly what we were going for, was it? I viewed a reaction as progress, but a bad reaction could prove to be too dangerous to proceed. We only wanted the wolf dead, so we started with the items least likely to kill Eren.

The first thing I suggested was something intangible and absolutely ridiculous by my reasoning, but it was worth a shot.

"They say if you call a werewolf by their full name three

times they will be cured," I half-heartedly offered when Luke had asked for the least dangerous thing first.

Luke watched me for a second, gauging my seriousness. I shrugged and absently petted Nyami's cone head. Luke turned and walked back into the house, latching the bolt behind him like it could stop a pumped up werewolf. It hadn't last time. It didn't stop me from hearing Eren's laugh when Luke attempted my suggestion.

Speaking of...What had triggered that reaction? Luke had said they'd been messing around trying to find a cure, didn't he? I could hear his voice, but the walls of the house filtered voices until only whispers remained. He came back out and shook his head, another method failed.

"Did you try an exorcism?" I asked, my mind churning to pull up harmless cures. So many were fatal or at the very least extremely painful to endure.

Luke tilted his head at me like he found that statement odd. "Can't exactly bring a priest in there. Dangerous."

I looked up thoughtfully. That blue sky up there held the heavenly realm in certain religions I'd be using in an exorcism, wouldn't it? Surely if that particular deity disapproved of my thoughts, he/she'd smite me where I stood. I wiggled my fingers in anticipation. Luke's head stayed slightly tilted.

Nada. I wasn't zapped a crispy golden brown. It was unhealthy, really. If the gods were going to eat me, they might get food poisoning. *Although,* I thought as I eyed a fluttering insect, *that butterfly is flying suspiciously close. A sign?*

Its dusty wings flapped madly as it flew in circles over my head. Was it drawing a halo? The circle was a little lopsided, but I chose to take that as a good omen. I needed a little positivity right about then.

My eyes continued to track the creature while I thought things over, but it veered off course. The moth spiraled down like a hit airplane and fell straight to the ground. Well, not quite the ground. A little safety net caught it on the way.

Too bad the safety net was sticky and a large spider was waiting on top. The moth was bitten and wrapped before I could decide whether I wanted to save it or not. The spider didn't look smug to have caught itself a meal, just mildly irritated at the moth's vain thrashing.

So much for a good sign.

Whatever, I didn't let it get to me. I proceeded to tell Luke the plan from the stump I was perched on, the same one he'd been chopping wood on earlier. "What if I were to do the exorcism? I mean, I—"

Luke's head reoriented itself violently. "No."

My eyebrows knitted together. "But, who else could you get to—"

Luke cut me off again. "No."

Nyami must have sensed my frustration, because she started rumbling lightly. I bent down to rub my hand through her fur. "Come on! I can—"

The voice that responded wasn't Luke's. "He's right. It's too dangerous." The owner turned toward me. "Hey, Kitten. Nice dress."

I hadn't noticed Eren in the doorway, but apparently neither had Luke. That figure leaning against the doorframe quickly consumed all of my attention. I'd been wrong before, I was going to do much worse than hit him.

My vision constricted and I bared my teeth like I was the dangerous one in this pairing. With the rage pulsing through me like angelfire in my veins, I felt dangerous.

Luke's muscular arm held me back as I lurched to my feet.

Biting back the anger that felt like a physical muzzle restricting my speech, I didn't manage to say a word. Luke, on the other hand, didn't have the same problem. "Eren, get back inside."

Eren didn't reply immediately, but he straightened up. There was no cocky grin. Deep black circles resided under his eyes, almost as bad as mine. "Listen, I...Can I talk to Leah alone?"

Luke didn't release me. "No, you can't."

I shoved against his arm, taking him off guard. I broke free, but Nyami reached Eren before I did. She streaked across the ground like a golden bullet and leapt, snarling.

Then she seemed to realize she had no idea what to do. She fell clumsily to the ground and began to run around Eren in small circles, barking all the way.

Some of the rage started to ebb, but I was left with an unhealthy dose. Still enough that I wanted to scratch out his eyes. I was afraid Nyami'd get hurt, though, and she was my priority. I called her back to my side.

She came willingly, relieved she didn't have to pretend to be fierce anymore. Her tongue lolled out of her panting mouth, slobber falling from her satisfied grin. I, on the other hand, was not satisfied.

While I crouched, tying Nyami's leash to the stump I had been sitting on, Luke barred Eren's path with his broad shoulders. "Get back inside."

Eren's nostrils flared. His eyes looked wild and angry at the command, but his words were anything but, barely audible. "I need to apologize. Just give me a minute."

I did not want a false apology from him. It'd tip me right off from considering homicide to committing it. Luke took one look at my face and gleaned as much.

He pushed Eren back into the house. Eren definitely could have resisted, but instead he cast a long, indecipherable look at me and let the door close between us.

Luke's gaze slowly shifted from me to the door. "I think that's enough for today."

The first true siege of the demons was easily something the humans with badges, suits, and white coats explained away. The violence, the sightings, the deaths...all had the facts minimized and the truth twisted. Anyone who dared to tell their tale was ridiculed, labeled for a mental asylum, and never heard from again.

From behind the screens in cozy little houses, the stories spun by victims were denounced as too outlandish. It didn't matter that dozens were singing the same tune: a song of a living blackness darker than night and its human puppets. No, anyone listening just squinted their eyes ever so slightly before leaving to go about their life, sometimes turning down the volume so the victim's tales could become the forgotten soundtrack of the observer's daily routine, sometimes turning the television off completely.

Out of many, all that they knew was a brutal uprising had occurred in a small town in Alaska. People from all walks of life, from all ages and ethnicities, rose and slaughtered whomever they could get their hands on. Fathers to sons, daughters to mothers, elderly to the young, siblings, cousins, neighbors, and strangers attacked each other without discrimination. And all it was to the unaffected was fodder for conversation.

Only one or two of the main inciters were possessed. It had to be, it was impossible for that number of demons to escape Hell in one area. In order to leave the dimension of pain and suffering, they had to find a weak point on Earth. A place where agony was had and an imprint was left. The worse the crime, the larger the gate. The town had known no horrors before this one.

Another handful were broken ones, the living humans with corruption boring large, gaping tunnels in their souls. The Corrupted. Their actions snowballed the event, and with each second and every drop of blood or tears the rift for the demons to crawl through grew wider and wider. Of course, for every demon that appeared there, on the mortal plane, there was more bloodshed. A wound festering, widening.

But the worst was that the majority of people involved—the majority of those fighting and killing—were just regular humans.

Well, they weren't regular any more. They found that hurting people they knew tended to change them. The savagery, the things they thought had resided only in their minds or behind bright screens—it all grew too much.

Snap.

A whole town was now broken. A living, breathing weapon for the demons, a spot of darkness not even full days of Alaskan sunlight could erase. A whirlpool began low in my gut, that sinking feeling when you know something irrevocably bad has occurred.

This was not war.

This was genocide.

The innocents were being picked off in bunches, families and lives getting crushed under the relentless waves of the demonic forces. I was the only stone in the path of this rag-

ing current, a lone soldier against Hell's army. It could not end well.

But I had been there when it'd happened, as one would learn if they had listened to the newscasts long after the witness testimonies had been dropped by the more credible news sources. A glowing woman, they said, killing the exotic animals on the loose. Others were less kind, and in their eyes I was the origin of the chaos rather than the result of it. All stab wounds were made by my sword.

Officials had a much more mundane reasoning: gas leak. The toxins had built up in the air of the town until the first act of violence ignited it. Of course, recreational drugs were also mentioned as a factor, and the melanic animals seen were supposedly all results of this hallucinogenic substance.

Fair enough, I supposed. I did not need undue human attention while I worked to prevent a second battle. I preferred my solitude as I stalked through the victims of the massacre, searching for the telltale mark of the demonic so I could trace the origin of this madness.

I had arrived in the thick of it, when neither beginning nor end was in sight. I sought to rectify that, to learn from my mistakes. The demons must have come slowly at first, when my advantage would have been greatest. As the rift grew wider, the demons crawled out at a greater rate. I needed to strike before that happened next time.

Next time. I shivered to think of it.

I was covered in battle scars, puncture wounds and thinly sealed tears in my skin, but I barely felt the mass of them as they healed. My pain and aching were nothing compared to the grievous strain on the inhabitants, so all my focus was on the ruins in front of me. I could not afford to be self-absorbed.

A large number of those involved were in custody, but it was impossible to put a whole town behind bars. No demonic presences were in the jails. They had fled to find new hosts or wreak new havoc in a place where they would have space to roam.

Space. It was all I could see. Not the endless mystery above me, but the emptiness around me. Nothing breathed, no one dared venture out. Cars lay unmoving in roads like slaughtered mammoths. The only sources of noise were a live power line sparking on the ground and the tiny, far away voice of a young news reporter looking for her big break.

There was nothing left for me here, and yet I lingered. Perhaps I felt my presence was needed as an apology. Perhaps I felt a desire to learn from the events that occurred here. Perhaps I was just guilty.

It didn't matter what I felt as the tugging started in my chest and wings lifted from my back. I stretched them once, quickly, but nothing seemed to eliminate the heaviness that pulled the feathers down, as if each individual one was bowing its head in mourning.

Despite this, I heeded the calling and flew.

Chapter Thirteen

The full moon was tonight. As the sky grew darker and darker I could feel the yellowish orb growing stronger beyond the horizon. It had been wishful thinking to hope that it didn't mean anything. I should have known that something I'd loved as much as a nice, magical full moon would be corrupted by the stain on my life.

Sigh.

I knew the day was going to be interesting when no one drew the sky. It was a blank canvas, just waiting to be filled in. A giant white dome above my head. I squirmed in my seat at school, dying to ask Luke just what tonight would bring. He took one look at me and knew what I was thinking. How was it that he could read me so well when I could only pick up the bare minimum from him? He shook his head and whispered, "later". Then he turned and coughed into his shoulder.

It was almost enough to distract me from the fact that this was my first day at school without Jeremy. Almost enough to distract me from the stares and whispers and the inferno of condolences from people who'd avoided me like the plague before. I nearly snarled when a dyed-dark haired, stud-wearing art student of Jeremy's former crowd put his hand on my shoulder. I was barely able to control myself.

I didn't want to be rude, but everyone was scraping

and scraping away at the shell I'd so carefully constructed. My skin tensed at every noise, my head thumping a tribal rhythm. I didn't know what would happen. I felt like I was simultaneously coming undone and being buried alive. I fingered my bag of tricks, but it didn't elicit any comfort. I needed a friend and I was two short.

The police were conducting searches of the woods, but they were no longer looking for a living person. After Jeremy, they were looking for Jessica's body. I still had hope, but it wasn't comforting. It was like a thorn in my heart, ripping every time it beat.

Then again, I'm pretty sure the rest of my heart was in bloody smithereens from the shotgun blast of Jeremy's death. A thorn wasn't too bad.

It was only when the celestial artist's afternoon off ended and he began to paint his creation with purple and gray patches that Luke called me.

As soon as I picked up, he cut to the chase. "Not telling you anything unless you agree to stay as far away as possible."

My brows lowered in protest even though he couldn't see me. "I can help."

I could *hear* his resolve. He was steel. "Your safety comes first."

I let out a frustrated huff of breath. "What about the safety of others? What if he gets out again?"

Luke knew exactly where my thoughts were. The same dark hole as usual. He tried to pull me out. "Won't happen. I won't let it happen."

I sighed, the spirit world stealing my fight. "Will you tell me what happened?"

I could hear a scraping noise on the other side of the phone. I couldn't quite place it through the static. "If you want to know, we need to talk in person."

My voice betrayed my more suspicious thoughts about leaving Eren unsupervised with the countdown ticking away. "Is it safe? I mean, we only have an hour or two before nightfall."

There was a gap where he didn't answer, but I heard a quiet bang followed by the scraping noise again. "Explain when I get there."

I didn't protest. The line went dead. Then I put the phone down very carefully, taking more time than I should have while my thoughts bounced around. I marched myself over to the front door and exited onto the porch. My mother was hovering somewhere inside, so I had to be out of earshot, but I'd learned better than to drag people into the woods.

My mind went instantly to the silver bullet I had tucked away. I knew, without a hesitation or a doubt, that if Eren came around here on all fours I was going to put it right into his heart or his brain, whichever worked. I wished I had the second one I'd thought I'd felt when I first found the manila envelope. In a way, though, one was a blessing. It meant I didn't have time to mess around with nonfatal shots.

I'd figured out the caliber of the bullet and everything. .30-06. There was a compatible rifle in the safe downstairs. As I sat there on the cold, wooden porch the thought of that rifle made me anxious. Something under my skin was squirming at that murderous solution, while another, very small part was somewhat...pleased.

I didn't have time to be disturbed or disgusted by myself. I knew, if it came down to it, I'd protect my loved ones no matter what. Even if it meant murder, which it would be if I shot a werewolf. That was the bottom line. No amount of moral sniffling could change that.

Luke arrived, cutting over my severely-in-need-of-a-haircut lawn. He moved funny, with less of his lupine gait than usual. Something was off. He pulled his hand up and coughed violently into it. Was he getting sick? Had the moon gotten to him as well as me?

I didn't think I was meant to see that hint of weakness, because he tried to fix his gait when he saw me looking. It didn't work very well. If anything, his failed attempt at fixing it had made it more apparent. His mouth was pulled in a tight line.

It was such an animalistic instinct to cover injury or illness that I caught myself wondering if I hadn't been wrong in the first place, that he was the werewolf. I had no proof the wolf was Eren besides his word, after all. However, I shook myself mentally because I truly did not want to doubt Luke. I trusted him.

I didn't wait a second after he got to me before getting on his case. In fact, I think I get negative seconds because I leapt up and moved to him. "What's wrong? Why are you moving like that?"

His breathing wasn't normal. It was quicker and audible. "Healing."

My hand twitched at my side, uncomfortable with doing nothing. "Healing from...?"

His hand went to his ribs. "The wolf collided with me to escape. Damage from that and falling."

Uncaring if one of my elderly neighbors peeping out the window would think it was a spontaneous sex session, I grabbed the hem of Luke's shirt and pulled it up. I gasped and he stiffened from pain.

Deep red and purple blotching covered all of his ribs on the right side, the one not covered in scars. He'd hidden it from me. It was bigger than my head. "Holy Hell, Luke. I think your ribs are fractured."

He took my hand in his rough one and tried to gently tug it away, like I was the injured one. I held on, unwilling to let the gruesome image disappear like a mirage.

"You and I were fighting! What if I had hit them?" I exclaimed, incredulous.

He shook his head. "Just bruised."

I wanted to slap myself. "How the heck did I not notice this?"

I could feel his eyes on me while mine were pointed at the ground. "You were distracted."

I didn't deny that, but I still felt like a terrible person to miss something so extremely obvious and painful. I could feel the confused furrows rise in my forehead. "Did the doctor tell you they were bruised?"

He let my hand drop. "No."

Disbelief sank into my tone. "Please tell me you went to the hospital."

He lifted the corner of his mouth at me. I softly punched his shoulder, the one furthest from his injury. "Why not? Are you an idiot?"

Luke's eyes met mine, a deep ocean blue in the fading light. They were slightly confused, like he couldn't follow my thinking. "Eren said he could hear you and a guy before he shifted. Knew what that meant. Said the wolf...the wolf wants you. Had to stop it."

My head shook involuntarily. My eyes darted just as wildly as my thoughts did. "Luke, assuming you yelled 'no' when Eren got loose and he ran full wolf speed to get there in seconds...How the heck did you get there with human speed and bruised ribs?"

The shoulder on the good side of his ribs twitched up a tiny fraction. "Running. Coughing. Crawling."

I blinked, processing the pain he must have chopped out of those statements along with the excess words. I didn't...I didn't know what to think. This friend, the one standing before me, whom I had once thought was to blame for Jeremy's death, had *crawled* to try and save us. "You are unbelievable."

He was at a loss for words, but I sure as heck wasn't. I could feel them bubbling up inside of me. They began to spill out of my mouth faster and faster. "And you are even *more* unbelievable, and not in a good way, if you think I'm going to leave you and your useless ribs in the presence of a werewolf during a full moon. Are you *nuts*? You'd be defenseless! Screw the knowledge you were trading for my un-involvement, I'd rather go in blind than let you do this by yourself!"

Luke's eyes widened as he realized how badly he'd screwed up handling me, which was Jeremy's specialty, not his. All my words were true. There was no way I was letting him put himself in such huge danger, nor was I willing to risk Eren getting out and harming anyone else.

He might have tried to argue against me. He might have tried to argue for me. But the second his mouth opened, I cut him off. "No, no, and no. Come on. We're walking back to your house. Actually, wait. Better idea. We are walking down the driveway and we're getting in my car and we are driving back. Don't argue, you don't have the breath to spare."

I started walking. I could practically hear his slow blink behind my back before his boots began clipping toward me.

A small smile split my face, a little, slyly victorious one just for me. For the first time since Jeremy's death, I felt useful. I was going to save someone that night; I could feel it humming in my bones.

When Luke had told me he'd secured Eren during the cure research, I hadn't really thought about what that meant. When I mounted the rotting wooden steps to enter Luke's creepy cabin, I showed no hesitation. When he opened an utterly destroyed trap door under a pale deer hide on the floor, I have to admit a little apprehension snuck in. It didn't stop me from lifting up the remaining splinters-on-a-hinge door and walking down the teeny-tiny staircase.

However, it was when I saw the huge circular holds drilled into the wall with lengths of thick chain dangling from them like upside down seaweed that I began to process just how badly I felt vulnerable. One length of chain had been torn in two, the middle gruesomely warped. I couldn't help but think of the sheer amount of power that act must have taken and just how it'd look on a medium other than chain.

The other chain pile was a lighter color and intact. Luke stood behind me and explained. "The day the wolf broke loose it went right through the steel ones."

I pointed to the lighter, shinier chains, though I had a feeling for what they were. I used my bad shoulder despite the itchy pain. "And those?"

Luke shifted from behind me to my side. "Silver plated."

My mouth thinned. "That doesn't hurt him?"

Luke shook his head strongly. It was clear he would have been much more loathe to do such a thing if it had posed a risk to Eren. "Weakens him a bit unless it hits a wound. If it does hit open flesh, it's even worse than the call of the moon."

I thought I knew what he was saying. It seemed the archaic rules were in place, as in shifting at the moon and weakness for silver. Only this time silver equaled uncontrollable shift rather than death. Unless...Perhaps it did kill, but in larger doses or with a more central injection site? I wasn't ready to throw away the safety that I felt owning a silver bullet.

I guess I didn't know everything. It was too late to find out, though, because music with a throbbing bass line interrupted my thought. The ruined door's minute light was brightened when the scraps were pulled up to allow a large shadow to lope down the stairs.

Eren smiled and spoke over the music he'd turned on upstairs. Avenged Sevenfold's *Nightmare*. How fitting. "You guys started the party without me? I'm wounded."

There was no hint of the apologetic Eren. I wondered if that version of him had been real. I knew I was mad at him, but I was truly taken aback by the wave of intense fury that rolled over me. I had never been this ready to scream and fight and yell.

I tried to bury it inside, but it rumbled around like the worst of hunger. Unavoidable. I tamped it down the best I could by shutting my mouth, but what I really wanted to do was use every cuss word under the sun and then invent a few more until I was satisfied. Only the breath-stealing sadness that came with thinking about Jeremy was able to restrain me.

221

I ran my teeth roughly over my bottom lip as a distraction.

"Does he come with a muzzle?" I asked Luke hopefully.

I was disappointed when he shook his head. "Careful. Anger might be another trigger."

Eren leaned up against the wall but still managed to tower over me. "Good thing I'm as cool as a cucumber. Right, Kitten?"

Restraint flew out the window. I picked up the heaviest set of chains I could find and chucked them at him like they were made of feathers. Anger did most of the lifting. Unfortunately, they also hit like feathers. Eren's lycanthropy allowed him to stand in place, completely unfazed as the massive chains smacked his stomach.

My head swung wildly as I looked for something else to throw. Before I could pick my next weapon, a hand settled on my shoulder, a strong suggestion. I wanted to growl in frustration, but my all-too-human vocal chords were having none of it. Then clarity hit me.

I relaxed against Luke's hold, and I put myself closer to him, hoping his presence would calm me. His warmth settled the goosebumps I hadn't known I had.

"Not your best idea," he whispered in my ear, though there was no point in trying to keep secrets from a werewolf. We all knew he could hear it.

I tried to shrug, but Luke's hand made it one-sided. "Not my worst, either."

I could feel his chest jerk as he held in his laughter. He released me. "Feel better once he's in chains. Almost time."

At that, Eren raised his eyebrows and winked at me. "Kinky, aren't you, to want a man in chains?"

I ground my teeth. "Let's start. You can't be too safe."

Luke nodded and collected the chains from where I'd thrown them. The silver links looked awfully lunar, and, if I was honest, thin. Hopefully Luke knew what he was doing, because the steel chain, which lay broken and mangled, was thicker than its replacement. It was fitting that the moon-like chain would be protecting us from the darker side of the moon tonight. Speaking of...

"What exactly is going to happen?" I asked, helping Luke pick up the chain and wind it through the circles protruding from the wall. The area surrounding the circles was reinforced with a newer stone than the rest of it. A new addition. I was glad the house hadn't come with a torture chamber at hand.

Eren wiggled his fingers. "Magic, Kitten."

It's strange how much I would have been enjoying this had Jeremy been by my side. A werewolf in my town? It would have been a miracle. I would have offered myself to be bitten, probably begging for it. Jeremy'd be making some stupid pun relating to the moon and the fact I was already a lunatic.

But he wasn't here. He couldn't be. His body was lying dormant in a wooden casket six feet under. His soul? Well, it was anywhere but here. I'd snuck peeks behind me in mirrors and peered into dark corners with no luck. I'd hoped to feel watched. But there had been nothing. He was truly gone.

And I hadn't turned due to that nip. False alarm. Which I was actually very, very relieved about. To become the same monster that slaughtered my best friend would be the end of me. I couldn't, however, keep the thoughts of what use the enhanced senses could have. An idea had struck me and stuck: What if Eren, in human form, obviously, could sniff around and find Jessica?

I'd have to ask after this fiasco. If I was lucky, Eren's senses might be stronger than those of the search dogs that had been combing the woods. Maybe he could pick up a trail and find her alive but confused. I did not allow myself to consider what else he might find.

Luke's voice snapped me out of my thoughts. "Wound on his arm, Leah. Don't touch it with that chain."

My eyebrows knit together. When Eren hadn't sported black eyes or a bruised cheekbone, I'd assumed they had healed rapidly. "No quick healing?"

"There is, from everything except silver," Luke explained.

I nodded and watched Luke for a second before mimicking how he wrapped the chain. Each end had a silver handcuff type deal, but the slack had to be wrapped around Eren before those could be put on his wrists. I wound them cautiously so my hand would never touch his skin.

Eren's eyes were on my neck. A yellowish hue clung to the iris, one that conquered more and more territory by the second. I thought he was zeroing in on my jugular until I realized that my shirt had slipped down and revealed a corner of the bite he'd inflicted. Today was the first day I hadn't wrapped the scabbed and scarred mess.

The corner of his lip pulled up like he was pleased, but the motion wasn't right. He'd grown awfully quiet, and I was starting to think Eren was no longer with us.

Then his whole body went rigid. He started to shake violently, the fine hairs on his arms standing on end. He jerked against the chains and I jumped in response, my hand releasing the chain I'd been winding.

"Don't!" Luke yelled, but it was too late.

We snapped the manacle portion on his wrist in two

off-sounding clicks just as the links of chain I dropped rolled down his arm and touched the scabbed over crevasse on his forearm. Eren snarled with not a hint of humanity in the reverberating tone.

I yelled something incoherent and drew the excess slack up over my shoulder, trying to reverse the effects. It mashed my own wound down hard enough for it to bleed, its cold stabbing like flames. The damage was already done. In the blink of an eye, the creature of my blood-soaked night-mares was lunging for me.

My hands came up, but they didn't feel right and fire was pouring into me through my shoulder and I wanted to scream but Luke pulled me away. I fell to the floor and tried to let my voice loose, but it came out so wrong. Not my voice. Luke yelled for Leah but I was quickly forgetting who that was and oh god my insides were on fire. The chains clinked as they held Eren to the wall, but I hardly even looked as I fell to the floor.

Pain.

Not Heaven. Nothing heavenly could hurt this badly.

I tried to put my hands to the ground, but they didn't work. I closed my eyes as waves of agony pulled on every hair follicle in my body and every muscle convulsed. But my bones...my bones were the worst part.

Please.

Snapping and crunching and grinding and growing. They writhed like snakes inside of me. I wanted to scream and scream, but things weren't lined up and no sound came out. My teeth strained and tugged from my jaws as my jaws themselves were pulled.

Stop.

I could feel my nails pull deeper into my not-so-much

fingers and skin roll over their thickening and curving mass. My spine arched and extended, new nerve cells screaming at their conception. My senses exploded, the assault hitting me like physical blows.

Rage.

The whole thing took less than a second, but the pain was enough to tide me over for a millennium. Everything had been robbed from me. I panted. The ground was warm from my heat. But the smells. Smells everywhere. One so, so tempting.

Kill.

Saliva dripped from my jaw. No argument here.

Consume.

The human smelled good. I could hear his heart pounding as he scrambled away. Each noise was an abrasion to my ears.

Capture.

Nowhere to go, human. Not in that corner. Jaws will rend flesh.

Madness.

The scent...Not human. Human, wolf, human, wolf. Human-wolf. Not prey. And another wolf.

Growling, loud and louder. Shook the skull. Wolf on the wall lunged for me. Jaws open, reaching. Shook with fury. My lips pulled back.

I growled. Wolf snarled harder, a challenge from the chains.

Dominate.

So easy. Wolf in chains was weak. My jaws at his throat tight enough to draw blood. He snarled and snapped at my snout. I tore open his face. Blood flowed, so good.

"No, no please. Not you, too! Leah!" the human yelled.

Prey.

Not weak prey. Strong. Difficult.

"Don't do this."

I bared teeth. Voices bit like gnats in the skull. Time to leave.

"Leah, I…I'm so sorry. All of it, my fault…"

Devour.

Elsewhere, where flesh would yield to blood and bone. Tainted air crawled into nostrils. Thick like fluid. Wolf and man and pain and silver, all in one. But the moon, the moon pulled. I went to it. A small stair-eating spring to get to freedom.

The wolf-smelling human's clip, although fast, was outpaced by his heart. Hands reached for my hide but new limbs carried me quicker than even the heart. Sharp spikes prodded from the hole and bit into fur and flesh. I snarled.

Taste.

Fur of the long forgotten outside the hole, covered in dust. But a glance deemed it unsatisfactory. Only fur, no meat. Stomach was a beast of its own, chewing inside. Must get to moonlight at any cost.

Run.

Footsteps pounded up the stairs, heavy and clumsy. Paws were fleet. I relished the pull of muscles as I launched away from the sound. Toward where moonlight filtered in. Fur fled as my shoulder rammed the barrier and I tumbled through.

Moonlight stole the pain, numbing my heaving flanks. Darkness parted before golden eyes. Blades of grass tickled the thick padding under my paws. I paused, taking in the scents of the outdoors. Pines. Creatures. Silver.

Threat.

Vibrations filled the air I breathed. Snarls, from my own

chest. Metal clicked loud enough for my flinch to spin me toward it. My ears pulled back as I faced the human with metal and a small, burning hint of death metal.

The contraption in the human's hands was steady, aimed at my rib cage. "I don't want to shoot you, Leah."

His words meant nothing, but the scent of danger from the barrel spoke volumes. With no warning, I darted away. The contraption didn't move quickly enough. The forest welcomed me.

Trail.

So did overlapping scents of fur and breath. Of prey. Some hid in trees, some underground, some far. None were accessible except for the faintest of wisps. It was unknown but warm. I would have it.

Nostrils flared. Pine needles lifted as I inhaled near the ground. The desirable scent was a flavorful ribbon constricting my brain. Tighter and tighter and tighter.

Track.

Human boots ran behind me. Blind. Easily avoided. I clamped down on the uneasy rumble in my throat. Took to the trail, lust for blood thickening with each beat of the heart. The human's struggling faded into the distance.

I would find my prey. I would kill it. The scent livened as the distance covered greatened. It was close, and large.

Stalk.

Bushes offered perfect cover. The berries on them were pungent. Slow, unaware life pulsed ahead. Forelimbs scraped the ground as I lowered. Dirt coated the fine hairs on my underbelly. The night made the mud indistinguishable from the darker hairs.

I crept forward, slowly, stealthily. I wanted nothing more than to

Leap
Tear
Devour
the creature.

It was a pale ball on the ground. Larger than me. Breath hiccoughed from its nocturnal shivers. A large blackberry stain surrounded the non-lethal mouth. Hair at odds with the new human's paleness absorbed the color of a moonless night.

The bushes announced my presence when I crept forward. The human who slept fitfully on her bed of leaves started. Her eyes widened uselessly. She smelt of metal, too, but her arms were constrained by it. She was weak.

"Hello? Is someone there? Please tell me someone is there!" She spoke, her voice cracking from sleep and stress. The sound raked against my skull like rusty nails.

Anger.

Closer still. Black and white was beginning to turn to mottled red. Vision diminished, but the other senses re-mained.

"Hellooooo? Please be somebody! I've been out here for days!"

Attack.

The back side of the human was vulnerable. That was what I targeted. Haunches coiled and forelimbs were ready to spring.

"Fine, then. Be that way! Stupid animals. Go away!"

Challenge.

The bush erupted. Jaws clamped down on the noisy human's calf. True to her nature, she let loose a banshee shriek. She fell and flailed, striking with her free leg. I felt nothing but blood running down my throat and the satisfying fissuring of flesh in my mouth.

A kick landed on my eye socket. I yelped and released, reeling for less than a second. The human tried to crawl away but didn't get far at all, not with the metal binding her hands. Standing on the ravaged leg brought her back to the ground. Fire lanced through my face and my mind.

Strike.

Paws carried me further than her scuttling hands and useless leg did in a fraction of the time. A quick snap at the human's face punctured one cheek and caused the lifeblood to flow in streams. Her teeth were visible through the new opening. Her hands flailed as her screams became shrill.

She caught my fur and yanked in desperation, not realizing it brought me closer. My canines bit deep into her jawbone and neck, adding a wet quality to her cries. I shook my head vigorously and was rewarded with a crunch I both felt and heard. The human slumped, deceased.

Feast.

I was in a sleepy little town, the type where neighbors could rattle off the schedule of anyone living within three blocks. On that day, no family dared venture into the frigid air. Even though the sun's crown was resting above the horizon, houses were silent and no children were out to play.

To the residents, there was no concrete danger, but whisperings from third degree friends were enough to shut everything down. Inside homes, families slept or stared, spellbound at television screens. The scene could have been normal, would have been normal.

If only the residents weren't comatose.

Well, comatose was not the right word. Those who looked to be sleeping drew deep, rhythmic breaths and showed no indication that they recognized my presence. Those that were awake, however, followed my movements with only their eyes. No sound escaped slack lips or stiff necks.

Each house was the same. Dark tendrils, invisible to the victims, wove in and out of eye sockets and hearts, crawling and feeding off their victims like the worst of parasitic infections. No amount of cleansing energy I attempted to radiate fixed them. The tendrils were too deeply entrenched. To destroy them was to destroy their host.

Only destroying the source of the rune-inscribed snakes would help. I recognized the seriousness of this spell work, the likes of which I had not encountered for a long, long time. The radius of the damage was nearly unparalleled. I could only think of one other who had this power.

But it was not the time for such recollections. I became increasingly alert as each abode I entered yielded the same results. I neared the end of the row of houses before anything changed.

A ringing cry blasted from the very last house. An infant screaming for its life. Wings burst free from my back and I was there in an instant, but the screams had been silenced.

In an underground room with no light source except myself, a woman held a child. Like everything else in this town, it would have been a nice scene. A loving mother and a neonate who had begun to enjoy her presence. The reality was not close.

The infant was slumping, becoming more and more lifeless as the woman whispered under her breath. Dark hair, struck through with white yet fringed with rust on the bottom, covered the baby's face as she leaned forward and blew.

From her mouth pulsed plumes of a dark aura, the same that wound through the remainder of the population. I moved to snatch the child from her grasp, balancing the art of delicateness and celerity as I gathered it in my arms.

Through the matted locks emerged a face younger than the hair led me to believe, but the eyes on this beast were cloudy. Thin, scabbed over symbols were carved into her skin, dotting her hollow cheeks and her forehead. When she blinked, one eye came back red from a symbol that completely punctured her eyelid and steadily leaked blood.

The dark aura of a demon pulsed around her, but no amount of exorcism or expulsion on Haldis' part could lead to her redemption. I could see nothing left of her soul, the blackness indiscriminate from the swirling mass around her. She'd succumbed.

I couldn't help but wonder if the demon in her was one of the few responsible for the Alaskan massacre. Because of the rare nature of demonic possession, how difficult it was for less powerful demons to make it through the gates of Hell, it was a good bet that they'd be the same. Claws of fear poked at my heart for that very reason. If that theory was correct, I knew this town would soon mirror the other.

Her arms flew out and her head lifted to the sky. Mouth open, she chanted. Words of a language long lost to humans, known only to the demonic realm. The words themselves swam through the air, pouring out of her mouth and extending toward me. The demon inside of her was feeding her power.

They didn't come for me, as I expected. Instead, they shot like bolts of lightning straight for the skull of the child. Turning to shield it, I took the brunt of the blow under my ribcage. I had to get the slightly wriggling life in my arms out of here, but when I moved, my side refused to cooperate. Numbness cut in deeply.

Everywhere the curse had hit, my muscles were locked. The left half of my back was paralyzed, my wing drooping until the white tip brushed the floor. Angelfire was working feverishly to rid me of the weakness, but it was not quick enough. Another blow would be catastrophic.

The witch growled, angered by my refusal to wither away. Her cataract-clouded eyes followed my hobbling movements, the left one still leaking pink stained tears. I could see that she bore carvings all up her arms, engravings marking her as property of the demonic and amplifying her power. Those were the reason that this girl, who must have been in her late twenties, looked like a feral elder.

More smoke plumed from the markings on her neck and around her mouth, sluggish yet lethal. As it emerged, pieces of the witch shrank like she was on the verge of collapsing inward. To channel this much power was killing her. Every vein in her body became more pronounced and writhed under her skin like worms as muscle was whittled away.

"I'm sorry," I whispered to the child in my arms. The spell had not been completed on him, so he was starting to awaken. I did not have any guarantees for his safety.

I did the only thing I could think of: I set him down.

He cried loudly, in long sputtering gasps. The witch did not turn her head to the sound, instead focusing her efforts on me. The baby could not go far, while I was capable of flying quicker than the eye could track. This made me the primary target, as I desired.

I opened my palm to the empty air and Haldis appeared inside combustion. The curl of dark spell work it had materialized in was consumed in a mad dash of fire that licked along the length of it until the flames reached the skin of the sorceress. Her mouth opened silently, flashing teeth ground to nubs, as her skin boiled at the base of the tentacle. I made a note not to use Haldis on any of her victims.

Light footsteps sounded behind me, the slap of bare feet working at a furious clip. The pattern was uneven, a slight drag-drop came every time one of the feet touched down. Despite this, when it reached the home where the demonically influenced human and I were preparing for war, the door blew off its hinges and clattered against the far wall above us.

Lurching footsteps descended the basement stairs. They moved slowly but surely, never once hesitating until they reached the bottom. Standing at the base of the stairs was a girl with a sharp nose and short spikes of ebony hair.

The left half of her body was slumped, barely pliable. Curse work wound around that side, but it was slowly dissipating. Her left foot was angled strangely, the weight resting on the wrong side, and it was battered and bleeding where it came into contact with the ground. Rubble was caught in the bloody wound. It was not yet broken, but she must have limped a long way through rough terrain to get here. There was a life in her eyes that was at odds with the paralysis making her limbs lifeless.

Looking between the two humans before me, I could see the similarities. They were one hunk of metal, separated by the heat of the forge to become a shield and a sword, the final products almost untraceable to the original source. These two were sisters, irrevocably drawn apart.

The newcomer did not notice me, despite the fact that I was the only thing illuminating the basement. The setting seemed eerily similar to the cellar I had been freed from by the Elemental spirits, with water stains on the floor and walls and no sign of inhabitance. I eyed the child in the corner, who was quiet but still breathing.

She was staring, mouth open but slightly asymmetrical in one corner, at her sister. "Josephina, what have you done?"

Her sister showed no recognition. Darkness poured out of her with a few guttural words, reaching closer to the haggard newcomer. Before the spell could reach the girl, she shouted.

"Enough!" she cried, her eyes flashing with determination. She spoke shortly in Latin, her words clipped by anger. When she stopped, the air around her pulsed once and the door rattled on its hinges, a display of raw power. The greedy tentacles were pushed away, but the bob-haired girl bit her lip fiercely, rolling it to the point of bleeding. She was more afraid of what she had done than of the danger she was in.

The dark caster was distracted. With a flick of my wrist, I threw Haldis at a nonfatal area of her shoulder, pinning her to the wall. She wailed as the power coursing through her fought and perished against Haldis' angelfire. She started to slump, weakening, but the heavenly blade pinned her upright. In the absence of her shadowy fingers, I approached.

The second I pulled Haldis out, her head snapped up, cloudy eyes settling on my own. Though her legs were failing her, she latched onto my ankle and began pouring the last of her demonic power into me. I swung Haldis downward as my knee failed and hit the floor.

I was stopped a centimeter into her neck by a cry. "Don't!"

Ah, the girl had noticed me. "If you are looking for me to spare your sister—" whose mouth was frothing a pink paste, "I cannot."

I heard the swish of her hair as she shook her head, a quiet wind chime. "No, nothing can save her now. I thought...I hoped I could, but it is too late for Josephina. That thing is not her."

That thing jerked as I lowered my blade again, preparing for a quick, clean slice.

The sister spoke up. "No! I need to...It needs to be me."

I faced her this time, fully aware of my appearance. I spread my wings slightly, trying to show her what she was not registering. This was my job. While the death of the power-rotted girl would weigh on my mind, my soul would be unaffected. The weathered innocent behind me did not have the same luxury.

But it was not my job to steal choice. "You will carry this burden for the rest of your life."

The girl was at my side then, her bloody foot in my field of vision. "I do not plan on living long."

She reached down as if to embrace her sister or caress her face, whispering in a soothing, almost loving way. Her fingers trailed her sister's mottled cheek, getting coated with bloody residue in the process. Another pulse of raw power undulated through the air. There was a swift crack and her sister's head lolled onto her chest.

She rose and left, walking past her sister's corpse and the crying baby without a glance, limping into the night.

Silence followed from the demonic front.

The dregs of the news on the Alaskan massacre were questionable in information and dismissive in nature. Yes, this was an isolated incident. No, it could not happen in our town. Misguided lies, all of it. After the media had grown bored of the story, whispers swirled. On a particularly dry day, they themselves were brought to light. The conspiracy theorists had latched onto this event and at the center of all their plots was me.

In their eyes, I was the leader of the black aliens, come to collect brains. I was an angel, and the blade I wielded was none other than Archangel Michael's sword. I was patient zero for the zombie apocalypse. I was the devil himself. Even so, these odd titles didn't perturb me. They were the only problem I could find at this point.

The demons were suspiciously silent. I had not felt a single call to action in days. While it was a relief that no one had been injured, killed, or converted, I felt grossly underprepared for the next attack. The experiments they had conducted left me edgy, unsure of the rules in this new game. They went from seizing individuals to groups to towns...I feared what was next. The ball was in the demon's court, and I did not know what its return to mine would bring.

I wandered aimlessly, not a hint of gold weaving through my veins. Time had passed since I watched the witch's demise by her sister's hand. The moon and the sun had greeted me, but the exact amount of times they had come and gone was unknown. I had not bothered to count.

I walked barefoot down a sandy strip. It carried me further and further from the main land, out into the ocean. The hem of the white slip I was wearing was coated in wet sand. Every other wave exploded into a kaleidoscope of droplets that painted my legs with salt.

I didn't mind. Physical discomforts barely penetrated my line of thought. From this far away, the scattered handful of people on the chilly beach looked like mere colored dots. One of the figures was wearing a bright yellow rain coat without the rain to call for it and had hair that reflected orange light, brightly visible even at a distance. A sore thumb in the crowd.

Some object, maybe a crab exoskeleton or a bit of sea-shell, clinked briefly on the rocks before hitting the sand. I thought nothing of it until it hit the sand again. And again. And again, despite the lack of strong enough waves.

Without a thought I dove into the frigid water. It enveloped me with a solid splash, causing my clothes to stick to my legs and bubbles to follow me down. Less than an instant later, a halo of sand chased me from where I had stood. Something heavy had pounced.

With a silent plea to the water Elementals, my eyes cleared to view the area around me as easily as day. From above, a form I was quickly becoming familiar with took shape. The feline roared, the clinking of shattered glass combined with the sound of animalistic rage.

The Rashtka.

There were no humans to protect all the way out here. No one to save but myself, the one being I could not help. I looked around, aware these few seconds were crucial. I had to find a weapon.

Under the water, the bottle almost blended with the algae growing on the rocks. After nearly missing it, I scooped it up by the neck and grabbed the hand-sized chunk of stone residing next to it. The subdued sound the stone made when it broke the bottle didn't signal the creation of a deadly weapon, but I had to make do. I kicked off the bottom to propel myself out of the water.

The force of it threw me into the air and over the Rashtka, something which I doubted a human could do. A fine layer of particles coated anywhere I hit the ground, my soaked clothes slapped me as I landed, but I paid them no heed as I whipped around and dodged the Rashtka's leap.

238

Claws like heated iron missed my head by mere inches.

I swung at the underbelly of the demon with the bottle. The jagged edges tore open flesh, but it knit together again without angelfire to validate the wound. Something that should have eviscerated the beast left barely a scratch.

I stood my ground, unable to flee for fear the Rashtka would turn and attack the people on the shore, who were not in danger so long as I was playing prey. Judging from the intelligence behind its eyes, it would do just that. I'd be left without my angelic blade, so the odds would favor the demon, but it wanted me to be done with, now. It had no care for what danger the fight might possess as long as it ended with me no longer in the realm of the living.

My voice rang loud and clear. "No words for me this time, beast?"

Its blood-stained teeth became more visible as its lips curled back in a mockery of a human smile. "The crunching of your bones will speak volumes."

Its voice grated, sounding as if the vocal chords were functioning after being burned to cinders. I wanted to cringe at the undertone of rending, grinding metal and shattering glass. I did no such thing.

Instead, I focused over its shoulder where a machine was quickly approaching. The noise was noticed by the Rashtka in almost the same instant. Using the distraction, I ran into the demon, biting back a scream as demonfire burned my arms and torso without my normal angelic protection. I pounded the heavy rock once, swiftly onto the Hell spawn's head.

It cracked, but only for the briefest of moments. Before it could recover, another crack rang through the air: the report of a gun. The demon was flung off me by the sheer force of the blast, and I was splashed with blood that burned like acid.

My heart beat once, twice, then gold flooded through my system. It was a first breath after almost drowning. A glorious release of instinct, something so natural it was almost painful to be without. The essence I had come to recognize, though falsely, as my own wound its way through me with the warmth of an embrace.

"Booyah!" shouted an all-too-familiar strawberry-blonde. Before I could yell at her to go the other way, the Rashtka was on its feet again. Where the dark paws touched the ground, sea life perished in a sweeping wave of green turning to brown.

The expression of glee fell off Katherine's face. She swore as she swung her leg back over the quad she'd come out on, pulling her knee up to take aim yet again. The gun rested on the yellow rubber of her coat.

My focus was split evenly between the threat and the threatened.

"Don't," I warned Katherine. Human bullets would do nothing against the Rashtka, with the exception of angering it.

My open palm endeared the sky and Haldis materialized in it. I relished the slight chill of the hilt as I put the trigger-happy girl behind my back, facing the demon. Unlike any natural animal, its sides did not heave with the exertion caused by the slug in its shoulder. Instead, it stood still as the night while minuscule, wraith-like swirls of darkness poured from the wound. They neither floated up nor were pulled down, but simply remained, hovering in the air.

The purr of the quad sputtered and died just as small clinking sounds started from the demon's side. The slug was expelled, dropping to the ground. I heard the key scraping in the ignition and the strained, stuttering moan of the machine as it refused to start again, but I did not look at it. Instead, I kept it and the girl directly behind me, vaguely wondering if I was going to get caught by a misplaced shot.

I tried to buy time for Katherine to escape. "Tell me why you came here, demon."

The only response was hellfire burning every one of my pores as the mountain lion collided with me, claws raking down my neck. I swung with Haldis, matching the catamount's blow with my own. Blood warmed my shoulder blades as it ran in streams I had no time to see to. The Rashtka was on me.

We tumbled, a mass of pain and weapons. The light around me hissed as the demonic shadows pushed through and caused my skin to crack in the least affected places and burn in the worst. Off the rocks we went, and water provided blissful relief for a split second before the sting of salt coated my eyes and flooded my wounds. The water did not slow the Rashtka as its mouth went for my trachea.

Without any conscious action on my part, Haldis pierced through its throat. The angelic flames pulsed through its body, blurring the lines that bound its writhing darkness into the feline form. In a sudden explosion that rocked the water, the Rashtka's demonic presence went every which way.

For a brief second, I thought it had taken my eyes. I saw nothing, but I could feel sharp points in the thick fluid that battered me with every wave. From below, other things began to bump into me in their ascension, surpassing my position in the darkness.

Then, I could see. The sun shone dimly, in a distorted fashion, above me. I leveled myself and flipped so that I was facing the sea floor. The darkness was not gone, but it was sinking quickly, with purpose. Even though it had spread to an area wider than my field of vision, it was contracting, coalescing as it got further down.

This was the essence of a demon. A sentient soul, twisted with hate, violence, and darkness. The Rashtka was not gone, not by a long shot. I chased after this darkness, desiring to vanquish it once and for all, but it had already formed a column and seeped past the physical dimension. It disappeared into the ocean's floor.

A different sort of shade took hold of the underwater world. This one, not of demonic origin, came from above. There had been things rising earlier, but it had not been what I imagined. Thousands of dead fish and marine life-forms crowded the surface of the water and blocked out the sun, like an eclipse of the sky.

Even more were still rising. Brushing past me to reach their perished cohorts. I aimed for a glimmer of light between the swaying bodies and swam to the surface with three powerful strokes, breaking through the barrier.

On the sand, Katherine was leveling her shotgun at me. Her eyes looked a little vacant as she took in the white underbellies of the creatures around me. For a second, I did not believe she knew who I was.

Proving me wrong, a glimmer reignited her eye. "Oh, it's you! Good god, I thought you were dead."

I hauled myself up on the stones and stood on the sand a good distance from her. Haldis had disappeared. I did not speak.

"Is it dead?" Katherine inquired, her eyes on mine.

I spared her the vague statement meant to clarify what death was to otherworldly beings.

"No."

Chapter Fourteen

When I first woke up, I thought I had turned into a yara-ma-yha-who. My head pounded, which would have been fitting if I'd been swallowed and regurgitated several times. My body felt wrong, like an arm pulled and pinned the opposite way it was supposed to go. What really sold it was that my skin was painted a flakey, unnatural red.

The truth didn't really hit me until after I rolled over on my bed of leaves. My groggy eyes opened to the morning light, blinking away the pain it caused my unadjusted pupils as I felt foliage in places I'd never felt it before. Sure enough, my only covering was my newly reddish skin.

I scrambled up and out of the warm sleeping spot so quickly I miscalculated and slammed my spine into a tree trunk. Ignoring the small burst of pain, one of my hands flew up and tentatively poked the surface of the opposite arm. A shower of rust-like dust floated down to the ground. A strangled little sound escaped my lips as I began to claw furiously at the browning red, knowing what it was.

The second my nails hit my flesh I flinched and covered my ears with my hands. I looked down at my arm, incredulous that there were no gouges on it. Surely I had torn something after a ripping noise that loud?

No, the skin was not adding any more color to the mix. I scrubbed my arms carefully, wary of the hideous tearing sound it was making, like someone ripping a pile of wet leaves in two. I was getting nowhere. I could *feel* the stuff seeping into my skin, tainting me. I could never remove enough.

That's when I noticed I was being watched.

The scraping sound of nails on skin had almost eclipsed my other senses, but they came back to hit me like a bomb. All at once, so many scents flooded me—warm and rotting and light and damp and coppery: so many so similar, so many so conflicting—that I began to wretch.

I gagged and gagged into the bushes, leaving a suspiciously pinkish paste. All the while, I could hear something above me: breath sawing in and out of lungs. An intruder waited impatiently, its scaly feet scratching back and forth over the branch it was perched on.

An ink black raven watched me with matching colored eyes. When it opened its mouth to caw louder than a gunshot, its tongue matched the color of my arms. A ruby gem. I leapt away from the noise, landing closer to where I had woken up. The ground underneath me squelched.

Then, my skull started to buzz with the droning of a thousand flies crawling in my ear canals. I slapped at the empty air around me, eyes closed in fear, before I covered my ears with my hands. It didn't matter. I could hear my heart pounding along with tens of hundreds of tiny muscles thrumming around me. I wanted to *scream*, but I couldn't take the noise, fear clogging my throat.

I dug my palms in harder and gasped at the pain it caused my skull. My eyes flew open, to see my hands—away from my head—were glossed with a fresh coat the same color as the flakes on my arms. As I watched and began to hyperventilate, the skin of my fingers was crawling up to cover a darkening nail. The nail itself was changing shape, elongating and curving.

I hid them under my legs, but that turned out to be the biggest mistake yet. With them tucked away, there was nothing to hide what was in front of me. That, by far, was the worst thing I could have seen.

There *were* flies. Many of them. But they weren't there for me.

They were swarming the bloody pile of bone and hair.

Raven hair to match the raven in the tree. Hair I knew very, very well. Jessica's hair. And if the hair was hers then that meant the skull with the flesh partially stripped off of it was hers and—oh goddess.

My chest heaved rapidly as I stared at the empty rib-cage. No lungs, no heart. Everything eaten. Consumed. Some of the patches of bone glowed yellow, like they'd been licked clean. One of the bones in her forearm was still pinned back by a pair of handcuffs looped around a young tree. It was the only place on the body that had any sort of meat left.

What sort of monster could do this? I shrieked silently.

The raven left his perch with an earth-shattering flurry of wings and landed near the corpse. It did not partake, but looked at me with its black eyes. Accusing. My vision got eaten by black dots like hundreds of those condemning eyes, swallowed until it was a mere pinprick and all I could see were feathers like oil.

I screamed then, wild and hoarse and unrestrained. I screamed until my throat constricted, until it was only a raw, heartbroken gasping.

Jessica, oh god, Jessica. Please no. Please. You can't. Fat tears poured out of my eyes, blurring my vision, but not enough to obscure her prone, skeletal form. Not enough to give her any semblance of life. I choked on nothing, almost grateful when the force of it doubled me over, taking the body out of my sight. Hyperventilation left me lightheaded.

I looked back up, my vision doubling. For a second, I saw two bodies side-by-side, one decomposing. My heart tore, the wounds from Jeremy's death merging with this new damage.

Even in my despair, I could tell the stretching feeling in the rest of my body was not just my emotion.

I could feel other things constricting, shifting. My skin felt like it had been run through a cold wash and shrunk. My teeth felt too long and my tongue felt too large. The insides of my eyes squirmed like I was looking into the sun, and the colors began melting away from the trees within my panic-restricted sight.

I knew what was happening. There was no way I couldn't know. The second my vision faded to black, I'd be consumed. The beast that had killed my Jeremy was there. The beast that had killed Jessica. It writhed inside of me.

No. *No, no, no! I can't let it out, I can't let it win!*

My fingers no longer felt like fingers under my thigh. It was progressing like a time-lapse of carcass decay, crawling, morphing, and taking over inch by inch. I could feel my canines stretch to greet each other. My irises bled out like a growing pool of divine ichor.

I knew that even a seed of moon magic, silver, or simple *desire* would throw me into an instant shift. All the changes taking place were like the stretches before a sprint. They were *nothing* compared to what was coming, but they made me feel like the world was closing in around me. I was losing it.

I stood up, heaving air into my lungs with greedy gulps.

The bare skin of my arms, puckered with hair standing on alert, rubbed a frigid rock face behind me. I flattened my slightly warped palm flat against it, the cool surface reminding me of the feel of Haldis' golden hilt.

The thought helped to center me, but was also accompanied with a bout of nausea. I pictured my eyes a molten gold all the way through rather than just the lupine iris-ring. I tried desperately to ignore all my senses, to shut the hypersensitivity out. I imagined wings spreading out of my back, ready to take me away from this cursed body. It didn't help. I felt feverish. Sick. Diseased.

I took a chance. "It's okay." I spoke to myself, instantly regretting it when it cracked like a beat of thunder and I pressed my exposed back up against the stone.

I tried again, softer. "I'm okay."

I held myself stiff as a rod, not moving a muscle other than the ones that were slipping around inside of me. I turned my head to the side and was sucker punched by the scent of...moss. Something I had never actively smelled before.

Without looking, I gathered a handful. I used the wet, absorbent material to start scrubbing at my arms more forcefully than I needed to. My panic was reduced from hysteria when the blood started to come off in small droplets, but the elevated beating of my heart spoke the truth my mind attempted to cover.

Pitter patter pitter patter, the blood said as it fell to the ground. My arms took on a greenish tint, but it was better than red. My little drum stopped beating and took up again, but at a slower rate. My nails stopped piercing through the damp mass, steadily retracting.

I felt like I had been burning in an inferno only to be

247

thrown into arctic tundra. The first few seconds of pulling inward—of retaking the form I'd held for seventeen years—was exactly the relief I craved. My body hummed with contentment, despite the chaos in my mind.

Then the frost set in as my mind cleared. I felt a deep numbness take up residence in my heart, pumping through my veins and into my extremities like the worst of drugs. I'd shut down. Shock, guilt, whatever. It was done.

I didn't know what had happened to my emotions, but I didn't particularly mind in this state either. I found myself wondering if the wolf had eaten my heart, too, but then I realized it didn't matter. That abused thing would only slow me down.

I could see the disaster my silver-and-moon induced rage had caused in all of its glory. Buzzing flies slid over broken bones, tasting desperately but not finding much substance left. The wolf had consumed all of the accessible flesh, leaving long, bloody trails where large chunks had been separated and chewed on.

Blood covered everything, but the deepest score marks in the bone marrow, where fangs had crunched deep, were drowning in the substance as it pooled and coagulated in the crevasses. The black hair was the most intact feature of the corpse, for even the skull had seen the wrath of jaws. There were holes in it where teeth had punctured straight through tissue and bone near the eye socket and temple. It looked like it was in agony with its detached and split lower jaw.

I was glad for the numbness as I saw a neglected pink and silver phone a few feet away from the body. I walked over and picked it up, carefully avoiding treading on sharp remains with my bare feet. The cracks in the shattered screen had been filled in with flyaway fluids from the attack.

I pressed the on button to no avail, as I expected. The thing was dead, and out of reach. Whoever had left Jessica here wouldn't let her text someone. The placement of it, within eyesight, was a cruel joke.

Maybe she would have texted me. Well, the good news was that I came. The bad news? I think that part was pretty obvious. I stood, staring at the mass of clothing, bone, and hair in front of me, never having been more grateful for letting my feelings disintegrate and then freeze over. It let me think without experiencing.

Experiencing was the last thing I wanted to do. Ice shard firmly in place, I walked toward the rising sun.

I could feel the pinch as something small and non-physical was pulled from my body to remain in that cursed place, under the watchful gaze of the raven.

Despite the rigidity of the ice within me, my body felt weak. Frail, the opposite of what I had been led to believe a werewolf should feel. Every noise, every scent, every sensation had me leaping out of my skin. I wished to trudge forward blindly, but my perceptions had never been sharper.

And yet, I still felt sick. Sick with the residue of what I had done, maybe, but it felt like so much more. Like my very blood was rebelling against me. I leaned against trees, using them as crutches as I moved forward. The view of the world was shaky, just like my limbs.

It almost seemed like it wasn't my muscles that were causing the problem. They worked fine, if not better than fine. As I pushed against a cliff face that I had been leaning precariously toward, it groaned and shifted within like I had taken a bulldozer to it.

No, I felt like I had when I was fourteen and was in bed with the worst flu I'd ever known, aching and exhausted. Except this was worse than that. My whole *being* felt heavy, like I could just sink into the earth. Every time I startled, the world would fly off of its rotation and I had to fight to keep from keeling over.

Inside, deeper than my organs, it felt like my soul was getting swirled, mixed with something foreign. It was too heavy for me, too volatile. My eyes rolled around listlessly, no longer seeing.

Then, just like that, I was no longer Atlas.

I hadn't done anything. I swear. The feeling of eminent demise just sort of...*Poof.* Magic trick.

Not going to lie, I was not ready to jump up and click my heels, but the remaining strain was bearable. The weight of this planet had been replaced with the weight of just one plump dragon. I could handle it.

I swayed a little, like kelp on a calm day, but I managed to walk straight. I didn't notice my surroundings until I was ankle deep in a creek. It was a very nice creek, if a little cold. I bent down to examine it rather than extract myself from it.

The sudden urge to sing struck me as I watched the water rushing over the stones at the bottom. I gave in because I had no thoughts to spare in order to stop myself.

"Took me down to the river—"

In a clearer eddy, I could see a little of my reflection.

"So I could drown, drown, drown—"

Without a clear color distinction, I looked like I had just rolled in the river sediment, nothing more.

"Looking up through the water—"

My voice broke a little as I started to wash away the filth

I'd missed, coating my face and chest and shoulders and hands...

"I kept sinking—"

With my face and arms clean, I was finally brave enough to face my reflection.

"Down—"

My eyes flickered: blue gold blue gold blue gold.

"Down—"

They settled on blue, but a blind person would have noticed my lack of humanity at this point.

"Down," I whispered, my words swallowed by the chaos of the silent forest around me.

Katherine was whining again.

"How can you be so calm? Shouldn't we be doing something right now, you know, like kicking some demon butt?"

I sighed, looking at her with eyes a false human shade. "We should not be doing anything. It's too dangerous for you to remain here."

Before the sentence even ended, Katherine was speaking, something she did very frequently. "You've said that before! I've told you, I'm here to stay. You couldn't get rid of me if you tried."

I could, very easily. And the more she talked, the more I considered it.

I spun from the railing I was leaning on, fixing her in my gaze. "Katherine, this is a multi-dimensional war. Heaven, Hell, Earth...Others like me have been able to contain the demons for centuries, but the tide is turning. Elementals, spirits, angels, Protectors, demons...The balance is slipping, and once it is lost, this plane will become a living nightmare. You must understand. You are not risking death. Death is guaranteed. You are risking the damnation of your soul."

Katherine hesitated for a second, and it wasn't difficult to see my long exchange had rattled her, as was my intent. Then, she opened her mouth, with less fire in her tone. "You think I can go back? Knowing what I do now? Just walk right back into some town and plop down and have my two-point-five children, never having it cross my mind that somewhere out there, there is a family just like mine being torn to shreds?"

No, she could not do that, any more than I could. She was too far in, and my futile efforts to spare her were not making progress.

She continued. "Besides, when I'm alone, that demon is never far. The mountain lion."

My gaze, which had looked beyond her, drew back to her face. "You've seen the Rashtka before this? Besides when you and that boy were attacked?"

She shivered, but passion occupied her heart, not ice. "Everywhere. It's at the edge of the woods, by my door, looking through my window...When I woke up and found it at the foot of my bed, I knew it was all starting again. I can't take it anymore. Trust me, going with you is safer."

My mind circled, puzzled. "For how long has this happened?"

She seemed eager to tell me. I surmised that it wasn't something she'd been able to say freely before. "It used to be a different thing. Much less substantial. It blended into the shadows, before that one night...."

The night when I'd found her in the woods, possessed and tormented by a corrupt spirit.

I informed her of such. "Right. The spirit I tore from your soul."

"A spirit? Not a demon? As in, a dead person?" she asked, confused.

I nodded. Like a switch had been flipped, she deflated. "Oh."

There was darkness in her past, it was clear. But my job was to combat the darkness in her future. "Is it still after you? The Rashtka?"

"That's why it was on the beach, but when it saw you it deviated. Why else would I go on a stroll armed?"

If it was true, I could not abandon her to the demons. "I will allow you to accompany me, as long as you promise not to attempt to run over a demon with an ATV again."

It took her a second to understand I was speaking light-heartedly. Once she did, however, she broke out in a grin that displayed two deep dimples on either side of it. "Hey! I thought that was badass!"

The memory concerned me, though. "Do you have other means of fighting demons? While impressive, the arms and the quad weren't particularly effective."

Katherine's fair cheeks heated as she twisted a strand of her hair. "Yeah, about that...How about you just get me one of those light saber swords?"

Whatever reference she was trying to make was lost on me. "An angelic sword can only be possessed by a Protector."

Katherine's hand dropped as interest reached her eyes. "And how many are there? Of the swords and the Protectors?"

It was a question I had not let myself dwell on, for answers were unobtainable. "I do not know. Perhaps there are dozens. It is possible it is just Haldis and I. I do not seek answers to questions that do not further my mission."

253

Katherine raised an eyebrow at me. "What a bundle of joy and free spirit you are! We'll need to get you a sense of humor, pronto. But first, how about some weapons that work? Any idea where to go for those?"

My chest kicked, a thump and a draw very familiar to me. The pressure built, urging me into action as gold danced outward from my heart. Katherine noticed immediately.

Her fair skin turned ghostly. "Umm...Please don't smite me? I swear I was just kidding."

I backed up a few paces, judging the angles on the dock we stood on. My wings materialized, a congealment of light almost opposite of shadow. "Don't worry, we don't have enough time."

"Time for wh—" Katherine screamed when my arms slid under her shoulders and I leapt, taking to the sky so quickly that anyone without a trained eye would have missed it.

Her shoe, a slim, flat-like thing, missed the railing by a few inches. I needed to get better at calculations if I was going to fly with a passenger again.

She didn't stop screaming, not even to close her mouth to keep bugs out. When she finally did cease that truly horrendous noise, it was to curse me and my ancestors. I was impressed by how creative she became with compound swears, muttering words with meanings I could not comprehend nor did I want to.

At the top of a nearby building, I slowed and put her down. Her short hair was in wild tangles around her face, complementing her shocked expression. It seemed she had run out of words. Her gaze trailed down the edge of the apartment complex, slightly glazed. Finally, she shook her head and looked at me.

"Just...Why?"

My head whipped around, knowing what was coming, but finding nothing. "Something is here. A demon. I believe it is after—"

What felt like a burning wall impacted my back, throwing me over the roof's edge. Katherine's angry shout followed me down as I spun, disoriented. I flared my wings and my descent stopped, but I heard scrabbling noises and a sharp yelp from Katherine before I could regain any altitude.

Something whistled as it fell, and I immediately soared upward to meet it. My eyes didn't register until it was too late that it was not Katherine who had been launched off the roof, but a dog-sized black form. It hit me square in the shoulder before I could readjust my path, and we both went down. I rolled on top, but the impact with the ground still made my entire being feel bruised.

I heard something snap, but sighed in relief when I saw the sound was made by Haldis cracking through the ribcage and shoulder bone of the lizard-like demon below me. Its acidic gore bubbled out over my fingers, hissing as it met angelfire. The creature evanesced away, and I rolled off its corpse before I inhaled too much of the toxic substance.

I craned my neck to see the top of the building, shielding my eyes with a free hand so I could see the figure watching me from above. Gravel bit into my palm as I lowered it, pushing myself off the ground. I looked again, just to make sure it wasn't a mistake. I shook my head.

Katherine was smiling.

"Sorry about that! I guess I'll have to aim a little better next time I kick a demon off a roof. Hey, you okay?"

I returned her smile.

Chapter Fifteen

"And where have you been, missy?" My mother's scalding tone washed over me as I exited my room, thankfully donning some clothes.

I didn't feel the hot rush of shame that those words normally inspired in me. I shrugged. "I felt sick, so I stayed over Luke's. I told you I was headed there, remember?"

It was the only plausible explanation. He was the only friend I had left. Although maybe not any more, since I was a monster. *Poor Luke, he tried so hard to protect me,* I mused. In the end, nothing could save me from myself, my own stupidity.

My mother blinked furiously while I stood immersed in my thoughts. She didn't realize how far away my mind was, how she'd have to cross over seas of writhing darkness to get to me. I was a midnight island.

"You could have just called your father or me. We would have picked you up. I don't want you spending the night at a boy's house, Leah," she argued. The words echoed in my skull like a song you enjoy, but with the bass all the way up. Vibrations that should be familiar, but meant next to nothing.

"Everything is fine. It won't happen again." At least I doubted it would. I didn't quite remember what had happened until I had woken up, but the animal instinct slowly raking its claws down my brain even at that moment was an indicator that it hadn't been pretty. I realized then that I didn't even know if Luke was alive, let alone if he'd cover for a nighttime excursion on my behalf.

I was surprised when vehement hope rose up and claimed my consciousness, temporarily thwarting the cold. I needed Luke to be okay. *What if I...?* But soon enough frigid waves pushed that thought from my mind. The hollow word reverberated in me. Dead. Luke could be dead.

"No, Leah. It's not. I understand that you've gone through worse things than anyone, let alone a teenage girl, should suffer. That's why I've been trying to give you a little breathing room. But, that doesn't mean you should turn to sexual impulses to—"

I leapt up, no longer able to ignore my worry for Luke. And what about Eren? What happened to him? He was just as much of a threat as I was. If he had hurt Luke...

My eyes started to glow, so I turned them away from my mother, who was still speaking.

Quickly, I found my cellphone. My mind overlaid its image with another phone, the screen shattered and filled with blood. I shivered as my hand curled around it.

Six missed calls, four of which were from Luke. Seeing his name on the tiny screen wasn't enough for me, however. I needed to hear his voice, just to know.

He answered my call on the first ring. His voice agitated and unconstrained. "Leah?"

I hung up and slumped against the bedpost. Relief flickered through me, before I realized how insane it was to be relieved you had not killed your best remaining friend. Jessica's corpse appeared in my mind's eye, and then a phantom image of Luke's followed it. The image of blood-

257

soaked manacles around the tree trunk was burned into my mind and my fingers itched again over the phone. I should call the police. Tell them…What?

Tell them that I'd stumbled across her in the night? And then, when they find my DNA all over the place, hell, probably even in the wolf's saliva? 'Oh no, I didn't chain her there, officer, I just killed her?' No, I couldn't. I swallowed once, hard. I shook my head and pieced together my blanket of numbness, succumbing once again. I didn't feel my mom's hand on my shoulder.

There was a squirrel on the front porch. I could hear its nails clicking on the treated wood, but quietly enough that I would have been able to block it out of my mind if I hadn't focused in on it. Like a clock's second hand. Now that I heard it, it was there to stay.

Then, everything shrieked. For the nth time, I flinched and hit the wall hard enough that my head banged it after my shoulders had already slowed me down. My mother's cool, soft hands wrapped around my elbow with surprising strength and pulled me forward, my supposed sexual digressions forgotten.

"Are you okay? Oh my god, you are burning up!" she exclaimed. I winced and wiggled my surely bruised elbow. The pain of it had faded by the time I finished with my exaggerations. Unnatural.

Another icy palm was on my forehead. "You really were sick. Go, take your temperature. I might need to call the doctor."

The home phone was still shouting. I lightly pried away her hand. "I'm going to get the—" *hideous screech machine, then throw it out the window with a tankful of gasoline and a lighter*— "phone."

I rushed to the kitchen, snatching the phone from the glossy black counter. The caller ID made my shield of numb crumple like a raft with a cannon-ball sized hole in it, though it felt more like I was descending into fire than water. *Jeremy's cell.* I fought desperately to regain my icy composure, but though it was not completely gone, it was in pitiful condition.

My voice hadn't even been slightly disturbed from the running, but it sure as heck was as I answered the phone with a quick tap. My finger sank through the edge of the plastic phone, smashing the casing. Thankfully, it still worked. "Hello?"

The voice on the other end of the line was equally breathless. Air puffed into a speaker held too close to a mouth, but it wasn't the voice I'd been simultaneously hoping and dreading to hear. "Miss Leah?"

The way my body reacted with both affection and fear at the same time was almost comical. Too bad I wasn't in the laughing mood. "Benjamin, are you okay?"

"I need your help, Miss Leah. He won't leave me alone." Of course he wasn't okay. Couldn't *something* be okay for once in this nightmare?

I could feel my resolve hardening inside of me. I'd make things okay, at least for him. "Who won't leave you alone?"

His voice quivered. "Please come. He's so scary now."

Ah, the man in the closet. This, I could handle.

"I'm coming, Benjamin. Give me ten minutes."

The waves of fear radiating off of him were palpable through the phone. "Quick, Miss Leah!"

I took the stairs three at a time in my haste to get to the next floor, then realized I had just done that with no effort and turned around to stare accusingly at the steps. It totally

259

was their fault. Not my problem that they'd been replaced with very deceptively stair-looking trampolines.

But that raised the question: what's real and what's myth with the werewolf thing? I was going to have to start a list. A secret list. I didn't need anyone reading it and sending me to the looney bin.

Werewolf things I know to be true item number one: Werewolves exist.

Or maybe they don't. Maybe everything was just a huge hallucination. *Brilliant. Great start to my list,* I thought as my car crunched gravel in Jeremy's—or, I guess, Benjamin's—steep driveway. Poor pebbles. I wondered where they wound up once my wheels ejected them from the hill.

I fingered my new and modified bag of tricks. I'd added Jeremy's EMF, but removed a depressingly large amount of silver items with a pair of tongs. I wasn't risking anything when it came to Benjamin's safety.

And besides, I was hoping this would be the same deal as before. I'd show up like a knight in psychic armor, vanquish the probably-not-real bad guys, and save a kid from nightmares. It'd be nice to have something be just play for once. Nice to be the hero.

I watched the windows as I approached the house, wary. I had a strong suspicion that Benjamin had called me without his parent's permission. One curtain in his room fluttered, but it wasn't pulled back. Another in his parent's room flickered with lights, possibly from a TV. Melinda's was still. Jeremy's window was only a slit from this angle. I was glad I didn't have to view its dormancy.

Unless I hadn't imagined a flicker of black behind the tiny piece of glass I could see. But, despite the way my heart thumped like someone had struck me with a drumstick, I knew that was too good to be true. I quieted my mind.

The front door was unlocked and soundless as I pulled it open. I was equally quiet as I snuck up the carpeted stairs. I had been right, there was a TV perched on what little I could see of Benjamin's parent's nightstand. It was on mute. A happy-looking soda commercial was flashing across the screen, full of smiling people on a beach. It was so outlandishly joyful that I didn't know how anyone could connect to it.

As I crept further, I could see that there was a foot hanging out from the crumpled brown blanket on the bed. Whispers carried, almost imperceptible. Just one word, over and over: No.

Something wasn't right.

I got up on tiptoes and approached Benjamin's room, surprised when my feet practically placed themselves. I made no sound, but there were also no sounds to cover me.

I couldn't hear any noises except for breathing coming from all rooms. The frantic whisperings had died off. As I approached Benjamin's room, I could tell his breathing was erratic. He'd draw in a few breaths deeply and evenly, like he was asleep, but then a few would clump together like he was hyperventilating. I ran the rest of the way, throwing caution to the wind.

I ripped the handle of his door off. I really didn't mean to, but I was left with the cool metal and a clump of splinters. I wielded it like a weapon. As I walked in, a strange rotten, salty smell bloomed around me. The room was cloaked in shadow, but I could see by the trickles of light snaking under the windows.

Benjamin sat so straight it was like someone had hooks in his spine. Papers and salt were scattered around the room like a hurricane of knives had blown through. I stepped on the faint crystals as I walked closer. Benjamin's head did not turn from the dark recess of his closet, a place where not even my enhanced eyesight could penetrate.

"Benjamin?" I called, softly. My voice sounded like a whisper to even my ears, like the darkness had the muffling quality of snow on sound.

He must have heard me, because he spoke. His eyes did not leave the dark, shifting void in the closet. "He's been waiting."

I stared at Benjamin, unnaturally still for anyone, let alone a young boy. "Who has been waiting?"

Benjamin's gaze finally shifted, tracking something creeping slowly toward me. My sight started to narrow like I was going to faint, but only on one side: the side Benjamin was watching. His eyes came to rest over my shoulder, glazed with an unsettling amount of white. His mouth opened, but he didn't answer me.

My heart thumped harder. "Benjamin, *who* has been waiting?"

A breath tickled down my neck, raising gooseflesh. A cold gust made my hair sway. The *swish swish* noise it made was louder than it should have been. Benjamin was staring at the area just above and to the right of the crown of my head. His neck was bent at what must have been an uncomfortable angle, but still he said nothing.

I was too close to panicking. I attempted to clamp down on it, to limit the potentially dangerous results, but fear bled into my voice when I repeated my question once more.

"Benjamin, *who has been waiting*?"

262

His shoulders convulsed, once. Then his eyes finally met mine, but devoid of any recognition. His mouth opened, but breath tickled my earlobe from behind me.

"I have been waiting."

I jumped, actually hitting the ceiling with my scalp as non-human strength coursed through my veins. I landed behind Benjamin and instinctively wrapped my arm around him, protecting him from the thing that filled the area I had vacated.

Benjamin was still once more, though I could feel how franticly his pulse was fighting. The thing—the swirling of darkness upon darkness, like smoke in the nighttime sky, only visible by the light it absorbed—stood before us. My hand fluttered behind me, a moth beating desperately against a street lamp.

I found light in the form of ripping an entire shutter off the window and throwing it at the darkest spot in the room.

For a second, I thought the daylight had saved us. Like in all horror movies, the bad things were limited to the dark. The only shadows that were left were Benjamin's and mine, twin and ash grey against his radioactive green carpet.

As I watched, his shadow bled out, growing darker and darker as it deviated from its host's form. Benjamin vibrated softly in my arms, but not enough to explain what I was seeing. His shadow split in two, one elongating to take a form I knew very, very well. Even without the features.

"No," I whispered, more to myself than anyone else. I could feel my eyes burning, simultaneously brimming with tears and flickering lupine gold.

Jeremy reached out a shadowy finger like he was going to touch my cheek, but stopped short just inches from my face. I felt a deep tugging, like my energy was being drained straight from my body. I fought the urge to wilt like a dying flower and hung onto Benjamin even tighter. I was scared I was going to hurt him with the force, but not a squeak escaped his lips.

Jeremy's form became more substantial. Familiar contours began to shape his face, but still I could see the closet through him, warped and haphazard. I remained frozen, wishing that my insides would abandon their tumultuous raging and mirror that rigidity.

It didn't happen. Jeremy dropped his hand quicker than my eyes could track and his head began to slide, ever so slowly, off-kilter. It was not cocked in questioning, but no longer able to support itself on the measly bit of smoke and bone left on his neck. He stared at me sideways, a rough mouth drawn in either anger or pain.

Don't let this be him.

A whirlwind of noise enveloped the room. Every electronic turned on instantaneously: the lights flickering and then blowing out as too much power surged through their circuits, the EMF in my bag started screeching full volume from behind me, a game console near my feet turned on and off and on again, and a compact alarm radio sent static and snatches of speech into the already charged air.

That same radio began to filter words like a ghost box.

"What...have...you...done...?" it screamed, never ending. *Done, done, done* repeated over and over, growing louder and louder.

I spoke with the most minuscule movements of my jaw. "Jeremy?"

The shadowy form was on me in an instant. His hand slid through me, through my chest, and I collapsed. Benjamin finally cried out and left his post as I convulsed on the floor, blind and terrified, but it was too late. The dangerous spirit was crawling through my veins. I was breathing him in with every inhale. There was no escape.

All I saw was darkness. All I *felt* was darkness. My physical sensations were split from me as my body became the vessel for another soul. I could not move, could not speak. I was trapped with this creature of darkness.

And then, I began to see things. Not Benjamin's room, not anywhere I'd been before. Deep, swirling vortexes of ash and smoke took center stage. Shapes emerged from within the stampede, jumping, running, fighting. They all converged on one unseen point in the center of the madness.

Then I was it. Right in the middle of the blitz, I was the only being of light. The fury bit with jaws I knew well and tore and ripped and *hurt*, yet when desperate fighting tried to pour out from my own being, the balled fists and flailing limbs I could see were not my own.

In fact, I was no longer sure I was myself. Through the hurricane of torment, I could see a girl standing just outside the chaos, lit from within. A weak, pulsing light held in check by the physical body, but a light nonetheless. Anything was a better sight than that prison of teeth and claws.

Relief flooded through the soul I knew then was not me. The vision of the girl that looked suspiciously stubborn with her chin raised and her hair flowing out behind her. The image clicked. That was me, and in that moment I was watching from none other than Jeremy's vantage point.

I wanted to cry. Jeremy, sweet and lovable and carefree, was trapped in this prison. *My* Jeremy, suffering for *my* mistakes. My carelessness. And yet, I could feel the spark of hope igniting within him at the sight of the other me.

His elation dropped sharply as something happened to the version of me we were both watching. Bottomless dread rolled through him in waves, pushing me out and back into myself with the force of it. So, of course, it was then happening to me.

I could see tiny wisps of a light, airy substance obscuring the tiny aura of light around me. It poured out of my chest, growing thicker and thicker with each heartbeat. It did not linger in the air, but rather fell down like a stream of water to pool at my ankles. After a few seconds, the buildup of smoke took shape.

A terrible shape. No wonder Jeremy had felt such betrayal when he saw it forming. It was exactly the same beast that made up the whirlwind of jaws around him, exactly the cause of all his suffering.

Next to me, tethered by a leash of smoke, was the wolf.

It was not one from the ring of teeth surrounding Jeremy, but my own. The chord connecting us pulsed with the thoughts of a foreign mind, but not a bloodthirsty one. The wolf eyed the scene in front of it with mild interest, then sat back on its haunches and opened its mouth in an exaggerated yawn.

This creature, which wasn't forced to submit to the moon or silver at the moment, was an entirely separate being from the monster I had witnessed—had *been*—prior. A current of rage swirled through me at its apathy.

The wolf leapt up as if it had been electrocuted and snarled, but it was not aimed at me. No, the wolf was snarling at Jeremy's captors, same as I was. The wildest, most reckless idea crawled out from the depths of my brain, aided by the aggression flowing from the wolf.

It was the only option I could live with.

I bolted straight for Jeremy's obscured form, straight into the spirals of teeth that looked like leaves of ash. Instantly, I was scored with dozens of claw marks raking down my flesh. I may have screamed, but there was no sound to be heard over the storm.

I struck out, my fists hitting like they were underwater. Every blow I landed was matched by two I received. Every time I managed to make a small pocket of safety in the front, a snarling, phantom wolf would rip into me from behind. I was experiencing Jeremy's own, personal Hell on earth. Every second since he had drawn his last breath, this had been what he experienced. Blinding pain and reliving the worst thing that had ever happened to him.

My hands dug deep into the flaky fur of one of my attackers, a sensation surprisingly real. It disintegrated into dried, bloody powder in my hands, but not before I managed to throw the beast as far as I possibly could.

Once it got more than a few yards away, it vanished. The darkness swallowed it and did not let go. The gears in my head started to turn. The wolves here were nothing if they were not close enough to Jeremy, which meant one of two things: these creatures either fed off his energy or they were products of his own soul's turmoil, a violent and physical representation of the trauma he had experienced.

A bite to the back of my knee delivered me onto the cool, nondescript ground. I struggled desperately, kicking out to no avail. When jaws grabbed my ankle, the thought of what would happen to my body rumbled through my head. If I were to die here, would the rest of me lay comatose? Wither away?

My ankle was released only so fangs could come for my

face. I kept my eyes open, staring at the shiny obsidian eyes of the constantly shifting mass of nightmares. My muscles coiled in anticipation of one last battle.

The wolf leapt.

And was thrust to the ground in a roiling cacophony of snarling. My wolf, a creature I realized was much lighter in color than the others, had entered the fray. An ash-like substance flew instead of fur and streams of blood were curling tendrils of smoke as the two moved in a frenzy of almost untraceable movement.

Other wolves turned away from me to circle around the fight and snag whatever bits of flesh they could. They howled and yipped, destroying the suffocating silence of this plane. I scrambled to my feet, shocked to find that the places where I had been bitten did not contain bloody puncture marks.

Though I knew without a doubt it could be done, it would take a heck of a lot more to bring me down when blood and flesh weren't there to betray me. Where teeth had gripped me, there was only a fading pain.

Then again, I couldn't exactly see my skin. Sight was not the dominant sense in this place.

I found myself wishing for Haldis. That blade...These wolves wouldn't stand a chance. I'd save Jeremy in a matter of seconds, and then everything would be all Happily Ever After.

I mean, not really. But it'd be better than this.

I kicked one of the roughly canine-shaped outlines on the edge of the circle, spinning it out of place. It leapt at me and I ducked my head and braced myself as we collided, a confusing mixture of hard and soft. I pushed forward, arresting its momentum and sending it flying. It tumbled through the air and disbanded with a burst of shaded night-time before it hit the ground.

Paws hit my back and I went down hard. Before teeth could sink into the back of my neck, I twisted around and kicked the beast in the sternum with both feet. It flew up with a solid *thump*, but never came down. Above me, it unraveled and stretched to match the black of the sky above us, painting over the stars that could have been.

It hadn't gone that far up. That shouldn't have been outside the sphere in which the nightmares were thriving. My head swiveled wildly, taking in the changes occurring around me. My wolf panted as it rose from a dust devil where chunks of obsidian turned to ash and floated like cherry blossoms in the wind.

And Jeremy...He was running. A full-tilt dash away from us, dissolving wolves in his wake. Only the fastest were able to keep up, yet it seemed the proximity to him that gave them their substance was slowly becoming insufficient. One wolf, realizing this, nipped at his ankles before planting broad paws on his legs. Jeremy fell and the remainder of the wolves descended on him.

My wolf and I bolted after them at speeds I had not known were possible; covering the ground like it had contracted in front of us. Fear and determination boiled in my heart, and I was sure if I could feel it beating it would be at a pace quicker than my own footsteps.

From the wolf, there was the predictable rage, but it was tainted. Through that chord binding us, I could feel my surge of protectiveness transform into the wolf's own possessiveness. It wanted to kill the wolves attacking Jeremy.

I was down with that.

Within milliseconds, we descended on Jeremy's attackers. I jumped straight onto the back of one, while my wolf growled behind me, all the hairs on its back raised, warning others off. I was knocked to the ground, but I rocketed back up and pushed it out of range, thankful I did not have to breathe in the resulting dead embers in the air.

Two to go, I thought as I stood up. A blast of still-sharp bits caught me in the face, a sudden explosion. I raised my arm to shield from quickly deteriorating pieces and glanced under it, too wary of a sneak attack to block my vision for long.

There was no need to worry. Only two forms stood there, still shifting in the aftermath of adrenaline: Jeremy and my wolf. Both eyed each other, but neither made a move. They were polar opposites. Jeremy's dark coating was melting off of him. He was obscured by a veil of gold while my wolf was painted in shades of grey and silver.

"Leah?" Jeremy called. He sounded confused, like he had just awoken from a dream.

Well, I guess the opposite was closer to true. He'd been living a nightmare. "I'm here, Jeremy. Are you okay?"

He embraced me, though the interaction was more emotional than physical, without a second thought.

My voice was soft, barely audible, scarcely able to believe this gesture of affection was real. "But I got you killed."

Jeremy laughed, a sound I cherished every second of. "Hardly, unless you secretly put a steak in my pocket to lure that wolf."

All of my emotions swam together, overwhelming me, but for the first time in a long, long while, bits of hope and happiness were undeniably present.

I didn't give in just then, knowing full well Jeremy was treating me far better than I deserved. "But—"

Jeremy backed away so I could see his fluid form more clearly. "Leah, that wolf could have killed you just as easily as it did me. I'm just glad it was me, and I'd do it all over again to keep you topside."

I blurted out the truth, unable to hold it in any longer. "I killed Jessica. On the night of the full moon. I didn't mean to, I don't even remember it, I just woke up next to her and there was blood everywhere and I just couldn't... Jeremy. How could I?"

Jeremy shook his head slowly, not looking at me. Words poured out of my mouth, burning like flames. I didn't even know what they were, just that they were so foul I knew that they'd consume me. The icy barrier I'd put between that horrible day and myself crumbled.

"And I just shut down. How could I be so calm? She died, Jeremy. She died and I didn't do a thing for her. I just left her there, in the woods she hated. Because I killed her. She can never leave that place, because I killed her. The silver, the moon, I shouldn't have—"

"Leah," Jeremy said, but I didn't react

He tried again, his voice soft. "Leah."

I was so swept away, I couldn't hear him until he shouted, his harsh tone cutting through the darkness.

"Leah! Enough! It wasn't your fault. I've learned a thing or two in here, and a wolf influenced by both a full moon and silver should have killed a whole town, not just one person. You had no control. Am I happy she's dead? No. But it could have, and *should have* been so much worse. And, now that you've helped me out of this, I can go find her and do the same for her. It's okay. Everything's okay, Leah."

I choked on my next words. "How could it be, Jeremy?

271

I'm a monster. I might…I might hurt someone else. I couldn't take that."

He shook his head. "A monster doesn't come running to keep a young kid safe from the boogeyman, Leah. You're too strong to give in to this. And, I think that wolf is just as stubborn as you. I know you can beat this. You won't hurt a soul."

I walked toward him my arms extended; hoping beyond what I knew was possible that he was right. His kindness tore away at the ragged, cutting edges of my darkest thoughts, smoothing them down until they didn't continue to infect the others anymore. They would never go away, but they remained nestled in the deeper recesses of my mind.

As Jeremy drew closer, I noticed I was starting to squint. The dismal black backdrop of the place we were in was fading ever so slowly from black to grey, reflecting the light coming from Jeremy's form. Soft. Comforting. I'd needed this.

I'd needed him.

"What's happening to you?" we chimed simultaneously.

I scrunched my forehead at him. "Me? You're the one who's all glowy-glowy."

His voice was enough to make me smile. "Says the spotlight to the lighter."

I rolled my eyes. It felt good to do it again, so natural. In the most unnatural setting and the most unnatural form I'd ever been in—what was that form, by the way? Just my soul, bound to the soul of a wolf, still connected to my physical form? *Eh, good enough explanation for me*—Jeremy still managed to make me feel at home.

Well, except for the part where I felt so dang *stretched*,

like a chord beginning to fray. I started to speak, but was cut off mid-word by a strange numbness of the mind.

I rubbed at my face with the palm of my hand. It looked so foreign in the dim light that I held it out in front of me and wiggled the fingers slowly, methodically. They were much brighter than they had been when I first got here, but nothing remotely similar to angelfire. I didn't realize I had zoned out until Jeremy's voice was right in my ear.

"Leah? Can you hear me?" he asked frantically, his tone making it clear that he had asked multiple times without getting a response.

My eyelids fluttered. "Mmph."

That confused me. I had planned for words to come out.

"This isn't right. You aren't supposed to be glowing like that."

Like what? I wondered. *I'm lit up less than* "you," was all I was able to get out in my protest.

Jeremy scoffed. If I could have seen his eyes through the gold haze, they would have flicked dramatically up and then to the corner before catching me again. "I'm dead. You know, the opposite of undead? It doesn't count."

I was glad he continued speaking, because I was not capable of hearing the entirety of his speech, let alone producing my own. I felt adrift in water, inconsequential in the waves.

"Oh, crap. If this is me, without a body..." My hearing trailed off, though I could tell he was still talking. "You'd be more like me..."

Jeremy jolted suddenly. "That'd mean you're dying. You stayed here too long."

I was glad he figured things out. I wasn't really caring at the moment, though. Some of the tension was starting to release. It felt nice. I was ready to be free.

Jeremy's hands gripped my shoulders, momentarily stunning me to the point where I actually looked at him, instead of the faraway area over his shoulder I hadn't realized I was gazing at. "You need to go back."

My gaze slid again, but this time with a purpose. The light was so bright. I spoke, just one soft, confused word. "Where?"

I think something was moving behind him, but I didn't recognize the fact. Jeremy was pushing on my shoulders. I was sinking into the ground like it was quicksand.

Except this was no regular quicksand. Everywhere it sucked at my ankles felt electrified, like it was shooting me with sparks. I squirmed, desperate to get away from the almost-painful sensation, but Jeremy kept on pushing me down.

When the electricity reached my waist, I started struggling for real. Jeremy, who was on his knees, effortlessly pinned my arms with his hands.

I was swallowed by the ground. Static raged inside my body, a raw *sensation* I did not want. It took my head and my neck, but just before I submerged into the increasingly uncomfortable spikes, I heard Jeremy clear as day. "Go. Tell Ben I'm so sorry and that I love him and Melinda. I'll miss you, Leah, but fighting life makes about as much sense as an amoeba entering a jumping jack competition."

And those were the last words I ever heard from Jeremy.

Katherine's second flight was better than her first, but not by much.

274

Luckily, the location was nearby. The flight only lasted a few minutes, but at the speed I went, I had to call upon the air Elementals to create a protective sphere around Katherine, so she could catch the breath needed for all that cussing and screaming.

The area I was called to was boggy, the type of place where houses floated on water full to the brim with mosquitos. I found the only piece of damp land—the rest could only be considered wet—and set Katherine down as gently as I could.

She still fell to her knees, heaving as her short, spiky hair swung to cover her face in small knots. "A little...warning... next time...please..."

I was already moving away. "Remain in place. I have to take care of this situation. I will ask the elemental spirits to protect you."

Katherine stalked after me like she wanted to follow, but her foot sank into mud so deep that she had to crawl backward to retract it, minus the shoe I'd worked so hard to save. I was gone before I could see her reaction.

I engaged the Elementals under my breath. "Spirits of water and earth, I ask for the protection of the mortal I have brought. If you do this kindness unto me, I shall do the same unto you, as has been our way."

Even though I was flying, I saw the clouded water leap up at me. Spinning in greeting. I nodded my head in silent gratitude as my wing tips glided above it, a few powerful strokes landing me where I needed to be on the deck of one of the floating homes.

The smell was ripe, a living thing that wormed its way inside of your skull and refused to leave. Swamp, blood, and sulfur smells wound hand-in-hand, none overpowering the others. *Already I could see the stains that were not mud on the wooden slats of the deck, so I didn't hesitate to enter, kicking the door off its hinges.*

The house crawled with unnatural shadows. They oozed off the walls, gathering in corners and doorways, watching. They shrank away from the angelic fire like a mist blown by a fan, but I had no doubt they would be lethal to humans.

The body in the corner proved it to be so.

As I spun, careful never to leave too many of the shadows in my blind spot, their cold fingers raked across my cheek. It was only then I knew what I was dealing with. These were not demons.

These were the Corrupted.

The humans targeted by the demons, twisted beyond recognition. They'd all been killed once their souls harbored enough hate and vengeance to keep them substantial after death, malevolent beings with the same purpose as the demons, but not nearly as focused. They killed when the desire struck them, and the desire never quite left. They were exactly what that spirit and the Rashtka were trying to make Katherine.

I lifted my blade, bright with ocean-like waves of fire. "I can offer you freedom from the evil churning your souls."

It was not life, it was not even afterlife, but anything had to be better than this existence. Even a non-existence. Oblivion and peace instead of rage and madness.

The things produced a whispery, shriek-like noise, like the beginning thrums of a cicada's wings. They pushed closer, growing bolder. Then, all at once, they rushed by me to exit through the windows and walls of the abode. I swiped at them with Haldis, but felt no resistance as it contacted those trailing behind. Some ignited in a quick flash of gold before disappearing, never to haunt nor roam again.

I was out the door before I heard a cough, a deep, wet sound. I raced back inside and found the man in the corner on his side, blood trailing out of his mouth in thin lines. Stress lines aged his haggard face, and his situation was making his tanner skin go gaunt. Unable to leave him, I appeared in his corner and laid my hand on his chest, sensing the weak galloping of a heart underneath layers and layers of a pulsing darkness, an infestation of the energy the Corrupted were emitting.

I didn't have enough time to heal him properly, but I could fend off the writhing mass of spirit inside of him. My hands pressed quickly, firmly on his chest as I projected angelfire into him, leaving as he gasped and began to draw clean breaths. I wanted to do more, but I recognized that the threat was still real and time was of the essence.

The Corrupted had not drawn me here, despite their cruel acts. Only a demon could do so, yet I had not laid my eyes on one. It must be at the center of this chaos, further in. My wings snapped out as I leapt over water to reach another of the swamp cabins, the air around it spinning on itself as if it were a scorchingly hot day.

The angelfire around me hissed and was pushed tighter to my skin as I entered the tumultuous aura of the place, the atmosphere so laden with the Corrupted that it was like moving through oil, thick and unforgiving. Up above, wings rustled as carrion birds watched and waited.

There was no need to break this door; it was flapping back and forth from the Hell within. I hit the ground running, Haldis' hilt strong in my hand. There was movement to my left and without a thought I slashed, scoring the demon across the chest.

The demon, some scaled creature that vaguely resembled a dragon, reared back its long neck, burning. Its demonic flames canceled out my own before the wound became fatal. I slashed again, two quick swipes, causing it to roar with fury, shaking the household. The sound almost hid the scrabbling behind him, claws on the wood.

The dragon lunged, its great fangs revealed to be as long as my hand and as thick as my wrist where they were covered by gums. Haldis flashed backward rather than forward, finding purchase in a demon's hide behind me as I ducked to avoid a frontal blow from those huge teeth.

I rolled away, straight into the carcass of the monster that'd snuck up from behind, which slowly broke off and fluttered away as if it were a collection of freed moths. Those moths burned on contact, but I stood my ground. I raised Haldis in front of me, not as a warning, but a promise. This demon would not do harm to another mortal.

My feet planted on a counter behind me and I launched above the beast. Haldis raked over the obsidian scales on its back, producing a hissing noise. The second my feet landed on either side of the dragon's long, prehensile tail I drove Haldis down. It found purchase in the dragon's softer flesh. Gold began to shine under the scales, but the fight had not yet left the creature.

The tail thrashed and hit me so hard I flew back up over its head. The wooden wall embraced me with a painful crunch, the sound signifying a wound fatal to humans. My vision was consumed by gold as the angelfire worked furiously to heal me, but every second lying prone, useless, was another second wasted.

Another demon, its form indistinct, slithered forward and lunged, lightning quick. I moved weakly to the side, but *it wasn't enough. The fangs came for me, dripping acidic venom.*

Then the beast rolled across the floor as a lung-sized chunk of rock hit it square between the eyes. I pulled myself up enough to see Katherine in the doorway, mist and dust swirling around her like she was a woodland faery.

Her face scrunched in distaste. "I hate snakes."

I drew myself up using the fake-tile counter, fearing for a second that I would fall from the weakness in my limbs. "And I hate demons."

The earth Elemental that had allowed Katherine to throw the heavy stone with such accuracy was causing swamp plants to bloom around her feet. It seemed it had taken a liking to her, and from the amazed smile on her face, she to it.

Still, I couldn't shake the feeling that something was terribly wrong. Not with Katherine, but the situation. As I gathered myself and walked painfully toward the serpentine demon, it became apparent. The Corrupted, the demons... Nothing in this place warranted such an onslaught. In fact, the humans in this house were upstairs, unharmed. I could hear them whimpering.

I dispatched the demon with a downward stab, Haldis sinking into the floor without leaving a scratch. A dark chasm opened, as it had done with the ursine demon. The snake was pulled forcibly through the rift, fire consuming it. Sparks flew down, like insects to a light. Then, in the blink of an eye, it was gone.

I forced my limbs to move, as jerky as puppet strings. "Katherine, there are humans above us. Keep them safe."

At first she looked honored to have a meaningful task, then she raked her assessing gaze over me, finding my well-being less than satisfactory. "I'm pretty sure you aren't in any shape to fight demons. I'll come with."

I shook my head, the movement sending shooting pain down my extremities. It was likely I had damaged my spine on impact, but both the Elementals and the angelic flames were rushing to undo the damage. Haldis needed me whole to continue fighting the battle. "Upstairs. They cannot be left alone."

I spread my wings quickly, testing for weaknesses. When I found none, I headed out the door. Katherine had realized she could not stop the inevitable and raced up the stairs to help the traumatized residents.

Outside, the Corrupted blotted out the sky. I flew just feet off the ground, trusting the celerity of my wings over the unsteadiness of my feet. Despite the haziness that covered all my eyes could see, there was a coalescence of darkness just ahead, standing out like a beacon in this newly grayscale world.

Up in the trees, a flock of ravens shifted and murmured like starlings.

From where I stood, I saw that earth and air Elementals were fighting vigorously to reclaim the huge black birds. The Corrupted were overpowering them from sheer number. It was so wrong to me, the perversion of something I had always held constant. The ravens, always so cunning and glorious, were being possessed by the essence of this world's impurity.

I realized then what I was seeing, the magnitude of this atrocity. A convergence of the Corrupted was capable of wearing the Earth thin, layering it with the despair and darkness needed by the demons to rise. These souls were taking to the sky as I realized this, infesting countless hosts to spread their forces to every corner.

The demons were coming. So many, in so many different places. Each bird before me was the slaughter of another town, the conversion of a hundred souls to darkness and the eradication of a thousand. The horrors I had witnessed would be nothing in comparison.

And I was utterly helpless to stop it. Haldis cut through the Corrupted, but it was like trying to scoop oil from the ocean with a pencil. Ineffective, pointless. My movements grew frenzied, only hastened by that knowledge.

My heart sank in my chest as the shadows began to clear, not from Haldis, but because the spirits were successfully possessing the ravens. I took to wing, desperate. I struck out at the inky birds with Haldis, willing to try anything. The spirits inside burned when the angelic blade hit them, leaving the bird a shell, empty. Before I could turn to the next, more Corrupted had filled it.

All at once, on some silent signal, the ravens leapt from their perches. Ebony wings spread far, darkness in every direction.

A ruby red tongue flashed as long, dark feathers brushed my cheek, not pausing as it sped forth, from whence it came.

Chapter Sixteen

Werewolfy list item number two: Lycans and cereal do not mix.

If you ever wake up with super strength, do yourself a favor and *do not, under any circumstances* try to make yourself a morning bowl of cereal.

Cereal is supposed to make the day less miserable. And, in my specific case, supposed to distract me from the fact that I still hadn't talked to my only friend. It does not work that way when the ceramic bowls are being inflexible wimps that shatter the second you pick them up. Then you've got shards in your hands and on the floor and No. Stupid. Cereal. to show for it.

Okay, I got my cereal eventually, but not until after the shards were pushed from my hands by swiftly-regenerating flesh. I may have also broken the milk container and then left the house in a storm of frustration.

It was raining outside, light enough that an umbrella felt unnecessary, but heavy enough that I was thoroughly damp within a few minutes. Walking felt infuriatingly slow, so I took up a jog. My sneakers squelched against the dirt road, then grass, and then leaf detritus as I moved along, not focusing on where I was.

My pace was a steady rhythm, one that easily combined with the music of everything else around me. My breathing was even, lungs not struggling to keep up with the rigorous pace. It was unusual for me to be able to run for so long, so I paused after my silly frustration had died down.

I found myself in the woods, but it was far from the spots I told myself I would not revisit. As much as I loved the forest, I doubted it could clear away the taint of what occurred there. And, despite the pain, I found I didn't want it to be swept away. Some things deserve to hurt.

Rain droplets fell in bucket-sized clusters above me, waiting until they gained enough allies before they jumped from interfering tree branches. They straightened my hair with their weight and dyed it darker.

Most noises and scents were obscured by the symphony of rain, almost enough to make me feel normal again. The remainder, however, were enough to convince me that was not the case. Muffled scratching, shuffling, and even a tiny, far-away snatch of human speech were audible from my location a decent way into the pines.

But senses aren't all there are to a werewolf, are they? I wondered, already forming hypotheses. Ideas popped into my head, bright and tempting. I *really* wanted to find out what I could do...Without wolfing out, of course.

Would it be that dangerous to try out human-werewolf mode? Wouldn't it be better to get rid of any surprises away from people who could get hurt? I'd made up my mind. I was going to nail down everything I needed to know as soon as possible, so there would be the least amount of...accidents.

I could not ignore, even with my teeny, cautious bead of optimism, the truth that I'd use that silver bullet before I'd allow the wolf to hurt anyone again. *This*, I thought, *is so it does not come to that.*

Of course, the easiest way to learn the secrets of the

werewolf would be to contact Luke. I didn't know whether to be concerned or relieved by his silence in the days prior. What did he think? Did he guess as to the horrible things I had done that night under the full moon, despite the fact that anyone but me who'd witnessed it was dead?

Was he afraid to see just what sort of monster I'd become?

So I was on my own. In the woods. Chained to a monster. *Or maybe not a monster, I mean it did help me save Jeremy...*

No way could this go wrong. None at all.

"Let's do this," I said to no one in particular.

Distorted senses were a definite. I didn't have to focus to hear a little girl talking a thousand yards away, nor the partridge working through the brush. I could smell so many things, secrets the forest hid in its shadowy corners. It was like suddenly being able to taste the air. Everything held a new, exotic scent. Even birch, which I could always recognize with the old sniffer, smelled foreign.

I held my palm up to the light. There were no wounds from my cereal mishap, not even the slightest, pinkest line. This I had to check out, rapid healing could make a heck of a difference and possibly even expose me. Although, when I thought about it, about the only person who would have believed I could grow fangs was me. The crazy one. I shook that from my mind and focused on the task at hand. I found a rock, unwilling to do anything that could be unsanitary. No palm slices for me, only a quick bruising.

I turned the cool stone over in my palm, finding the smoothest side. Once I got that, I nailed it into my calf bone. I let loose a small "umph'" at the impact, then waited. The pain fled in a matter of seconds. The area tingled, a bad itch, before settling down. Nothing. No discoloration, not even a tinge of red.

"Well, that's useful. I think," I muttered.

"Pretty sure it's not healthy, though," said someone behind me, voice thrown by the deluge.

Without thinking, I whirled and chucked the stone at the source. It whizzed like a rocket before missing the person by a hair and exploding a section of a poor, defenseless tree on impact. *Holy deities, I could have just killed someone.*

And then, of course, the rotten tree decided to fall on the both of us. Again, instinct had me leaping away. One push carried me over yards of brush and sticks; wind flicked my hair over my shoulder. It felt like flying for a brief moment.

Then I touched down, two solid feet planted on the ground and a hand for support. A perfect landing in my book: my feet didn't even smart on contact with the sodden earth, and the mud I kicked up flew behind me, not on me. A small thud sounded near me before the huge, splintering crack of the tree brought silence to all else.

I spat out of my mouth the hair that landing had thrown in my face. I stood up and came face to face with someone I definitely hadn't been expecting, despite the scent winding through the air. Unfortunately, he'd dodged the tree, too.

"Why are you here?" I barked, slightly angry that he had caused me to almost kill myself by almost killing him.

Eren eyed me appraisingly. "I guess there's no doubt you're a wolf. You reek."

I rolled my eyes, surprised to feel how harsh the motion was. An angry jerking rather than a soft-hearted gesture of affection. I could see what he meant, though. The air spun with his decidedly lupine smell.

I crossed my arms over my chest. "I wouldn't be talking,

furball."

Eren raised his dark eyebrows. "I like it when you're feisty, Kitten."

His scent was infuriating and his words rang as loud as an avalanche in my ears. I couldn't stop my mind from whispering the word that now applied to both of us. *Murderer*. Instead of grief, anger flared strongly. Even as a human, I could feel a growling growing inside of me, a fierce need to dominate. From his stiff posture, I surmised he felt it, too.

It didn't stop the smug grin from pulling at his lips.He stepped closer. Despite the cold and wet, he wore a dark t-shirt. "Aww, don't be like that. Is that any way to treat someone who came to help you?"

I wanted to step away, but the wolf would not accept such an action. Instead, I took a small step closer. My personal space bubble moaned at the intrusion. "I think I have it handled, thanks."

Those were satisfying last words. I spun on my heel, loving the finality of the *crunch* of leaves under my feet.

I didn't make it a yard before Eren called out, "I know you killed someone."

I froze, mind and body. "Now Luke, he thinks you fought the wolf. That you, in all your innocence, are still the sparkling angel you've always been. He doesn't want to think his first friend in months could...Well, you know where that goes."

I focused on my breathing, not the failure weighing down my chest.

"I know it's not true. I know what it feels like, Leah. Under the moon. With silver burning in your veins. There is no fighting."

I shook once, a quick spasm. A weakness. A confession.

I raced to cover the slight, bristling. "I still don't see why I need you, puppy dog."

Eren ignored my lame attempt at getting a rise from him. "You need me to stop you. Might feel okay, now that the moon is waning, but the second it grows full again your wolf will writhe inside of you." He paused. "Then it'll be outside."

He didn't make some sort of crack, and the smug grin was gone. He was serious, and I couldn't help but believe him.

Feeling like I was making a demon deal, I cleared the terms. "What exactly do you propose?"

His stance was of a strange type, simultaneously slouched against a tree yet looking as rigid as a golem. "I'm just offering help."

Help was something I could sorely use. Anything to prevent another tragedy. However, I could throw Eren farther than I trusted him, even without the werewolf strength. My consciousness stuck on this point, but it was barely an issue. Lives came first. I just had to know what I was dealing with.

I was in a state of disbelief. "That's it? No strings? You aren't going to call this in like a faery favor later?"

Shiny white teeth glinted at me from the shade of the pine. "You see me sticking around you long enough to do that? That's sweet. Really. I'm touched."

"Listen up, you cocksure canid—" I held up a hand to stop his complaint about my phrasing. "If you screw me over somehow, I will kill you."

I can, right now, some part of me whispered. I wasn't sure if it was wolf, human, or some blend of the two.

Eren never stopped smiling. I got the sudden mental

image of chipping those gleaming teeth with my knuckles, but stored it away before it could do any harm.

The incorrigible wolf winked at me. "Looking forward to it."

Then he spun around, walking away without waiting for me to follow him. If he thought I would trail behind him like a lost duckling, he was sorely mistaken. I put on a quick burst of speed, much faster than I had known I could run, and caught up to him.

My hand darted out to meet his shoulder, but was met with...Nothing. A flash of color and he was gone.

I stumbled briefly, losing my footing but failing to go down. I arrested my momentum and stood there, confused. Teleportation was not a skill I'd known werewolves to have. I gave a tiny inhalation of surprise when I realized my error a second too late. No teleportation here.

"Really, Kitten? I thought better of you," that cocky voice said from above me.

The hem of his shirt flapped like the wing of a frantic bird as he jumped down from the branch he was perched on. Little pieces of bark rained down on my head from where his feet dislodged them. I didn't know whether to be impressed by or pissed off with how high he'd jumped. I chose the latter.

I glared at him. "If you keep calling me kitten, I will jump rope with your intestines."

He clapped me on the back, overly hard. "That's my girl."

I bristled with the urge to yell that I was not his *any-thing*, but settled for hoping I'd morph into Medusa so my eyes could turn him to stone. No such luck.

Eren turned away. "Come on, let's see just how wolf

you are."

He ducked under a low-hanging branch and loped forward at a slow pace. I took delight in watching a teeny-tiny spider drop from above and crawl on his shirt, unnoticed. I gave the brave arachnid a curt nod of respect.

I took in air that was tainted with trace amounts of exhaust. The woods were thinning. For some reason, Eren was leading us into the town center, the only part of this area that had two buildings within fifty feet of each other.

My brain whirred as I verged on sensory overload, suddenly surrounded by too many sensations to process, even with the drizzle softening them. My skin crawled with discomfort. The wolf, who was far from sleeping, did not want to leave the safety of the woods.

I paused, hesitant to push myself further yet completely confused as to where the boundaries were. I hadn't fully shifted at Benjamin's, despite the copious amounts of stress pumping through my veins. There had to be more to it than that.

But what? I was in the dark, and that was not a fun place to be when the topic was yourself.

It was hard, so hard, to disentangle my mind. I didn't know where I began, or even if there was any untainted *me* to separate. My thoughts were rimmed with an ever-present primitive edge and my emotions were so screwed up I didn't want to touch them without a shotgun.

Maybe it was bad I felt I needed a shotgun. Maybe I just needed anger management classes and a squeezy stress ball.

I doubted it.

I supposed that might be normal for someone who recently lost one friend, then murdered another.

Helping Jeremy move on hadn't absolved me from his

death, though his kind words had helped lighten the load. It had, however, made me question how truly evil the wolf was. Kill one, save another...It seemed more like the laws of nature than any sort of demonic possession.

Still wasn't forgiving it. Me. Whatever.

I froze slightly before the town came into sight. "Have you ever purposefully shifted outside the moon?"

Eren stiffened, his posture somehow displaying exactly what he was thinking before he said it. Venom infused his voice and posture. "Do I look like someone who is okay with murdering on a whim?"

I scowled, then tilted my head just slightly. I wanted to snap at him for his scathing tone, but I couldn't stop my memory from dragging me away from the current situation. I wasn't going to risk it, not even close, but I wasn't sure the wolf was all that feral outside of the moon's pull. I could remember feeling its calm and seeing its pink tongue loll out as it yawned.

Eren grabbed my shoulder, bringing me right back to him. "Don't even think about it. I don't care what you are hoping. It doesn't have a soul. You don't have one anymore. Do not ever consider shifting on your own."

I bared my teeth ever so slightly at the direct command, then under his assumption that my soul was lost. Who said I believed in souls? Maybe I thought people were run by tiny, chained Mothmen flapping their wings next to wind turbines in a person's chest.

I shrugged my shoulder from Eren's grasp just as he was releasing it. The guy wouldn't shut up. "Don't be ridiculous."

Simultaneously, both of our eyebrows drew together.

"How did you—" I started as he said, "Wait, did you—"

My turn first, otherwise we'd talk all over each other

and get nothing across.

"No, I didn't say any of that. What did you hear?" I questioned, my eyes widening as the possibilities trickled through my brain. We'd had a one-sided conversation that we'd both fully understood without even thinking about it. *Oh my spirit guides, you've got to be joking me.*

Eren swore loudly enough to startle a few squirrels. "Undo it. Undo it right now. I am—" more swears, "not going to—" the expletives were getting truly colorful now, "*telepathy* with—" a sailor would feel inadequate at this point, "*anyone*, let alone you!"

I just smiled at him, one of those awkward, overly-innocent, I-have-no-clue-what-you-are-talking-about smiles. He gleaned my meaning and calmed down. "It's not that, is it?"

My turn for orders. "Turn around and tell me what I'm thinking."

He wanted to argue, but he could tell I wasn't doing it for kicks. I was serious. Didn't stop him from grumbling as he turned his back.

I pulled up a vivid picture of a manananggal trying to belly dance. Poor things. Torsos are required for that type of activity.

Eren cracked the knuckles on one fist. "This is stupid. How am I supposed to know...Oh."

I grinned, but neglected to tell him he could turn around. I liked him better when I couldn't see his face. "Exactly. If telepathy were involved, not only would we be hearing specific thoughts, but orientation wouldn't matter. I've got a theory."

Eren's composure slid over him like a shadow as he turned around. "Don't keep me in suspense, Kitten."

I choked down my annoyance. "Wolves can't speak, Eren. I think we're just talking the way they do. Reading body language and translating it into emotions, intents, and very simplified thoughts subconsciously. It might work that way with everyone, but then again, it might just be us, with our altered gestures and behavioral patterns."

Eren looked like I had taken a flounder out of my pocket and slapped him with it. Actually...He didn't really look it. I doubt anyone other than his closest friends or relatives would have been able to pick up on the slight shifts in his facial muscles. Even if Eren tried to dispute it, I knew my theory was correct. Unfortunately, I was not observant enough to pick up naturally on anything but the most exaggerated gesticulations.

I spread my arms. "Come on, Eren! Don't be dull. Tell me what I'm feeling. I'm an open book."

He squinted at me, drawing back slightly. My brain translated that to mean he was slightly overwhelmed by what I was proposing and wholly uncomfortable. Sucked for him. But, because he was thinking it, my mind ran down the same track. I held as still as possible, willing myself not to betray how suddenly itchy I felt in my own skin.

Eren's lupine grin was back in place. That kid fed off fear like it was his only sustenance. "Well, right now, it seems you're jumping between cockiness and...What's that? The infallible Leah feels wariness? Embarrassment? Ooh, and a little deeper? Could it be...Oh."

He quieted. He'd found in me exactly what I was seeing in him, the only constants to the emotional roller coaster of the werewolf. The grief, the self-hatred, the guilt. The things that don't leave you. Ever. The things that can be unseen but never unfelt.

I gritted my teeth and pushed forward, surprised to feel the slight burn in my eyes. I was not going to cry. I refused to. Eren did not pursue the subject.

I reached the edge of the town and was surprised to find it had changed. I supposed I was the source of all the differences, but it was still disorienting. The vintage clothing store had never smelled so strong. Decaying garments might as well have been dancing around me, along with rubber from all the soles of the hiking boots in the nearby wilderness shop.

A few people bustled about, despite the weather. A girl a little older than me was walking a tiny dog with a pink bandana wrapped around it. An elderly couple ambled leisurely with one oversized umbrella covering both of them, the older man's cane clicking loudly with each step. A mother held the hands of her small children, twin girls from the look of it, which made her stoop over so that her spine was at an awkward angle.

It made me realize I hadn't seen people in forever.

Actual people with actual lives. Amazing. I wished I was kidding when I was taken aback by how normal everything seemed. I continued down the steep slope that led to the only paved road in the town, drawn eagerly.

Eren walked beside me, but disapproval flowed off him in waves. He didn't think this was a good idea at all. I guess his genius plan had been to stick to the wood line. Deep down, I agreed with him. It was reckless and stupid to bring two wolves so close to potential victims. I just...I just wanted to absorb some of these people's normalcy. Just to feel a little again.

I gave in. Everything whirled and magnified within my head, almost infuriating, but things started to rise to the surface. Every couple of steps, the puppy's collar would jingle especially loud as it jumped up and down in puddles. When the elderly woman reached out her hand, her husband accepted it with a quicker heart rate and a comfortable smile.

I neared them all, taking it in with long strides. Wind spiraled around me, stirred up by my clip but unusual for the calm day. I was about to walk past the harried mother and her two daughters when I froze, stock still. 60 to 0 in 0.2 seconds.

If Eren had been human, he would have slammed into me. As it was, he managed to halt enough where his shoulder barely brushed mine. I fought the urge to shake it off as I processed why the alarm bells were ringing in my head.

Just quiet enough for the family not to hear, but noisily enough for me to want to cringe, Eren spoke. "What's wrong?"

I finally was able to put my finger on it when I saw the toddler in the black dress stumble ever so slightly, using her mother's hand for support. "I think there's something wrong with the girl."

Eren flared his nostrils. "She smells weaker than the rest. More reason to leave."

I was insulted at his lack of trust, but it was quickly off my mind. "No, don't you smell that? It's getting stronger. I think we need to do something."

Eren shook his head and leaned backward. "I don't know what you're talking about. We need to go."

I pulled on my sense of smell, willing it stronger and letting a teeny-tiny bit of the wolf push forward to do so. I wasn't leaving someone who was injured. Not if I could help.

Out of nowhere, Eren grabbed my arm and shoved me against the brick side of a nearby store. "What, are you stupid? Don't you get what you're doing?" he growled, clenching his teeth.

My nose scrunched as my upper lip pulled back. "I just wanted to make sure she was okay! I did nothing wrong."

His hand was still on my shoulder, squeezing tight. "Don't lie to me. I know exactly what you were thinking."

I was about to yell that he didn't know crap, but he was right. He could read my intents in my body language. It'd be excruciatingly difficult to lie.

I angrily pushed his hand away. "Do that again and I will claw out your eyes."

I was also going to rip off that ever-present grin. "Anything you desire, Kitten."

I strode away from his hold for the hundredth time that day. That kid had a serious touching problem for someone so antisocial.

I strode up to the woman leading the sisters. Unsure what to say but determined to help somehow, I spoke.

Luckily for me, even though I hated myself for thinking that way, the girl in the black dress stumbled again, briefly.

"Oh!" I exclaimed, actually a bit surprised. "Is your daughter okay? She looks a little pale."

I was about as smooth as a burr, and the mom picked up on that. Her eyes hardened as she glanced up at me, wary of ulterior motives. She pulled the twins closer to her sides and spoke quickly, roughly.

"She's fine, dear. Thanks for your concern," she said, a polite dismissal.

But she wasn't fine. Almost before her mother finished the sentence, the girl collapsed. Her tiny shoulders thudded against the ground and her arm was wrenched upward by her mother's hold. Her eyes rolled back into her head.

Each thud was a bird hitting a window.

The mother was on her knees, shouting. Then, so was I. Except I was shouting into the mother's cell phone, which I had jacked from her pocket.

911 was on the other end of the line. "Hi, yes? Seizure, send help—"

With less than a second's hesitation, Eren was next to the girl.

He ripped a long chunk from his dark-colored shirt. The sound of it was lost in the commotion. Crumpling it into a ball, he shoved it into the side of her chittering mouth. The noise of her clanking teeth stopped.

Eren explained though I didn't ask. "Stop her from biting her tongue."

Then he rolled her onto her side, careful to make sure most of her mouth was open. Fluids passed through, their scent extremely foul.

The mom was trying to hold her girl still. Eren lifted her hands off. "Ma'am, it'll be over in a second. You don't want to hurt her."

Eren did want to. The lines of his face, though downturned, were tainted by the strain of an internal dominance match. His wolf wanted to devour the weak child. Eren wanted to help.

Mine was edgy, adding thoughts of hunger and flesh to my mind. It was not overpowering, just present in an uncomfortable way. Images and suggestions from an invisible voice. *Why?* I wondered.

It was not the time for wondering, not when yellow was flickering in Eren's eyes.

I grabbed him and drew him up forcefully, casting him behind me. I motioned for him to stay and added a flash of teeth as a warning for the wolf before taking his place, though the girl was no longer convulsing. The ambulance could not come quickly enough as Eren paced predatorily behind me.

It came, causing spectators to scurry away like it was an akaname with its tongue lolling on the ground. EMTs rushed out and loaded the girl on a stretcher while her head lolled weakly. They buffeted her mom with questions as she was lifted into the ambulance, but got nowhere as she was doing the same in turn. With the girl safely loaded, I grabbed Eren's wrist.

"Go," I commanded, and we sprinted away, up the street. From behind, I tugged on him so we would move at a human speed rather than a lupine one. Within seconds, the trees embraced us, casting their shadows over our backs like a loving parent wrapping their coat around a shivering child.

Both of us put on a burst of speed, and I couldn't help but feel exhilarated despite the dire situation. I had *never* run this fast before, even though I'd thought I'd hit the limit this morning. My legs' pumping produced a delicious tension. I felt like if I just leapt up, I'd soar. Those big, golden wings would shoot right out of my back.

If only my sins didn't weigh me down.

I stopped, and so did Eren, despite me not telling him to do so. His normally dark eyes were growing lighter as lupine genetics flooded his own. The tension rolling off him was palpable, as was the reversion of his thoughts. The shift wasn't stopping, and that was freaking him out, which was pushing it forward. A vicious cycle. He was going to lose.

The sound of my voice surprised me. "Hey."

Eren looked at me then looked away. I knew he was close to the breaking point, and after that the actual transformation would take about as long as the blink of an eye. Right now, he was fighting it, but I could tell he held no hope. He expected to wake up coated in blood. Maybe mine. His eyes shone with torture.

He swore suddenly, then shoved his fist through the nearest tree. It shuddered and moaned when he extracted his hedgehog-esque hand. The pain from the splinters impaled in his fist didn't seem to ground him any more than the sluggish trickle of blood from the already-healing wounds.

I held back my wince at the appearance of it, leaking blood. "You could have killed a tree spirit right there."

Eren growled, low and inhuman, "I could have killed anyone in that town right there. I could still."

He swore vehemently enough that even the trees flinched. I debated how to proceed as the well-defined muscles in his arms twitched, either from the impending shift, nerves, or a combination of both.

I took on a more casual, relaxed posture, as if I wasn't looking death in the eye. "You may think I'm nuts, but I wasn't deceiving you earlier. I honestly think that outside of the moon or silver, our wolves might just be...wolves."

Eren didn't seem like he was paying much attention, but I continued to talk anyway. "A couple of days ago, something happened that I can't really explain or validate, but it gives me hope. I think hope is something the two of us desperately need."

I still got no response. Eren paced in large loops, sometimes in my sight, sometimes not. When I didn't see him, I never lost his location. My ears tracked and recorded it with almost no effort on my part.

I kept at it. "I'm not saying we should take unnecessary risks, especially when the cost is so high, but, come on. We, as once-decent once-human beings, cannot function if we're free falling into the chasm of self-hatred. I doubt the wolf knows what to do with such complex emotional input. The things are probably confused out of their minds."

Eren's loop carried him in front of me, frenzied energy following him like the tail of a comet. I snagged him, swiveling him toward me.

"Stop shifting," I commanded quietly but not without power.

Eren sneered. "Doesn't work that way, Kitten."

I stared right into the emerging gold in his eyes, one of the clearest signs he was close to breaking. "I wasn't talking to you."

He blinked, once, looking at me like I'd lost my marbles. I mean, it wasn't really that inaccurate, just vaguely insulting.

"Calm down. There is no urgency to this situation. No threat or prey you need to take," I insisted.

If I thought it was safe, I would have let my wolf inch toward the surface a tiny bit. Maybe that would get the point across better. But no, I was not enough of an idiot to make possible the worst case scenario: two rampaging werewolves. It'd be like unleashing the apocalypse in this dormant town.

Eren stood rigidly, but he was no longer pacing. "Eren, you can't push open a door someone's pushing from the other side."

He flashed his teeth, but not in a menacing way. "Application, Kitten?"

Huh, he was learning. At least 56% of the things I said had an application to the situations in which they were said. *Good dog!* I praised in my thoughts, aware even that was pushing it with this whole reading body language thingie we had going on. Thankfully Eren was distracted enough not to notice my tease.

I spelled it out for him. "You have to get the wolf to back down."

Eren shook his head, a longer piece of his dark hair falling loosely over his eye before he angrily brushed it back up. "Impossible."

I rolled my eyes. "*You're* impossible. You two are a good match. Now just try it." *Oh crap, I just called him and a murderer a good match. I'm so dead. Bye, world, it was nice to know you while it lasted—*

Eren's voice had hints of a growl in it. "How?"

I bought myself some time with a very see-through stalling method. "I just have to do everything, don't I? It's your wolf. Tell it that now is not the time for wolf things."

Eren stilled, visible in my peripheral vision. He vibrated with energy. I was the opposite, cautiously still and attempting to radiate calm and cheeriness. I said nothing. Wind ripped the rain from the sky and threw it sideways across my face.

"Would it help if I made stupid faces at you? As a distraction?" I asked as I brushed wet hair off my neck. I didn't receive a response.

There were a few more seconds of silence, then he sighed. His eyes were his normal shade of light brown, not anything inhuman.

"I may want to strangle you," he said, "but I no longer

want to rip out your throat."

I threw my hands up in the air and wiggled them in a celebratory manner.

"Progress!"

"Jesus Christ. I didn't think a demon could just explode like that!"

Katherine paused thoughtfully. Her fingers rose to her chin as a small smile rose on her face. "Is there even a Jesus? Do you know?"

I blinked and continued walking. I tried not to let frustration seep into my tone, because it was not her I was mad at. It was the demons. Every time we would approach one of the Corrupted-bearing ravens, they'd pop up en masse to stop us from reaching it. "I suppose I don't, same with Heaven and Hell. Most of the terms I use are adopted, a succinct way to get most of the point across."

Her shoes slapped the gravel as she lengthened her stride to catch up, unwilling to run. The distance closed between us as our distance from the disintegrating demon bits grew.

"I'll never understand that. How are you not curious?"

I didn't have an answer, so I did not speak. Katherine's short hair bobbed as she turned her head to eye me, but all I wondered was when she'd had the time to dye it a mess of purple. It had the effect of making her seem like she wore an amethyst as a hat.

She sighed, the silence prodding her to speak as it did for most humans. "We need to find something I can use as a weapon against the demons. I hate being on the sidelines. I did not sign up to be your personal cheerleader."

"Nor I your babysitter."

A muscle in her cheek twitched. "Then we better find a place, and quick! But where would we go?"

I pondered this. All too soon, my thoughts met a conclusion. "I saw a cabin, once. In a field. On one side was a forest and on the other was a cliff."

Katherine raised her eyebrows. "And?"

Her impatience brought along a warm feeling of familiarity, rather than the annoyance I had expected. "The aura around it was peculiar. I'd never felt so strong a neutral radiation from a structure, nor a person."

Katherine made a 'continue' motion with her hand.

"I know not whether it contains a magic that could help, but it contains something. I don't believe it to be particularly evil. We will go to it and reveal its true colors."

Katherine snorted, then nodded as if pleased with her unladylike display. She'd have to work much harder for her actions to beset her pixie-like appearance, however. "I guess that's better than nothing. How do we get there?"

I motioned to my nonexistent wings. "We walk. A quick pace will put us there by sunrise, unless we need to divert our attention to one of the demons."

Katherine blinked three times as I picked up the pace, preparing for a long haul. Her pointer finger rose, found the rising sun, fell, then rose again. "Ah, Protector? I know time doesn't mean too much to you, but it's sunrise now. I don't suppose the place is around the corner?"

I had forgotten human stamina couldn't compare to mine, even in this form. Already Katherine's face was puckered from trying to keep up with me on her shorter legs.

I stopped moving. "No, I meant tomorrow."

Katherine panted slightly, but hid it well. "I'm going to

let you in on a little secret. It's called public transportation."

The map of bus routes looked like the spidery, black veins of someone possessed. Katherine prodded me, trying to ascertain which one to catch, but all I could tell her was that we were headed northwest. From the way she waited for me to follow up, I believe she thought I was joking with her, but I had never been more serious. Nor more confused.

Finally, she picked one out on her own and we waited, huddled at the stop. It took long enough I became anxious and wondered if we should have walked after all. Eventually, though, Katherine's savior arrived, hulking metal shell and all.

"Give this to the driver as you enter," she ordered as she handed me money.

I did as she requested, but I couldn't help thinking the overweight man I handed it to looked like time had pickled him, all lumpy and sour as a hint of the burning cigarette he held wafted around him. He promptly sneezed on the cash, spittle flying.

I turned my head away and Katherine pushed me down the aisle, ushering me into an uncomfortable, ratty seat before sitting down herself.

"You're lucky it's so early in the morning. Normally these are much more crowded," she informed me. I acknowledged it by nodding as I stared at the absent eyes of the girl on the advertisement across from me. A bus goer nearby caught my eye, revealing a male's face much younger than I had expected. His blank stare held no more life that the ad girl's had and he quickly dropped his gaze and retreated into his hoodie.

I noticed the same reclusion from the others who boarded and dispersed to all corners as if repelled by each other. Their faces were flat, their backs hunched... Yet not a single one of them was Corrupted. Just worn down by time.

"What is wrong with these people?" I asked Katherine. "They are free from all spiritual threats, yet so unhappy."

Katherine shrugged. "It's just how people are. It is early in the morning. I doubt anyone wants to be up, let alone picking up the kids, heading to work, or going to a conference."

It was so foreign to me. I'd always spent my time saving the innocent and fighting the demons, with time between lost to trance-like wandering. Not once had I imagined that those I freed or those who were untouched by evil could be so... gray.

Where was the passion? The gratitude? Why were they not content to have loved ones or jobs worthy of spending their time on?

I wanted to ask Katherine, but I had a feeling she did not know. I settled for watching the land pass me by, admittedly much quicker than it would have on foot. Katherine tried to make idle conversation with me, but I could see my attempts to be polite and entertaining were failing.

By afternoon, however, a feeling had me launching out of my seat.

Tingles rolled over my skin in waves, causing all my littler hairs to rise. I sprinted to the front of the bus and my sure footing thwarted any bumps in the road, but accidentally sent a discarded soda can flying into the leg of another passenger.

"My apologies," I threw over my shoulder absentmindedly, not bothering to pause.

My eyes were on the trees on the horizon, across a stretch of barren field when I put my hand on the driver's shoulder. "Please pull over."

He flinched and shrugged my hand off violently. "Return to your seat. The next stop is in Galbranth, another twenty minutes."

"Stop now, sir," I insisted. All those with their bowed heads decided I was more interesting to watch than their phones. Katherine slunk up behind me, but held herself low as if to duck under the stares.

"Miss, sit down!" the sagging bus driver commanded, but his voice was soft and cracked from hours of disuse.

Katherine plopped down in the nearest seat, mumbling to the older lady next to her. The elder pulled her floral purse closer to her chest. "Sorry, I really don't know her—"

I found the device that he'd moved to let us in and gripped it, taking a split second to analyze it before depressing the button and throwing it to the side. Wind whipped through the newly created cavity, even as the driver slammed on the brakes and pulled onto the fine grasses beside the road.

I didn't wait. I could feel the fingers of whatever magic lurked beyond growing weaker, and I wouldn't risk losing it.

The ground was hard and unrelenting as I rolled across it, my skin catching on thorns and rocks. The brakes of the bus screeched as I pulled myself up, not bothering to brush off the dry, clinging weeds.

A few yards down the road, there was a thump as another body hit the ground, and yet another as the bus door slammed shut. The enraged pickle slammed on the gas as he led the rattling metal can away from us.

Katherine's voice chased it. "Sorry!"

305

She hissed as she drew a breath in, examining a shallow scratch on her arm where something had snagged her when she ran out. By then I had picked up on a few things, enough to know the noise was less in pain and more as a declarative statement.

She looked to the stand of trees across the field, almost perfectly in the center. "This better be worth it. Although, I have to admit, that was a little fun—"

She cut herself off as she turned toward me. Her eyebrows pinched down. "Your arms!"

I glanced down to see I was more torn up than I had expected. Blood crept out from my forearms to my wrists. I flexed my fingers, and though it stung, I was relieved.

Katherine continued in my silence. "That looks terrible. How are you supposed to walk all the way over there?"

I tilted my head at the oddness of the question. "With my legs."

Katherine's face unknotted and a smile gave way to raucous laughter. "This is so crazy. What am I even doing?"

I drew my shoulders straight and didn't bother to mask my words with human behavior. "Currently, you are accompanying an angelic being on a quest to obtain something a mortal could use to fight against the demons. However, I will never forbid you from leaving. An ignorant life has many merits."

Katherine blinked, but the smile remained. "The way I see it, I'm here in this butt-ugly scrubland with someone who's supposed to be some heavenly big shot, but doesn't know how to get off a bus without practically bleeding to death. No, hon, you need me here."

I started walking without responding. Katherine crunched through the brush behind me, sighing and mutter-

ing under her breath when burrs made her calves look like assorted cacti. Every once in a while, a particularly resilient branch would slap at the wounds on my arms, which stopped them from scabbing.

"Do you really think it's good to leave a blood trail?" asked my talkative companion. We had drawn nearer to the pines, enough that they expanded before us, taking up almost all of our vision when we looked straight ahead.

"If anything demonic comes, Haldis will assist me. Besides, not often do they follow weak prey. They like to be the ones that create the weakness."

Katherine rolled her eyes. "What about a bear or a mountain lion? I had to stash my shotgun before we took off."

My mouth twitched. "I would fight a hundred bears before a demon."

The ground beneath me felt like it was twitching, but Katherine seemed unaffected. She shrugged. "I mean, without my gun I'd die either way, so..."

I shook my head slightly in amusement. "All right, if you insist."

I knelt down and placed my hand on the earth. The frenzied pulsing intensified, completely overwriting the usual drumbeat of the Elementals. Even the air shivered. My eyes narrowed. I tried to beseech the spirits despite this.

"Earth spirits, I ask your help to—"

I ripped my hand away with a grunt and put it on my forehead as my skull vibrated violently, scattering my thoughts with pain.

Katherine's hand grabbed me tentatively. "You all right?"

I shut my eyes, but found no relief in it. "There is some... spell work...ward...curse on this area. It won't let me communicate with the Elementals. I suspect anything more, or less, *than human is affected by something this extensive."*

Katherine knit her mouth. "Then is this the place we want to be? Isn't it dangerous?"

The forest line was at our feet. Beyond was concealing shadow. It didn't swirl in an ominous way, as I was used to. "This is exactly where we need to be."

It occurred to me that our long trek through the scrub had left us extremely visible to whomever could be concealed in this grove, leaving any stealth useless. Still, I entered warily and walked in a crouched position, which Katherine adopted.

The second I crossed the invisible border made by the trees, I felt like the vibrations stole my thoughts completely and hollowed out my insides. I did not mention this to my companion.

"Up ahead. I believe we might find what we are looking for. We'll make a grid."

Katherine nodded, but after only a few steps it became clear she was growing more distant.

"Katherine?" I called.

She paused, then drew her head back as she saw the distance between us. "Why are you walking that way? I thought you said to look ahead of us?"

"I did say that. And I proceeded in such manner."

Katherine looked down at her feet, then in front of her, where the field gleamed a shiny brown. "Why..."

She turned to face me, then started walking again. Within seconds, she'd made a circle and glided back to the mouth of the forest.

I ran after her and took her arm. She flinched when I touched her, then took in her surroundings. "Oh, crap."

"I'll lead you there," I offered. I took her hand and pulled

her in the opposite direction.

She shook her head every few seconds, but complied. "This is so weird. I feel like the world is spinning when I walk straight. This place must have some serious mojo."

In the distance, something growled before letting free an animal scream, then falling eerily silent. I broke into a run, tugging on my link to Katherine.

She tugged back. "Shouldn't we be running away from that thing?"

I didn't stop. "If it's dead, something killed it. It didn't sound natural, so something here is able to kill the unnatural. That is what we seek."

Katherine kept my pace, her stride swallowing leaves. "Did anyone ever tell you you're nuts?"

"To be honest, I've never had a prolonged conversation with a human before. Ravens were quite talkative, though, but not much for insults."

I could sense her expression without looking at her. "Just for the record, you're cuckaloo."

"Thank you?"

The rest of the conversation was cut off when I stopped short. Katherine bounced off my braced form, cussing under her breath.

She huffed out in annoyance. "That was—"

I placed my hand over her mouth to stop her words, but it was most likely too late. Our cover was long since blown.

Her head craned up to take in the house before us, a stone shack that looked as lopsided as it did abandoned. To refute my thoughts, however, a candle was lit in the single window. It emitted a thick, heady smell and spilt wax onto the salt line beneath it.

The door had an iron handle, which I approached. I

motioned to Katherine to be prepared for anything. She nodded like she understood, but I could tell from the crinkles in
her forehead that she was thinking she'd be useless against
whatever magic would be thrown at us here.

There were no steps to climb before my hand was on the
handle, which thrummed with the same over-intensified
energy that littered the place. I gave Katherine a three second
countdown.

One.

The metal was warm in my grasp, like I was gripping
another's hand.

Two.

No lock forbid it from turning as I twisted it, slowly.

Three.

Through the inch-wide gap in the door, something shone,
much too close. My pulse spiked.

"Get down!" I yelled at Katherine, all but tackling her
before she could respond. The huge blast of a shotgun blew
heated air over my back. My ears screamed and rang, but the
disorientation didn't stop me from rolling across the ground
before a second shot scattered the earth between us. Katherine did the same, except in the opposite direction.

On my back, I planted my feet and launched up, through
the doorway. The barrel of the gun was hot in my hand as I
grabbed it and pulled, met by an unbudging resistance.

It was equally surprising to me to see the skeletally thin
man on the other end, and to hear the click of a handgun
cocking before the cool metal touched my temple.

The ancient man lifted an eyebrow. He was old enough it
was yellow instead of white, yet his arms never once shivered
from holding the weight of two guns, not even with me pulling on one.

A shadow blocked out the door frame. "Easy there, tiger. I wouldn't want you to waste any more ammo missing us. That and it'd be a shame if we came all this way only to kill you."

The man's lip twitched, but I was inclined to believe it was a spasm, not an indication of a smile. "Who says I missed?"

There was a second's pause before I heard Katherine pat herself down, checking for wounds. "I do?"

He jerked his head, rapidly, like there was no time for this foolishness. It continued to amaze me how quickly he moved, and even though magic pulsed in the air, I could tell his was the hyper-vigilance of someone who'd seen war.

Katherine followed the motion of his head, where his ice blue eyes held a spot on the ground. In his gaze, a spirit Katherine was blind to withered away, its essence scattered by whatever had been in the barrel of his gun.

Those pale irises might look unseeing, but they saw much more than they should.

"Now," he said, pulling the barrel of the pistol slightly off my skin, not to let me off the hook, but to make it harder for me to shake it off now that the initial threat was delivered.

"I'm going to shoot you. These bullets are silver. There isn't much that survives them," the man told me matter-of-factly, but I was too busy trying to calculate if I'd die from a bullet to the brain. He knew I wasn't human, that much was for sure. I decided it most likely didn't matter in this scenario, anyway.

"And if I survive?" I questioned, my eyes darting to take in the rest of the room, searching for weapons or options.

He didn't even blink. "I'll shoot you with something else."

The safety didn't need to click off. In fact, I doubted it was ever on.

A wooden table cluttered with neglected papers and a meticulously marked map was just outside of my reach. Katherine saw me looking at it and stealthily approached it. If I could make a grab for the small desk, it'd be a hefty weight to swing, but I was not quicker than the pull of a trigger.

"Do you have anything with which you could shoot demons?" I asked my captor.

A roar came from below, accompanied by a ground-shaking blow. There was no mistaking the bellow of an ursine demon.

I met the eyes of the elder. "You have one here? You need to let me handle it. I do not care what magic you wield; it will kill you."

He coughed violently, but something told me the motion carried humor. "That's my pet."

I shook my head. "Your...pet?"

Sarcasm dripped from his words. "Named it Fluffy."

If I couldn't feel the power of the wards around me, I would have left this man who was simultaneously unhinged and sharp as a tack. "It can't harm you to aid us. We search for weapons a mortal can wield against demons. Please."

There was no indecision in his light blue eyes, only calculation. Katherine paused hopefully. "We'll leave quickly, and you won't hear from us again."

"I did not live this long by trusting people," the elder insisted, but he slung his shotgun over his shoulder.

He turned, but despite the fact his back was to us and his handgun no longer rested at my temple, he didn't feel any less dangerous.

"I've forgotten courtesy. My name is Abelard Bauer," he

informed us before lapsing into silence. It seemed Bauer did not care to know our names. His steps creaked as he descended into the basement. Katherine looked at me and shrugged before following him down. I went along.

Incensed by our presence, the demon roared a greeting as we reached the bottom. The cement walls were dank with moss-like growths, unpleasant to the touch. Angelfire failed to catch within me, thwarted by whatever forces were in play. Bauer, with his nearly sightless eyes, still managed to descend the easiest of us all, disappearing from sight.

I blinked at the emergence of stakes protruding from the wall. They penetrated the slavering bear's thick hide, burrowed in deep. When the incensed demon so much as twitched, dark gore slid down the spikes into containers at the bottom of the wall, the smell fowl and sulfurous. Bauer removed one of those jars swiftly and was the only one not to flinch as the demon roared at him.

He brought it over to a work bench where a rusted reloading press sat. I approached a ten gallon pail underneath the table and saw, when I peeked over the rim, that it was full of a clear liquid and bullet casings. They glimmered tantalizingly at the bottom and when the liquid shook with the vibrations of our movement, they shone like angelfire. Numerous jars of the demon gore littered the dusty area around it.

Bauer drew out a drawer from the table and its contents glittered like gold. He eyed Katherine. "What do you shoot?"

Her shoulders sank when she saw all the brass casings before her. "20-gauge shotgun, preferably."

Bauer grunted, which might have been a good thing or bad. There was a clang as another drawer opened, this one filled with the colorful plastic of shotgun shells. Katherine *shared a small smile with me, pleased.*

Bauer wasted no time. "Casings and shells in the holy water. Bullets and BBs in the demon blood. Primers in Oil of Abramelin. Put very little of this—" he held up a greenish powder, "mullein in the powder when you load it."

"Won't the demonic gore counteract the holy water? What is its purpose?" I asked, suspicious.

Bauer's bushy eyebrows rose. "The demon can't fight itself."

Katherine's mind was on a different track. "We don't have a mobile reloading press. How could we do this?"

"Simple," Bauer stated.

Katherine nodded him on with her head, waiting.

"You don't."

She scrunched up her face and glanced at me to see if I understood. No such luck.

Bauer's hand twitched on his pistol as he gathered small, thick containers full of each ingredient. "Just rub a little of everything on the outside of a live shell. Dry it off before you fire it."

He shoved the ingredients into my hands. "Goodbye. Do not come again, or I will kill both of you."

In a blink, we found ourselves right outside the front entryway. The iron-handled door slammed shut with a bang, one the precariously leaning building could hardly afford.

Katherine glanced at the shells in her hand.

"Those ravens won't stand a chance."

Chapter Seventeen

I may or may not have been skipping school. I mean, come on. Going to school when you're a werewolf? That's crazy talk. To be honest, I couldn't justify fidgeting in a class all day when I knew there was so much more out there. That and there was a chance I'd snap and eat someone.

I wasn't about to go somewhere with such a huge crowd of potential victims. I also wasn't sure Luke would react very kindly to my presence, which would probably hurt like a jerk. I just wasn't feeling the whole thing.

My parents thought I was sick. The thermometer read a fever at all moments of the day, but thankfully, the doctor I'd been dragged to proclaimed it to be a virus and sent me on my way. No super-secret government lab for me, it seemed. The temperature was helpful to me, however, because as soon as my mother and father left for work I was free to drop the ill charade and take off into the woods, even though I had to practically beat them off with a stick to get them to leave me home alone.

Eren met up with me each day. He taught me little things, like how to not crush anything I grasp, but I think his main reason for coming was to get a rise out of me. I honestly didn't know where either of us stood on the hatred-friendship spectrum, but I believed it wasn't at either extreme, which was something I could deal with.

That day, I was the first to arrive. It wasn't that unusual; he made me wait pretty much every time. I occupied myself by wandering, knowing full well that when Eren showed his ugly face he'd be able to catch my scent. The extra distance he had to travel to find me was his own fault for being late.

I ambled along a stream bank dotted with mossy rocks. I could hear each and every disturbance in the water as it strolled around the bend, but it didn't bother me. I was getting better at selectively blocking out my new senses.

I skipped over the tops of the slippery stones, trying to tamp down my pleasure at the ease with which my feet were placing themselves. A foot or so into the water, the rocks became submerged. I didn't even hesitate to jump the twelve-foot gap to the opposite end, pushing myself up for maximum air time.

It felt great for about half a second. I could all too easily imagine wings unfurling, catching the air, and feeling the delicious tug of the feathers as they shifted together.

Then I felt pain.

Something crunched as I hit the ground. There was the tiniest delay before I realized my foot felt like it had attempted acupuncture with razor blades instead of needles. I yelled some meaningless words as I hobbled away from the area, not letting the foot touch the ground.

A warm hand steadied me, then let go as soon as I stopped wobbling. "What the heck is a killing kelpie?"

I looked up at Eren, who seemed to not care that my foot was leaking blood and impaled with the remains of a glass beer bottle. My eyes were tearing a little from the sting of it. "Umm, what?"

Eren stood there, useless as a bump on a log. "That's what you yelled. 'Killing kelpies'."

I drew in a deep, prolonged breath and fluttered my eyes shut. "I landed in a pile of glass. What was I supposed to say?"

Eren enlightened me. What his linguistic vocabulary lacked, he sure made up for with expletives.

His list never petered out, but he stopped suddenly. "Should probably come with me. We need to pick out the pieces before the skin closes on them."

Eren started walking, leaving me to figure out how I was supposed to keep up with a werewolf when I only had one foot. My pride would have probably stopped me from saying yes if he had offered assistance, but still. It would have been nice of him to try.

Eren wasn't nice.

I used the chilled bark of trees as my crutches, shooting forward in great leaps. The process would have been a little fun, like a game, if every jarring movement to my foot didn't feel like a dozen snake bites. I kept pace and the walk wasn't that long.

"You know, it's probably better for you to walk on that foot," Eren suggested without turning around to look at me.

My nose wrinkled at the thought of feeling the pain of landing over and over again. "What, are you nuts? No way!"

Eren shrugged and that stupid body reading thing we had going clued me into the fact that he felt what he said was supposed to help me, but he wouldn't argue. It was my foot.

I made it the rest of the way just fine. My foot had stopped bleeding. It didn't even hurt that much. Still, I wanted to be safe rather than sorry. I followed Eren into his dilapidated little cabin.

As soon as we entered the doorframe, we were in the kitchen. The animal pelt looked slightly out of place now that it was daylight, and it was sagging in the middle where the wood beneath it had been damaged. I almost thought the trapdoor would be more secretive if it wasn't covered.

The room was about as clean as it could get for a home with two males in it. The floor had only minimal mud on it and the walls were mostly smudge-free. Something gurgled suspiciously from the sink drain. The countertops were cluttered with dishes, albeit clean ones. Eren brushed them into a corner with a sweep of his broad arm.

He nodded his head toward the cleared space. "Sit."

I folded my arms. "I'm pretty sure there's something living crawling up your drain. I'm really not about that. I mean, rats aren't fun, but that nasty smelling drain sludge-water? Disgusting. So a rat coated in said nasty smelling drain sludge-water? No, thank you. And besides, my foot feels fine."

Eren glanced down purposefully. "Then why haven't you put it down?"

A loose board cracked like a gunshot. Both of us perked up, as if caught red handed. My head whipped around and my gaze landed on all-too-familiar eyes, a pair I wasn't expecting.

My mouth fell open and I could feel my face crumple, just a little bit. The safe little world I had built, the one where werewolves weren't monsters, where I hadn't killed, started to deflate. Everything rushed back to me. Luke knew. He was pausing because he was debating whether or not to banish me or kill me. Oh goddess, he was going to shoot me and I'd die and my blood would never come out of the floor and that wouldn't look good to potential buyers down the road and— "Luke, I—"

My words were muffled by the plaid fabric shoved in my mouth as Luke enveloped me in the largest of bear hugs.

"Don't ever do that again."

For a second, I stood still. Those words clinked around in my skull, refusing to settle down so I could register them. Then, I smiled so wide I practically bit the shoulder my face was shoved into and my arms flew around Luke. My friend.

I only broke the embrace because I couldn't breathe. My cheeks hurt from the grin.

"Thank you," I said, not caring that none of the exchange made sense. The feelings were enough.

And then there was Eren, Destroyer of Mood. "Aww, how cute! Luke, I told you I'd keep an eye on her. You should be in school. Now, in case you haven't noticed, Leah's foot has healed over multiple glass shards. We have to get them out."

Too bad you can't minimize people like you do with apps. "If it's healed over, isn't it good?"

At the same time, Luke swore with a knowing edge dragging his voice deeper.

Eren grabbed a fillet knife from a rack next to the burbling drain. "Take a look for yourself."

Eyeing the knife till the very last second, I grabbed my ankle and pulled it up. I blinked for a second, fluttering my eyelashes at a rate that could only be described as seizure.

"Flipping púcas!" I muttered under my breath.

Eren whistled next to me. "That's a good one. You should have walked on it like I said."

He was right. The entire bottom of my foot was an angry red, but there were no wounds. It had healed entirely with the glass inside the skin. Some pieces protruded slightly, either emerging from the sole of my foot like an iceberg out of water or forming suspicious lumps underneath.

Eren turned the fillet knife slightly in his hand. The light

319

from the blade caught me in the eye. Luke noticed. "Don't know if it's the best idea for you to do that."

His tone said he certainly did know, but Eren ignored it. "You'd be too much of a pansy about it. The wounds will close before you can get anything out."

Oh crap, I thought, *they're arguing about who should slice open my foot.*

"Rather not have her foot turn into a hamburger," Luke insisted.

Eren smirked. "Why not? We could have a barbecue later."

I cleared my throat and their eyes landed on me. "Actually, I'll be doing this one." I snatched the knife from Eren's hand adding, "thank you very much."

The boys shared a glance. Eren crinkled his eyebrows and Luke shrugged. That was about as good a go-ahead as I was going to get. I plopped myself down on a beat-up wooden chair, which creaked embarrassingly loudly.

I raised an eyebrow. "Either of you got a bucket? I'd rather not bleed on your floor."

Eren left to grab one, and I was alone in the room with Luke. I wasn't sure what to say, or whether to say anything at all. Seemed like he was having the same issue. Before either of us opened our mouths, Eren was back. Yay for social awkwardness.

Eren dropped the bucket in front of me with a loud clatter. "Go to town."

I pulled it closer and inspected it. It wasn't filthy, but it was far from clean enough to be used in surgery. Whatever, it'd have to do. I pulled it closer and rested my ankle on it with my foot turned sideways. I sucked in a deep breath.

Then I lowered the blade to my skin, hoping for a

second either of the boys in the room would shout and ask what the heck I was doing and say I had misinterpreted them big-time, so I wouldn't have to proceed. Neither did.

I realized then that Eren could probably sense my discomfort and Luke could probably see it, so I didn't hesitate, just pressed down with the blade.

My breath hitched as the skin split. I stopped almost immediately, sure I had gone too deep. When I examined it, however, I found that I'd made about a paper-cut-sized indent, which closed the second I lifted the knife.

This is going to be worse than I thought.

I considered how bad it'd be to just leave it, but that seemed worse than just taking it out.

All righty then, I mused, *no mercy from the edge of the blade.*

I stabbed downward with a ferocity that startled everyone, me included. A muffled gasp escaped as the blood flowed freely. I could see the dark brown of the glass, a long plate of it. Before I psyched myself out, I made two more quick slices and yanked, yelling as the shard tore flesh. I panted, glad to be done.

Eren broke that little happy delusion of mine over his knee. "It's not over yet. At least two larger pieces and four or five tiny shards."

I got to work.

I didn't even get a bandage. The only sign my foot had once looked like it had gone through a meat grinder was the bucket full of blood and the towel I had bitten clean through.

321

And the reward for my pain when it was all over? Eren shrugged and Luke said, "guess you are a werewolf" in a wishy-washy, almost unreadable tone of voice. Thanks, guys.

Either way, I was glad to have Luke back. His presence was comforting. Where Eren was an unstoppable force, Luke was an immovable object. He instilled a sense of hard-won calm where he went, and I couldn't get enough.

The two of us had departed from his house, leaving Eren behind. There were words hanging in the air and both of us felt their urgency, but neither of us wished to speak them.

"Guess you figured out I stole a silver bullet?" Luke broached, starting the conversation near the topic we both knew we'd need to cover eventually.

I crinkled my eyes, drawing a blank as to what he meant. "When did you steal a bullet from me? And how was I supposed to figure that out?"

Luke tilted his head. "Interesting. Don't have any memories from the first shift."

I'd come to the same conclusion. That entire night was a blur of pain. It took a split second for the gears to click together in my head, but when they did, my head snapped up. I hadn't realized I had paused until I saw Luke striding ahead of me.

I put on a burst of speed. "Hey, wait up!"

I really hadn't needed the speed. I overshot Luke by a couple of feet before turning around and poking him square in the chest with my index finger, stopping him.

I retracted the finger. "I think it's story time, yeah? Fill me in."

Luke shrugged. "The package you found with the letters.

Had two bullets. I took one."

Ah, right. The manila envelope. The one I had entirely forgotten about but possibly held the cure to the disease I was currently infected with. That package. Holy Amaterasu, how did I forget the letters?

Luke lowered his head slightly. "I apologize for not telling you. Didn't want to bring you into the craziness. Wanted..."

I knew I should be mad, but he sounded so defeated. I didn't need telepathy to finish his sentence. He wanted a last resort, in case everything else failed. I couldn't help the shrug that came to my shoulders. When dealing with life and death, this matter just seemed so petty.

I'd put two and two together. I knew where I would have seen the bullet: the barrel of his rifle, aimed at me. I wondered briefly why I was learning this then, not firsthand as it entered my ribcage. Why had he not fired at me?

Must not have had a clear shot, because I had Luke pegged as a deadeye.

My mind whirled on to revisit a topic that had nearly slipped my mind. Again. "Luke, we need to finish looking at those letters. There might be something useful in there."

Luke nodded, but said nothing. We turned down my driveway and greeted an exuberant Nyami at the door. That silly dog hadn't blinked an eye when I'd come home a werewolf, even though my scent wasn't remotely human. My palm rested on her cone head as we both moved forward, up the stairs. Luke had to fall behind us, as the railing pressed pretty narrowly.

The steps complained loudly, but we made it to my forest green room soon enough. I beckoned Luke in as Nyami curled up on my bed. I tried to subtly kick some of my magic-themed clutter under the bed before he entered, but there was no space left. The stuff I put in pushed more things out the other side. A test-tube of iron dust rolled across the floor, freed.

"Umm..." I stuttered, rethinking the location. Luke, however, had started to roam, taking in the sights of my own little World of Weird.

Luke lifted up a pair of earrings, carved from bones. "What are these?"

I smiled. "Two representations of the Nyaminyami." Nyami lifted her head at that, before plopping it back down with a thud.

Luke didn't question it, but instead picked up a necklace with a frog charm on the bottom. "And this?"

I reached for it, spinning the engorged form toward me. "That's the Australian Tiddalik. He drank up all the water, greedy little thing."

He placed it down carefully before looking at a figurine on the front line of the clutter. "This is?"

I laughed. "Loki from Marvel Comics."

Luke blinked twice before breaking out a lopsided grin. "Oh."

I turned my back on Luke to scrounge for the letters under my bed. The process was surprisingly quick, and I was able to get back up again without making a complete fool of myself, a new accomplishment. I sat down next to Nyami, who jostled along with the bed.

I handed it to Luke. "Here, take a look."

Memories were resurfacing, ones from the day I had found the manila envelope. I started to feel sick to my stomach as snapshots of Jeremy, darkness, and pain flickered through my mind. When the moment of confusion in the basement surfaced, distorted and choppy from the possible blow to the head, I stood up abruptly.

Something was wrong. My veins felt like they were pumping congealed blood, and my head started to pound, right in the center. I walked out of the room with a barely audible excuse and traversed the squeaky floorboards to the bathroom.

I squeezed my eyes tight as I entered, regretting the decision to flick on the light. My third eye was beating out a steady rhythm and my nausea grew. *I thought werewolves weren't supposed to get sick?* I questioned, making a mental note to add whatever the heck was going on to my werewolf list once I made sense of it.

I reached for the counter, but my hand spasmed before I put it down. My nails bit into my palm before my hand opened once more and I laid it down flat. My gaze found itself in the mirror.

Gold.

For a split second, I thought I saw both of my eyes being overtaken by gold, in the manner of my dreams. When I blinked, they were gray once more, but a trail of crimson was making its way toward my mouth. A nosebleed.

I wiped it away just as Luke knocked on the door I hadn't remembered closing. "Leah? Are you all right?"

The blood flow didn't continue, and my stomach started to settle. As quickly as it was on me, it subsided.

"Peachy," I claimed as I opened the door.

Luke gave me an odd look, like he wasn't sure whether or not to press forward.

I patted his shoulder as I passed, though I might have missed a little. Stupid tall people. "Don't worry about it. I'm not exactly a damsel in distress for you to save."

Luke shrugged, but his tone was down-to-earth. "Everyone needs to be saved at some point."

I didn't know how to respond to that, nor the hidden implications. I wasted too much time on thinking how to that I missed the opportunity. The subject dropped and I took up residence on my bed, shoving Nyami over to make room for Luke. She dropped her head in my lap as I extracted the papers, handing half of the thick wad to Luke.

I found where I had left off and continued, losing myself in the story-like text, all too aware of the gravity behind the fantastical words. The scrawling text made sure to write out, in detail, how to use the items enclosed. There was an entire section on the wolfsbane, from using it for wards to killing a werewolf. The silver bullet, however, was clearly for one purpose.

I reached the end of my section too quickly. Despite the sheer volume of paper, the one thing I desired was missing: the outcome. I wanted to know the end of the tale. Did the lovers live? Did the wolf? Was there a cure?

I flicked the last page over, which broke off mid-sentence, into Luke's. I poked him. "Anything?"

There were only one or two papers left for him to read, and they were considerably lighter in color than mine. From a different source. Luke looked at me with indecision in his sea blue eyes, but only for a split second. Then, he filled me in.

"Last pages are newspaper clippings. Two articles and an obituary," Luke informed me, his tone heavy.

I nodded. "Go on."

Luke's eyes skimmed the text even though he already had read it. "The first article is about an animal attack. A girl named Helen Palentina was fatally injured in her own home. Suspected a pack of wolves. Big mystery. The obituary is hers."

"And the second?" I asked.

Luke continued. "Second article is a missing person's report for her brother. They thought the wolves took him."

In other words: the werewolf had eaten his sister and fled.

I let out a big gust of breath before speaking quietly, to myself. "So much for a happy ending."

I knew sleep sparingly, most nights I was a companion to the moon. The ravens that bore the Corrupted traveled day and night, so we did not have time to rest. The bags under Katherine's eyes, however, ripped that decision away from her.

It seemed the camping-style equipment she'd purchased no longer afforded enough comfort. A part of me couldn't help but wonder if it was more than just the proximity to the hard, cold ground that did it. If, perhaps, the stress was growing too much.

I looked over at her, taking the opportunity as one of the many intermittent street lights passed above us. Katherine's eyes were glazed, but they didn't cease their listless movement. Her jacket, which bore an amazing sampling of filths—dirt from our more remote hunts, grime from the more urban, blood on the cuffs of her sleeves—slipped down to expose her right shoulder. It was a mess of broken blood vessels from the recoil of her shotgun.

Her fluttering eyes were barely open enough to reflect the neon lights of the motel we'd arrived at. I watched as Kath-

erine entered a small room, spoke to the man inside, and was rewarded with a key to room 24. She gave me a small wave as she made her way toward the room and I nodded once in response.

I sat outside the motel in the cool night air while Katherine rested. The far-off swooshing of wings above grated against my mind. I shook my head, clearing it of the lingering feeling of being watched. Haldis' cool hilt solidified in my palm, and pulses of angelfire climbed throughout my body. When I breathed in, the flames ignited and coated my skin in a fine, shimmering blaze. I leapt and kicked off the grimy, brick coated wall before taking to the sky knowing that Katherine would be safe for the time being.

Unable to delay any longer, my eyes found their target, a streak of black nearly indecipherable from the shrouded night sky. The wind whipped around me, stinging like hail where it brushed my skin. The raven saw me too late, and its hasty turn meant nothing.

Haldis, my faithful companion, flashed through the air so swiftly I doubted the Corrupted felt pain before it evanesced into nothingness. The corpse of the raven, however, I knew was long past feeling, even as it hit the ground with a final thud.

The next morning, I found Katherine at a small creek behind the motel. Brown sludge had built up in the center, around what looked to be a large litter barricade. Katherine sat with her back to me, unaware of my presence. She held her phone in her hand, and on it were the outlines of a group picture.

I sat down next to her, lowering myself into the filth that lined the muddy bank. Katherine sucked in a quick breath and flinched, but then relaxed when she saw it was just me.

Her smile was weak as she faced me, and her eyes didn't meet mine. "I said sunrise. You're late."

I tilted my head, watching her. "I wanted to give you more time to rest."

She sniffed and drew herself straighter. "We don't have time for rest. We need to find those Corrupted before they do whatever the hell they're planning to do."

I looked out over the water, at the early morning sun, already so strong. "You do not need to do anything, Katherine. This isn't your fight."

Katherine looked at me sharply, but I still gazed out at the water, offering her what tiny privacy I could.

"I told you, you can't get rid of me that easily. I'm here to stay."

"Katherine, you could die. I will do everything I can to protect you, but I can't promise anything. This war will never end. We might beat the Corrupted, but the demons will still roam."

Katherine bared her teeth at me, fire burning in her eyes. I moved my head back an inch, surprised.

She cut off any words I was about to say. "And what about you, huh? What if you die? You expect me to sit passively when my family is at risk? Everyone I know is on the line here! And everyone's fate rests on your shoulders? That's not okay. That's not fair. I'm not letting you do this by yourself. Just because I miss my family, doesn't mean I regret a single decision I've made. It's because of them I'll keep fighting."

She poked me in the shoulder, hard. "And because this is not something anyone should do alone."

I let out a breath I didn't know I was holding, and smiled

at her. Shaking my head, I stood up and extended a hand.

"Good. I think your shotgun might come in handy with this next one. I think the flock hasn't diverged yet up north."

"Perfect."

She gave a last glance to her phone, to the smiling faces, before turning it off and putting it in her bag. She returned my smile and took my hand.

Chapter Eighteen

I hadn't turned the television on since I'd become a werewolf. Honestly, every time I saw its flickering lights I was transported right back to a time when Jeremy and I had been perched in front of it, eyes glassy as we binged on terrible horror movies way past our bedtimes.

He had always been terrible with movie talking, making puns left and right.

"Are you tele'n me he didn't see that coming?"

"They are no longer werewolves. They were wolves."

I stopped because I didn't want to hear about his death, but then that reason paled in comparison to the newer one: I was afraid they'd find Jessica.

I knew they couldn't trace it back to me, or at least were very unlikely to, but I was walking a fine line between feeling too much and too little. If I saw her smiling face flashing up on the screen, I'd fall. I'd stop functioning or be consumed by grief and madness.

So when I waltzed downstairs and saw a news channel on, I froze. The ceramic bowl in my hand, full of strawberries, tilted, spilling one before I righted it. Bending over to pick it up ended much too quickly, and I was forced to face the TV. I could see a portrait photo on the screen and a bright red banner on the bottom. I started to freak out, just a little.

331

Or a lot. I read the banner first, but it was relaying unrelated information about mysterious deaths for which I had no focus. I tore off the Band-Aid quickly and tilted my face up to meet the center of the screen. My pulse was in my ears as I filed it as definitely not Jessica. My heart rate barely started to lower before it kicked up again, even swifter and more forcefully than before.

The face wasn't Jessica's.

No, it was Benjamin's.

The bowl shattered.

I slammed my fist repeatedly against Luke's door, sending splinters flying and impaling a few in my hand.

"LUKE! EREN!" I yelled, ignoring the blood seeping from my wounds. I was frenzied, writhing inside my mind. My fingernails were turning dark in front of me, curving. Uncontrollable.

My head pounded louder than my hand, but not loud enough to obscure the tinny drop of a utensil inside and Eren's, "Oh crap, she's really going for it."

Luke opened the door almost instantly and blinked at the sight of me, my gold irises flaming. "Leah?"

I shook head to toe, but I didn't know if that was from nerves or the transformation looming above me. "Benjamin. He's gone. He's missing. I need to find him. Grab your gun. With the silver. I'm going to find him. Please, please, I need to find him."

I turned on my heel, darting for the woods. Before I got off the rotten front steps, Luke's hand caught me. I was moving too fast, though, and barely managed to turn around and stop myself from pulling him off the stairs.

Eren appeared by my side, lightning-quick. "Whoa! Hang on there, Kitten. Why the shifty eyes?"

I didn't know if he was referring to the color or to the fact they couldn't stay in any one place. WoodsErenLuke-woodsLukeEren.

"I'm going to do it," I stated. They were missing the point that time was ticking. With every second, Benjamin was...Well I didn't know. And that made it worse.

Luke tilted his head as he tried to follow my thought process, but Eren was already updated through my body language.

Eren's expressions were flickering almost too quickly to trace. "Nope, not happening. Bad idea."

I curled my toes, not all that surprised when I felt the curving toenails catch and rip into the soles of my shoes. I didn't have much time left. "Luke gets the gun. If anything goes wrong, he uses it."

I moved too swiftly and unexpectedly for either one of them to catch, in the wood line before I completed my last words. Both sets of feet pounded after me, but I heard Eren yell.

"Luke, do as she said!"

The gun, the silver. Yes. Necessary. I was glad when he turned around, but it was only a small part. Getting increasingly smaller. My thoughts were dimming as more primitive ones rose to the surface, so I trimmed away all but one: *I have to find Benjamin.*

Eren chased after me but it was too late. A second that felt like an eternity was all it took.

A flood of discomfort, like the pain you feel if your joint is locked and you have to extend it to fix it. My fingers quit functioning, gathering darkened, hardened flesh underneath and changing shape.

My skin felt pricked with thousands of tiny needles, opening each and every pore. Mid-stride, fire poured into me. My muscles writhing, clamoring over shifting bones and pointed edges. Things I did not want to imagine reshaping and resizing, organs swimming around inside.

My bones bent like heated steel, malleable under only the most extreme pressure. Yet somehow, as pain coursed inside and my mind emptied, it felt...

Natural.

My paws hit the ground, not a stride broken. I pushed forward, the ground flying beneath me.

Free.

Except the boots pounding behind me. Too fast, but downwind. The scent did not carry. Threat? Possibly. My legs flew faster, sights and sounds flying by me as if warped.

I didn't know what was behind me, but what I did know was that I had a scent in mind, one imprinted into my memory in a place of darkness and fear.

Trail.

There would be one, back at the source. Had to be. There was no plan for what had to happen when I arrived, just the knowledge that I must. Yes, I'd push forward.

The scents were intriguing, everything under the sun. Green and wet, brown and decaying, sharp and strong. Yes, the last one. The smell of fear, oh so familiar. I did not recognize the falsely rotten smell intertwined with it, but the faint smell of sage and salt tickled my memory. I turned toward it.

Track.

My paws moved at a furious clip as I loped toward the

scent, but that speed was enough where the boots behind me faded in intensity and then ceased to be heard. In a matter of minutes, the scent grew stronger and stronger until it taunted my tongue.

But an unnatural *boom* sounded, a slammed car door.

"Leah! Where are you?" I could not place the voice, just that it was familiar.

Another voice this time, one that made growls want to rise in my throat. "I don't think she's exactly fit to respond."

There was a line of harsh words from the same male. "How could she be so stupid?"

The first's noises continued, with a little bite in them but a lot of worry. They entered the woods together, the second leading only because he seemed to know where I was.

Run.

But I couldn't. If I ran, I couldn't follow the scent I needed. And I needed to follow the scent. I stood still for a second, the instinct to get out and the one thought in my mind combating.

Inhale.

Good, rotten and salty and sweet and bitter, that was the one I wanted, and it went deeper still in the forest. Four scents most crucial: two threats that smelled oddly of wolf, one unknown, far away, and my target. In the same direction, a raven cawed.

Prey.

I tore my thoughts from it. If I was lucky, the scent I was following would be prey. Warm, bloody...I hoped it would run. I wanted the chase. To earn the meat still hot.

Stalk.

I approached my target, while others stalked me. I darted through the trees like a phantasm, but never seemed

335

to shake the pursuers, even as the scent of fear and feathers grew stronger. Maybe the ravens were eyeing my prey.

Hunger.

It could not be silenced, a hole needing to be filled. Good thing I could see the tiny morsel of clothing and flesh, staring at the bird that tempted me so, on the ground, crumpled.

Consume.

But no, the thought grated. The bird was fair game, but the little one...As uncomfortable as a thorn in the paw. Before I could choose, though, the crashing in the underbrush approached behind me, too quickly.

Leap.

I did, knocking the young human to the ground. He thrashed beneath me, delicate as a pup.

Click.

That's what the device said as the burning metal—silver—was loaded into the chamber. The intruders were here. Threats. They wanted the one beneath me.

Protect.

He was mine. A pup, not a food source. I bared my teeth and let my snarls vibrate the earth as the threats drew closer, the smell of silver searing me.

They made such strange noises. The one with the silver never took his hands off the machine, keeping it aimed at me. "Leah, you can't do this. To him or to yourself."

I snarled harder, gathering the young one behind me so he could not be subjected to the silver's bite.

The other human looked confused, the expression itching into my conscious.

Wrong.

But why? It was so hard to think with the silver's invisible presence. But, as a flash of memory took over my mind, I found it was not impossible. I knew both men, and while I was unsure whether or not I should kill the unarmed one, who smelled of a rival wolf, the other was only surrounded by warmth in my head.

"Leah," he called, his voice low, his eyes seeing mine through the scope, "don't do this."

The tone was not lost. Imploring, but I strained to comprehend the meaning, too far gone. As my eyes darted to all exits, I knew I could never drag the pup away swiftly enough to escape. The young one fought no longer, more still than was natural.

Survive.

I had one feasible option. Darkness consumed me as the pain swept through my being, clawing and crunching and crushing me until I collapsed with two legs instead of four.

We were leaving a trail of dead ravens at our feet, Katherine and I, but it wasn't enough. They'd spread to every inch of the place, crossing the continent with surprising speed. While tracking one, the others would cover miles, carriers of the virus that was sure to cause an epidemic of the soul.

I felt neither joy nor remorse as Haldis pierced them, or as Katherine swept them from the sky with her shotgun, which was finally of use. Even active, the birds were dead, the spirits inside of them too great a darkness for the ravens' essences to handle.

They were meat puppets, decaying even on the wing. It was harder for me to find the Corrupted inside of them than demons; their call was less of a tug accompanied with a feeling of certainty and more like listening for a whisper in a crowd.

We walked down a country road, evergreens flanking us as I listened for that whisper. Up ahead, I was almost certain. There was also something...Other with it. Not the same, but nearby was a muted tug, such as with a demon but weaker. Disguised. It was one of the very last.

Either way, the direction was forward. However, the dog in the yard we were passing did not know that, and was whining in a goofy way as we passed, begging to be pet. It had a strange impression surrounding it, but I had no time to spare in idle investigation. Katherine, however, bent to its will, running her hand over the dog's golden fur as we passed, but leaving it at the edge as we moved forth, no time wasted.

If I could fly and hear the whispers, we would have arrived much, much sooner to this sleepy little town, which was about to experience a rather rude awakening. That was, if I could not destroy the Corrupted there before they weakened the place in such a way that a door from the demonic realm could open.

That would spell disaster.

The remaining ravens were a handful of bombs all over this continent, perched and ready to expel flames that could not be quenched. I entered the pines to my right as I heard a deep, throaty caw far in the distance. Katherine plunged in behind me, unslinging her shotgun and holding it at the ready.

I summoned Haldis, which was willing to appear when we found the Corrupted, as long as humans were in danger. Because I had Katherine with me, that meant any Corrupted in the area was fair game. Without her, countless humans would have already perished.

Pine needles glided over my skin. A few found their way onto my eyelids, only dispelled by a rapid blink. Katherine's gun barrel wove in and out of saplings as we stalked closer, the both of us too desperate for any action other than to head straight for the danger. Worryingly, as we moved closer, the whispers died out all at once.

Not close by, the kicking roar of a truck halfway in the junkyard blocked out all quieter, woodsy sounds. The chugging pickup passed behind us on the road and I noticed the strange aura surrounding it from our far-off view point, too. This one was much brighter and much more enticing than the dog's had been, but again I refrained from pursuit.

It was apparent we had come to the right place when a sulfurous scent tinted every breath we took. The leaves were torn up as if a dust devil had blown through, roots and bits of earth visible through the mess. In places, the ground was scorched and high plumes of spiraling smoke rose.

When I looked at Katherine, it was clear she could see none of it. She stumbled at my sudden pause and I had to lay a hand on her puffy, winter-jacket-coated shoulder to keep her from toppling over. The height difference almost made me go with her. As I straightened, the leaves beneath us scuttled over each other, the sound not unlike the scurrying of rodents.

Katherine shivered, aware of the situation on only a subconscious level. The tension kept her voice at a whisper. "Why did we stop?"

I motioned her forward, and we crept between the trees to approach the center. "Something went wrong here. Terribly wrong. This place has a spiritual imprint as if—"

My words cut off and a small sound escaped from her lips. "Oh."

Between two maple trees of massive stature lay a raven, its wings spread out as if in flight, but the rest of it tellingly limp. On each side of it, the ground was scorched. To Katherine, it looked like the bird had been on fire, setting the surroundings ablaze. To me, well, it looked like the bird was centered in a mass of squirming, ever-shifting symbols.

I blocked Katherine from proceeding further, pushing her back out of the symbols' reach. "It's too late. It's been done."

Her tiny shoulders drooped. "You don't mean...?"

"What we have before us is a gate to Hell," I affirmed.

Katherine drew in a deep breath before straightening her spine. "Remember when I first met you and you said that possession was only for the direst circumstances?"

She didn't wait for a response. "I think this counts as a dire circumstance."

I did not deny the truth of her words. "That it does."

My eyes idly circled a spot not far away where there were small burn marks, like those of a lopsided, oversized cigar. While my mind whirred, I almost did not process them. Almost.

I raced over, careful not to approach the shifting symbols any more than necessary. As I drew nearer, what I was seeing became apparent. Footprints, with little clouds of decay around them. A demonically possessed human had been here.

"Is that what I think it is?" Katherine asked.

I nodded as I tried to piece the scene together. Unless a demon was extremely powerful, it wouldn't leave trails like that without using massive amounts of energy. Then, it would just be a side effect, a bit of residue cast off. Had a powerful demon been awakened by the corrupted souls? Or did one need to be present during whatever ceremony or ritual took place to open the gate?

But the footprints...They led in, not out. A human vessel then, brought to amplify demonic power and to give them a foothold in the corporeal realm.

Just then, an eerie silence descended, as if someone had pulled the plug on the sound. The whispers, I realized, had stopped. This was the resting place for last of the Corrupted. I had miscalculated. There were no more. We'd been so close... We'd almost stopped them. But time had run out.

Katherine's words just barely registered at first. It seemed I had missed a bit. "So? Would it be?"

I tilted my head slightly. "Would it be what?"

She rolled her bottom lip, getting a few residual lip gloss sparkles on her teeth. "Would it be time for you to possess someone?"

I sighed, not because she had asked the question, but because it had to be asked. "It's dangerous, Katherine. While the benefits would be great, the risks are formidable. I am not a spirit, nor an angel or a demon. I would have to ask Haldis to transfer my soul, my being, into another. Most humans cannot survive an overload of such energy for long. And their soul? It could be forced out or altered. There is very little chance a person would enter and exit the same as before.

"However, our options dwindle. I hear no more whispers, Katherine. The Corrupted here have completed their mission. Soon, Hell's inhabitants will rise. I fear we need every advantage we can seize."

Katherine's face hardened, the corners of her eyes tightening. She blurted out her piece as if it'd been bashing at the gates of her mind for quite some while. "Okay, then. Possess me. If it's going to save people, I want to do it."

Her words struck me like a physical blow. I had not

formed many attachments in the years I had existed, but suddenly, I could not bear the thought of risking one who'd already gambled so much to help me in my quest.

I understood the gravity of what she was offering better than anyone else could. To face such a danger, especially after the pain she'd endured when being possessed by a corrupted spirit...Her bravery spoke volumes.

Those sentiments did not translate directly into words, as they were very foreign to me. The words themselves were evasive, so I just shook my head.

Katherine's mouth dropped open slightly. "You can't be serious. Why not?"

"You'd die," I proclaimed truthfully, and left it at that. I wasn't lying: it took a special type of human to host one like me without unravelling. That, and Katherine had already lost portions of her soul to Haldis' cleansing at the end of her spiritual possession. I did not know the dangers of possession from experience, but the facts were burned into my mind despite this. I would not question them.

Katherine's mouth twisted. A fire burned in her eyes.

"Then what?" she spat. If she'd been anything other than human, I'd have been afraid she'd end me.

I explained my plan. "We'll find someone who will suffice, as quickly as possible. I'm going to need you to keep an eye on him or her, because the first days will be difficult on both sides. To be honest, we may not even have days left. I have to hold my place firmly enough not to be ejected, while not too unrelentingly so that I can avoid removing the soul already in the body."

Katherine, as usual, seemed appeased as long as she had a solid job to complete. Her anger burned brightly but quickly. "Fine then, let's get moving."

She spun and started walking away before realizing she had no clue where she was going. "Uh..."I started moving toward her, but slowly so that she took my steps as a reassurance and was able to reclaim the lead. I followed her out and we came again to the degraded road, yet this time she paused to wait for my word on where to go next to find the vessel.

I remembered something. "Up the street, where that dog was. It had an unusual trace imprint on it."

Katherine cocked a reddish eyebrow. It conflicted with her newest hair color, a spunky flame red that was beginning to fade. "You want to possess the dog?"

My mouth tugged. "No, but whoever left the imprint on the dog may be a viable option."

At her blank stare, I explained. "An imprint is like a trace aura left behind by a person. Different qualities can be displayed in an aura, most notably corruption in the way of holes. This one in front of us is in decent shape for a human's, and displays minor psychic qualities. Good for channeling spirits, but an extended stay is risky on anyone. Ideally, I would like one with less corruption, but we don't have time."

Katherine clapped her hands together, though whether it was from excitement or to kill a mosquito I was not sure. "Sweet, let's check it out."

The dog was equally wriggly with excitement the second time around, but the air around the house was filled with an exhaust-like scent. The rusty truck in the driveway matched the gasping backfire I'd heard in the woods. Hadn't an aura shown strongly through it when it passed? Yes, I believed so.

Good, this might be easier than I'd thought.

It was, exceedingly so. The front door was not only unlocked, but open a crack. From inside, male voices drifted out.

One had a harsh, cynical edge to it. "You're just mad you couldn't carry her up the stairs like a damsel in distress."

The other was lower, a learned calm. "You're just mad I brought a blanket to wrap her with."

The first laughed, the sound starting as suddenly as it stopped. "Come on, brother. I'm not that bad. You know it."

"Give me the comforter. Kid's cold," the second said, sounding like he was thoroughly uncomfortable with the idea of both the "kid" and the kid's temperature being outside of normal.

There was rustling as he complied. "He's looking at me funny. Why do you think he hasn't said anything yet?"

"Probably scared of your face. Don't blame him." Ah, these two were actual brothers then. Not many others banter like that. The first man growled, the sound raising the hair on the back of my neck with its lack of humanity.

His next remark had very little bite. "What now?"

"Give it an hour. Two, max. If Leah wakes, she'll know how to help him. If not, we bring him home. Tell the half-truth. Found him in the woods."

The conversation carried on. I motioned for Katherine to serve as both the watcher and the distraction outside, so that if anything went awry she could help. Her mouth twisted slightly to the side as she looked at me.

"I have no idea what state either the human or I will be in when this is done. Most likely, no news from me is good news."

The corner of her mouth didn't relax even a tiny bit. "Then how long do I wait? Do I try to talk to the person you possess? Where do I go?"

I put my hand on her arm. "There's a small inn not too far from here. If you don't think you'll need to intervene,

344

head there."

I paused. "I'm going to head in, but be safe, Katherine. If demons start showing up and I am unable to help, get out of this town by any means necessary."

Katherine grinned. "I'm not exactly someone who gives up that easily."

I didn't want to break her small pocket of happiness, but we were running out of time. "You don't exactly seem like someone who is willing to die in vain, either."

Katherine inhaled and nodded, grudgingly acknowledging the truth to the words. I found myself wanting to delay, but every second I spent then could be one I had to sacrifice later. Instead of any more words, I simply bowed to Katherine, inclining my head toward the ground as I bent at the waist.

"Thank you," I said as I straightened and walked through the doorway.

Wood flooring creaked the second I stepped inside. In another room on the bottom floor, the two men I'd heard were arguing about the morality of eating the inhabitant's food without her knowledge. As silently as I could, I crept forward. I had to eliminate either of them as the potential vessel I sought.

Only one of my eyes peeked around the corner. I held eerily still, not willing to have my cover blown. From my vantage point, I could see that the blonder man leaned against a counter while his brother was paused with his hand halfway into the refrigerator. The dark haired one, stockier than the other, finished their debate by shoving an entire sandwich in his mouth.

Both of them had peculiar auras, unlike anything I'd seen. Spiraling around both was a trace amount of the imprint I'd seen in the truck, but it was clear neither was the source of it. The one with blue eyes had energy around him that pushed farther than most, but didn't interfere with the auras of anything within the radius. A presence made clearly apparent despite its silence. Unlikely to leave imprints, especially the one on the truck outside.

His incorrigible sibling could have been a vessel, if not for the holes in his aura. Little marks of corruption riddled him, a telltale sign he had been the center of many evils in his lifetime. As a matter of fact, both of them had holes, but the blond's were smaller and less corrosive-looking. Less self-loathing to tear them further apart every day.

It wasn't corruption of demonic origin, not yet. That would come if I didn't find a vessel soon. I turned away from them and stalked silently up the stairs to my right. When I entered the hall, it was readily apparent that I was nearing my target. The door furthest had waves of power coming out from under it, shimmering like air over heated tar.

I opened it with as little noise as possible, despite my conclusion from the boys' conversation that the occupant was sleeping. When I entered, it was like standing while a low-level earthquake rocked the ground, and it was easy to see why.

Magical artifacts, spell-working ingredients, ward materials, and lore books littered every surface. On the wall, the eye of a hamsa stared at me, cold and unblinking. When I entered, dozens of dowsing pendulums swayed from the ceiling. New additions, judging from the incomplete pattern they formed.

There was no doubt the girl on the bed in front of me was the one I sought. Her imprint was on everything in the room, like she left a little bit of her soul on each thing she touched but had much more to give. Her face was turned to the side, *her eyes closed, and her breaths even.*

Her aura was a similar color to mine, except it faded from gold to leaf-brown in some places. In the darkest areas, the aura had cracked, spidery lines running through it. Not ideal, but I believed it would work. I hoped so.

"Haldis," I whispered, summoning the blade. It took its time to appear, enough where I began to believe it would not come unless there was a demonic threat.

Instead it materialized slowly, as if to ask whether or not I was sure. When I nodded, I found its cool, metal hilt was fully formed in my hand. Angelic flames poured over my wrist and up my arm, tugging lightly at me. Haldis faded out slightly, taking its non-corporeal form. I wouldn't leave a visible mark on the girl, but I feared the pain would still be great.

I lightly took her wrist, wrapping mine around it as gently as possible. She didn't stir. Over the back of her hand, I placed my own, lining up each finger, guided by a knowledge I couldn't explain. I drew a deep breath, aware it could be my last in this form. Seconds passed.

Then I drove Haldis through the backs of both of our hands.

The blade slid in without a scratch, but as waves of agony rolled over me I would have welcomed physical pain. Golden fire worked through the girl's veins, pumping with each heart beat from me into her. With every pulse I felt weaker, smaller...The world faded from focus.

I felt like every organ of mine was being pulled out and forced through a straw into the one lying beside me as Haldis reduced me to my very essence. Her eyes flew wide open as she gasped, gold pouring out through the irises but pausing there. It was like I was ever so slowly shifting vantage points, and as I drew nearer and nearer to those eyes they were over-

347

come by angelic flame.

The force of it was enough that she arced off the bed and never quite touched back down, hovering there as inside, I fought not to disband, to simply cease to exist. I wasn't quite sure when it happened, but soon it was I whose sightless eyes stared at the ceiling, and it was from my shoulder blades that wings, oh-so-familiar to me but so foreign in this new form, spread outward.

Then she turned out the lights.

Chapter Nineteen

"Told you I heard something. She's awake."

I groaned, my thoughts as hard to stop as water trickling through my fingers. I rolled away from Luke and Eren, planting my head firmly back down on the pillow as my head flared with pain. The throbbing ache was made worse by the movement.

I didn't pretend to myself that I'd have any luck falling asleep. "Don't you two know it's creepy to stare at someone while they're unconscious?"

I could hear the smirk in Eren's voice without opening my eyes. "All in a day's work."

Luke spoke simultaneously, uncaring when his words crossed over Eren's. "Sorry. Need you to talk to the kid, and maybe bring him home, if you're okay."

Was I okay? I thought so. But if so, why exactly was I passed out with—I reached up to touch the offending mess—sticks in my hair? When I pulled on the stubborn twig, it refused to budge and the tension on my scalp felt like a fist beating my head down. Luke gently pushed my hand away and freed the offending shrubbery from my hair, able to do it better from his vantage point.

Sure that nodding would only bring more head discomfort, I settled for a simple, "Thanks."

Eren snorted. "Lovebirds."

I made my eyebrows do the sexy caterpillar dance. "How about it, Luke? A little tongue tango?"

Luke looked extremely confused and leaned back ever so slightly, making a filler noise while he failed to find words. It seemed tongue tango was the furthest thing from his mind, and I couldn't help but be glad we were on the same page. Eren's guffaws sounded like a bear's heavy breathing, and I couldn't help but to join him, my own, lighter laughter adding to the mix.

The brightness of the dim room no longer felt like needles to the skull, so I took that as an all clear to get up. I knew I was deathly wrong when my stomach rolled, trying to crawl up my esophagus. I swallowed down the bile and cut off whatever comment Eren was going to make by standing up.

The room see-sawed like I was in an underwater cave rather than a space with solid, unchanging walls. I grabbed onto the thing nearest to me, which happened to be Eren's thick bicep.

His words were teasing, but his rigid stance spoke nothing of humor. "You all right, Kitten?"

"Fine. Now both of you get out so I can put on—" I glanced down at my attire, clearly selected so neither of the boys would have to dress me, but I'd still be decent, "something other than a backward bathrobe."

They complied, although both looked a bit worried. I practically fell against the door handle when I went to shut it, and mentally heard myself apologize to it. *Sorry.* 'Cause that's just how sane people roll.

I threw on the first thing I found, uncaring. I closed my eyes to center myself, but they flew open in confusion when my cheek hit the ground. The solid *thunk* reverberated through me.

My thoughts flew to the pain I'd felt in the hazy post-shift faint, and I couldn't help but wonder if werewolves could get sick. Still, my wolf hearing was able to pick up Eren's and Luke's conversation downstairs. Eren must have heard me hit the ground, and was restraining Luke, stopping him from checking on me as he heard me scramble to my feet. They had decided with whispered words that it was decidedly not normal.

But then again, hadn't that been one of the first things I'd said to Luke? I'm not normal?

I walked out the door, into the hall. I tried not to stagger, but I had to trace my fingers against the wall in order to keep from overbalancing. I found myself wondering if they'd spiked my drink last night, and then found that I drew a blank on almost everything after rushing over to Luke's place.

The kid that Eren mentioned...Benjamin? Had I found him? Hope bubbled in my chest so suddenly and fervently that I couldn't help but suck in a quick, excited breath. Dizziness forgotten, I barreled down the stairs. The steps didn't even have the honor of having my feet pound them during my descent. I simply jumped them. All fourteen of them.

In the living room, a form was bundled up on the couch. Without any command on my part, my face broke out in a huge, lopsided grin. I ignored the raging undercurrent of déjà vu as I knelt in front of Benjamin. For a second, the area around him blurred like a dark migraine aura, but I blinked it away, just like I was doing with the stinging sensation in my eyes.

Benjamin was paler than I thought was possible for someone with Native American roots. His eyes fixed on me and widened, some indecipherable emotion flickering to the surface. One that should be too complex for the limited experiences of someone so young.

My heart squeezed as I thought of the possibilities. Even with him alive, I could have traumatized him. I could have injured him. Oh Allah, I could have infected him. What had I been thinking?

I knew the answer to that question: I hadn't been.

Scratchy words interrupted my thoughts. "Miss Leah?"

"Benjamin! Are you all right? Why were you in the woods?" I asked while trying to keep the frantic tones away from my speech.

He sniffled and nodded. "I thought I saw something, Miss Leah…"

"What was it, Benjamin? What did you see?" He didn't answer, just looked out the sliding glass door.

I shook my head. "Okay, you can tell me later. Just never, ever do that again. You hear me?"

He nodded once more. Then, even though he was a few years too old to do so, he held his arms out for me to pick him up. Without hesitation, he was in my arms. Warm and solid. Real. He was safe.

His head was on my shoulder, drooping. "I'm going to take you home, okay?"

He nodded.

I started walking, oblivious to the two brothers standing awkwardly in the hallway unsure of what to do. I blinked, and for a second I thought a dark cloud descended over my vision. *Wrong*, my mind whispered.

Then it was gone, and as I opened the front door I motioned to Luke and Eren.

"Come on, fellas. Time for a road trip."

352

Ringing the doorbell at Benjamin's house was like knocking on a crypt. I regretted it almost instantly, but steeled myself. This was something I had to do. And besides, it wasn't like I could keep Benjamin indefinitely. I could barely take care of myself, let alone another person.

The flowers on the concrete patio were unusually cheery, spots of red and orange that seemed to suck the color out of everything else rather than provide any excess. Rosalind had practically lived on the porch in the summer, making sure the flowers were healthy.

At that moment, they seemed obsessively starched to perfection, each one straightened by its own, individual rod. The stems were starting to outgrow their straightjackets, however, and their heads tilted haphazardly in a jumbled mess. A new attempt, forgotten.

Only someone with wolf hearing would have heard the door open the smidgen it did. I could see a slice of the hall, bare. Nothing suspicious about it except, well, there should have been a person there, opening the door.

The shuffling caught my attention. One eye, a cold brown, appeared much lower than expected. Melinda.

"Benjamin? Is that really him?" she whispered, watching through the doorway. She didn't push it any further open or closed.

A shadow loomed up behind her, slithering across the wall to draw closer. I shivered as a pale, bony hand clasped Melinda's shoulder and pushed her out of my sight. Rosalind Bellevue filled the gap, widening it to fit her whole body, while not enough where I'd have any delusions about being welcome to enter.

353

Her breaths had a slight whistling quality to them. She reached out and scooped Benjamin from my arms.

The door was almost shut before she said anything. "No, Melinda. Of course it isn't Benjamin."

More locks than I remembered the door having clicked into place the second the door rested in its frame. Those clicks spoke of finality, but I was far from done. I stood, shocked, but my brain had already pushed past the that-used-to-be-the-woman-who-gave-Jeremy-double-grilled-cheeses-in-grade-school-so-I-could-have-one phase and onto the plan-making phase.

Know thy enemy.

And I did. I could hear it, shifting behind the walls of the house. I had to help Benjamin. He wasn't safe. The flower's pungent odor dipped for one second, allowing a rotten smell to drift from the house. My enemy i—

Demon.

The word roared in my skull, so loud and forceful I grabbed at my temples. Sinking to my knees, I vomited into the nearest flowerpot. Almost all of it was foul-tasting bile. The minuscule amount of food left in my system was barely enough to taint it.

I was definitely sick, and definitely grateful that Luke and Eren were waiting in the car at the bottom of the drive-way, out of sight and hopefully out of Eren's hearing range. I slid down onto the cold cement of the porch, relishing its ice-like effect on my feverish skin. No one would notice if I just stayed here, curled in the fetal position, right?

I knew I was wrong when the car door slammed. I pulled myself up, my arms childishly weak. The world rocked back and forth, but I wasn't sure if I was actually moving or if it was just perceived. It seemed to me that it would be easier to surf on a kappa than walk just then.

My ears rang, a shrill, unavoidable sound. It grew more insistent as footsteps drew closer, crunching up the gravel of the driveway. In my off state of mind, it took me a second to realize that it wasn't actually my ears, but my cell phone, ringing in Luke's hand. The stupid phones had gotten me twice.

I quit my internal pity-party and tried my best to walk in a straight line toward him, but it was like a ghost was draining my energy field. Like the worst of drugs. At least this time, I knew neither Luke nor Eren were responsible.

Every other blink the shadows around the house twisted and elongated, a rather sinister game of peek-a-boo. There was, undeniably, something wrong with me. *Lycanthropic update number three: you don't need shrooms to get high as a kite, but the trips are pretty bad.*

Luke reached me, but the cell phone had ceased its whining. I grabbed it quickly and hit redial so I wouldn't have to answer the questions forming in the deepening lines of his face.

I should have looked to see who it was first. That would have been the smart thing to do.

"Leah, honey? Where are you?" My mother's concerned tone dunked me in a pool of shame, though I didn't know the exact reason yet. I hadn't even been accused of a crime. It was just a side effect of having so many secrets.

I hated how calculated my answer had to be. I ran over her work schedule in my mind, used it to determine she probably wouldn't be back for another three hours, and flew with that.

"I'm at home, Mom. What's up?"

There were a few seconds of silence. "No, I'm at home.

I wanted to talk to you about Benj...something I saw on the news this morning."

Well, I done diddly screwed up. I drew attention away from the mistake by playing stupid. "What did you see? On the news?"

She cleared her throat, the sound odd and out of place. "Not now. There's a...friend? Yeah? ...For you here."

There was a problem with that statement: anyone I could remotely consider a friend was either here or six feet under. My lips flattened in confusion.

I didn't get a chance to respond. "She says you two were assigned a group project? In history?"

That raised many red flags, a whole churning sea of them. I hadn't been in class, let alone assigned a group project. As I made up my mind, weighing the danger of both the situations before me, I felt the strong, steady pulse of whatever instinct made me think the word "demon" retreat. I wasn't sure why, but I took that as a sign that the more immediate danger was at home.

I hiked down to the car, swaying less like I could feel the world spinning and more like a bush in the light breeze. A manageable, coverable amount. My soul didn't feel like it was the ball in a Ping-Pong world championship any more.

I pondered the danger my mother could be exposed to. The muscles in my arms contracted at the thought, small, pre-shift tremors, but controlled. Eren watched me like a hawk, but remained silent. He wouldn't interfere. Whoever was at the house wanted me, and I was sure as heck coming.

I ushered Luke into my scratched up car's driver side with a pointed nod and claimed the passenger seat as my own, mouthing the word "home" to him. He understood and started the vehicle, rolling us out of the driveway at a pace far too slow to satisfy my churning thoughts.

I settled for casual, despite it being the opposite of what I felt. "Yeah? Okay. I'll be home in fifteen."

It would be more like five, but if the person in the house could overhear, this would buy me a few precious minutes of time and put surprise on my side. From the lack of fear in my mother's tone, I knew she didn't feel the situation was dangerous, but I felt my crash course education into the darker side of humanity left me paranoid, and for good reason.

I covered the receiver with my hand. "Luke, step on it."

Chapter Twenty

Eren didn't have the patience to wait in the car. I didn't have the patience to open the front door stealthily. Luke didn't have the patience to let me walk in first.

Therefore, when the door slammed against the wall hard enough to knock out the stopper, my mother and the threat/guest found themselves staring at a muscle sandwich with me, invisible because I was shorter than both of the brothers, as the jam in the middle.

Behind me, taking in a scene I couldn't see, Eren's shoulders began to relax. I shoved my way out of the barrier the boys had formed around me and saw exactly why he'd judged the threat level to be lessened.

There was someone in the kitchen, laughing politely at whatever my mom had said. She turned around and faced me and my mind started to itch. Like it wanted to supply me with some information or memory, but didn't want to breach the surface.

As I stared her down, my mother asked the obvious. "Um, honey? What is that man doing here? And—Oh! Hi, Luke! Haven't seen you in a while."

Eren introduced himself, but Luke and I were fully absorbed in watching the stranger. I remembered the pixie-like features on the girl before me, but from where? I would have thought I'd remember someone with blue hair. "These two are my other partners for the group project."

Pixie-girl didn't even blink. That solidified my suspicions. She wasn't from school, and whatever project she'd made up was a fake. She wanted something from me.

I smiled as sweetly as I could, aware it most likely looked like I was baring my teeth. A long, subtle inhale told me the girl was wholly human, but I didn't dismiss the possibility of danger then, not even close. Next to the pixie-girl was a case that looked like it was made for a camera tripod, but a suspicious waft of gunmetal came from that direction.

"Let's go upstairs to get started, shall we?" I was proud of how calm the words sounded until Eren shot me a warning look. I'd slipped into ice queen mode without realizing it. Crap.

Pixie-girl's eyes hardened, and she hefted the case she'd brought into her arms. Good. I wouldn't feel bad about throwing her out of a window if she was armed. I gave Eren a shove to get him moving, then another when he was on the stairs, but that one was because I was pissed.

I hissed softly in his ear. "Just because she's a girl does *not* mean she isn't a threat. If she makes a move, I'm defenestrating her."

Eren was less subtle than me, and spoke at a mock whisper both the humans behind us could probably hear. "What's she going to do, Kitten?"

I fought to keep the growl out of my voice. "If you'd quit eyeing her like a horny prepubescent, you'd smell the shotgun in that case she's carrying."

It was strange. I hadn't known it was a shotgun until I said it, but it seemed so right. Something scratched under the surface, so I rolled with it.

Eren, inhaling, swore as he came to a conclusion similar to my own. I took the lead and brought them all to my room, where the windows were the largest on the second floor. Like the wolves' hunting formation, I stood in the center, facing the door as Eren entered and moved to the right and Luke entered and moved to the left. When pixie-girl entered, she shut the door behind her and faced us, crossing her arms.

There was one long, excruciating second of silence. Then, pixie-girl and I spoke at the same time.

"Obviously, you aren't here for a history pro—"

"Yeah, um, I'm not going to beat around the bu—"

We both silenced ourselves at the same time, but I waved her on.

She nodded, appreciative. I got the vibe that this was a little too formal for her. "Hi, I'm Katherine, and this is going to sound crazy, but time is running out and—"

Holy cow, is poison ivy on the brain a thing? Because when she said her name, my mind went up in itchy flames. "Wait."

Her eyes widened, baring the same hope they'd had when she'd first seen me. Katherine held still and waited for me to speak, as did the brothers, who both looked slightly confused at my outburst.

My shoulders dropped, each fraction of an inch clicking my muscles as if they were being lowered by cogs.

"Gyrating garudas," I muttered under my breath. Eren, the only one who could hear it, stifled his laugh.

I turned to Luke. "Were there any major events in the news in the past month? I haven't been watching."

His eyebrows sunk down, but he still answered. "Jessica missing, Benjamin's disappearance..."

I rushed in, sorry for the rudeness but all too high-strung as my mind put the pieces together. "Worldwide."

He nodded. "Alaskan massacre, possible temporary paralysis bioweapon testing on an island outside of Canada, dangerous swamp gas discovered, with casualties..."

I stopped listening. I already knew each item on the list, stripped bare of the excuses covering them.

I'd been there.

I was over four years old. I could connect the dots and color in the lines to reveal the picture before me. Okay, I was missing a few, but once you've got the horns, tail, and pitchfork, it's pretty easy to fill in the devil. Katherine, dreams coming true, and puking into flower pots led me to a similar conclusion.

Demons.

Katherine saw the look in my eyes and the slackness of my jaw. "You understand what's going on now?"

I nodded, my emotions at war inside me despite my calm façade. "I believe I do."

Eren opened his mouth. "Then would one of you pretty ladies fill the rest of us in?"

"In a minute," I replied, reaching for my bag of tricks hiding between the mystical clutter on the dresser. "I assume that if Katherine's here, then there's something nasty about to go down elsewhere."

Katherine's eyes glittered as she smiled at me. "You'd be assuming correctly. Care to help me take on some demons?"

I smiled back at her, but it was tainted with steel and sadness as I grabbed my bag of tricks, slipping my fingers over the cool silk in my palm. "With pleasure."

I followed Katherine out the door, throwing a glance at the boys over my shoulder before waving at them to follow.

Luke looked lost. "Are we not throwing her out a window?"

I made a quick excuse about needing film of the school for a video project, plausible because of Katherine's apparent tripod case, and we set out. The relief on my mom's face, glad for both my seemingly improved social life and for the newest announcement on the television, that Benjamin had come back home, made me feel guilty. I shook my head as I closed the door. This needed to be done.

We crammed into my car, which suddenly felt tiny. Luke sat next to me in the passenger seat, and both Eren and Katherine were crammed in the backseat. Eren didn't seem to mind his position next to her, maybe even a little too at ease with it, but every time he gave her a glance she gave a more meaningful one to the shotgun perched between her legs.

I quickly introduced everyone, but I could tell Luke was brimming with silent questions even as I did so. He tilted his head at me. His light eyes met mine, and dang if I didn't take it as a challenge, just like the day we met.

"Explain," he ask-ordered.

I tried my best, hoping he'd take my words at face value. "We're stopping at your house, and you are going to have to grab any pistols you have, and that .30-06. Take the silver bullet, too. Oh! And maybe Katherine has some rock—"

I heard a *swish* in my ear, and I could see Katherine grinning as she shook a shotgun shell undoubtedly full of heavy rock salt. "I've got you covered. In fact," she pulled out a few baggies of all different colored substances and a small bottle of what was undoubtedly holy water, "I've got you *more* than covered."

I liked her. I liked her a lot.

It took all of thirty seconds to pull into the clearing that served as Luke's driveway. He put his inquiries on hold and hopped out without a word, disappearing into the dilapidated cabin.

The car was silent as we waited for him to return. It struck me, suddenly, that if this was happening, I had people outside this car to worry about. Hesitantly, I lifted my cellphone out of my pocket and hit speed dial.

The sound of metallic grinding drifted through the line, and I didn't even have to say hello. "What're you calling for, honey? Something wrong?"

Dang those paternal instincts. I was treading on light ground. "Hi, Dad. Mom knows, but I'm working on a group project and I won't be back until late. Did you want to go somewhere with Mom tonight? You did say you two wanted to check out that Italian place."

I was suspicious, he was suspicious... "Oh, that's nice of you, sweetie, but it's over an hour away from here."

I didn't know if that was far enough, but it would have to do. "You've been working hard. You deserve it. Well, I guess I'll be seeing you later, then? Loveyoubye!"

I hung up on his protest. A long sigh escaped me, but I had to hope I had done enough. Katherine turned to Eren and tilted her head, her cropped hair spilling over her cheek. "Why isn't he grabbing a gun?"

I felt like I could trust her, but my throat constricted violently at the thought of spilling our secrets aloud. "Ah, he and I have...special skills."

Eren cut me a sharp glance for that statement. "Whatever this is, it does not warrant that."

Katherine's head didn't un-tilt. "What are you, like, a bomb expert?"

Eren rolled his eyes upward in contemplation. "Something like that. The body count's about the same."

Katherine seemed to be mentally recalculating. At the same time, Luke strode through the doorway, looking every inch a chiseled action hero with a pistol in a belt sling and his signature .30-06 slung over his shoulder.

Katherine maintained the same expression. "That could be useful."

Without a word, Luke reached through the open car door and offered me the pistol. I shook my head, knowing that if I used my greatest weapon, if I shifted, the pistol would lie on the floor for anyone to use, possibly against one of us. Or, that is, anyone or anything with hands.

Eren looked at Katherine like she was nuts, and I almost felt sorry for him. He was in so over his head.

Luke managed to compact himself and his guns into the teeny tiny passenger seat, and asked where we were going with that silent, questioning expression of his. I mirrored it at Katherine.

She stated the instructions like she had them memorized. "End of this road, two lefts and a right. In the woods. Also, mind handing me that ammo for a sec? I'll add a little something...special."

Luke didn't move for a second, but Katherine gave him a quick summary of the how's and why's of blessing bullets. Without a word, he held them out in the palm of his hand, his huge fingers dwarfing the glimmering clips. Katherine got to work.

I put my body on autopilot for the drive, my mind whirring. Plan? I needed one. But still, I had to keep on glancing at Katherine to make sure she was real, that she hadn't disappeared just like the dying sun had a few minutes prior. I shook myself.

"Okay, Katherine, what exactly are we dealing with?" I asked, my knuckles tight on the steering wheel, bending it with my werewolf strength.

She didn't look up from what she was doing, mixing together the herbs and holy water with foul smelling black gore—the first truly demonic thing I had seen. *This is real.* "A weak spot was opened. Well, a giant portal, really. In the woods, the Corrupted took a raven host, and somehow the ritual or whatever was completed—"

Eren piped up. "Man, don't you just hate when that happens?"

Katherine's mouth pressed into a line at the realization the boys were not up-to-date. "Quiz time. What do any of you know about what I just said?"

Luke blinked. "Wasn't something I learned in school."

I smothered a chuckle as I turned my headlights on, having forgotten to even though dusk had firmly settled over our sleepy little town. "Right. So, um, I know everything. I think it's a clairvoyant type deal? Except, you know limited to dreams? Not sure, but I've had dreams of you and the—"

Katherine laughed, high-pitched and tolling, like a giggle. "Are you saying I'm the girl of your dreams? You're cute and all, but I think it might be best to postpone our relationship until after the apocalypse."

Eren did a double take, which made Katherine laugh even harder. "I'm bi, sweetie."

His eyes darted to the side in deep contemplation, but his thoughts were practically audible to me as he processed the information. He shrugged as he came to the conclusion that as long as he was still in the running, it was all good.

Apparently, that was visible to those without our super-special werewolf communication, because Luke craned his neck at Eren and the corner of his mouth slid up.

He shot a quick glance between the occupants of the back seat no doubt thinking about what an explosion the pair would be. "Not likely."

Eren huffed. When he crossed his arms, the muscles bulged out like they wanted to jump from his skin, but they didn't slither along in the werewolf fashion. "Okay, keep explaining? Rituals and pervy dreams?"

I tried to draw a deep, calming breath through my nose, but only managed to drag the scents of the occupants of the car inside of me. A small, unaltered voice in the back of my head whispered to me, urging me not to tell, that it was my secret, my dream in all the senses of the word.

"So, dreams. Every night, I see the two of them, Katherine and the Protector, traipsing around hunting demons. Saving people. But demons, they radiate this hellish fire, right? Come into contact with it, it'll kill you. Get near it for too long and your soul starts to decay, deteriorating until the energy collapses in on itself.

"I think," I shot a confirmation-seeking glance at Katherine, "that pretty soon, if we don't already, we'll have demons here."

Katherine nodded. "From what I've heard, they're coming through a weak spot caused by the Corrupted—never mind that now, it's a little too late and the information isn't crucial—"

Luke's hand was on my lower shoulder, which I hadn't realized was vibrating until then. I wasn't sure if I was falling apart or if I had finally found the missing piece. Wasn't that supposed to be obvious?

The warmth on my shoulder was reassuring, even if it was patchy over my scars. So was Luke's voice, and his lack of doubt in me. "Life or death?"

"I wish. Life or damnation."

And that was when it hit me: Eren wasn't the only one out of his league. We all were. We were all so screwed.

Luke nodded at my comment, and I stared at him in disbelief. "You're just okay with that?"

Eren piped up, leaning forward to put one of his hands on the side of my seat back. The other one found the intricate mess of scars at his collarbone and scratched absentmindedly.

"Kitten, that's where we're all headed anyway. Might as well enjoy the ride." He paused before he added, "not that I quite buy into this yet, though. No offense."

Katherine jolted suddenly, her gun's barrel scraping the car door. "Wait, sorry, you just drove past it!"

I hadn't thought to slow down when I reached where she'd indicated. No, I'd been on autopilot, my body taking me straight to the home all-too-familiar to me. The one that, apparently, was less than fifty yards from the hellish gate.

My heart sank like a stone, cold, hard, and lifeless.

"No," I whispered, flooring the gas, uncaring about how any of this would look to a police officer.

Katherine made a confused "um" sound as I sped into Benjamin's driveway, violently twisted the key, and leapt out of the car. I marched forward, blinded by worry, before spinning on my heel and meeting her head on.

"The Protector. Where is she?" I demanded, regretful for my sharp tone, but unwilling to waste time apologizing when Benjamin's soul could be on the line. After I barked out the question, though, I felt deflated. I had never been the Protector, not even in my dreams.

I refused to let that fact make me useless. My eyes darted, seeing the layout of a rough plan overlaid on reality. The Protector would take the demons, I would search the top floor right-to-left for Benjamin and the rest of his family...

Katherine seemed to sense the urgency, but had few words to put up quickly enough for me. "Wait, what?"

"The Protector," I insisted. "Angelfire, wings, Haldis? She needs to be here."

Dawning understanding widened her eyes, and I was glad one of us could make sense of this cruel twist of fate. "I think there's been a bit of a misunderstanding. She isn't here, in that sense—"

My plans caught fire before me and I swore, the creativeness of it making Eren smile despite the grim situation. He'd taught me well.

I stomped out the mental flame and went with the charred remainder, unwilling to delay. "We don't have time to waste. Come with."

I motioned for everyone to follow and took off, not bothering to limit my wolf-hastened gait. At the front door, the one that had been shut in my face only hours earlier, I tried to weave together my battle strategy. It was still hazy and vague, but that's how things tend to work when your enemy is unknown. Well, that and when the only thing that could kill said unknown enemy was unavailable. Shouldn't she feel the call?

The front door splintered like the tail of a shooting star when I put my foot through it.

Words ripped out of me like barbed steel. "Katherine,

clear the bottom floor. Rock salt only. Luke, with her. Eren, perimeter. Let nothing escape. You see anything off, and I mean *anything*, you call for me. Understood?"

The fact that Eren's signature smirk had left his visage was all the confirmation I needed before I took off up the stairs.

I could hear scuffling in the master bedroom. I knew, *I knew*, that something was happening in there. But I didn't even hesitate as I passed it, running straight to the room with the door that had already borne my abuse.

That made it easier to pull open, but not to take in the sight before me.

Everything was broken. The room was covered in colorful explosions, bursts of white powders and brown wetness and rainbow shards. All the things I'd brought to protect Benjamin, all useless puddles of dust. I wished I could have missed it, but the tiny drops of blood scattered throughout didn't escape me, not for a second.

The last of the droplets resided under my left foot, ceasing before they went into the hall. Benjamin had left. No one remained in that disaster zone.

A body squirmed against the floor in the bedroom down the hall, the carpet fibers shifting loudly enough to sound like tearing fabric to my werewolf ears. I could hear tiny, hiccupping sobs from the room to the left. My decision between them was made before I weighed the outcomes.

Melinda's doorway was clear, but I couldn't help the thought that I would have preferred to tear it down and use it as a makeshift weapon. My fingers were itching for the pistol I'd refused.

Opposite the sticky shadows that clung to the house,

every light possible seemed to shine from Melinda's room. They were blinding and I couldn't fight off the image of a restrained mental patient staring up at the ceiling light, unable to move.

"Melinda?" I called, softly. Something shuffled in the corner, and I saw a girl there, curled up in a ball.

Her hair was in massive tangles, a nest. "Melinda, sweetie, is that you?"

Again, the shuffling. It was the sound of her drawing further into herself, so stiff and shrunken I thought the vertebrae I could see were going to snap before my eyes.

My heart broke. "Melinda, it's me, Leah. Please, I'm here to help you."

I approached her, slowly. She trembled so rapidly and subtly I didn't notice it until I drew closer, but once I had I could not banish the observation. I tried to reconcile my image of her, hands on hips and chin held high, with what was before me.

I reached out, uncertain, my hand hovering an inch off her shoulder. "Hey, Melinda, hey. It's okay. I'm going to take you out of here, all right? I—"

She twisted suddenly, like her upper body was on an axle. I barely registered the flash of metal as she slashed me with the knife she was carrying.

I cried out as my hand was scored deep by the cooking utensil, and felt the panic surge as I noted the silver surface of the blade. I felt my irises bleach out to gold and felt the wolf raise its eager head.

Then the plug was pulled, lights out. My breath didn't burn with the scent of silver because there was none. The blade was steel.

I could have cried in relief, but Melinda was doing

that for me. Pregnant tears rolled down her face. Her wide
eyes, murky and bloodshot, found mine. The knife fell
from her hand, but she only pressed further away from me.
She closed her eyes, ushering out a new wave of tears, and
pressed her cheek flush against the wall, waiting.

I snuck my hands around her quivering body and lifted
her up, even as she began to hyperventilate. She stiffened, as
brittle as straw when I drew her closer to me and wrapped
her in a hug.

For a few seconds, it was as if she'd frozen: her tears were
the only things about her that moved. Then she moaned
and her head dropped to meet my shoulder, her neck limp. I
gathered her in my arms, a task easier said than done with the
gangly child, and carried her out of her illuminated sphere.

Her hands clenched together behind my back as I
walked down the hallway, but I knew already that their grip
would have to be broken. Things still slithered on the floor
of Benjamin's parent's bedroom.

Katherine and Luke were on the stairs, climbing up.
Katherine's shotgun was balanced in her right hand, while
Luke's rifle was over his shoulder and his pistol was at ready.

Katherine's eyes roved over the girl in my arms. "Bottom floor is all clear. I assume outside is as well, because
Eren had nothing to say."

I could hear the lone figure in the room move across the
floor, too heavy to be Benjamin. A bang came from the bedroom, something hitting the wall near us. Melinda flinched.
Katherine's shotgun was up instantly.

I tried to pull the girl away from me, but Melinda held
on tighter.

"No!" she yelled, her voice high-pitched and animalistic.

Luke evaluated the situation. "Stay with her."

Katherine nodded, her chin on the stock of the 20-gauge. "Yeah, we've got this one."

Protests bubbled up in my throat, but I tamped them down. "Be careful."

They inched toward the entrance, silent as creeping death. Luke reached for the handle, his huge hand dwarfing it. Katherine counted to three with her left hand in the air.

When the last finger fell, Luke yanked open the door and Katherine plowed in first. Luke filed in behind, pistol in hand.

I took it as a good sign no shots were fired in the first few seconds.

I stalked closer, trying to see in the gap while preventing Melinda from doing the same. I flinched when Katherine's pale arm appeared in the space and widened it, blindly shoving the door against the wall. "You might want to see this, Leah."

"Melinda, I have to go in there. Stay here, all right? It'll be okay. I'll be out in a minute," I cajoled.

I don't think she felt safe, but I felt her shiver at the thought of entering the master bedroom. She sniveled as I set her down on the floor, but stood on her own, leaning against the wall. Her dark skin was bleached unnaturally pale, but her eyes held a spark of life, or maybe madness, in them. Her little fists clenched even as she hiccupped from her doubled breathing.

Her mouth worked before she managed to get out a small, "okay."

I drew myself straight and pushed forward before the doubt could collapse my spine. Once over the threshold, shadows embraced me.

Chapter Twenty-One

I don't know how I'd missed the stench of it while walking past. Inside, it was like living tentacles of the foul odor crawled through my airways, threatening to rip me apart. Thick, human scent, as if the air itself was dirty. Underneath it all was the brine of tears and sweat.

The salt from those had not been enough to keep the evil at bay, it seemed.

There were no lights on, but my augmented vision cut through the dimness like a blade. Luke and Katherine held still as I approached the crumpled form on the floor. I knelt, my knees hitting the floor quicker than if they'd given out.

I reached out my hand to Rosalind, who hissed as my skin brushed hers. She shimmied away, redness covering her flesh where it didn't leave the carpet, and I saw something flicker white, then black, then white in my peripheral vision.

Carefully and more slowly than I could afford, I turned my head to meet it. In the corner, a pocket of pitch blackness, a rocking chair stood as still as its occupant. Even once my eyes found his, my ears picked up no sound. No heartbeat, no breathing, nothing. The blood that had run down his neck was cold and brown, staining his shirt and the ground below him. Only the large incision on his neck held the ruby hue.

Yet Cole Bellevue's eyes still darted, back and forth, back and forth within his rigid body. One second, his eyes were on me, the next, the window. White, brown, white, brown.

Rosalind moaned on the floor, lifting her bloodstained hands to her face as realization shattered me. Her eyes, with a gaze as vacant as her husband's was pointed, roved over the corpse, which had stilled. Small whimpering sounds bubbled in her throat, growing and growing until they burst forth in a scream that made everyone in the room flinch.

I watched her bare hands thump the carpet, leaving stains. I was out of the room before the banshee's wail had ended. Melinda, with her hands over her ears, followed me without a word, but Katherine's words cut through the air.

"What do we do with her?" she posed.

Rosalind gasped, having run out of breath to expel. I spoke over it. "Leave her. We need to go, now."

Katherine opened her mouth and then closed it, only opening it again after she had peered into the corner with the rocking chair, where Cole's eyes finally stood still, free from whatever had possessed him. "She's a murderer! We can't leave her."

I blinked slowly, my eyelids heavy with choices and consequences. "She murdered no one. We need to get outside, and quickly."

I let out a hint of the suspicion I'd been holding, fearing the implications would make it real. "We haven't heard from Eren." *Or Benjamin.*

Luke's eyes grew wide, panic striking them like lightning. His boots slammed against the stairs as he went down, leaving while I fixed Katherine with a meaningful stare. I ran after him and onto the porch, Katherine behind me by only a second's delay.

"Eren," Luke called. "Eren!"

I'd never heard him raise his voice, and that almost shook me more than the body in the bedroom. Almost.

I grabbed Melinda's shoulder, steering her toward my car. "Stay here, please. You'll be okay."

A curl of ebony hair hid half of her face, but she didn't move it. "What about you?"

One corner of my mouth drew back. "I'm going to fix this. Then I'll come get you."

I shut the door behind her, hating the finality of the clicking locks. Behind the tinted windows, she was just a blur of motion as she hunkered down.

I ran, my speed driven by necessity but my path aimless despite the rising urgency in my bones. The sound of my fleet footsteps mirrored that of Luke's and Katherine's, further away. The woods were eerily quiet, no creature dared to raise its voice. That is, except for Luke shouting and the werewolf growling.

Eren. He was close. Close to me and close to the edge.

"Eren!" I yelled, and hoped my cry would carry to the others, alerting them. I had no time to tell if my feeble attempt worked before I launched myself forward, leaping off rocks and tree stumps in an effort to cover as much ground as quickly as possible. Branches I didn't care to avoid stabbed at me, opening bloody gashes in my face and my sides, but it didn't matter.

He came out of nowhere. I skidded to a stop, leaving huge, muddy furrows in the ground. For a second, I thought I'd happened upon a stranger. A man who did not lean casually, but stooped, drawn lower by the weight of the world. One who did not smirk, but bore a grimace carved by years of pain.

All that, before I could even see his face. Eren did not stiffen as I approached. He showed no sign of recognition, but spoke to the unseen.

"And if I..." He hesitated, spitting out the conclusion only after a second of silence, "accept?"

My heart beat blurred my vision with each pulse. I moved toward Eren, sneaking around the edge. The white scar on his collarbone and shoulder stood out like an accusation against his red-flushed neck.

He wasn't alone.

Of course, I knew he couldn't be. I knew he was talking to someone, but I just hadn't wanted to believe it. A spike of dread lodged itself in my heart. If tension didn't perfume the air and the muscles in Eren's back did not swim beneath his skin, I would have been glad when the small figure before him came into focus.

Benjamin.

Neither of them looked at me, but a slow, creeping smile began to warp Benjamin's face in a way I had not seen before. The spike of dread twisted violently, a painful wrenching.

I felt like I was sinking. "Eren, whatever he is saying, don't listen to him."

He flinched, the only sign he could hear me. Benjamin's upper lip lifted further, but it was a cruel mockery of anything human. Fabric protested as he drew a knife, a small kitchen ornament, its tip stained dark. The second it was out its scent rushed my senses. Burning. Silver. Blood.

The tiny blade fit his hand perfectly. "You know my offer is merciful. Your tarnished soul calls to me, and if you allow me to deliver it now, I *will* spare them. My word is my oath."

My mouth dropped open in protest, rage dragging its claws at my rationality. "You can't believe him! He's talking about dragging you *to Hell,* Eren!"

Benjamin turned to me, his eyes black orbs, lightless and inhuman. Pieces started clicking together. My sweet, sweet Benjamin was possessed. He had been since we found him in the woods. His father's corpse was still leaking from stab wounds in his own bedroom. His mother mourning the dead as if she had not killed him. She hadn't.

Where was the Protector?

"It's a demon, you can't listen to it. It lies! There's a loophole, somewhere," I insisted, begging Eren to turn toward me, to see the truth in my eyes. "Please, you can't hate yourself this much."

The Protector would know what to do. She'd save the innocent. Send the demon back to Hell.

He whispered, barely a breath, "That's where I'm headed, anyway." He sucked in a deep breath, as if the intangible air could fill him. "Might as well do something good in the process."

Innocent. That word didn't apply to Eren. Or Benjamin, now.

I could feel myself on the verge of shifting, my eyes flooding with gold. "I won't let you! We need you, here, now, to stand and fight. To save hundreds, not a handful! Think of Luke, *he* needs you!"

Eren was on me in an instant, his eyes wide with torment.

"I need to do this for him!"

I bared my teeth and raised my voice to match his. "Don't, for even a second, think your brother would—"

Eren growled, the sound crescendoing to a near scream

I picked words from. "I killed them! I killed them! Our mother, his father. The first shift, I—I fucking ate them! He wasn't even there. As I murdered them. Then he was and I tried to kill him, too. My own brother. What sort of monster...Oh god, when I woke up, she didn't have a face. Just hair. Gold hair. Both of them. And the eyes, the eyes, always had been blue, but never so cloudy—"

He was gone, his words shaking as his own eyes were focused on something I couldn't see, in his memories.

Like a slap to the face, I was viewing the same, but not from his perspective. The Protector's. The dream I'd had, not too long ago, with the timber wolf and the pool of blood ever-expanding. Tears flooded my eyes. Luke and Eren had come here to flee from what he'd done.

Eren was still talking, incoherently. He stopped suddenly and looked me in the eye. "Monsters like me deserve to rot in Hell."

Luke busted through the tree line, Katherine on his heels. His expression switched from worry to relief to confusion, then realization and fury as Eren closed his eyes and shook, unable to bear the sight of him.

"Eren, don't—"

But he didn't have to. Our argument had left us blind, our senses tuned to each other. The shadow that was Benjamin rose from behind Eren and, before I could shout, stabbed his silver blade across Eren's palm with inhuman strength.

"Don't!" I screamed, but it was far too late.

Eren folded in on himself, his bones crunching and snapping in a quick cacophony before he emerged, wolf.

His snarling tore through my head, and as I looked from the canine to Luke to Katherine and finally to Benjamin, something in me clicked the same second Luke chambered his silver bullet.

I don't know exactly if it clicked out of place or in, but everything changed around me.

The world grew fuzzy then crystal clear, but shadows and light clung to everything, an abstract aura. I was used to hyperaware senses, but those were just that: senses. It didn't compare to the sudden intrusion of everything I felt, of not only hearing the leaves scrape in the treetops but knowing them, almost seeing each jagged edge as they rubbed together high above.

All things were alive. A breeze spiraled lazily, making itself known, ready to assist. The earth pulsed beneath me, a heartbeat. Alive. Moisture budded from the air and dripped down my fingertips, tear drops of their own.

But most of all, fire. The shape so familiar to me, my nightly companion, slowly and steadily awakened in my palm. Haldis, glowing with a pure gold blaze, enraged and invigorated. Its flames licked up my arm, through my veins, until my heart flickered to life, thumping to a foreign rhythm. Familiar feathers spread from below my shoulder blades, waving in and out like light on the ocean's surface.

My mind fractured. The wolf, whose thoughts had become familiar to me, the boisterous id to my ego, fell silent. Never would I be rid of it, but for the first time since I'd touched the silver, its influence was no more than the feeling of a presence.

The Protector's mind spread through mine, engulfing me.

Katherine's attention shot rapidly between the werewolf, a threat unknown to her, and Benjamin. She did not spare a glance for me, yet half her face was lit with the light I was casting.

"Long time no see, eh? About damn time you showed up."

I was paralyzed, yet my lips moved of their own accord. "You've been busy as usual, Katherine."

It wasn't even my voice. Luke, whose rifle was pointed unwaveringly at his brother, even with the safety off, opened his closed eye and drew his brows together, confusion melting his features. The rifle inched toward me, an involuntary twitch, before landing on the wolf that was spinning in circles, assessing threats and victims while singing its brutal song.

Luke called out, hesitantly. "Leah?"

The wolf heard the noise and leapt for him, its jaws open. For the briefest of seconds, or maybe a timeless moment, I saw Jeremy overlay Luke's features, and fall to the same strike. But when he came to rest, twitching on the ground, it was Luke's throat that jumped up and down as blood poured.

My mind turned to liquid fear, but my body sprang into action. My feet placed themselves, a steady one-two before I, too, was in the air. My unoccupied palm grabbed the furred neck of the beast and both of us tumbled out of Luke's path.

My mouth moved of its own accord, though if I couldn't feel it I wouldn't have thought it was me speaking. "Katherine, contain the demon while I deal with this one."

"Salt rounds only!" I yelled, before realizing no sound came with it. It was only in my mind.

I'm sorry, Leah. I was trying to avoid this, rocketed around my skull. One mental blink while I rolled with the wolf and my confusion dissipated.

Benjamin was not the only one possessed here. I was the vessel of the Protector.

I didn't have time to ponder it as the wolf's claws lashed

at my skin. I felt the pain all the same and gasped internally, but the Protector just grit her teeth. My teeth. Whatever, it wasn't as important as the beast trying to take a chunk out of me. Her. No, no definitely me.

The Protector planted my sneakered foot on the lupine form beneath me, and the shocks from his growls rumbled through my leg. Even as the wolf thrashed and snapped at my ankle, my foot held firm. Haldis shone brilliantly as the Protector spoke.

"Whether you are wolf or man, you, creature, have a soul. Yet your madness makes you a threat to these humans in a time when they have never been more threatened. I cannot allow such a thing. I offer you redemption or death."

The angelfire surrounding me did not burn it, but it had the werewolf squirming in more pain than a shoe to the chest could bring. The Protector answered my unasked question.

This one is heavily corrupted. The presence of angelfire enrages the darkest parts of his soul. I do not know if he can survive an angelic cleansing.

Maddened Eren only fought more vigorously, and I knew there was no compromise left in him, and his humanity slowly trickled from the hourglass.

"Shift, boy. You need to be human to understand the consequences of your decision."

The Protector straightened as she fell in line with my thoughts, realizing the futility of words against silver.

She nodded and spoke aloud. "Then I have no choice. I apologize."

Luke, torn between the two scenes, realized the danger of the situation in the same second I did.

When he yelled, I yelled with him. "No!"

381

But Haldis plunged down, its non-corporeal blade sinking into Eren's heart. Angelfire spread through him, hissing as his very soul caught flame. The wolf let loose a high pitched whimper-scream and its gold eyes rolled until the white was visible. Seizure-like convulsions wracked the body below me, which suddenly looked small. I beat my fists furiously on the mental barrier, desperate to stop the torture, but I knew it was too late.

I couldn't even cry as the noise died in his throat and his paws quit kicking. He gave one last, violent exhale.

Suddenly, the Protector was shoved against a tree, and the cold barrel of Luke's rifle was pushed against my sternum. He breathed heavily as if to compensate for the breaths his brother did not take, and the desperate fire in his eyes matched that of Eren's pre-shift. His smooth, steely composure exploded in a thousand fragments. The safety clicked off, the sound louder than any words could have been.

His voice was a rumble, the low and dangerous thunder of an oncoming storm. "Get the hell out of her body."

Katherine shook her head, still staring down Benjamin, whose demon, for reasons that probably had to do with her barrel full of rock salt, had not fled. Its smile told me it was more than pleased with the way things were unfolding. Its first push was all that was necessary. We were tearing each other apart.

"Luke, don't," she warned.

But he was far beyond caring about the opinions of the entity who'd murdered his brother. My heart broke. He'd been so loyal. He'd followed me, trusted me, and I'd plunged him into a world of nightmares and stolen his brother from him. The only family he'd had remaining.

There was no threat implied, only a promise in his words.

"Get. Out. Now."

The Protector met his eyes with her inhuman ones, but even with all her wisdom she seemed at a loss for words. "I—I am sorry, but I cannot comply."

In this world of black and white, it's the gray that hurts the most. I wasn't sure if the bruise pending on my chest was from the end of the .30-06 or the chasm I felt right in the center, leaking out its darkness.

"Luke, don't do anything irrational," Katherine warned.

He ignored her. "I will not ask again."

The Protector straightened and I could feel the decision she made. It was the same as always. In this Technicolor world, she saw black and white. Or, more accurately, black and gold.

"The demons—"

"Shut up!" Luke roared. I knew he was going to shoot me. I prayed that the Protector would be able to mend my flesh, but in a way, I was prepared for the alternative. I closed my mind's eye.

The Protector remained motionless, silent. Waiting. Just when I thought I'd yell, for what little good it'd do unheard, there was a sudden release of pressure on my chest. I became aware again to see Luke spin away from me.

He let out a long, shivering breath, hitched with either budding sobs or deathly fury. "I won't hurt Leah."

A whisper wove through the trees. "You'd...better...not."

Both the Protector's, my, and Luke's heads rose to find the origin. Against a tree, low to the ground, the wolf was gone. A shaky Eren took its place.

Shaky, but very, very much alive.

Chapter Twenty-Two

A hush fell over all of us, broken only by Eren's labored breaths. For a second, no one moved. Then Luke's gun was slung over his shoulder and he slammed into his brother in the most aggressively loving hug I'd ever witnessed. From the sudden, unabated joy that coursed through me, I knew that if I had a body under my own control, I'd make it a group hug.

Luke looked like his brain had sunk into his chest, leaving his thoughts hollow and his heart overwhelmed. The dulled look remained in his expression as he eyed the Protector, but it was vastly preferable to his anger.

"You okay?' he asked Eren, still wound tightly.

Eren stole the fight from him by speaking, his voice already stronger. He smiled, for the first time without malice. "Human."

He cleared his throat and continued, his posture weak but relaxed. "Thanks, Sparkles. I think you did me a favor. I can't feel it any more. The wolf. And I guess I should thank you, too, Kitten. If you're in there."

The Protector reaffirmed her grip on Haldis, in gratitude to it. "The wolf's entity must have hoarded most of the corruption. You may be rid of it entirely, now. But be warned: your soul was not pure. Where it was corrupted, it is now weak. It will take time to heal, and further taint will worsen your condition. Physically, mentally, and in your soul."

Katherine, who hadn't budged the entire time, cleared her throat. "I'm glad you're not dead, Eren. I truly am. I'm even up for a little hey-he's-not-dead party after this, but we have to deal with the demon right now. You up for that?"

The Protector watched as slowly, both boys nodded their consent. Luke monitored his brother, his protective streak running strong, but Eren shook his head, already refusing to leave before Luke suggested it. Used to this rejection, he turned to me.

"Leah," Luke said, his eyes still made of icy steel, "is she okay?"

The Protector paused, carefully, and focused her attention on me. My thoughts were bare, and I couldn't squirm away or hide my discomfort.

I do not desire to cause you such distress. If you wish, I will leave, but I do believe you know the consequences of that. I do not know how or why you were able to watch my activities, nor did I even know it was possible before this day, but it is fortuitous despite its mystery. You know the importance of my work. Our work, now.

My imagination knew them all too well. It was impossible to stay away from sticking the faces of those I loved and cared for on the countless bodies left by the demonic. Bleeding, dying, decaying. I couldn't do that to them.

There was only one question left to ask. Baring my thoughts, I sent all I knew about Jessica to the Protector. "I need to know. Was she...?"

The Protector's response was immediate. *It was likely she was taken and chained by one of the Corrupted, due to her mother's position of power.*

Then I'd failed her. Completely and utterly. But as I

looked around me, at the faces of those I held dear, I knew there was still a chance.

I'd give anything to keep them safe, including myself.

I will relinquish control for as long as you'd like. Do with it as you will, but know—she directed my head to look at Benjamin—*every minute wasted is another demon exiting the damned portal. You know what they are capable of.*

It wasn't even a question. As I rose to the surface, the angelfire died. When the last, swirling remnants left my skin and my eyes, I felt loss. Like just one leaf on the tree: tiny, insignificant.

Luke straightened as my eyes lost all gold, and rushed over to give me a supportive hand as I slumped, unprepared to support myself.

I didn't wait for him to ask. Instead, the words poured out of me in a long rush. "I'm okay. We need to let her do this, Luke. The Protector is our best chance. Trust her."

Luke's strong hand tightened involuntarily. "We could find a way, Leah. If you can't—"

I closed my eyes for a quick second, and splayed my fingers, already missing my autonomy. The decision was made. "There's not enough time."

Angelfire flooded my system, shoving me back into myself quickly but not harshly. Every heartbeat pushed it further, until the Protector stood tall. "We need to start."

Luke moved quickly, but it was clear he followed my warning and not the Protector's. All gathered in a semi-circle around Benjamin, who, if you didn't stare at his eyes, looked small and innocent.

The smile gave it away, too. Twisted and cruel far beyond what Benjamin had earned. The Protector moved closer, circling around the back. Haldis' angelfire spun and twirled in anticipation. A spring of discomfort welled in me.

"Wait," I called, but only the Protector could hear me.

When she moved closer to the possessed Benjamin, my discomfort turned into alarm.

"Wait! Stop! He's been possessed for too long! If you try to purify him, he'll die along with the demon!" I beat against the mental barrier, but was shoved aside like a pup.

It's most likely too late for his soul. I need to make sure the demon is dealt with.

"Luke! Eren! One of you, please!" I cried, but they couldn't hear me.

There wasn't a hint of worry on their faces. The same thing had been done to Eren, hadn't it? And that turned out well. I told them to trust the Protector. They didn't know. This crazy world I dragged them into, they didn't know the rules. And Benjamin was going to die for it.

No.

No, he wasn't. I wouldn't allow it. I *couldn't* allow it. Both the rational human and the primal wolf pieces of me agreed on this, fueling my strength and my desperation. I banged my fists against the mental barrier, exerting my mind in a way I didn't know possible. My whole being ached from the strain.

The hand holding Haldis didn't even twitch. Eren watched the Protector with his brow slightly furrowed, and for a second I thought he would say something, like he sensed the rage I felt, which would have been oh-so-apparent if I was in control.

But I wasn't, and I couldn't rely on his wolf instincts to save me when there was cautious hope that wolf didn't even exist anymore.

I could feel my own wolf like it was curled up next to

me, its warm body heating mine. We were shoved in this dark corner of awareness together, away from the blaze of angelfire. Our position gave me an idea.

I poked the wolf. Just a prod, but I could feel its curiosity rise.

"Wake, wolf. Rise and help me," I insisted, but while I could feel its attention on me, my words were useless.

I didn't pause, I had no time to. I forwent words and let the wolf feel what I was experiencing, the blinding fear, bitter betrayal, and my own flame-like anger hitting it like a blow. I wasn't proud of myself for it, it was almost like kicking a puppy, but when the wolf's emotions surged to match my own, I knew I had done the right thing.

Both of us strained and fought, not needing physical claws or teeth to push against the Protector. It felt like lifting the weight of the world through telepathy, a pressure so great I thought I would compress into nothing and be crushed by it even with the wolf bearing half of the strain.

Then, it snapped.

I thought for a second we had lost, that I'd been crushed into a pinpoint of darkness. It took me a moment to realize that I was staring into Benjamin's black, soulless eyes. I flicked my own away.

I flicked my own away.

I gasped when I realized it, and the sound actually made it to the air. Heads spun in my direction as the angelfire was snuffed out like a candle.

It didn't matter. I didn't need it anyway. I dug into my pockets as the thing before me spoke.

Its voice was a raspy croak so at odds with Benjamin's small mouth I thought it came from behind him. "And who are you?"

I found what I was looking for. My bag of tricks was warm and familiar in my palm. I pulled out a small, wrinkled piece of paper, the words too small to read without my adrenaline-enhanced eyesight.

I smiled. "I am your worst nightmare."

I began to read, my words soft at first. "Exorcizo te, omnis spiritus immunde..."

Benjamin stiffened, but laughter, not a demon, poured out of his mouth. "You, girl? You are no priest. Nothing more than an overzealous youth."

The Protector did not fight against the position she held, cramped in the same way I had been, but she was there, attentive and active. Her curiosity about my plan circled me. When she lightly prodded at the barrier between us, a light stream of blood trickled from my nose.

She didn't mean me harm, but she poked again.

I am no priest either, she claimed, *but I feel as though our shared, heavenly mission might make up for it.*

I nodded at the unheard voice, but it didn't tell me anything I didn't know. This was not just me fighting a demon, this was me saving Benjamin. I drew in a deep breath, ignoring the way it hitched.

Despite the Christian exorcism, I pulled out a long piece of braided sage and a small smudging feather from my pouch. I'd never used the matches that accompanied them, but I thanked the spirits when my first strike yielded flame.

"...omnis incursio infernalis adversarii, omnis satanica potestas..."

Benjamin twitched, once. He blinked rapidly as I fanned the smoke from the sage toward him.

"...in nomine Dei et in nomine Jesu Christi..."

When the thin wafts of sage hit him, his right eye

started to trickle blood. *This is safer for him,* I told myself. It has to be. But no reassurances could clear the icy fingers in my chest.

His veins writhed under the skin of his face, like worms squirming as they burned. I bit my lip to keep from crying out.

"Benjamin defende...Spiritus Sanctus habitet in eo."

There was just one more. One more line. I prayed to every god, every entity I'd ever heard of to save him, *just save him please.*

My voice rose with each word, until it was no less than a scream. *"Maleficiam umbram dimitte et pium hominum absolve!"*

Benjamin shuddered forward, slumping until his face was unseen. The only sound was the steady *drip.*

Drip.

Drip.

Of blood, falling from his nose and his eyes.

Oh god, Melinda was in the car. I was going to have to tell her I killed both of her—

My screams had died when I knelt before his prone form, but it wasn't because I had given up. Far from it.

My hand shot out and snagged the collar of his shirt. I pulled it forward and my other hand flew out to catch his chin, holding it upright so that if his eyes were open, they'd be on me. I removed some of the bloody crusts that had formed and pried one eyelid open.

Black as night, it slithered in its socket to take me in. I growled, high and agitated.

My hand clenched on his clothing. "Listen to me, Hell spawn. This is the end of your miserable existence. You will exit your host. You will crawl or slither or scrape by for a

390

few seconds and shroud yourself in darkness to heal how I have already weakened you. But right as you feel the wind chasing you, the earth beneath your feet, *you will feel the pain you've caused me, sevenfold.*"

Benjamin's lip curled, but I couldn't tell if he was in there still. "But who is to say your pain is over?"

Then he shuddered, and the muscles of his throat drew tight. His head lifted in a silent scream. Out from his mouth, thick as oil but light as the wind, rolled darkness.

The cloud of it rose, expanding, before it reached the size of a large bear. It fell all at once, making no sound when it hit the humus. Recognizing what needed to be done, I threw back the barrier between our souls and thrust the Protector to the surface.

The demon had formed a droopy horse, its legs crooked and wavering. Haldis cut straight through it, into the earth. Waves of flame overtook the shadow and expelled it with a brilliant burst of light. The ground quaked as it fissured, sucking in the remaining strands like a greedy mouth.

For a minute, there was silence. The silence so quiet your ears make up for it by ringing to phantom bells. The heavy breaths of my companions betrayed their frayed minds. The Protector consulted me and made one last statement before relinquishing control, allowing me to tend to Benjamin, the only one who breathed quietly, if at all.

"This was only the first. We have to shut that gate before others arrive."

I pulled up Benjamin's small face and lifted it toward me. His cheeks and forehead were feverishly hot. That's a good thing, right? Aren't the dead cold?

But when his eyes did not open and his neck remained limp, my heart stuttered. I put my fingers on his jugular and almost fainted in relief when I felt a pulse.

The Protector spoke softly to me, internally. *You saved a life I thought forfeit, Leah. For that I am grateful. You must watch the child, though. His soul is full of holes. If not for the plasticity of youth, he would surely be one of the Corrupted. As is, memories will plague him as living nightmares.*

I've done away with all his monsters so far. This will be no different, because I will be there for him, I replied silently.

Luke crouched next to me. He saw the decline of my shoulders and asked, "All right?"

I inhaled roughly, suddenly aware of how clogged my nose and throat were. "I don't think any of us are all right, but he's alive."

I drew my sleeve under my eye, where moisture had leaked out. Before the half-tear had soaked into the fabric, I was making a plan.

I couldn't bring Benjamin to the demonic hurricane we were about to plunge into, but I would not leave him this weak and alone. I glanced at each person surrounding me.

I couldn't leave Eren with him. He'd do no good guarding without a weapon. Though Luke had handed him the spare pistol, I could tell from his heavy-handed, stiff-armed grip that he had not used one before. Why would he, when tooth and nail surged free at the touch of adrenaline?

The question of how much forgiveness he'd allow himself now that he was rid of the wolf flitted through my mind as I watched Benjamin in my arms. Both of them had been possessed by something when they'd killed, yet I didn't see Eren's scars fading any time soon. I could feel Jeremy's gaze on me, from far away, as I made the decision I'd never questioned: I'd protect Benjamin from anything, even himself.

I shook my head to clear it of these thoughts. The future was only something I had to worry about if I survived. My eyes met Katherine's.

"I left Melinda in the car. If I bring Benjamin there, can you tend to both of them, make sure nothing happens?" I asked, but my tone was firm enough she couldn't have argued if she wanted to. I knew she understood that "make sure nothing happens" was synonymous with "anything that so much as moves near you, pump it full of lead".

Each second I wasted another demon crept out of the portal. Another life taken, another loved one stolen. We had to move. I couldn't see the demons yet, but I could feel their mounting presence, like smoke on the wind. When Katherine nodded, I gave her Benjamin with murmured re-assurances. He blinked at me, slowly, uncomprehendingly.

I didn't want to leave him, but I had to. Selfish choices were fantasies to me, and I dared not subject innocents to this ever-expanding nightmare in exchange for a few moments of peace, no matter how tempting.

An ink-black wing wheeled above me, and the memory of blood-matted hair of the same color reemerged unbidden. It did not slow my steps as I ran toward the spot the Corrupted raven had touched down. Boots pounded behind me, but not a complaint was uttered.

That was, until a small, swift body darted out of the underbrush. The black cobra raised its hood and hissed, striking at Luke, who leapt back in surprise. I spun, but before the Protector's lights could flicker to life, the snake kissed the end of Luke's barrel. Though it looked shadowy, just a step under corporeal to human and wolf eyes alike, the threat was clear.

Boom. Burning snake guts scalded my cheek. Eren stiffly

sidestepped as the eyes and upper jaw of the snake flew up and over his shoulder. It thudded like a fallen nut.

"Ow," I said, but less in my own pain and more in sympathy with the exploded serpent.

Luke pulled a handful of Katherine's blessed ammo out of his pocket and nodded to them before putting them back. "I like these bullets."

The wispy black essence of the demon stayed in the corpse, swirling. It was bound by whatever magic had shattered the body.

I pursed my lips. "I think I do, too."

I turned to Eren. "You've got the good stuff, too?"

He shrugged. "It doesn't matter much if I can't hit the broadside of a barn."

We were all moving again. I sprinted as quickly as humanly possible so that Luke didn't fall too far behind, but Eren was lagging slightly as well. Not all traces of the wolf were gone, but it was definitely diminished.

I had to toss my words over my shoulder and hope the wind would carry them to the brother's ears. "Well, as long as you don't shoot us, you're good!"

Eren's hand twisted upward, and his mouth twisted as he yelled. "Not really! *Not* killing you is not the same as being able to kill these—"

He was cut off by the close retort of a shotgun. Katherine.

I couldn't afford to stop, and before I could even process the blast Eren fell like a downed tree. I thought maybe the shotgun had done him in, but a lynx-like demon rose over his back like the sun greeting a new day. Except, you know, this sun was lacking the signature smile of a children's drawing and chose instead to replace it with a mouthful of needles primed and ready to deliver demonic flames.

Luke swore and doubled back for him. Instead of firing on the feline, Eren sent it flying with his fist. The light-weight cat spun head over heels until it collided with a tree trunk, but showed no sign of damage when it landed grace-fully on its feet. It darted for him again.

Luke made a grab for the creature, but at close range his rifle was as good as useless. Eren, on the other hand, would've been fine if only he thought to use the pistol in-stead of his limbs, which were scratched and slightly toasted from the dark flames. I came running, drawing from my wolf side to move more quickly.

Luke stopped me with a command. "Close the gate. They won't stop otherwise. No good here."

His eyes never left the darting, black form. When it was flung backward once more by Eren, Luke caught it in the ribcage with one of his spelled projectiles. Ash flew from the demon in a small stream, up and then down.

As yet another demon charged from the brush, I real-ized Luke was right. I shouted quick warnings before I left, but they fell on distracted ears.

"Eren, be careful. Your soul is unbalanced. It can't take much of this. Luke, remember to protect yourself, too. They're smart. They will attack you when you are occupied guarding your brother."

Luke's eyes were shot with the same red that was un-doubtedly running through the kicking vein in his neck. He blinked and his hand extended toward me, then dropped. "Don't do anything heroic."

I nodded. "Not until you've got my six."

It was understood and accepted, though we didn't

exactly have time to stare soulfully into each other's eyes or shake on it. A shotgun blast resounded yet again in the background. I felt my heart sink, but my feet only flew quicker, carrying me away.

The woods shifted from green to gray as I drew closer, the leaves wilting and dying from the pulsing decay in the air. Each breath made my lungs feel like they were rotting. The skeletal limbs of trees held no leaves to block the sun as I approached the center of it all, yet it felt like not a single ray of light dared to challenge the shadow of this place.

Demons crept around, as thick as a low-lying mist. I plowed through sharp boughs of trees, ignoring the sharp *snap* they gave and the *thud* when they hit the ground. It was too similar to the sound of breaking bones.

I glanced off one that sent me spinning, but when I tried to move forward, it brought me to my knees, its hold on my sleeve secure. I tried again to rush away, only to realize it was not a branch that held me, but the beginnings of a giant web, which extended far above me in the treetops.

The strand stuck to my shoulder wiggled at my escape attempt, and the vibration rode up to the mess of fibers above me. I thought the sticky, vaguely human-sized cocoon of silk near the top would stop it from spreading, but when my line's tremor reached it, something thrashed inside, with too many legs to be a person.

Unless it was multiple, smaller humans. I shuddered at the thought.

The web above it shuddered violently as whatever it was desperately tried to escape. I searched the land around me, looking for a way to get up there without becoming lunch, but it was short lived. When the movement of the strands reached the very tip, eight glossy eyes as large as my fist twitched above the heap of a trap.

Those orbs watched all as the huge arachnid descended on its captured quarry and its fangs appeared from behind the white glob. Each was the length of my head and the width of my forearm. They sunk into the squirming mass without a sound, but the animal inside shrieked its last breath.

The sound was horrible enough to cancel out the relief of it being non-human. The animal fell silent when its legs stopped kicking, the whole thing having lasted just long enough to be excruciatingly painful but not too long that it was inefficient. When the spider lifted its head, a thick, black tar-like substance dripped onto the white silk, hissing as it rolled down.

Corrosive, I noted, but I didn't have much time to process it before a softball of the substance flew at my head. I ducked so hard it was really more of a face-plant, then scurried up onto my knees. The adrenaline was making my head pound in time with my heart.

The Protector was suspiciously silent. "Ah, hello? Angel-on-my-shoulder? I could really use your help right now."

The Protector replied shortly. *Busy.*

"With *what*?" The last word was a bit of a screech as I threw myself to the right to avoid another spitball.

Preparing you to close the portal. As she said it, my stomach roiled. A little sprig of blood started to drip from my nose.

I moved too far and was thrown back like a slinky by the web that was attached to me. My breath whistled out when I hit the ground on my back.

I bared my teeth, which she likely couldn't see. "If you kill me I swear to god—"

Worry about the demon killing you first.

397

I hated to admit she was right, but when yet another projectile was launched, it splashed me in the arm, right through the shirt I was wearing and onto the scar I'd received the night of Jeremy's death. I wiped the blood away from my lip and set my gaze on the eight-eyed one above me.

I angled myself to make a smaller target, allowing the web to hang slackly between me and the pine I was bound to.

"You kiss your mother with that mouth?" I asked, but this time I was ready for the answer.

When the bubbling liquid flew my way, I sidestepped and used my lupine reflexes to put the string binding me in its path. The sizzle as it dissolved was satisfying, but when I was free, my only thought was, *what now?*

The arachnid had no such qualms. It descended from its throne like surefooted lightning and stopped in front of me.

"Um...Nice spider? Don't eat me?"

That brought up the memory of a certain snapping turtle and I would have laughed if, you know, I wasn't staring into the eight eyes of death.

Both of us moved at the same moment, the spider forward and me to the side. As it lunged, I leapt in the same direction and launched off of a tree trunk. Soaring through the air, I realized I had not thought my trajectory through at all, really, because instead of flying *away* I flew directly *into* the creature's abdomen.

If you ever wanted to know what it feels like to kiss an oversized, demonic tarantula, I'll fill you in: painful, more painful, and hairy. I was spitting out the nasty, barbed hairs when the spider reared, sending me to the ground. As I landed, the spider speared my arm with one of its legs, thrusting it downward with such force I heard a solid *snap* a second before the pain came.

I growled, the sound as far from human as it could get. My free hand shook as my fingernails were covered by skin, sharpening and darkening until only a curved claw was left. I slashed at the leg holding me, feeling a quick bite of pain as my nails pulled before breaking through.

The spider, unbalanced and bleeding burning gore, lurched forward. Its fangs dropped to mere inches above my neck and dribbled demonic venom on me.

I screamed as it burnt my throat and collarbone. The portion above my windpipe burned through the skin before I could blink, with the intention of burning a hole straight through. It wouldn't stop until I stopped breathing.

There was only one option that had me alive when this all ended. Well, one option that gave me the *chance* to survive.

I shifted.

I was barely done lobbing my clothes toward the final destination before it was on me. I relished the pain, embraced it. It was not weakness, it was strength. The snap of my bones as they reshaped, the seizure of my muscles before they released, the pull of my skin as it reoriented...It was simply *delicious.*

And the spider. It just stared, as if it's multiple eyes were tricking it, all of them had succumbed to a phantasm. A demon, hellish in nature, murderer, corrupter, deceiver. It looked at me as if I was all that was foul with the world.

Strike.

My eyes burned with gold fire, but not the angelic type. I tore into the part of the demon nearest to me, leaping high to clamp my jaws around the remainder of its stump leg.

The bristle-like hairs made the inside of my mouth bleed, and the black gore that came with them burned the wounds. The leg joint came away in my bite, a satisfying *crunch* that released me from my dangling position. My paws had barely touched the ground, only to leave again as I dodged the strike of those head-long fangs. Leaves sizzled as stray venom hit them. The sound of it made my hackles rise.

Threat.

I darted underneath the belly of the beast, biting at any flesh I could grab. A kick from one of the remaining legs hit my side like a mace, rolling me head over heels.

Pain.

It drew my thoughts further away from me, clouding my mind in the opposite way that my senses were sharpened. The Protector said something, but the words were scrambled uncomprehendingly. Like trying to catch rain with splayed fingers, her words slipped through.

Fight.

The spider spun quicker than even lupine eyes could follow and struck for me. Ribs creaking in protest, I rolled. A small snatch of my grayish fur ripped out when it caught a bush, but the adrenaline pumping through me didn't allow me to feel it, nor did the rapid healing, which was silencing the groan of my rib cage. A snarl ripped free as I attacked the meaty part of the spider's abdomen.

Survive.

There was less rage than desperation pumping through my veins. Ebony gore sluiced off the creature in clumps, but it showed no sign of slowing down. That is, until my muzzle bit deep.

Rend.

There was something there, underneath the layer of stinging hair and burning fluid, something that pulsed with life. I tore it to shreds. The visceral fluid splashed my eyes and burned my throat, but I ripped my head side-to-side anyway, the discomfort inciting me.

Burning goo bubbled against my nose, eating away at the skin. The spider twitched beneath me, its barbed hairs scraping my underbelly. It lurched to the side with only three appendages and skittered, but when it finally hit a tree trunk, it fell with a noise like a rock off of a cliff. Its head, thrust down by the failure of support from its body, cracked against the ground.

Hold.

But I knew my prey was vanquished when its fangs drove into the earth like stakes and the body softened like a rapid decomposition. When I jumped to the ground, my back paw sank into the remainder and came away coated in a wet film. I tried to put it down, but it didn't hold much weight. I limped away from the remainder of the spider.

Cover.

I found it just in time, before the arachnid exploded into ash. A sudden gale picked up the pieces and drew it over my fur, toward something ahead of me. The small part of me that retained my memory only provided one word to describe it.

Danger.

Footsteps echoed all over in these woods, things walking and crawling and slithering and skittering. The pounding *danger, danger* warning in my head allowed no time for me to lick my wounds, nor did the heavy slap of boots slipping over rocks.

Human.

The word rose, unbidden, and I wasn't sure if it was bad or good. Neither was I sure of the intent of the two of them staring at me.

One of them held a long device of steel, but traces of silver rose from elsewhere on him. My teeth gleamed freely when the scent of it scalded the inside of my nose.

Foe.

The wariness calmed as quickly as it came when I realized that rifle was pointed at what I'd killed, not me. Both of them smelled of wolf, faintly. The stone-filled expression of one and the way the other's hand was twitching in and out of a fist eased my mind.

Friend.

The voice of the lighter one was familiar, but his words were not. "Leah? I think you should shift back now."

His calmness struck a chord in me, but I did not shift back. I cocked my head and watched him, *really* watched him and the other. It wasn't hard to sort the drive rising up in me, even with the unease caused by the shuffling of the burning creatures around me, drawing closer.

Protect.

I spun, putting my back toward them in order to face the real threat. I limped forward, my rear paw stinging in pain. From inside, a different pain brought me to the ground, growling and struggling to rise.

Intruder.

A voice rang again, clear as a bell. I snapped angrily at the air next to me, but caught nothing. I scrambled up and darted away as quickly as my slowly healing foot would allow. The dark spots of gore stung as I stumbled onto them, like a swarm of bees.

Weak.

In comparison, that is what I was. I shook my head, trying to rid it of the spots in my vision. The complexity of the emotions toward whatever was inside of me didn't translate well, just evening out into a baseline pressure. I did not comprehend what it was urging to me to do.

I crawled forward, and the boys behind me lightened their tread as they followed my lead. Nothing, however, could make us invisible to so many eyes. A scream, the sound of animalistic alarm combined with screeching metals, grinding stones, and crackling flames took the valley, and everything exploded all at once.

Move.

The dark animals erupted from every corner. I dodged them with difficulty, teeth flashing. The humans, however, remained rooted in place, twisting and turning to pick off anything that moved too close to them. Within seconds, they were coated with soot-like remains as the perverse animals' carcasses dispersed in the wind.

Wrong.

I had my own coat of ash, the substance somehow heavier than its natural counterpart. It weighed me down while my teeth tore into a small, rodent-like creature, severing its spine before I tossed it. It rolled into the gaping, churning maw of earth in the center of this decaying ring of trees.

Stay.

But nothing staunched the flow of creatures. Vaguely, shadow wolves danced over my vision, as did the face of someone lost, the one I'd freed from their snap and tear. I shook away the memory, but it left me incensed. I crushed the skull of a strange, dark bird, but a loud blast made my head pivot. My flank stung, little trickles of blood pouring out. The angrier man was aiming his smaller, less imposing but no less deadly, weapon near me.

His words were tainted with strain, but not much anger.

"Missed that one, my bad."

I was stung again as the malformed thing he'd shot burst and sank into the ground. I chuffed lightly at him, but it ended in a whine of pain as the intruder twisted something deep within.

Struggle.

But the frustration built up, the threat inside was too much to deal with when I was being clawed and pecked and bitten by the hordes of black shapes around me. I spotted the bundle of clothes I'd lobbed over and ran to it. A familiar expansion of the mind occurred, and with it came the faintness that accompanied the change back to human. I clung to consciousness, knowing that to pause was death.

The roar of demons wasn't a lullaby, it turned out. Dizzy, I managed to throw on what I'd thrown over, minus a pair of underpants that had gone missing. The clothing looked more like rags, spotted with holes that hadn't been there before, their edges burning me where they touched my skin. I ignored it. My flesh could heal. It was my soul that couldn't.

The dizziness was too much to have been caused by the shift.

"What are you doing, Protector?" I asked as I snatched up a hand-sized beetle of some sort and dropkicked it into the horizontal gate. It dissolved into the writhing shadows, a living night.

I called out to Luke and Eren, who looked a little shocked to hear my voice wholly human. "The gate works both ways! Whatever you do, do *not* fall in!"

That may be an issue, said the Protector. I was so relieved to understand her I almost didn't comprehend her words.

When I slammed both palms into a poorly equipped

seal-like blob on my right, it tumbled down the hill and into the portal. As it rolled, though, it made a high-pitched squeaking sound that seemed to me to be about the same as the sound my brain's gears were making, grinding together.

I grit my teeth. "If you expect me to let Luke or Eren get dragged in, you are sorely mistaken!"

No, she said, *I expect you to jump in.*

Chapter Twenty-Three

I won't force you, the Protector told me. Her words rang true.

My voice and thoughts were strangely calm, even as I continued to dance with the demons. "But this was always the end goal, wasn't it? Everything you've done so far, you could have done without possessing someone."

Something stabbed into the back of my calf, but whatever the Protector was doing had a small amount of angelfire pouring through my system. It was able to stem the flow of the poison in my leg, and my werewolf healing took care of the rest.

The *crack* of the scorpion's exoskeleton under my bare feet was satisfying, if not painful. My breaths, though quick, didn't seem to be bringing enough oxygen. They were thin and carried the scent of burned flesh as thick as if I was forced to breathe through a veil of it.

Yes, all except this. My essence alone is not enough to combat the Corruption lurking in that bridge between worlds.

I was well assimilated to the Protector's methods. I'd expected something on this scale. There was no sting of betrayal, not a hint of anger. I was done being angry.

"So what you're doing now...?"

I'm purifying whatever I can of you so your own soul will not combat us on our descent. There was steel in the Protector's voice. Her resolve mirrored my own.

There was one thing tickling at my mind, though. "And the wolf?"

It's not like it was with the boy, the Protector explained. *His darkness was greater, and more confined to the lupine portion of his soul. Yours is less corrupt, and has it evenly distributed between wolf and human. It's unlikely I can 'cure' you as I did him.*

Air whistled as it flew from my nose and my scar throbbed. I didn't know whether to feel disappointed or relieved, but I could figure that out later. One of Luke's bullets hit a demon above me, one I had not seen while I was focused on the things crawling closer on the ground.

Worse than the ones headed in my direction were the ones heading in the opposite, leaving to do unspeakable things to innocent people. It struck me that I had not heard the blast of Katherine's shotgun in quite some time.

I turned around to see Luke and Eren. Something had bitten a chunk out of the top of Luke's ear, a small stream of blood trickling from the semi-cauterized wound. His trigger and trigger finger were dark with the glimmering fluid, as if he has touched the hole for only the briefest of seconds before firing another round.

The hand in which Eren didn't hold his pistol gleamed yellow at the knuckles, where bone poked through. His arms were covered in scrapes and burns, just like his brother's. I guess he'd lost his healing along with his wolf.

Luke dropped a clip from his .30-06 and swore as his replacement came up empty. When he shoved it into his pocket, it clinked against all its other unfilled brothers. He checked Eren's ammo, assuaged to find a few rounds left.

When something vibrated in my pocket, I jumped and

clawed at it. It was only my phone, however, and my desperate attempts at killing it pushed the connect call button.

My wolf hearing picked up the yells on the other end of the line. My parents. A chorus of growls rose, and the sound of two animals tearing at each other. When it fell silent, whimpering was all that was left on both sides. *They shouldn't be home. I thought I could spare them.* My stomach twisted violently as I realized what had brought them into this house of horrors.

My father's voice spoke in harsh whispers. "What are those things?"

There was movement, and a higher-pitched whine rose above the others. Not human. My mother's soft voice was scratchy and strained. "Nyami, baby...It's okay, good girl... good girl..."

The tinny tones of the phone made a bang sound like a gunshot, but the clinking afterward could only be pieces of drywall raining down. There was a scratch of fabric against the speaker and the line went dead. I hit redial, but met no salvation.

Luke stalked toward me, sending smaller demons flying from the tips of his steel-toed boots. Ash flew from him like an afterimage. His hand landed on my arm, the callused surface scraping comfortably as he gave it a squeeze. Both of us saw the panther approaching us as the same time.

The Rashtka's eyes flickered with glimmers of flame. An aura unlike anything I'd seen surrounded it, following its movements. There was a hideous screech of metal on metal which made Luke and I flinch.

It took me a minute to figure out it was laughing. My hands twitched at my sides, itching to cover my ears, unable to imagine a worse sound.

Until it roared.

The metal was still there, but shattering glass and raging flames combined with it to produce an unearthly sound. The worst were the human screams that underlay it. I had never heard such pain. I couldn't bear to think of their origin, but the Protector held back no truths.

It has gorged itself on souls, destroying them slowly, like a source of fuel, she said.

Luke watched the Rashtka, so enraptured he didn't notice I talked to myself. "Fuel to destroy you, I assume?"

And you in turn, the Protector agreed.

The plinking of Eren's gun stopped as he shouted toward us. "Where did they go?"

All demons had fled at the Rashtka's roar. Their absence brought no relief, as I knew they'd only find new victims.

That, and the only way they would have left was if they were sure we were as good as dead. Their faith in us was just so comforting, but I had my own faith. I had two with me I could call my brothers, and one whom I knew better than I knew myself.

Luke caught my eye, still alight with lupine gold. He took out his last bullet, the silver one. The only bit of the lethal metal he possessed. Even chambered, its fumes made my eyes water. He pulled the trigger.

The magically-enhanced bullet seemed to fly in slow motion, pushed by flame and impatient air, inching closer and closer to the Rashtka. The silver sank in the black fur, disappearing into the beast's forehead. For a second, nothing happened.

A breath.

Two.

Before shadows poured from the wound, water cascading

down. For a split second, I thought we'd won. That it would burst into ash and retreat to the depths of Hell, where it belonged. It wavered for a second and its fur rippled.

Then the invisible heat rising off of it intensified in a huge wave, shaking the ground like an earthquake. Every line of the beast screamed of fury, but no weakness to be found.

We were doomed.

All of a sudden, I shook like a rung bell. My vision blurred and the dirt I stood on rose up to meet me. My eyelids flickered, strobe-lighting the world around me. It was the Protector's last attempt to purify my soul, but the ringing in my ears and the way I felt like I was tilting as if I was on a boat spoke to the fact that there was probably not that much soul left.

When my knees scraped open upon the ground, my eyes cleared enough for me to see the burning rubies of the Rashtka's eyes, only inches away. Its breath crisped the flesh of my neck. My fist, shaky and weak, struck its chest uselessly.

"The Protector could not kill me. What makes you, a mortal, think you can d—"

Luke's boot had more of an effect. He kicked the cougar in the throat, pushing it away from me, but only a short distance. Eren's pistol immobilized the beast with a few quick shots to the ribcage, but it was clear it wouldn't stay down for long.

Luke lifted me to my feet as if I weighed nothing, but a fresh bout of blood escaped the cuts in his arm. He held me close for a second to whisper in my ear. "Can't win. Leah, run. Find your family. Get out of here. Now."

The cold steel of his gaze was the opposite of the demon's. So determined to protect me, but all he'd done was given me the perfect opportunity to do what I needed to do.

I did run, but not away. The swirling gate seemed to move toward me as I bridged the distance between me and it. Dread exploded through me as wisps of smoke curled around my ankles, tugging me into the center as steadily as if they were tangible ropes. It was all I could do to turn around and shout.

My voice didn't waver. "Rashtka, if you think you can take me, now's your chance!"

The beast laughed again as it stalked closer. Its feline body was long, lithe, and deadlier than a bullet, but fear had long since left me.

I knew of too many gods to pray to any specific ones, so I left whispered words for the Elementals. "As surely as the demons corrupt the souls of the innocent, they pollute your winds, rot your earth, muddy your waters, and taint your fires. Spirits, help me or they will bring death to us all."

A kiss of wind pulled back a strand of my burned and battered hair. The rustling near my ear was the only sound available to me, even my heart seemed to have stilled.

Then the breeze turned to a hurricane and the sky writhed with lightning, striking down with reckless abandon. Tremors shook the ground as trees toppled, the sudden rain pouring from the heavens churning the earth to mud. I watched it all with wonder and awe.

The Rashtka leapt for me as the darkness yanked my ankles. We plunged into the abyss.

I burned.

The darkness had a thousand fangs and a thousand claws and a thousand eyes. The growl of the Rashtka was joined by swarms of other demons, slicing at my ear drums. I was no longer in the woods, I was no longer in existence. My eyes were useless, my sense of touch and orientation obscured by the choking smoke and the searing pain on all sides. I was in a sea of flame, where the endless waves were filled with the demonic.

My hands lost feeling first, then my feet. The numbness crept up, my thoughts slowing until they were all semi-lupine in nature. Instinctive, yet I wouldn't lose sight of my goal the way I had lost sight of the sun in this pit.

Neither part of me, the wolf nor the human, gave up. I felt the Protector's essence split from me, leaving me suddenly cold despite the hellfire. Her presence remained close and soon angelfire flickered over me, coating my soul protectively.

I reached out and grabbed it, feeling the pulse of its ancient sentience regard me. Without hesitation, angelfire burst to life across all that was me, repelling the nightmares around me with light I couldn't quite see.

But it wasn't strong enough. Even with the combined strength of the angelfire produced by both the Protector and me, it wasn't enough. The Protector was a being forged by angelfire. She had nothing more to give. Haldis' awareness prodded at mine, a feeling foreign enough to me to be as inexplicable as suddenly seeing a new color. Its strength aided me, but I still grew weaker.

Time was lost, but the army of shadows only marched closer and closer. Words evaded me, but images blew through my mind as if riding in a busy gust of wind.

Katherine, the gleam of her eyes matching that of the barrel of her shotgun.

Melinda, her face obscured by shadow inside my car.

Benjamin, clinging to his sister with his eyes glazed but wide, watching the woods.

My parents, fear consuming the confusion in their voices.

Eren, his signature smirk dancing across his lips as a bullet of his flew true.

Luke, a muscle jumping in his jaw the only thing contradicting his determined, cool demeanor.

The demons could not take them from me. I threw everything into the angelfire, feeding Haldis my soul as fuel. I didn't hold an ounce back, not even when my consciousness dimmed to nothing, no dark, no light.

I closed the damn portal.

I woke with my back on the ground. Mine, not Leah's. It was the same form I'd held during most of my stay on this earth, or at least similar enough. Every inch of my being ached and for a second I just let the darkness swirl behind my closed eyelids. When I opened them, I was staring into the sun, surrounded by swirling clouds. Rain kissed me.

Before the intense light could imprint its image on me, a shadow above blocked it out. A demon was battling the wind currents above, spiraling and screaming as it was driven down. It was reduced to only a flash of wing as it plummeted into the disappearing portal, writhing and bloated with demons being sucked down.

The Elementals had heard Leah's call. They purged the earth with mudslides and lightning and great masses of floodwater from mysterious sources, banishing the demonic back into their realm. Howls and snarls of wolves, real wolves, echoed over the rolling hills. Darting gray forms drew closer and closer through the pines, driving black shapes back into the spiraling pit before disappearing. The weight of their unseen eyes didn't lift.

The last of the Hell spawn circled the gate like blood spiraling around a drain. I fought my way through the remnants, but by the time I arrived, all that remained on the ground was a faint, soft glow over the bare earth and skeletal roots.

Behind me, brush rustled. I spun to face it, but my heart pumped only blood and not a hint of angelic flame. Katherine emerged battered and bruised, but wearing soot like war paint.

She smiled wearily. "I don't know what you did, but it worked. All are safe at Leah's house. Found people there. Alive, thanks to that guard dog of theirs..."

None of us truly heard her. Luke and Eren appeared in my vision, so coated with ash and gore I almost mistook them for demons. Eren tried to scrape it off, but Luke looked like he was an obsidian statue. I wasn't sure he was breathing. He stared pointedly at the spot where the gate had closed.

His words were a whisper lined with ice. "Where is Leah?"

My eyes jerked across the land, but an awful sense of foreboding bubbled in my throat. My search fruitless, I turned back to Luke. The bitter flavor of victory vanished from my mouth and I didn't taste much of anything at all.

When I followed his gaze, I saw the faint, golden aura I'd awoken next to rising. It became vaguely columnar before taking on a loosely human form. I expected the visages of my companions to be ignorant of this spectacle, but all in the clearing watched with greedy—and guarded—eyes.

I knew what it was right away, but the others, unused to seeing energies, regarded it with looks that ranged from suspicion to confusion to sadness. Katherine's shotgun was perched on her shoulder, but she had not flicked the safety off. Eren's focus darted up and down from the tree tops, trying to see if it was just a trick of the light. The realization that it was not was carved into the lines on Luke's face as he swallowed heavily.

We were all still for a breath. Then, almost imperceptibly, the withered flora beneath it started to move. Like an incoming tide rushed through them, they extended their grasp with audible pops and groans. The roots were filling up with the vitality I thought had forsaken them.

The power of the Elementals thrummed through the air, centering on the partial spirit in front of us. Glimmering gold, the remains of Leah's torn and wearied soul spread life to the forest of death and decay. It started with the small bit under her, but as her soul ripped free from its position, life grew as if to touch her.

Green shoots wiggled out from under our feet and the sky came alive with the rushing of wings. Dead pine needles fell like rain as newer, verdant ones dislodged them from their position. Leah's untamed spirit moved quicker and quicker, falling to a blur low to the ground.

It circled us, darting around our legs one, two, three times. The ground budded with fungi, saplings, and even small wildflowers, beautiful and resilient. Warmth bubbled up in me from the tender display.

The golden spirit rose again, scaling a healing pine in large, swooping leaps. At the very top, the light brightened to resemble another sun, one painless to our eyes. Elemental spirits rushed to mend the land wherever its glow was cast, far beyond our line of sight.

It dimmed as quickly as it had brightened. Waves of light dispersed, shimmering in the sky. When they'd cleared *enough to see the figure in the center, it was already fading. In the glittering sky around Leah's soul, I could almost see more figures, further out. Waiting. Watching, like we were.*

In a blink, the sky was clear. The newly sprung grasses swayed in a gentle breeze, their whispering the only noise. My eyes were the first to unhitch themselves from the heavens, but they instantly lowered in grief. They found the scarred circle in the earth, the only area marring the new, beautiful grove.

Battle torn, bloody, and bruised, we did not fit in either. There were two lines of ash cleared off of Luke's face, and the pain in his eyes told me they were not likely caused by the miracle we'd just witnessed, but what it had cost.

Eren coughed, the sound harsh and jumpy. His face was obscured as he turned it away. Katherine's cropped hair was the only part of her that moved, hiding her pallid face in snatches.

Luke spoke first, his voice fading in and out of a hoarse whisper. "Leah...she killed them? All of them?"

I wished I could lie to him. "For now."

He heard what was unsaid. Eren's gaze met mine, his sclera so red I had to convince myself his eyes were not lupine gold. Anger flared in his tone, but it had no target. "And then? When they come back?"

Katherine stepped forward, all of us facing each other in a loose circle. She looked to me. "Then we fight them, whatever it takes."

Leah had known that well. Eren's upper arm muscles bulged, pulsing as he shut his fist. His words flew from his mouth, as quickly as wind but as set as stone. "We'll kill them with you. Every last one of them."

My head cocked slightly. "You two have done enough

today. You've experienced horrors and pain and loss. Your part has been done. Why would you do this?"

Luke's cheek twitched, his jaw working. Hatred and love battled in his heart, but they pointed in the same direction. The setting sun gleamed in his watery eyes, looking, for a minute, just like angelfire.

"For Leah."

Concealed deep within the pines, the raven croaked his assent.

Acknowledgements

To be honest, anyone willing to put up with my insanity deserves my fullest appreciation.

For this book in particular, however, I have to thank my friend Arpita Jajoo. I think it says something about a person when they can hear out crazy ideas like mine without batting an eye. Whether that's a good or a bad thing to have said about you, I'm not too sure. Either way, there wouldn't be a book without her.

As for the rest of the Nerd Herd, thanks to Emma Lampropoulos, for being the Lizard King; and Leah Miller, even though I can't quite remember what she helped me with...

For taking and editing my photo, thanks go to Jen Zhu.

Other than that, I have my mom to thank for allowing my wonderful and wacky ways to blossom (mostly by not murdering me when I asked the age-old question of "what's for dinner?"), and I have my dad to thank for showing me the woods, which, in my mind, I've never quite left.

Thanks to my sister Morgan, who did not inspire Jessica, but mostly because anyone who came for her would have gotten a softball to the face.

And of course, a huge thank you to Christina Celentano, my publisher, for making all this happen. It's been better than I ever could have hoped.

Finally, I thank anyone and everyone who read this, whether they only made it through the first chapter or they've read it 27 times. I hope I've added a little bit of pleasant insanity to all of your lives.